WASTED

WASTED

A STORY OF LOVE GONE TOXIC

BIFF THURINGER

CHRONIC PUBLISHING | Epigraph Books
Rhinebeck, New York

Paperback ISBN: 978-1-948796-30-9
eBook ISBN: 978-1-948796-31-6

Library of Congress Control Number: 2018954096

Book design by Colin Rolfe

Chronic Publishing, in conjunction with
Epigraph Books
22 East Market Street, Suite 304
Rhinebeck, NY 12572
(845) 876-4861
epigraphps.com

CHAPTER ONE
EMERGENCY 911

As much as she had been looking forward to it, Sheila McNally was mortified that her death was turning out to be such a public spectacle. She knew the entire Western world was watching on TV as she girded herself to go down in a slow-motion reverse mushroom cloud of twisted steel, plaster and burning jet fuel, accompanied by Jesus knows how many hapless secretaries, pencil-necks and municipal martyrs with whom she had little in common. She was surprised that her primary emotion at this climactic moment was a gnawing, self-conscious embarrassment at having fallen short at everything she'd ever done. "What a fucking waste," she thought to herself. "I deserve this."

Still, she had one last chore to attend to. Hurling silent curses at a deity she had long ago given up on, she dialed her home number on her sketchy cell phone, which even when jetliners weren't flying into the building seemed powerless to connect to one of the world's largest cell towers right next door. She was sure Nate would be sleeping the sleep of the guilty, trying to forget what a scumbag he was. If only he wasn't such a weak-willed, skirt-chasing, piece-of-shit failure, she would have married him, or would have at least wanted to live for a few more months until she had finished digging up filth at USE.

Intense heat and smoke billowing from the central stairwells was driving people toward the outer walls. Four men threw a legless onyx conference table through a floor-to-ceiling window and huddled there, yelling and flapping their shirts and suit jackets. Sheila closed her door and locked it as her home phone rang mercilessly. Why didn't the fucking machine pick up? "Nate, stop jerking off and pick up, Goddammit!" An orange mist crept beneath her door. The temperature suddenly rose to the level of the hellish Helsinki Room at the 12th Street Russian Baths, where Nate had screwed that pregnant masseuse. "Fucking bastard."

*   *   *

For Nate Randall, staring in stricken silence out of Sheila's sepia tinted bedroom window with her last angry, unfinished words ringing in his ear and her hated corporate Babel crushing her into hamburger before his eyes, the world of shit she had been trying for years to warn him about suddenly came into being. He would, as countless thousands of others were obviously thinking at the same moment, never be the same.

Still, none of this should have been a surprise. As her reluctant nihilist-in-training, Nate had grown to share in Sheila's oft repeated opinion that it was only a matter of time before some grinning, death-hungry Son of Allah would perform a catastrophic act of anti-American symbolism; most likely bringing what she termed the "Twin Penises of Progress" down with all hands on board. As proof of his love and, thanks to her, his conversion to the paranoiac faith, he had even placed a bet with her on the date of the event, but had been off by a year. Sheila's guess was right on the money.

Being a pessimist was unnatural to Nate. As a result, life was always more of a struggle for him than it was for Sheila, who at least had her certainties and her nagging death wish to comfort her. Even under blissful conditions she was a defiantly wretched soul, which unfortunately was what had attracted him to her in the first place. She knew the human race was going down the toilet, and wanted out. As bad as his own behavior and attitude were, he was unable to shake the fantasy that things were somehow supposed to improve; for himself, for Sheila and for the rest of humanity.

Naturally, she was right all along, he thought ruefully. About the human race, which he now had to agree was headed straight for the abyss. About himself, who had been exposed during the last fortnight as a classic lout and a lying, disease-spreading creep. And about herself, a woman clearly marked for an early exit.

How could he have missed it? He had met her in a bar, for Christ's sake. Constitutionally edgy, paranoid and cranky as a badger, Sheila required a foul, contraindicated bouillabaisse of cocaine and opiates in order to simmer down to a boil. Alcohol was no help at all, not that that stopped her from testing her half-Irish liver. She would become dangerously self-destructive whenever she drank too much, which was every night. Under those circumstances, the very fact of her moving to New York and going to work for the satanic Universal Silicon Enterprises on the 97th floor of an obvious deathtrap like the World Trade Center was patently suicidal, as was her taking up with a germ-infested scuzzball such as himself. She might as well have tattooed a target on her forehead with a sign that said: "Aim Here."

* * *

As it transpired, Sheila had been acting out especially badly for two weeks, sobbing and screaming and threatening to annihilate herself, ever since she found Nate's top-secret woman list under the trash compactor. The list had confirmed, in inexorable USE black-and-white laser ink and including dates and rating points, that for the duration of their five-year relationship Nate hadn't been very adept at keeping his dick in his pants. Worse yet, Sheila saw her own name on the list, mired in fourth place behind two of his ex-girlfriends and a nameless Nebraskan "milkmaid" he had met while on the band's last tour.

The woman list, besides being a bad idea, was essentially an ongoing pack of half-truths Nate compiled to make himself feel as if he had experienced some kind of a life, when all he'd really done was squander his middling talents on a tantalizing but ultimately fruitless quest for second-rate pop stardom. It had been six months since the band splintered after having been dropped by Arista, and he wasn't making it as a freelance studio hack. A hundred bucks here, two hundred there, then nothing for three weeks. He wasn't doing so well as a small time booking agent/club promoter either. Three nights a week he had to fill some beer-stained sty up on Bleecker Street with mostly talentless rock bands who dragged their friends in from Jersey to drink and fight over the paucity of harassable females. Out of five to ten bucks a head Nate had to pay for the bands, the security and the sound guy and considered himself lucky to come home with fifty a night and no black eyes. If it weren't for Sheila supporting him with her filthy corporate lucre, he'd have been back on the street delivering packages or hustling fares in a pedicab.

With his graying temples, his aversion to success and his carefully nurtured commitment-phobia, Nate Randall was far from what one would call a catch, even before being outed as a filthy fuckpig. But he knew that Sheila, despite being darkly beautiful in a hollow-eyed, brooding sort of way, was no catch either, and had as much trouble hanging onto a man as he did staying out of female quicksand. Besides being a drug-swilling, alcoholic, chain-smoking emotional yo-yo, she had enacted far too much household legislation based on her psychotically paranoid conception of what germs are capable of. Nonetheless, Nate had recently realized that, despite her long and growing list of peccadilloes, she was the smartest, funniest, most sexually and emotionally electrifying woman he'd ever known, and that he in fact loved her. He had successfully curtailed his extracurricular activities for two weeks straight and was about to ask her to marry him when she found his infernal woman list.

* * *

Among the things Nate loved most about Sheila was her furtiveness. It was like living with a double agent. He found it stimulating that he never knew what she was up to, and fooled himself into thinking she didn't care about what he did either. She never talked directly about her work as a PR drone at USE, except to say that it profoundly depressed her. Over too much coffee in the morning she would wax elliptically about the impending collapse of modern civilization and how we were "slowly poisoning ourselves with applied science." She described America as a nation of "technology-blinded lemmings" who deserved to die. Gradually it had become obvious to Nate that she was on a secret mission of some kind, and he made a game of trying to investigate Sheila's shadow life without tipping her off.

Nate's happy suspicion that Sheila was a potential whistleblower on the evil USE Corporation was all but confirmed when one day the apartment door was open and he sneaked in while she was on the phone. "I'm going to bring down those fucking assholes," she was spit-whispering through clenched teeth. "I can't believe they think they can get away with this shit. I've got a filing cabinet full of stuff that will fucking destroy them. I've talked to Jim at the *Times*, but he says they won't touch it. He says nobody will, because it would 'blindside' the economy. Fuck the economy. Innocent lemmings are dying."

"Who was that?" Nate said as she hung up, failing as usual to startle her. "A friend."

Nate was not Sheila's friend. She trusted no one, Nate least of all. She was always lurking around her high-class apartment, hiding things and looking for porno and other items he might have hidden—which was how she found the woman list. Theirs had been a relationship based on a mutual dismay with the opposite sex, built up through years of prior experience having been cheated on, jilted, emotionally abused and otherwise fucked with.

The woman list had settled it. Somehow on Monday night they had fought through the tears and recriminations to a point where they even managed to make tear-greased, passionate love, but by Tuesday morning a murky veil had fallen over Sheila's face. "Don't ever do that to me again," she hissed on her way out the door. "Tonight I'm going to kill myself. If you're here when I get back, I'm going to have to kill you, too."

"Yeah, right. Why don't you stop talking and get on with it already?" Nate immediately regretted the remark as the door slammed shut.

Whether either of them was serious or not, there would be no last kiss. Nothing to remember but a flat, beaten look on Sheila's uniquely beautiful Portuguese/Irish face, and the fact that the laundry-care tag was sticking out of her sweater. "I'm going to miss that sweet can," Nate thought numbly as he drifted back to sleep.

* * *

An hour later he awoke to the sound of a thousand sirens howling. It was 9:50 a.m. He turned on the television. "Two hijacked commercial airliners have crashed into the World Trade Center...firefighters are battling blazes in the north and south towers...a third hijacked jetliner has crashed into the Pentagon..."

Fuck. Sheila! She hated her job and was usually late, but not today. Thanks to Nate she would be facing her longed-for end in the last place she would have wanted to be, trapped in her despised 2 World Trade Center tower, the dehumanizing architecture of which she often termed a "Franken-bauhaus clusterfuck." She was petrified of the elevators, the doors of which often opened inappropriately halfway between floors, scaring the crap out of the occupants. She told marginally credible stories of how the entire 97th floor would vibrate when either of two 300-pound co-workers would waddle to the ladies' room, or how during a high wind you could look out at the other monstrous slab and see it swaying 20 feet in either direction.

His heart pounding uncontrollably, Nate picked up the phone and dialed her work number, which was out. He dialed her cell number, which was busy. He pressed redial. Busy. Redial. Busy. Fuck, fuck, fuck! He opened the blinds of the bedroom window, with its panoramic view of the burning towers just 12 blocks to the southwest beyond the faceless, windowless, shit-brown telephone building. He had always hated that view, and now he knew why. He saw what looked like falling bodies of people who had hurled themselves to escape the unbearable heat and smoke. Sheila?

The phone rang. Nate answered, shuddering involuntarily. "Sheila, Jesus Christ!!!"

Her voice was calm and measured, clear against a wall of static. "Good morning, Natie. Apparently you've been looking out the window. We're trapped up here. Looks like I'll get my wish. Fuck you. That's not me waving a white flag. I'm going down with the ship."

"Sheila, I..."

"Shut up and listen, asshole. I'm toast, but maybe you can do something useful for once. In my file cabinet. Next to the phone stand. Combination. 22-35-13. The Amorphous folders. Call...Shi-" Suddenly a shower of steel girders exploded from the left side of the south tower as it folded slowly upon itself like a thousand-foot-tall accordion into the streets of Manhattan, carrying Sheila and untold numbers of other doomed, disconnected souls down with it. The emotional shock wave that comes to those unaccustomed to mass annihilation hit Nate Randall in the solar plexus like a spiritual medicine ball. The phone went dead, along with the TV and what was left of his no-good, cheating heart.

"Sheila!!!"

Knowing there was no point, Nate got dressed anyway, put on a pair of ski goggles and wrapped a scarf around his tear-streaked face, ran down the 10 flights of stairs and unlocked his bike, holding on to one thought like a mantra: 22-35-13. He sped downtown on West Broadway, slaloming to avoid the throngs of plaster-and-asbestos-caked refugees streaming north. Skirting roadblocks, he ended up on West Street, which was clogged with firefighting equipment and the detritus of Dante's imagination. The sidewalks were littered with burned and bloody body parts: heads, limbs, torsos...a pretty lace bra still cupping a severed breast. Sheila? 22-35-13. Fighting back tears and acrid smoke, Nate turned right and headed toward the river to try and maneuver around the back of the Financial Center toward the south side of the trade center complex.

He'd gotten as far the boat basin when the north tower collapsed. The force of it knocked Nate off his bike, even though he was on the lee side of the American Express building. Plaster dust and burnt jet fuel choked his nostrils beneath his useless scarf. Disoriented and passing out from asphyxiation, he stumbled to the promenade bordering the Hudson, crawled over the railing and jumped in, thinking, "22, minus 35, plus 13 equals...zero."

But that was all good news, compared to what came after.

CHAPTER TWO
EX MEN

For 24 hours after his world imploded, Nate lay in a St. Vincent's Hospital bed, alternating between moaning like a homeless lunatic over Sheila and swearing at various masochistic *Attack on America* marathons, as a platoon of overworked Samaritans tested and treated him for respiratory system dysfunction. Every so often he could smell the benzene, PCB and sulfur dioxide-laden stench from the burning hole downtown, and late at night when the drugs wore off he would awaken himself coughing and puking up blood. When the saintly, disinfectant-scented night nurse finally succeeded in getting him calmed down and sedated, he tortured himself quietly to sleep thinking about what might have been Sheila's left breast lying in its twisted C-cup on a West Street sidewalk.

Nate had been fished from the mouth of the river named for Henry Hudson by the stunned crew of a replica of the long-dead captain's 1609 ship *Half Moon*, his lungs half full of fetid river water, the other half encrusted with skyscraper dust and complex petrochemicals, and eventually deposited on a gurney in a hallway at St. Vincent's Hospital. He had lost his favorite hat, his glasses, his bike and his girlfriend, and felt as guilty to be alive as any of the losers blubbering their pathetic stories on TV. At least no one from FOX showed up for a bedside interview. They wouldn't have wanted to hear what he had to say anyway.

After being stabilized and diagnosed with a variety of respiratory maladies, only one of which (chronic bronchitis, from the years of playing bad music in smoky bars) he'd ever experienced before, Nate was armed with a grab-bag full of industrial-grade antihistamines, expectorants and painkillers and released into the brave new world.

With a steady southerly breeze pushing the plume from the smoldering ruins slowly up the length of Manhattan, the air circulating through TriBeCa and SoHo, up through Greenwich Village and Chelsea and over to the Lower East Side was heavy with singed hydrocarbons and particles of decomposing flesh. To Nate the whole city smelled like a condom had caught fire in a sailor's ass. The St. Vincent's neighborhood around 13th Street and Eighth Avenue was eerily quiet, save for the intermittent siren blast and the muted whining of the scores of fancy, disgruntled young altruists loitering about expensively after having been told by some red-eyed official to go away. Feeling that history would be written without them, they were irritated that everyone who might have needed their precious blood was dead.

Most people just meandered, walking zombified into the traffic-less streets, looking as if the wind had been knocked out of them. Many of them wore masks or scarves over their worried mouths and noses. The only sense of purpose on display from anyone not wearing a uniform was that of a scruffy entrepreneur pushing a shopping cart bristling with newly minted American flags.

Nate shuffled along with the other shell-shocked and confused, trying to get back downtown to Sheila's, but was rebuffed at Canal Street by a miniature African-American female cop and a trio of skinheads wearing camouflage National Guard outfits two sizes too big for them. Their preposterous Wehrmacht-style helmets looked as if they were crushing what was left of their brains.

Despite repeating the protestations that had successfully gotten him past earlier checkpoints, Nate was turned away with two blocks to go. The driver's license in Nate's still soggy wallet showed his old P.O. box address in Albany. "If you get caught down there looking like shit without authorization, you'll be shot as a looter, sir," one kid drawled as the other two twitched and smirked like Appalachian inbreds.

"You'll be all right," corrected the gentle cop lady, smiling beatifically. "Just get someone to vouch for you and we'll see what we can do."

"Thanks, officer," said Nate, still smarting over the reality of an emaciated little fascist from Oneonta standing guard over his neighborhood, telling him where he couldn't go. "Maybe somebody should check *your* pockets, cracker," Nate muttered uselessly into his hospital-issue mask as he walked up Broadway toward Rico's. "God bless America. Fuck."

* * *

Until he moved in with Sheila five months earlier, Nate had for two years lived with Rico Exman, the band's lead singer and primary sex symbol. Nate missed the apartment—four high-ceilinged rooms with a shower like a fire hose on the safest block in New York, rent free to Rico and his two cats for the past 13 years thanks to a tangled lawsuit over a forgotten tenant strike. It was on East Third Street directly across from the Hell's Angels headquarters, and when Nate lived in it there was a Haitian ganja supermarket in the basement directly below. Every night Nate's cluttered bedroom would fill with smoke from the Haitians' Santaria rituals and he'd have to hide in the kitchen if he didn't want to get high or sick, or both. There was a beautiful cloistered patio in the back, where he would sit and read and drink beer and make friends with the Haitians' chickens and bunny rabbits in the sun-dappled shade of the locust trees. After a while he didn't bother getting too close to the critters. He noticed that they would become increasingly mangled—missing feathers, tails and then a limb or two—before disappearing altogether, replaced by a fresh batch.

Moving back in with Rico was something Nate said he'd never do. But this was an emergency, and the two had stopped pretending they were enemies more than three months earlier. Rico had forgiven Nate for starting the inevitable mutiny that broke up the Ex-Men, and Nate had forgiven Rico for being a self-involved culture-appropriating blowhard who couldn't help pissing people off. Rico had hired a new band of fresh young kids whom he could browbeat and low-ball to his heart's content, and Nate was booking him every chance he got, because the bastard still had his fans, even with that bald head.

As he approached down the block, Nate tried to ignore the gathering Ground Zero aroma and noted the changes on Third Street. The Hell's Angels had commandeered the greasy old bicycle garage out of which Nate had worked the messenger and pedicab rackets in times before the band got hot. A group of the outlaw bikers loitered menacingly—under the circumstances almost comfortingly—on the sidewalk in front of their storied headquarters, forcibly administering the entire street's unique parking laws, as usual. In homage to the Angels' many friends among the neighborhood's martyred gendarmes and firefighters, their clubhouse façade was festooned with a missing persons' shrine, a tattered, Iwo Jima-sized Old Glory dug out of the downtown rubble and a colorful gallery of scatological posters defaming America's new scraggly-bearded enemies.

There were other, more disturbing developments. Sadly, the exotic snake and lizard shack on the corner had metamorphosed into a Starbucks. And the Haitians were gone, replaced by a repugnantly sleek Internet café crowded with trust fund babies in Caesar haircuts, who feigned cool detachment as they nervously plotted their escapes from the festering purgatory that New York had overnight become for them.

Nate suddenly and painfully recalled the Haitians' fate—a memory he had apparently been blocking out. They had been busted in a raid on the same day he moved out to Sheila's. He remembered having felt an uncharacteristic burst of empathy for the three dreadlocked brothers chained together on the bench inside their store, glowering at him as he wrestled his ugly sofa bed down the steps and into the van by himself. "It wasn't me turned you suckas in," Nate had blurted. "Must've been somebody didn't like your skunky dope. I'm just moving in with my girl downtown."

The jailbound troika had been neither amused nor mollified. To reassure them that he truly wasn't a lousy rat worthy of a personalized voodoo ritual, Nate had given one of them his new phone number at Sheila's, which the man made a point of calling when he got out of Rikers a week later. Sheila, God rest her opportunistic soul, had intercepted the call and struck up a conversation, quickly determining that he dealt more than just pot. Upon eliciting that the dealer had a line on some pretty high-grade Colombian coke, her tired eyes had lit up like Roman candles. Thus through Nate's chickenshit act had Sheila become a steady client.

Nate's sad realization that this new drug connection had accelerated Sheila's emotional deterioration, coupled with his certainty that she had been driven into a psychotic, suicidal Nirvana by poring over his woman list, plunged him into unfamiliar fits of guilt and self-loathing. Worse yet, he was sure he had rammed the last nail into her coffin with a few thought-less, sleep-slurred words on the morning of September 11. The fact that a fully-fueled airliner had been driven by a maniac into her workplace didn't enter the equation. Religious extremism and centuries of bloody bickering over a few hectares of arid wasteland had nothing to do with it.

He would never admit it to anyone, but deep inside, Nate knew he was to blame for Sheila's death. Somehow, he had to atone for it. Accused, tried and convicted in his own mind, he sentenced himself to community service. He would complete Sheila's work, and save her "innocent lem-mings" from whatever fate her despised employer had assigned them. But first, he had to save himself.

* * *

"Yo, Nate."

"Hey, Rico. Thanks for putting me up."

Rico was tall and angular; catlike. He had always looked and acted like a Hanna Barbera cartoon character to Nate, but women routinely wanted to crawl into bed with him, probably because of his sleepy Isaac Hayes baritone. Now, however, Nate noticed something was off. Rico looked tired and even more gaunt than usual.

His voice was ragged and phlegmy. "No problem. You're like a fuckin' hero already, you crazy old fuck. So sorry about Sheila, man. I'm serious."

An acrid vapor hung in the hallway, even stronger than the smell in the street.

"Yeah, I really loved that psycho bitch. I let her get to me and now she's haunting my dreams. You know, Rico, it reeks in here. Like the fuck-ing Meadowlands."

"I know, it smells like Mrs. Goldman's sixth grade," croaked Rico. "It's from when the wind blows north. It's hard to get rid of, like this part of the street is in an air pocket or something. I've been staying out at my mom's, where at least I know the stink is from an all-American dump. I gotta keep out of New York for a while."

"Is that where you've been? I've been trying to get another date out of you for the last two months. And you canceled your last gig."

Rico looked troubled. "Yeah, well, sort of. Sorry."

Rico grew up on Long Island in the shadow of its tallest peak, the ancient, steaming Atlantic Park landfill. Most of the thing had been paved over with blacktop, and a vast, gleaming shopping mall had been constructed atop it in 1996. Methane vents still flamed on its grassy slopes in order that the shoppers far above wouldn't be blown to smithereens. One of Sheila's pet conspiracy theories was that Rico's tumor-ridden extended family was evidence of a "cancer cluster," caused by years of illegal toxic dumping at the mobbed-up dump. She further maintained that the perpetrators were shielded from trouble and abetted in their crimes by a man she called "the highest ranking Mafioso in the U.S. government," Atlantic Park's favorite son, Senator Rudolf Viggiani.

Nate had to admit there was probably something amiss in Atlantic Park. Besides Sheila, no one he knew was more tainted with the pall of death than Rico. Rico's father had expired of a particularly cruel and virulent form of brain cancer, and his uncle and sister were nailed by lymphoma. His mother had beaten breast cancer years earlier, but had just noticed a shiny new lump in her armpit. And it seemed as if Rico was always trotting off to the Island to visit some leukemia-afflicted high school pal in the hospital, or to attend the funeral of a fallen comrade.

And now Rico didn't look so good, either. "You all right, little buddy? You look a little peaked," ventured Nate cautiously.

At that, Rico's already troubled face fell even further. His eyes began to water. His voice lowered to a barely audible rasp. "Natey, don't tell anybody. I'm not all right. I found out four months ago I've got Hodgkins. I shaved my fucking head because I'm sick, dude. They're zapping me three times a week and I feel like shit. I look like shit. My fucking hair is gone, and now my girl is gone. Fuck her anyway. She had a flat ass. My mom is dying, but I might beat her to the punch. I got a new record coming out next month and my first tour since you fuckers left, and I can't even sing. If the label or my manager finds out, I'm fucked. Fucked."

Rico folded onto his sagging couch and started to sob softly—for the first time ever, as far as Nate knew. Nate didn't quite know what to do, so he put his arms around his stricken friend and tried to comfort him—another jarring precedent that would probably never occur again. Rico felt like a sack of kindling in his arms. "Aw, man. That's all right. That's OK. Just look at us now, a couple of bad motherfuckers, yo? You all ugly and bald and radioactive and me uglier and balder and crying over a dead sociopath who wanted to kill me. The city is a deathhouse—fucking asbestos, rent-a-soldiers, rats and body parts. These are the end days, my friend. A swell time to be alive. Consider yourself lucky."

As the desiccated husk of his best friend finally let out a hoarse chuckle, Nate began to cry, too.

CHAPTER THREE
GROUND ZERO

With the city in a virtual lockdown and nothing much else to do, Nate decided he would try to be a better pal to Rico for the few short weeks the poor son-of-a-bitch had left on earth. It would be good practice in honing the sort of altruistic skills he would need for his new role as a selfless crusader for the human condition. As he could barely recall having ever cared for anything or anybody in his life, he figured now would be as good a time and place as any to start.

Since getting sick, Rico had given up performing and reduced rehearsing to the point that he had too much time on his hands. In the vacuum of empty, hope-stifling days pierced by sad, frightened, pain-wracked nights, he had come up with a life experience to-do list—a sort of Herculean set of labors to complete before wasting away entirely. With some trepidation Nate offered to help implement the list, despite his private opinion that Rico's proposed last wishes were at best tragicomically unattainable, and at their worst could get one or both of them killed.

The first thing to do, thought Nate, was to prioritize. Rico was obviously beginning to deteriorate at an accelerating rate and the list was far too long. If they got through even half of it, they'd be lucky.

He grilled Rico on specifics. What was the most important thing in the world to him? What sorts of things could he do now that he might not be able to do in a week? Luckily, a number of Rico's requests which would have been out of the question just days earlier—getting tickets to "The Producers" and a Madonna show, as well as obtaining dinner reservations at

Smith & Wollensky—were suddenly within the realm of possibility, thanks to the sharp dip in demand caused by the city's post-traumatic depression.

The 50 grand of Sheila's money in the bank account Nate had shared with her wouldn't hurt either.

Other proposed junkets, like a trip to Shea to see a Mets vs. Braves game and a visit to an Upper East Side brothel for a three-girl special—something Rico ruefully termed his "final hat trick"—would have to be postponed, and indeed might never happen. Baseball was suspended indefinitely in reaction to the terror attacks, and Rico's once legendary hard-on may well have been suspended permanently due to the slurry of boner-softening chemicals in his bloodstream.

But that was fine with Nate, because first there were Rico's two premier final requests to attend to, which were by far the most lame-brained, most dangerous and most difficult to pull off. Labor number one—a predictably mean-spirited, chicken-shit, self-obsessed thing to want, thought Nate—involved a particularly cowardly form of revenge, with virtually no participation from Rico. It merely required Nate to darken his skin with Au Courant, dress like a Moroccan homeboy and follow Rico's shallow-hearted, flat-assed ex-girlfriend around for a day to try and scare her silly without getting arrested.

"Man, I just gotta know she's scared of something, too," said Rico. "I want her to know how it feels."

"You just can't give it up, can you, you last-word motherfucker," said Nate, shaking his head disapprovingly. "It's no wonder you have cancer."

Nonetheless, Nate did as he was asked. Wearing a hooded jacket, a tricked-out fez and Doctor Thompson aviator sunglasses, Nate tailed the unfortunate woman for hours as she tottered around on 125th Street in a pair of ridiculous platform clogs, shopping for more ugly, crippling footwear. He lurked in her peripheral vision, twisting his mug into what he wrongly assumed were various sexual predator faces, until she finally noticed him leering obliquely at her from behind a revolving shoe kiosk. Once he had her attention, he made sure she saw him again and again, and succeeded in driving her like a frightened dogie through the sparsely policed uptown streets and subways. Becoming progressively unhinged, she eventually sought asylum in a Sugar Hill precinct house—despite carrying a purse that was presumably full of crack, according to Rico. "You turned the bitch out, yo," said Rico upon hearing the good news, laughing until he began to cough green bile. "I wish I coulda seen her face."

* * *

Their second and potentially most noteworthy labor—a criminally conceived 3 a.m. sortie into the smoldering underbelly of Ground Zero—was achieved over Nate's fervent objections. The last thing Nate wanted to do was go anywhere near the site of his latest personal Waterloo, much less to perform a felony against America that could land him in jail for 20 years. He'd already left his heart and his health in Battery Park two days earlier, and he was afraid of seeing Sheila's bug-eyed, blood-caked death mask staring out from under some subterranean shard of 98th-floor concrete. But Rico's still robust natural charisma and cancer-fueled desperation were like a double-barreled battering ram, smashing Nate's lamely presented arguments to pieces.

Rico's excuse for wanting to make the trek was the exceedingly remote possibility of finding buried gold. His "good friend" Pedrino, a toothless hustler who lived in a truck in a parking lot behind CBGB and who tapped Rico weekly for funds, had spun a complex saga concerning forty million dollars in red-hot bullion, entombed deep in the bowels of the trade center ruins. Rico believed this junkie to his dying core.

The mythical hoard was apparently locked in a secret room, defended by a small army of flattened Brinks guards. "It's definitely not a vault; the door says Room 411," Pedrino had confirmed. "Mo' Better was down there two days ago and saw it, but he got busted."

Mo' Better was a legendary one-eyed subway denizen with a history of underworld derring-do; another reason for Rico's chemo-addled brain to get excited. Rico just wanted to see the dust-covered lode with his own eyes, and perhaps lift a brick or two to give to his mother. "I know it's down there, dude. It's on the level below the concourse, right under the Duane Reade where we used to stock up on jimmy hats. It was the only joint had Sheik Ultra-Thins. Remember, Natie? Near the Cortlandt Street train stop. Pedrino says we can get in through there." He was strangely animated and his eroding face glowed like the last brightening of a candle before burning out. "I know you'll do this. You're as fucking wack as I am."

Rico was indeed insane and a born asshole, mused Nate, but he was also correct. In his current emotionally weakened state, Nate was uncharacteristically impressionable, and was neither prone nor particularly competent to examine the consequences of a foolhardy act. He had, in fact, just returned to Rico's house red-faced and exhilarated from performing a prosecutable misdemeanor.

This new junket would just be another rung on the rickety ladder to either self-destruction or immortality; Nate didn't care which. "All right, fuckface, I'll go. But if we get any heat at all, I'm leaving you to die alone."

"Thanks, my brother. You won't regret it, I swear."

"Yeah, we'll see."

The next morning Nate bought a used bicycle and a new chain-lock at George's and rode out to a contractor's supply store in Astoria, where he picked up a couple of lighted miner's helmets, two double-chambered respirators and an industrial-strength pair of bolt cutters. He packed these items, along with a detailed subway and street map from off the Internet and a 50-foot length of lightweight nylon rope, into his and Rico's battered old messenger bags. Setting the alarm for 1 a.m., the adventurers decided to rest up for their quest by downing a half bottle of Jack Daniels and pouring acid on each other's old wounds. Rico was reminded that he had been balding long before he got cancer, and that Nate had once dogged a Nubian stewardess out from under his nose at a show at Nell's. Nate's jabs were countered by Rico's drunkenly cruel boast that he had nailed Sheila first. "She was too fucking tight," he crowed recklessly. "I had to put it in her blown-out…"

"Fuck you, asshole," interrupted Nate, having none of it. "I always thought you were gay."

"Fuck you, old man. I may die first, but I already got more pussy than you ever will."

"More butt-hole, you mean. Fucking sodomite."

After slapping each other ineffectually for a half-minute that seemed to stretch into an eternity, the two failed, piss-drunk rock stars passed out face down on Rico's cat-hair-blanketed living room rug.

* * *

Upon awakening, neither Nate nor Rico had any recollection of their little spat. As the simmering whiskey had cleared out all self-doubt and common sense along with their short-term memory, they were raring to go. They decided to bicycle downtown as far as they could before taking to the tangled mass of hopefully empty lower Manhattan subway tunnels on foot for the final leg. Keeping to the unlit side streets and back alleys they knew well, the two highly untrained spelunkers—wearing the same absurd black ninja outfits in which they had nine months earlier been prancing around onstage at the Paramount—were able to avoid police and National Guard checkpoints. They were challenged only once: by a brown-uniformed, unarmed Chinese rent-a-cop standing guard in a private parking lot as they cut through from an alley below Houston Street. "Hey, where you think you going? Come back here!"

They ignored him and sped south on Suffolk, veering closer to the East River to avoid having to cross over Canal Street which, they knew from watching Channel 2 disaster news, would be bristling with manned roadblocks. Whenever they spied a cluster of soldiers or police officers ahead of them, they doubled back a block or two and chose another route.

Once past the Manhattan and Brooklyn Bridge overpasses it became easier going. The dimly lit streets still belonged to the residents of the self-contained neighborhoods surrounding the South Street Seaport—a forgotten area that had been cut off from the rest of the world by police barricades and highway and subway closings. Making what was even for him a precarious mental leap, Rico observed that, save for the strangely bustling 24-hour Pathmark Supermarket glowing like the U.S.S. Enterprise in the plaster-dusted night, "this was what the Warsaw ghetto must have been like."

"I'm not so sure about that, Rico," said Nate. "Looks more like Krakow to me."

"Shut the fuck up."

Farther on it soon became clear that fully armed death squads would be loitering on every street corner in the sliver of lower Manhattan from Broadway to West Street, presumably with the governor's orders to detain—or assassinate—potential looters such as themselves. From Battery Place up the stricken left coast of the island to Canal, every thoroughfare and square was floodlit like Super Sunday. The area around Battery Park had been converted into a vast staging area and was besieged by an all-night two-way traffic jam of rumbling trucks carrying God-knows-what, to and from Ground Zero through the Brooklyn Battery Tunnel. Armed assault troops were everywhere, with itchy trigger fingers and nothing to assault. As his mind was in the process of dying, Rico easily noticed things that weren't so apparent to Nate. "Look how short all these motherfuckers are," he whispered. "How we supposed to win a war with a pygmy army? I thought they had a height requirement."

"I guess they're saving all the tall ones for Afghanistan," offered Nate. "Takes a special breed of soldier to turn the desert to glass."

Diminutive though they were, these "pygmies" were armed, and they were everywhere. Trapped in a triangle of darkened streets near the south-eastern tip of the island, Nate and Rico had to abandon their original plan of sneaking into Battery Park to storm the gates of the South Ferry 1/9 station.

They secured their bikes in a pitch-black alley off Hanover Street and, keeping to the darkest shadows, slithered toward the M subway entrance at Broad and Pearl Streets. Directly east of the disaster site—downwind of it on September 11—this area was a post-apocalyptic wilderness. Every surface: vehicles, streets, sidewalks, mail and newspaper boxes, blacked-out traffic lights and buildings, was covered with four to six inches of what looked like volcanic ash. Nate knew his own heart was doing donuts in his chest, and he presumed Rico would be an even bigger mess; he feared that perhaps one of them might jeopardize the mission. "You okay, Hercules? You want to call it?"

"Fuck you, punk," was the spit-borne reply. "Let's go."

As this apparently non-critical section of downtown had been over-looked in the occupying army's general security plan, the nearest check-point outpost was blocks away. Nate and Rico hid behind a construction fence and waited nervously for a routine patrol to go by before making their move.

The heavy chain around the entrance's iron gate was no match for Nate's medieval bolt cutters. They quietly unwrapped the chain, slowly opened the creaky gate and slid inside, then closed it up and re-wrapped the chain with the severed link hidden in the interior. They groped their way down two flights of stairs before daring to take out their miner's helmets and turn one of the lamps on.

Nate hoped his Internet research would prove correct that there was a complex series of old, unused tunnels leading over from the Broad Street station to the Wall Street 4/5 station. After a couple of false starts, breaking into what turned out to be a locked, unmarked restroom and following a passage 300 feet to a dead end, they located the entrance to this presumably rat-infested maze, which was clearly marked with a red-circled minus symbol accompanied by the words "No Entry."

As they were about to enter, a ray of light flickered from beyond a street-level grating in the tiled station ceiling far overhead. "Who goes there?" a distant voice demanded.

"Con Ed!" yelled Nate impulsively. "Gas leak!"

They didn't wait for an answer, and bolted down the old tunnel as fast as they could, almost hurtling into a railing-less abyss. Around the first curve in the passageway they encountered a fork. Following his sense of direction and his nose, Nate chose the left-hand passage, and they slowed their pace down to a leisurely lope, wishfully keeping any potential vermin at bay by growling softly and shining their headlamps back and forth, giving themselves neck cramps.

Whenever they reached a point of decision, Nate chose the largest passage or, if the dimensions were roughly equivalent, the opening from which the rankest odor emanated. He kept a careful mental log of their progress, stopping to retrace all their previous steps upon reaching each new intersection. Flawed as his reasoning may have been, all the passages led to the same destination anyway, and within minutes they stumbled into a well-maintained section of tunnel. Soon they were in what was obviously a station chamber, the signs on the supporting posts of which confirmed: "Wall St."

They proceeded with lamps off, feeling their way along the walls to the south end of the station, where Nate knew there would be a fork in the 4/5 tunnel. The right hand track was where, in better days, the #6 trains, having terminated up at City Hall, would come down and split off to make a loop in the nearby 1/9 South Ferry terminus complex in order to head back north. Nate and Rico would take this tunnel and, if unmolested, hook up with the 1/9 line going north, which would lead them directly into the concourse level of the trade center, near the legendary Duane Reade. Pedrino had sworn to Rico that the 1/9 route from the south, although filled with debris, was clear enough to walk through.

The burning, acrid stench was growing stronger and the atmosphere in the tunnel was becoming markedly thicker. Nate's eyes began to tear up, and he felt the familiar gag reflex between his nose and throat. He popped two Sudafeds and an Advil and began to break out the respirators. Rico coughed violently. "That really stinks," he said. "I have a headache. Are we close?"

Nate gave Rico an even stronger dose of meds and a shot of Jack from his flask to sedate him. He took a long pull of his own. Fixing his lamp on his friend's twitching, sharp-featured face, he was struck that in this dank, subterranean environment, as Rico's eyes bugged with tension and his mouth foamed from his coughing fit, the animal nature beneath his weakening human façade was being revealed as never before.

"Rat."

"Where?" Rico's eyes bugged even wider from the electric spasm in his chest.

"You, kid. That's what you are, a fucking sewer rat. I just figured it out."

"Mother *fucker*. You scared the shit out of me."

"Sorry, man. I've just never seen you in your element before." He handed Rico a respirator.

"Fuck you."

"If we find gold, I might let you—if you can even get it up. Let's go, we're almost there."

* * *

Tunnels and underground infrastructure had always fascinated Nate. As a four-year-old boy he'd had the Bejesus frightened out of him by an unsupervised viewing of the sci-fi classic "Invaders from Mars." The movie featured scaly, catlike, 7-foot-tall Martians who burrowed a warren of tunnels beneath the young protagonist's rural home for the purpose of preying on the cerebral cortexes of his parents, among others. Besides being the basis of a youthful religion Nate devised in order to exorcise its brain-thirsty monsters from his subconscious, this film also permanently piqued his curiosity about what lies beneath any seemingly benign, unprepossessing surface. He later spent blissful swathes of summer each year tunneling in the soft, sandy earth in the scrubby pine barrens that stretched for miles around the suburban Albany neighborhood where he grew up.

Once a glacial moraine much like Long Island or Cape Cod, this inland seascape had been a paradise for a fledgling excavator. In the process of rooting for dinosaur bones, Martians or buried treasure, little Nate would dig enormous, perilously deep holes, often reaching the water table 10 and 20 feet down. After dinner and on weekends he would pilfer wood, nails and other materials from the many Tuscanini Brothers housing construction sites in the quickly expanding subdivision, dragging the booty into the scruffy dunes to line the walls and build roofing supports for his growing Plutonian empire.

As he shuffled through the death-scented caverns beneath Manhattan with his dying best friend, all of these childhood memories and more came rushing back to Nate, bringing forth a fresh spate of silent tears that temporarily rinsed his irritated eyes. Relieved that in the inky blackness Rico couldn't see him, Nate marveled at the sudden realization that, prior to three days ago, he hadn't seriously wept for 12 years. Comparatively, he realized, he had now become a blubbering fool. He felt exactly as if someone had taken a sledgehammer and smashed a gaping hole in the brick wall he had carefully constructed around his throbbing, naked heart. He felt violated and frightened, dangerously exposed, achingly sad and transcendently ecstatic, all at the same time. He figured he should probably patch his busted wall up as soon as possible, but decided not to do anything about it for the time being. It was good to actually feel something for once.

* * *

Nate was awakened from his reverie by a muffled shout from Rico.

They had made it through the South Ferry turnaround without incident, and were heading north through the 1/9 tunnel. A loud, steady rumble permeated the void around them, from the heavy trucks and equipment passing above.

Rico had been spooked by what he thought was a glimmer of light in the passage ahead of them. Nate hadn't seen anything, and as they crouched motionless with lamps off the tunnel was blacker than a moonless night. After a few moments commiserating in hushed tones, they decided to press forward slowly without illumination, keeping to the right side of the tracks, where they could duck behind the limited protection afforded by the tunnel supports and hope for the best if anyone came through.

After two minutes of unimpeded progress in pitched darkness, they began to trip on stones, wood and other debris. This and the fact that they were afraid to turn a lamp on for even a split second slowed their pace to a crawl. As they moved slowly forward, using their hands as well as legs to climb over unseen obstructions, the dark, narrowing space was suddenly pierced by a slender beam of light from a source a few hundred feet ahead.

Squatting behind a boulder of concrete, Nate and Rico pulled the wheezing respirators down off their faces, held their breaths and waited. The single light source jiggled and bounced, its beam focusing on nothing in particular. Its proprietor, stumbling through the partially collapsed tunnel with as much grace as a blind gazelle in a shooting gallery, emitted a series of muffled expletives as he presumably barked his shins on various sharp objects. As the intruder passed by just 10 feet away, cursing, coughing and muttering, the flashlight he was carrying illuminated his sweat-beaded countenance for an instant. The man's weathered ebony face was clearly adorned with a tattered eye-patch.

"Mo?" blurted Rico. "Mo' Better?"

"Whoa! Don't shoot! I give up!" cried the man, his flashlight clattering to the ground.

"Mo, it's OK, it's Rico." Rico took off his helmet, turned its lamp on and pointed it onto his own face. Nate did the same, so as not to shock the man twice.

"Shit. I thought you was official," Mo exhaled. He picked up his flashlight and, after shining it up and down to check out both Rico and Nate in their entirety, collapsed onto a hunk of cement. Holding his light between his still-shaking knees he fished a filthy, half-smoked blunt and what resembled a 40-year-old Mickey Mouse pez dispenser out of his pants, and lit up, taking a luxurious drag. "Damn. Looks like we got us a ninja treasure hunt. Y'all get caught down here lookin' like commandos you'll be doin' more than two days in Rikers like I did."

"Pedrino told Rico about the gold," said Nate, "He said you were down there and saw it. Did you?"

""Well hold up, now, shorty. If I did, I sure as shit wouldn't tell you."

"You told Pedrino," said Rico.

"I didn't say shit to Pedrino," countered Mo, staring a dagger with his good eye. "Motherfucker just frontin' again, that's all. Ain't got time for no monkey-ass junkie."

"What's in the bag?" queried Nate, noticing the small heap at Mo's feet.

"None o' your damn business," returned Mo. "I'm late. This meeting over?"

"Come on, Mo, baby," cooed Rico hoarsely, turning on what was left of his street charm. "How many times I give you a taste when you needed it? We brothers; you even said it more than once. I just want to see the shit and take my sick mama a Christmas present."

"I thought you was Jewish," replied Mo toothlessly, either smiling or sneering, Nate couldn't tell which. "Aww, Fuck it. Jus' don't tell nobody you seen me down here. I ain't found no gold, but I means to keep comin' back until I do. They got sweeps coming through all the time, so you got to be careful. I got jacked up last time I came down here, and spent two days lookin' at a light bulb, sayin' no, no, no. I told the suckers I live down here in a cave, and I look so fucked up they believed me. You motherfuckers won't be so lucky, and neither will I, if they catch me again.

"Y'all better stay clear for now. There's a white-suit squad in there, looking at some real nasty shit."

"What kind of nasty shit?" queried Nate, suddenly interested.

"Fuck-all if I know. Wasn't there two days ago. A big wall musta busted from all the heavy shit goin' down upstairs. Looked like rusty old barrels, millions of 'em, spilled all over with acid and shit. Real Toxic Avenger shit. All orange and green and steamin' up like a motherfucker. Some started on fire, an' they was puttin' it out. Fucked up my eyes and made me sick. I couldn't hit it, so I had to quit it."

"Shit," said Rico. "You didn't find no gold? So what's in the bag?"

"I hit up the drugstore, yo. A little something for my nerves."

Despite Mo's urging to the contrary, Nate and Rico opted to resume their quest, at least for the time being. They made arrangements to meet up with Mo in two days at the corner of Second Ave. and St. Marks to compare notes. After telling them what to expect and informing them of a couple of surefire alternate escape routes, Mo continued on his way. "Hope them shits help you breathe better'n I could," he said helpfully, pointing to the respirators dangling on their necks. "They got that whole messed-up section lit up with floodlights right now, so watch yourself. God bless."

* * *

One of the things Mo had mentioned in his briefing was the route through to the concourse level, which they would never have found had they not run into him. Much of the Cortlandt St./World Trade Center station just ahead was filled with rubble. However, an overhead ventilation tunnel, accessible by climbing a mound of collapsed ceiling, led to an outlet on the north end of the station, which was only partially destroyed. Mo had left a coil of rope tied to a grating at the other end for letting himself down.

They accomplished much of this claustrophobic passage by feel, turning their lamps on only intermittently to catch their bearings. The smell was so strong in the crawlspace they could no longer risk taking off their respirators. They would have to deal with the stinging in their eyes later. How Mo' Better's lungs had withstood this toxic Hades without his passing out was a mystery to Nate. Maybe it was the weed.

Because, despite the deluxe respirators, Nate and Rico still felt as if something very bad was happening to them. Breathing became extremely laborious, as their air passages filled with protective mucus and water to keep whatever poisonous particles had gotten into them at bay. Tears flowed freely, and the exposed skin of their wrists, necks, and upper faces began to itch and burn.

Once they lowered themselves down using Mo's rope on the other side, the air quality improved markedly, and they resolved to push on. The station, stairwells and turnstiles were nearly unscathed, and were as eerily accessible as they had been at rush hour on the morning of September 11. Emerging in the darkened concourse, they cautiously played their lamps around the area. Far to the left (west), pieces of the collapsed exoskeleton of Building 1 could be seen glinting in a vast mass of rubble. Directly around the area where they were standing, for what looked like a short distance to the south and for a longer distance to the east, the concourse and storefronts looked much as they would have during a power blackout, except for the ubiquitous layer of dust.

After getting their bearings, they proceeded west along a wall of stores, which opened up into the open mall area at the center of the concourse, where the food court and Path escalators were. Amazingly, although debris was everywhere, the massive bank of escalators was still intact. Climbing carefully down the steep, treacherous, rubble-strewn footing of one of these conveyances brought them to the mezzanine level, where they then turned around and proceeded in a southeasterly direction. They hoped to find Mo's magical back-door route to the subterranean section of Building 4, where he had estimated the mother lode to be. Mo had said that finding a stairwell in the concourse level of the collapsed Building 4 itself would be impossible, as it was entirely filled with the remains of the building.

As Mo predicted, they were thwarted by what they encountered next. Rounding a corner in a hallway off of the Path complex mezzanine, they saw ahead of them a brilliant orange glow emanating from the slightly opened set of utility doors at the dead end of the passage. "That's it. Let's go back," said Rico.

"OK. But I want to see something first. Stay here, and run if I yell," said Nate.

"No way, motherfucker, don't leave me alone."

"I'll be right back. I just want to check something out."

Gold, schmold, thought Nate. His secret obsession was to verify with his own eyes Mo's account of an underground toxic chemical spill bad enough to require a hazmat brigade in an environment where tens of thousands of gallons of jet fuel, PCBs and asbestos had already burned into the atmosphere. What was the point? During one of her anti-USE tirades, Sheila had alluded to the existence of "millions of barrels of toxic waste" having been illegally dumped in mob construction sites around the Northeast. He had to wonder if the World Trade Center was one of those sites. Now *that* would be news.

"Nate." Rico's eyes shone in the orange glow.

"What, Rico?"

"I love you, brother."

"I love you, too, buddy. Now don't freak out. I'll be right back, I swear."

Leaving Rico huddled in the hall, Nate edged up slowly toward the doorway, keeping in the shadows. The closer he got, the more he could see through the opening. The room beyond was an enormous vehicle access bay, with loading docks along the left (east, Nate reckoned) wall. The entire cavernous area was floodlit by arrays of portable lights, under which scores of hazmat workers were working. What they were working on lay directly before him: a 500-foot-wide section of the massive south wall had collapsed into the interior, along with many tons of fill that had formerly been packed behind it. Along with the dirt, rocks and stone were, if not quite "millions," many hundreds, if not thousands of rusted, oozing 55-gallon drums. Even through his mask, Nate could identify the odor. It was exactly the same stench he and Rico had suffered through while coming through the ventilation passage a half-hour earlier. They must have been crawling right over it.

* * *

A deafening roar erupted behind Nate. He whipped around in time to see the world falling down on top of the section of hallway where Rico had just been standing. "Rico!" There was no use. A cloud of dust billowed toward him down the corridor—more ceiling was caving in. If Rico were still in there, he would be crushed beneath 20 tons of food court. If Nate didn't run, he would be, too.

Nate pulled the heavy, damning bolt cutters out of his messenger bag, tossed them backward toward the dust cloud and ran out of the hallway into the brightness. Three white-suited hazmat workers were running toward him. "Collapse!" he yelled. "Man down!" Gesticulating wildly toward the door, he jogged toward the trio until they were about 50 feet in front of him, then made a sharp cut left and sprinted for the loading docks.

"Hey!" he heard from behind him, as he ran for the nearest bay, at least the length of a football field away. Other white shapes ran toward him from the work area. In their clumsy moon suits, none of his pursuers were any match for him, despite the fact that his helmet and his respirator weighed him down considerably—and that he was still technically hung over from his afternoon cockfighting session with Rico.

Rico! Hopefully someone would find him and pull him out alive. Forcing thoughts of his friend's frightened, imploring face from his mind, Nate vaulted the lip of the loading dock, turned on his lamp and headed for the nearest exit. He didn't stop running through the pitch-black hallway beyond. He may have left the hazmat workers in the dust, but they would be calling somebody and there would no doubt be a hastily organized National Guard manhunt for a black-clad ninja fool who had left behind a dead partner and a monster set of bolt cutters.

He decided to take a left turn whenever feasible, hoping to find an alternate route back to the PATH complex. Except for a layer of dust, the section of sub-basement he was running through seemed structurally un-scathed by the destruction. It was apparently a utility and service-oriented labyrinth, packed with storage rooms and banks of freight elevators for the businesses in the concourse area above.

Sensing tumult in the hallways behind, he kept the pace brisk, until the beam of his lamp fell on a doorway, illuminating the room number: 411. "I'll be dipped," Nate said aloud, stopping in his tracks. Remembering all the movies he'd seen in which greed killed the asshole who wouldn't let go of a bag of gold as it dragged him to his watery grave, he decided to leave well enough alone. "Rico, you were right on it," he couldn't stop himself from thinking. "You knew it, little buddy. Fuck."

Somehow, Nate regained enough composure to get himself moving again. Pushing through a doorway at the end of another long dead-end, Nate found himself in a large open space. He could hear sirens wailing and whooping faintly somewhere far above him. Giving the area the once-over with his lamp, he could see he was at the northern end of the PATH mezzanine. He ran for where he thought the lower stairwells would be.

They were still there, just as they were when he used to visit that chain-smoking belly dancer in Jersey City back in 1991. He hopped the turnstile and ran down the dusty stairs, onto the platform. A ghost train lingered in the blacked-out station, as if waiting to transport the deceased across the Styx to Hoboken. He ran down the platform to the end, where a section of ceiling had collapsed on top of the train. Squeezing past the last car, he jumped down onto the track bed, which was submerged under six inches of water. After sloshing a half mile down the tunnel, he heard commotion far behind, and stepped up the pace.

He estimated he was at least halfway under the Hudson, wading through four feet of rising water and wondering if he would survive, when he saw lights ahead of him in the tunnel. Edging closer along the wall, he approached cautiously, at this point hoping to get caught rather than face drowning or a bullet in the back. It was apparently a work detail, and he was directly upon them when they noticed him. He thought fast.

"Hey, fellas, have you seen my partner? We got separated."

"No," said the burly foreman, eyeing his get-up and messenger bag suspiciously. "And who the hell are you? This area's restricted."

"I know the area's *restricted*," bluffed Nate. "Where the hell do you think I just came from? I'm with a Con Ed emergency unit. We had a leak situation we were looking for back there, and my partner and I got separated. He's got our radio. Have you seen him?"

"No, sorry. Look, pal, why don't you just hang out here and we'll call somebody to see if they can help you."

"No thanks," said Nate, trying to smile nonchalantly. "I almost drowned back there. I'm cold and I want to go home. How far is Jersey?"

"About a half mile. It's a good thing we were in here pumping this shit out, or you'd probably be dead."

"Well, I have to say thank you. I prayed for a miracle, and it looks like somebody up there heard me. Thank you, friend."

"All right, chief. Just be careful. Fred, you call somebody to meet him at Grove Street and open the gate so he can get out."

Trying to remember the Jersey PATH map from 10 years earlier, Nate sloshed onward. As the water level lessened, he moved faster, finally breaking into a dead run. After a spell, he came upon a major intersection.

If he went straight, he knew he would end up at Grove Street, and after that Journal Square. He imagined his pursuers having reached the tunnel-pumping crew by now, in which case there would probably be a squad car waiting for him. He turned north, and ran for ten minutes until he reached a station. The platform overhead was lit, but empty. Signs said "Pavonia Newport."

Still paranoid, he ditched his helmet and respirator, crouched low and, staying in the shadows beneath the lip of the northbound platform, slowly crawled the entire length of the station, trying not to excite the rats. He had remembered where he was, and he knew what he had to do. He would continue on to Hoboken, a major rail link that was probably open and crowded, and into which he could disappear.

* * *

Only after Nate was in a taxicab heading out of Hoboken toward the George Washington Bridge did he allow himself to think about what had happened. He looked back at the golden rising sun hovering magnificently behind the billowing gray plume where the twin towers had stood, and began once again to weep.

Nate's cab driver, a gregarious Muslim whose hack license bore the name of Muhammad Adjani, noticed Nate's distress. "It is terrible, what these people have done," he said. "This is not Islam. This is evil. These people who did this will be punished by God."

"Yes, I suppose they will," agreed Nate, without expressing the remainder of his thought: "But what about the rest of us?"

As undersized National Guardsmen charged with protecting Manhattan from further attack pulled over vehicles piloted by dark-skinned road warriors, Muhammad Adjani's American flag-festooned cab slipped right through the Homeland Security dragnet. The soldiers' profiling decision was made easier by reason of Muhammad's middle-aged Caucasian cargo who, despite his disheveled, black-clad appearance and the pain on his face from all he had been through for the last 72 hours, looked thoroughly, unthreateningly American.

Time would tell how wrong this assessment was.

CHAPTER FOUR
SOUL SURVIVOR

When Nate checked the 5:00 news that evening on Sheila's $5,000 flat-screen TV, he saw a report that a piece of heavy equipment had fallen through the Ground Zero work area. An unidentified man working in one of the levels below had been found alive under the resultant rubble. "Alive" would be putting it strongly, however. The man had been in critical condition with severe head and spinal trauma, a punctured lung and multiple fractures, and was sent to Mount Sinai in a coma. The broadcast image of the victim's heavily bandaged, obviously decimated face showed nothing that could be easily identified as human, much less Exman-esque.

Nate knew the man was most likely Rico, but was in no mood to jump for joy. Rico's time was up in a matter of weeks anyway, and his dreadful injuries would put a serious crimp in whatever quality of life he had left.

Nate obsessively considered his own Catch-22 predicament. There was no way he could involve himself in Rico's situation, or even tip anyone off. As concerned as he was for his friend, Nate's first concern was for himself. If he showed up at the hospital or told anyone what had happened, he would be nailed. Whether the man they found was dead or alive, the authorities would surely still be looking for his partner in stupidity.

The media had been told that the victim was a rescue worker, and did not report his being charged with any crime. There was no mention of any escaped colleague or witness to a massive toxic waste spill. Nate doubted there ever would be, just as he doubted that Rico would ever recover.

Luckily for Nate, he had insisted that he and Rico empty their pockets of ID before their jaunt. Assuming the worst—that his friend wouldn't come out of it—it would be days before someone figured out who he was, unless someone working the hospital ward was an Ex-Men fan. Rico's friends and what was left of his family were used to him dropping off their radar; there would be no missing person's report for authorities to match their battered John Doe up to. If Rico did awaken, Nate was reasonably sure his friend wouldn't rat on him. Rico had many faults, but disloyalty was not one of them.

Also serendipitous was the fact that, due to its dicey nature, Rico had not shared his wish list with anyone but Nate. And Nate, as far as anyone save Mo' Better knew, had been a non-entity in Rico's life since the band broke up. Still, the first thing Nate did later that evening was go over to Rico's and eradicate all recent evidence of himself from the premises, including the damning list. He didn't want to stay at Sheila's again—it hurt too much to sleep in that bed. Adjusting his expectations of comfort, convenience and cleanliness to the level of his quickly eroding circumstances, he rented a $99-a-night room at a hooker hotel on West 35th Street, and prepared for the worst.

What was it about lists, anyway? If he got out of this, vowed Nate to himself, he would never write anything down on paper again.

Of course, that would turn out to be a lie.

* * *

Paranoia had crept into Nate's already battered psyche, taking over the top spot. To counteract it, he drank whiskey and ate take-out Chinese food. He cowered in his frayed room all day watching "America Recovers," fantasizing about being chased into an alley where bricks would fall on his head. While nodding off, he continued to obsess over his situation, multiplying the dangers exponentially in his fitful dreams.

The loose cannon in all this was Mo' Better, Nate thought. Although nearly agoraphobic with dread, on Sunday he risked going downtown to the corner newsstand at St. Marks and Second Ave. at 2 p.m. to await Mo for the scheduled debriefing. Pretending to browse, he hid behind the pages of a *New York* magazine for a half-hour, debating internally about what, if anything, he'd tell Mo about Rico, as the Pakistani owner glared at him suspiciously.

Mo failed to show, which due to his status as a reliably unreliable street person should not have been unexpected. But Nate was nonplussed. Upon leaving the store, he began to feel he was being followed; much in the same way, he thought, as Rico's ex had sensed him stalking her. Despite performing what he imagined were evasive actions that would expose a clandestine pursuer, he caught no one actually following him. Nonetheless, the feeling of being hunted persisted.

As soon as the Wall Street area was opened up after the weekend, Nate ventured back downtown and retrieved his bike from its hiding place, leaving Rico's where it was. If by chance anyone ran into him and asked if he knew what Rico had been up to, he would feign ignorance. He continued to look over his shoulder, and rode against traffic on one-way streets whenever possible.

On Tuesday Nate's self-imposed flophouse exile was broken only by a few carefully plotted sorties: to the liquor store, the newsstand and the bank branch at Broadway and 24th to all-but-empty his and Sheila's account. After spending the night worrying about being robbed, on Wednesday he traveled around to different check-cashing venues and American Express offices buying traveler's checks.

During this bleak period of near-insanity, using a relatively rational section of his brain, he started thinking about where in the world he might want to go next. Because as far as Nate Randall was concerned, New York City had become a ghost town. As vast and cosmopolitan as it was, it was now too small. The city had achieved the status of his twin hometowns of Albany and Boston, which were places to be avoided: grim repositories of dark memories and failed past lives, rife with dangers both real and imagined. As he had done so many times already in his life, Nate Randall would have to disappear.

* * *

Disappearing would be easy this time, because Nate was already falling through the cracks. He had no real job, no home of his own, and wasn't registered to vote. He hadn't paid income taxes in five years. He was the oldest person he knew who had never been called for jury duty. His girlfriend and chief benefactor was dead, and his best friend in the city was either similarly deceased or was an unidentifiable vegetable in a charity hospital ward.

Nate had lived in New York for a decade, yet was unknown outside a small circle of music people, alcoholics and lowlifes. He was as much a creature of the streets as Mo' Better or Pedrino, only luckier: he was a white man in America, with an undeserved, unearned $49,200 in traveler's checks burning a hole in his pocket. He would be all right, as soon as the coast was clear. There was no hurry.

Still, Nate's post-traumatic limbo stretched on, with no end in sight. Searching for clues to his future, he watched television, where it was reported hourly that huge jackpots were being amassed to heal the wounds of the various classes of World Trade Center tragedy survivors. In spite of his disgust with himself for even thinking such thoughts, Nate couldn't help wondering idly if there would be a taste of the pie for himself.

He decided to forget about it. Even if he escaped prosecution or eternal damnation for his recent crimes, Nate was a carpetbagger of a survivor who had never belonged downtown in the first place. His legal relationship to a bona-fide World Trade Center victim was a mere fading glimmer in his eye on the day of her death. He certainly wouldn't rate as a first class tragedy fund recipient when the man began doling out the blood money. Sheila wasn't a cop or a fireman, and the list makers wouldn't know Nate Randall existed; his name wasn't even on her lease. Sheila's parents—rich and connected upstate Republicans—would reap whatever foul benefits had accrued as a result of her death.

Nate was already starting to feel better about himself for his relatively weak mercenary streak when the water broke: the morning news reported that John Doe had been identified as Rico Exman. The poor chump had awakened briefly, long enough to croak out his name and his mother's phone number, and the pain was so excruciating that he lapsed back into unconsciousness before he could refuse to answer another question.

Hospital officials said he was still in critical condition, and that he was in the final, fatal stages of Hodgkins disease as well. He had two days to live, at most.

News outlets began to milk the story of Rico Exman the budding rock star turned selfless cancer victim, almost too sick to walk, who nonetheless was so moved by the suffering of others that he sacrificed his own ebbing life to lend a hand combing the rubble at Ground Zero for survivors.

Partially relieved, Nate immediately got in touch with some old band members and put together a posse to hide within while visiting his friend. Rico hadn't yet been transferred out of the intensive care unit to a hospice unit and couldn't be seen, but scores of people had already gathered in a waiting area and were holding vigil. Nate pretended he was as shocked and dismayed about what had happened to Rico as the rest of them, and through his tears surveyed the area for undercover police or federal agents. There didn't seem to be any.

Rico died right on schedule two days later, a week before his 31st birthday, hooked up to a respirator and surrounded by remnants of friends, family and flowers that made his pallid skin break into a rash. On television he was effectively, if improperly, eulogized as yet another martyred volunteer hero.

* * *

With his friend's brief resurrection and death, Nate's debilitating fog of guilt and paranoia lifted, if only slightly. Under the circumstances, the police and FBI obviously had much bigger fish to fry than finding and punishing the mysterious associate of a fallen enigma.

Nate emerged from his cocoon and began clearing his belongings out of Sheila's apartment. He knew it would soon dawn on her real estate management company that he was nothing but an unemployed gigolo, and he figured they would not welcome his continued ability to gain access to her $4,000-a-month crib. She had already paid until the end of her lease in January, so the money was effectively the realty's and they could re-rent the place to anyone stupid enough to move to lower Manhattan in the dawn of the Age of Terror. They could have it.

After the band broke up Nate had continued paying for a large room at Gotham Mini Storage, in order to mothball all of the filthy, beer-stained musical equipment Sheila didn't want lousing up her apartment—and as a hedge against what was never a certain future with her. Because he had first rented it when he was flush with money from the record deal and expected to amass even more obsolescent electronic crap, there was enough space left to cram everything he owned, and more.

He had so much extra room, in fact, that he found himself ransacking Sheila's place so as to foil her fat, scheming sister Julia from picking over the bones of their lives together. He went far beyond removing his own few belongings and some shared photos and mementos. He also helped himself to assorted booty that had technically belonged to Sheila alone, telling himself that she would have wanted him to have them to remember her by, and that she would have hated for Julia to get her chubby hands on them.

Sheila had surrounded herself with lovely antiquities to ward off insanity and depression. She was quite a shopper, and was well known in the expensive knick-knack bazaars of SoHo and Dutch Hollow, where she and Julia had grown up in horsy splendor.

Misting over with the memories Sheila's treasures evoked, Nate, as unauthorized executor of her estate, filched a good number of them. He looted her bronze bust of a man she had once tried vainly to explain to him was Sextus Empiricus, the obscure codifier of Greek Scepticism. He annexed her Egyptian tapestry and her 19th-Century leather-bound volumes of Shakespeare. All this and much more was carted off to Gotham Mini Storage, where it would doubtless add immeasurably to Nate's guilt, sadness and inability to let go.

On Nate's last tearful day in Sheila's apartment, as he was picking up her filing cabinet loaded with stolen corporate secrets, the horrid Julia came by. She was a troglodyte. A bloated, Bizarro version of Sheila, she sweltered under a great sculptured helmet of jet-black hair, her puffy eyes dripping with mascara and oceans of eye-stinging perfume, the ozone-depleting mist from which temporarily blotted out the smell of the still smoldering ruins down the street. Her unimaginably dense, squarely built body strained the seams of a ridiculous floor-length sable coat.

Posthumous jealousy of her better-looking dead sibling was stamped on Julia's stony face like a Kabuki mask. A New Jersey housewife and prolific breeder who was two years younger than Sheila, she had always maintained a frosty distance from her sister and her lengthening train of loser boyfriends. She had openly despised Nate for five years and had no trouble showing it, even now. The feeling was mutual.

"What are you doing here?" she sniffed, casting a suspicious eye around the room. Nate had left enough trinkets and big-ticket items lying around to satisfy her that he wasn't a grave robber. Nonetheless, despite his disdain for the woman, his heart was racing.

"Reminiscing. Actually, now that you're here, leaving."

He lifted the filing cabinet onto a dolly and started to leave.

"Whose is that?" she demanded.

"Mine. Whose do you think?" he lied.

"There could be important papers of Sheila's in there. Her will, perhaps? What's the combination?"

"Bug off. Her will's in that shoebox over there. Don't worry, she left everything to you."

Julia stared at the Gucci shoebox, which did in fact contain Sheila's will. Drawn up six years earlier, it was a simple document that left her entire inheritance to the Sierra Club and specified that she be cremated. Nate felt a *frisson* of ironic satisfaction that Sheila had already achieved half of her postmortem goals. He wished the Sierra Club luck in implementing the other half; they would need it dealing with this crew.

"If anything's missing, I swear, I'll sue," said Julia, scoping the room like a hungry raptor.

Luckily, thought Nate, the bitch had no idea how much crap Sheila had amassed.

"Go ahead. Sheila would have wanted it that way."

"Bastard. She told me what a cheat you are."

"Did she."

"You killed my sister. If it weren't for you she wouldn't have stayed here. I hope you rot in Hell."

"Mmmm. I'm sure I'll see you there."

As Nate loaded the filing cabinet into the double-parked rental van, cursing Julia's fat face, he failed to notice the dark blue 1998 Lincoln Town Car idling at the curb next to a fire hydrant a half block away. When he got in the van and drove down the street, taking a right onto Church, the big Lincoln pulled out and followed the van at the last possible moment, running the yellow light.

Lost in a particularly vivid memory of Sheila's laughing face as she purposely peed on him in the shower, Nate never once looked in the rear view mirror.

CHAPTER FIVE
MOVING AND STORAGE

The Gotham Mini Storage in Soho was a beehive, overrun with TriBeCan and Battery Park City refugees in addition to the usual crush of itinerant street vendors, musicians, artists and space-challenged apartment dwellers trying to use the facility's only double-wide elevator. If a cynic ever doubted for a moment that Manhattan remained a melting pot, a visit to this ecumenical, colorblind city-within-a-city would set the infidel straight. The seeds of the constant barrage of world-beating cultural trends coming out of the city during the 1990s were often sown in conversations between tenants of Gotham Mini Storage during interminable stints waiting for the elevator.

The lobby was, in fact, where Nate had met Rico 10 years earlier. The Ex-Men may not have quite made it, but they sure as shit had started a trend, thought Nate. The ultra-funky, rap-influenced hardcore rock sound they had introduced at the seedy, cocaine-happy Nightingale Bar in 1991 and had taken to the big leagues was now all over the fucking radio like a plague. Fuck it.

Nate's storeroom was on the third floor and he wasn't about to lug 250 pounds of inadmissible evidence up the stairs. He settled in the queue behind an East Asian gentleman in a harlequin suit, who was tending a six-foot-tall spherical cage apparatus that looked like a miniature Unisphere with a strap-in cockpit seat from a World War I Sopwith Camel suspended in its center.

"What is that?" Nate couldn't help asking.

"A human bowling ball."

"Nice. Are the pins human, too?"

"No. The pins are upstairs."

"I see."

Despite the collegially diverse environment, that was about the limit of Nate's sociability for the day. He was still feeling vulnerable and withdrawn. While waiting for the elevator, he unlocked the filing cabinet—22-35-13—and opened the top drawer. He fumbled through the "A" section, looking for anything labeled "Amorphous." He didn't find the folders right away. They were mis-filed—or so he thought—in the "B" section, behind "Bill," for Bill McNally, Sheila's father. Nate wondered if Sheila's mental filing system could have been as haphazard as the contents of this cabinet were and, if so, whether her sloppily administered, unreliable memories could have been at the root of her emotional problems.

The first folder was thick with indecipherable documents: incorporation papers, delivery manifest reports, scores of memos written in what may as well have been Aramaic on USE letterhead and on the business stationery of a trucking company called Janssen Moving and Storage, and other such arcana. There was a letter from the New York State Department of Environmental Conservation (DEC) that seemed to be communicating that a request was being denied for the Janssen company to store paint in one of its warehouses.

"What the fuck?" thought Nate. If a smoking gun implicating USE in some kind of corporate atrocity was hidden in this load of undifferentiated mumbo-jumbo, it was news to him. He had a feeling he was engaging in an exercise in futility that would only prove how crazy Sheila was.

Gradually though, and with difficulty, Nate began to piece things together. As the elevator queue inched forward, he stubbornly read through page after page, using the filing cabinet as a stand-up desk and pushing it forward on its dolly with his feet. His head hurt. He felt like he was back in school. He cursed Sheila's name more than once, then caught himself. "Sorry, baby," he whispered. "I'll stop."

"What's that?" queried the bowling man.

"Nothing. Sorry."

An hour later he was into the middle of the second "Amorphous" folder, and glanced up to see that the waiting line had barely moved. Although there were still fifteen carts, loaded to Joad-like proportions, arrayed in front of him—in addition to the human bowler, whose Jupiter-sized bowling ball alone would take up the entire space in the elevator—he was far from annoyed. Something in him had changed. He was becoming slowly, inexorably obsessed with the task at hand. His head no longer hurt, and his heartbeat had regained some of its lost authority. Because what had begun as a pursuit for clues to Sheila's madness was becoming a quest for knowledge that she alone may have possessed. She wasn't fucking crazy, he thought, she was *right*.

"Thank you, baby," he muttered under his breath to his dead fiancée, trying once again to stifle a burst of tears. "I love you for this. I really fucking love you."

"Pardon?" asked the bowler, eyeing him suspiciously.

"It's OK. I'm OK. Thanks."

* * *

Among other things, Nate had discerned from Sheila's files that Janssen Movers was no ordinary moving company. In fact he doubted that it was a moving company at all, in the classic sense. Originally named Amorphous Corp., the company had been created in 1980 by a pair of ex-USE engineers to be the prime contractor for transporting waste chemicals used in the production of computer components at the USE Corporation's two city-sized manufacturing plants up in the Hudson Valley. Janssen maintained a permanent multi-million-dollar annual contract with USE to remove these chemicals, no questions asked. It seemed that in the 1960s, USE had gotten itself in big trouble, having to spend nearly a billion dollars for various cleanups after having been caught pouring toxic chemicals directly down its own factory drains into the Mid-Hudson region's ancient aquifers. The company again was on the losing end of expensive litigation in the 1970s, after its chosen mob-run hauling companies were caught sullying the area's giant "sanitary" landfills with USE waste products.

This was very big business, apparently. If the trucking reports, company profiles, press releases, news clips and other documents in Sheila's files were to be believed, many millions of gallons of toxic waste annually resulted from the manufacture of silicon chips and wafers during every stage of their production by USE's white-suited clean-room technicians. Tons of chemicals would be used during processes such as photolithography, patterning, etching, junction formation, oxidation, layer deposition and metallization: acetone, arsenic, benzene, cadmium, hydrochloric acid, lead, methyl chloroform, toluene, and trichloroethylene, just to name a few.

A USE promotional flyer jammed in a folder between two memos about clean room procedures crowed about how chip manufacture was necessarily one of the most anal-retentive processes on earth. Indeed, each tiny microchip element would be dipped into a petri dish containing a few ounces of lethal miracle solvent. After one single element was dipped a single time, the chemical content of the dish would be considered spent, never to be re-used.

In a folder labeled "Good Luck, Lemmings," Sheila also had filed information and news articles regarding a class action lawsuit against USE by 99 cancer sufferers and 14 mothers of kids with serious birth defects. The litigants all claimed to have worked for protracted periods in the company's clean rooms in its Hudson Valley East Waterkill plant during the 1980s, and their various forms of cancer were consistent with experts' predictions of prolonged exposure to perchloroethylene, benzene and other clean room chemicals.

The lawsuit and its repercussions had been national news in 2000, with even knee-jerk USE boosters like *Digital Century* magazine wailing that USE could "easily be bankrupted in the manner that Dow Corning had been by the massive class action over failed silicone breast implants."

Lawsuits or not, USE's clean rooms were still operating at full capacity as of July 2001, according to Sheila's files. The daily output of dirty solvent from countless petri dishes was being poured into 30- and 55-gallon drums and loaded into Janssen trucks—an average of three semi trailers per day per plant—for direct transport to a recycling plant in Buffalo, some 350 miles away. Or, as other documents in a third "Amorphous" folder seemed to be saying, maybe not. There were reams of New York State DEC memoranda complaining of "gross inconsistencies" and "statistical manipulation" in Janssen's mandated reporting of deliveries to the Buffalo facility—apparently the only one of its kind in the Northeast. For some reason, it seemed that the Janssen folks, rather than trucking the stuff to where it was supposed to go, were stockpiling it in their three giant ware-houses without approval from the state environmental authorities. Nate wondered: To what end would a moving company divert millions of gal-lons of dirty solvent just to keep it lying around?

The used chemicals being ostensibly transported and recycled were mostly powerful petroleum-based solvents—the kind of stuff that would eat the chrome off a trailer hitch and, according to some of the badly filed literature in the folders, give you cancer. USE went through a lot of ben-zene, the main ingredient in the burning jet fuel that was currently sting-ing everybody's eyes around lower Manhattan. USE chip-manufacturing technologists were also particularly fond of employing tongue twisters like perchloroethylene, trichlorethylene, trichloroethane, toluene, polyvinyl chloride and methylene chloride.

Additional literature in the folders described each chemical in detail and explained exactly what it was used for in microchip production, as well as its common uses and dangers. Besides being a prime ingredient in jet fuel, benzene, a "known cause of leukemia in rubber workers" with an unfortunate tendency to show up in large numbers of buried drums, could be found in paints, inks, adhesives, rubbers, glues, old spot removers and furniture wax. It was presumably what the actress Laura Dern kept trying to get high on in the classic film satire about America's abortion quagmire, "Citizen Ruth."

"Unfortunately, benzene is also one of the primary antiknock ingredi-ents in gasoline," wrote one clever stoner in an exposé article Sheila had clipped out of *Weed Aficionado* magazine, "a fact that gives fits to those trying to prove the existence of cancer clusters. At any rate, it's a good idea not to breathe gas fumes while filling your tank, even if they do smell nice and get you off. Over time, they could kill you as dead as any rubber worker."

Acetone, used to clean chips after the process called "photoresist," can cause comas, kidney, liver, and nerve damage, increased birth defects and lowered ability to reproduce in males.

The multi-named Perchloroethylene (a.k.a. tetrachloroethylene, PCE and "perc") was contained in dry cleaning fluid, metal degreaser, water repellent, paint remover, silicone lubricant, adhesives and spot removers. Like other clean-room chemicals it had also been found with increasing regularity in illegally buried 55-gallon drums and in big nasty blobs in aquifers across the nation. The EPA also classified PCE as an animal carcinogen, saying it caused liver and bladder cancer in rodents and was a "probable" human carcinogen as well.

USE employed PCE almost exclusively as a chip-cleaning solvent until the early 1990s, when it was replaced by trichloroethylene (TCE), allegedly another commonly dumped by-product of clean room technology. It causes liver, lung and testicular tumors, kidney cancer and leukemia in rats (and "probably" humans, too, according to a U.S. Environmental Protection Agency report).

Upon discovering one standout among literally hundreds of thumbnail-sized DEC hazardous waste site reports in the file, Nate found that acetone, PCE and toluene, another poisonous solvent, had other, more exciting uses. Mixed with globs of methylene chloride, a large plume of acetone, PCE and toluene was still, in the year 1999, seeping along the bedrock near the contaminated well of a private home on the outskirts of Dutch Hollow, where in 1991 a big regional cocaine manufacturing operation had been busted. Like most other places where chemicals like these were found to have been spilled, poured or buried in barrels by the thousands, the poison was still there, never having been cleaned up. In most instances, no one had a clue as to how it got there. According to the state's environmental "superfund" rules, if the feds or the state didn't have a perpetrator to hang the blame on and charge for the cost of cleanup, it was more expedient to plow the surface of the site over, cover it with gravel or blacktop, and pipe in water from someplace else.

Nate found it odd that, even though most of the newer toxic sites were clustered within five to 10 miles of one or the other of USE's Hudson Valley plants, there had been no federal or state investigations or actions involving USE since 1980.

Nate could imagine Sheila's disgust upon finding that her home county of Roosevelt—to the naked eye a green, rolling paradise, but in a small corner of which both of USE's Hudson Valley plants were located—was one of the most toxic in the state. According to a statewide map and report in the file prepared by a public interest research organization out of Albany, beautiful Roosevelt County was home to more than 70 large-scale toxic dumping sites. Most of them were of unexplainable origin. The number and scale of toxic sites was more akin to those fouling Hudson County, New Jersey, home of the legendary Meadowlands toxic swamp—or those poisoning Rico's cancer-ridden home county of Nassau on Long Island. Poor Roosevelt County suffered more known toxic waste dumping grounds than Albany, Schenectady, Rensselaer, Greene and Columbia counties combined. Nate knew what Sheila was getting at with her inclusion of this information. Whatever polluting heavy industries those places endured, they didn't hold a candle to USE.

* * *

All of Nate's considerable capacity for obsessive, compulsive behavior—which in the past had only been successfully harnessed once, in mastering the guitar—was now focused on this new task. Even as his head filled with esoterica, acronyms, facts and figures, he craved more. Day was turning to night when the human bowling ball rolled into the elevator in front of him.

Meanwhile, a page from a semiconductor industry-bashing article Sheila had torn out of a lefty environmentalist rag provided Nate with a comprehensive, if highly opinionated, historical perspective on toxic waste:

> *"So what exactly is 'toxic waste,' and why is it so bad?*
>
> *"While it often includes red-bag hospital waste and radioactive materials, the bulk of what is termed 'toxic waste' in the U.S. is generated by the petrochemical industry and the hundreds of other industries, like semiconductor production, that use its end products.*
>
> *"The petrochemical industry was launched in the latter half of the 19th century, when techniques began to be developed to exploit the various hydrocarbon chains contained in crude oil. Since then, nearly every technological step forward has been accompanied by a seriously hazardous by-product, and most of the end products are highly toxic in and of themselves.*

"Samuel Epstein, in his book The Politics of Cancer, *tries mightily to explain, writing: 'Petrochemicals are the quintessence of a 'process industry' in which a small number of primary constituents from crude oil are converted into a large number of intermediate chemicals in a still larger number of large scale end products.'*

"Epstein goes on to reveal that the manufacture of chemical-based products such as paints, solvents, synthetic fabrics, plastics, pesticides and drugs has increased exponentially through the years. As a result, the production of synthetic organic chemicals in the U.S. increased from a billion pounds in 1940 to 30 billion pounds in 1950, to 300 billion pounds in 1976. With the advent of the silicon revolution, driven by the boom in electronics and personal computers, the need for the kinds of killer solvents and other complex hydrocarbons used in the manufacture of computer microchips has driven the nation's production of toxic chemicals to even dizzier heights.

"Toxic waste comes in many forms: from newspaper and magazine ink to the spent chemicals used in industrial dry cleaning operations, from the PCBs used in refrigerator manufacturing to waste oil and dirty solvents from trucking, shipping, airline, train and bus fleets—and to the hundreds of millions of gallons of toxic chemicals gone through annually by the semiconductor industry to produce its precious chips.

"As most industrial manufacturing has been migrated to second and third-world countries by companies looking for cheap labor and less stringent environmental rules, the semiconductor industry has risen to the top echelon of polluters on U.S. soil. Not legally reusable or cheaply or easily recycled, the semiconductor industry's spent solvents are fouled with PCBs, arsenic and other contaminants. These substances are now seeping their way into the nation's air and water, causing significant health problems that strain our medical establishment's ability to keep up."

* * *

A few minutes later the elevator showed up and Nate rolled his treasure inside. An extraordinarily attractive young redheaded woman pushing a cart loaded with boxes of adult diapers joined him, as did a large man with a florid face, lugging an enormous duffel bag. Nate, experiencing the first rush of sexual energy he had felt since September 11, managed a wan smile at the young woman, who smiled back brightly, disarming him. Her smile disappeared when, feeling emboldened, he said: "Are any of those for sale? I seem to have soiled myself."

The red-faced gentleman, whose eyes were obscured by an ungainly pair of wrap-around sunglasses—the kind retired Floridians wear on top of their everyday specs—studiously ignored the botched flirtation, and as Nate slunk off the elevator, the man disembarked too, with the doors closing on the woman's confused scowl. "Don't worry," said Nate, to no one in particular. "I'll get it back."

Turning toward him, the man chuckled in a deep baritone, saying in a curious streetwise brogue: "You'd better, my friend. You sure screwed that one up. You had it in the bag. She was watching you the whole time you were waiting on that line."

"Really? Shit. She was?"

Without further comment, the burly stranger turned on his heels and disappeared around the corner, dragging his heavy duffel bag and chortling to himself.

As the old hormones sloshed around in his bloodstream for the first time in many weeks, Nate considered going after the girl, apologizing to her and using the negative feelings he had aroused in her to manipulate her into the sack. The tactic had worked before.

Yet even as his cock began to stir in his pants in anticipation of the chase, it was being overruled by a new master: his slowly awakening brain. In a sharp departure from his past behavior, Nate managed to calm himself down. He unlocked his storeroom door and wheeled the filing cabinet inside. He pulled out another "Amorphous" folder, sat down on a carton of books, and resumed reading in the dim light of an overhead bulb.

Because as exciting as the return of his old sexual persona was, there was something even more stimulating going on. He could always get back to being a profligate ho-bag; there would be plenty of opportunity for that. But for the time being, Nate's one-track imagination had been captured by something else. He would follow it to its logical end.

Nate was overjoyed that he was actually beginning to understand what Sheila had been trying to get at in her oblique, elliptical way. Although it wasn't stated anywhere in her mass of redundant documentation, it was becoming clear that she was attempting to build a case against USE, Janssen and other entities for polluting the sylvan landscape of her childhood on a far more catastrophic level than anyone could ever imagine. She was backhandedly accusing them of burying billions of gallons of toxic chemicals over the last 35 years under everything imaginable: malls, parking lots, schools, subdivisions, superhighways, sports stadiums, golf courses and even graveyards. The motive for their doing this, she was saying, was to save money and maximize profits.

Nate suspected that Sheila was also trying to show something even more insidious—that the companies involved had created a billion-dollar shadow industry in dirty toxic chemicals. He wasn't certain that her research had actually proven anything, but he had a new respect for her diligence, heart and intelligence. And what he had seen in the bowels of Ground Zero didn't hurt his acceptance of her extreme point of view. He was hooked.

* * *

Two items in the file hinted at how Sheila had become such a foaming radical in the first place. The first was a brown, faded, folded-up newspaper article from the old *New York Sun*, dated August 17, 1964. The article concerned an 18-year-old Irish-American lad who had been arrested after being wounded in the leg during a shootout with police. He and his cohorts had been foiled in their attempt to rob a deli in Manhattan's Hell's Kitchen district. They were suspected to be members of the neighborhood's notorious, ultra-violent "Westies" gang, then being led by an urban Robin Hood named Mickey Spillane. The young man's name was William McNally. In Sheila's mind, at least, this gun-toting Irish punk was her father—the same man she had once told Nate had sexually abused her from the time she was 11 years old.

Reading the article made the hairs stand up on the back of Nate's neck.

The second item was a "personal and confidential" letter from the president of Janssen Movers to the USE Corporation's vice president of its

Silicon Technologies Group, one Harvey L. Cathcart. The letter thanked Cathcart for the company's decision to place an indefinite moratorium on what Nate understood from other internal USE memos and PR material was a program to shift the silicon division's dependence on petroleum-based solvents to a non-chemical, laser and sound-based technology. It praised the USE Corporation's "dedication to continuing longstanding relationships," and promised that the Janssen Company would "continue to provide quality removal services long into the future." Cathcart and his wife were invited to spend a weekend at the Janssen Company's resort complex at the Jersey Shore, as well as to a pre-season New York Giants game at the Meadowlands.

The letter was signed by the Janssen Moving and Storage Company's president: William T. McNally.

* * *

It was 8:55 p.m. and Nate was starting to fade when he found, stuck in the back of the drawer, a USE-formatted three-and-a-half-inch floppy diskette labeled "Adventures in Pollockistan: How USE, the Government and the Mob Conspire to Give You Cancer — Copyright 2001 by Sheila McNally and Reginald Thurston Brown."

The government? The mob? Reginald Thurston Brown?

Hopefully, thought Nate, he was holding in his hands the Rosetta Stone to Sheila's files and to her life. It suddenly came to him exactly what he was going to do. He was going to Dutch Hollow, to tilt at windmills.

Nate put the diskette in his pocket and locked the cabinet, daydreaming about his plan of action. Somehow he would have to ingratiate himself with the unsuspecting rubes of Dutch Hollow and environs, as well as with Sheila's family and with the prevailing subculture of USE company men and women. He would slowly infiltrate their lives and ferret out the truth in what Sheila had described. He would find and interrogate this Reginald Thurston Brown person.

As Nate distractedly slipped the big American lock-bolt through the metal holes in the door and jamb to secure his room, a shadow fell over him from behind. He turned around in time to see a beefy, beet-red face half concealed behind an incongruous pair of aerodynamic sunglasses, looming swiftly toward him like a moon-sized killer asteroid. And then his world went dark once again.

* * *

Nate awoke to the sound of déjà vu: sirens screaming. His head swam with pain. A smoky, acrid smell irritated his nostrils, and as he staggered to his feet he could see tongues of flame lapping at the ceiling over the bank of storage rooms behind him. The pain behind his eyes was blinding.

He saw a floodlit exit sign and stumbled toward it. His head throbbed crazily. He could taste blood. Pushing the exit door open, he realized he was only seeing with his right eye. He reached up and felt for his left. It was wet and sticky.

In the stairwell he slipped and fell. He got up again, reeling from dizziness and pain, and retched violently. As he began to pass out, a strong pair of arms reached out from below him and broke his fall.

The next conscious memory Nate had was of waking up on a stretcher in an emergency triage area. A woman in a nurse's uniform and a swarthy policeman in a baseball-style cap were ogling him unabashedly. "He'll live," said the nurse.

"That's good, because he's a witness," said the cop. "Let me know when I can talk to him."

* * *

For the next five days Nate was once again remanded to a St. Vincent's Hospital bed; this time with bandages over both eyes, watching soap operas through a pinhole. The right bandage held a plastic cup with a small hole drilled into it over the right eye, to keep his good orb focused straight ahead. This, the helpful nurse said, was to prevent the detached muscles around his busted left eye from getting caught on one another from trying to move it in tandem with the right.

The punch from the giant Leprechaun had broken the orbit bones behind Nate's left eye and nearly detached his retina. He would probably be able to see, said the doctor, but he would be even uglier, with some scarring from the heavily stitched cuts around his eye and the probability of a permanently dilated left pupil. He would have to go through whatever life he had left with one brown eye and one blue eye, like David Bowie. He should consider himself lucky, said the doctor.

In fact, he did. Nate had been questioned by police in the early morning after, and had apparently answered in a manner that satisfied authorities that he was not the perp who had set off a firebomb in the Gotham Mini Storage building. Besides destroying the third, fourth and fifth floors of the building, the conflagration had killed three people.

Although Nate didn't remember being asked for permission, the tabloid dailies ran Nate's bandaged face on their front pages, along with a police sketch based on his description of the suspect and photos of the other three victims. The fire had taken out yet another heroic New York firefighter during his last week of duty before retirement, as well as a well-known performance artist and an aspiring young opera singer. Even through the pinhole, Nate recognized the two slaughtered civilians: the human bowler and the redheaded girl. Sedated with enough codeine to kill a small laboratory animal, he was blissfully unable to cry.

Later Nate realized that nearly everyone he'd felt a twinge of humanity toward during the last three weeks was dead, probably as a result of their association with him. The paranoia that had so tragically deserted him over the last 48 hours returned with a vengeance. It would never leave him again.

"I *was* being fucking followed," muttered Nate Randall to himself, fondling Sheila's computer disk. "I've got to get serious here."

CHAPTER SIX
TRUST YOUR NOSE

Out in Atlantic Park the local death merchants were still so busy with the funerals of commuting firefighters, money managers and secretaries who had died in the September 11 holocaust that Rico's poor ailing mother had to suck it up and put in a phone call to her old high school sweetheart, Senator Viggiani, to get him to maneuver a weekend slot for her son's memorial service.

The fete, held in a soulless concrete temple in the teeming Jewish foothills of Mount Atlantic Park Mall, was packed with mostly female Tulane alumni and other young professionals who made up the bulk of the Ex-Men's considerable New York area fan base. Introduced to the band during its series of swings through New Orleans, many of these Long Island princesses had become Rico groupies over the years, and could be seen spouting gushers of remembrance for the 10 minutes of true love they had each shared with him in one dressing room lavatory or another. The clueless boyfriends at their sides were also fans, remembering only Rico's onstage performances as he would manfully pretend to direct the band's trademark staccato horn hits and endless, boring choruses. After the show, while their girlfriends had been sucking Rico's cock in the bathroom, these losers had been too busy buying Ex-Men CD's, T-shirts and hats—and trying to chat up the buxom mailing list girl—to notice.

More than a few brand-new fans who had never even met Rico—weeping aficionados of tragic heroism who had first heard his story on the 5:00 news—were also present and adding to the din.

There was, as they say, a lot of love in the room that day.

All Rico's band members, past and present, and all of the eclectic extended family he had assembled over the years were there. Those who were given the opportunity to speak told colorful—if only partly intelligible—stories that brought laughter and tears to the assemblage. It was a lot like the old TV program "This Is Your Life," as played by the Cosby Kids. Nate was so moved by the spectacle that he imagined himself dying young in order to have such an experience for himself; but he knew it was already too late for that.

Even Rico's mesa-rumped, uninvited ex-girlfriend was present, dabbing at her runny nose and the clown-like mascara stains streaming down her smooth caramel cheeks with a soggy, balled-up wad of kleenex. Whatever her motives for leaving him, she had apparently loved him, too.

Misty, red-rimmed eyes were the order of the day, and not only from allergic reactions to the dense, stinging mists emanating from beneath the shopping mall up the street.

Rico's mother, a petite fireplug of a woman who despite her recent physical travails remained a force to be reckoned with, erupted in tears during the cantor's wail and stormed the dais to commune with her son's bony ashes, nearly toppling the urn in the process. Senator Viggiani, subbing for Rico's dead father, brought the house down by somehow patching together false reminiscences of his subversive role in Rico's mom and dad's union, along with patriotic homilies to the trade center fiasco and egregious plugs for his upcoming reelection campaign. "I'm dedicating my uphill fight to Rico Exman and those like him who pour their hearts and souls into following their bliss, no matter what the odds," he concluded, his voice breaking dramatically. "God bless Rico Exman for what he meant to all of us, and God bless America for what it means to people like Rico." As he broke down and wept, the confused yet awed assemblage broke down with him.

Although it still hurt his left eye to do so Nate cried, too, remembering how the world would once again be a far poorer place than it already was. With top-notch flakes like Sheila and Rico dropping like flies in their youth, it suddenly became clear to him why the highways of Florida and Arizona were choked with pinch-faced, slow-moving old sticks-in-the-mud. The people who survived the longest were those who were too thick-skinned and stupid to feel the pain of living. Like cockroaches, stinkweed and kudzu, they had the least to offer, and were the hardest to kill.

In a world such as this, thought Nate, Sheila and Rico didn't have a chance—and neither, if he didn't get his broken heart wall back up soon, did he.

* * *

A mild winter was turning into an early spring. As one of Sheila's wisdom teeth had recently been sifted from the dust at the Fresh Kills landfill, her own standing-room-only funeral was scheduled for the Sunday following Rico's up in Dutch Hollow, at a charming English-style country church. Having taken extraordinary pains to watch his back and avoid being followed out of the city, Nate was already settled in at a local motel under an assumed name, and was looking around for an apartment and a job.

He had visited the village many times before, back when Sheila was still living at home in the year following her graduation from Vassar. Once again he felt the strong kinship with the place—something he had earlier attributed to being with her. The feeling was only partially dampened by his gnawing paranoia and by the interminable, uncomfortably sad memorial service, where every voice teacher, equestrian trainer, lesbian soccer coach and guidance counselor in Roosevelt County rattled on about what a "pearl" Sheila was.

Also of particular concern at the moment was the blight of a baker's dozen of Sheila's former flames—both male and female—who had descended on the event to pay their anonymous respects. Even the few whom Nate couldn't identify from his memory of Sheila's hilarious, dead-on impersonations of them were recognizable from the cocaine-blanched pallor of their skin, the ungainly hardware clogging their lips, noses, eyebrows and ears and the way they struggled to avoid his glance. Nate couldn't fathom how in Sheila's mind he had fit into the continuum of such a pantheon of ghouls. He didn't really want to know.

In the middle of the ceremony, the well ran dry. Embarrassingly, Nate had chosen to run out of tears at the worst possible moment, in full view of Sheila's assembled family and peers. As soon as he noticed Sheila's battle-axe of a mother studying him for signs of human feeling, his sense of emotional failure compounded itself with a bad case of the nerves, freezing over whatever untapped lachrymal reservoirs may have existed. Panicked, he feared he would permanently lose his recently resurrected ability to weep.

He needn't have worried.

Sheila's uncharacteristically teary sister Julia was there with her goombah husband and their raft of ill-behaved children. Nate mused that she was likely most upset at her own glaring deficiencies when compared to the veritable angel being relentlessly eulogized from the dais. Once every few minutes she would cease her slobbering and glare in Nate's direction.

William T. McNally, thankfully, sat with his massive leonine head bowed and never even opened his eyes.

* * *

Later a phalanx of Sheila's older townie friends, a few of whom he had met and caroused successfully with in years past, invited him to the Delafield House, a local watering hole, for some much needed drinks. Here he renewed an acquaintance with Augie O'Malley, the ex-spousal equivalent of Sheila's best friend Emma. An ageless, craggily handsome Irish/Italian sort with a roving eye and a decent sense of country irony, Augie possessed the borderline alcoholic's gift for making a stranger feel at home. So at home, in fact, that Nate gambled and let slip a few scraps from the growing manure pile of secrets that had been festering in his soul since September 11.

Upon verifying his sneaking suspicion that Augie was indeed a pot-smoking pinko liberal and no friend of USE—rare traits in a Roosevelt County resident—Nate dropped a few hints as to what Sheila had been investigating, and that he intended to somehow carry on her work. When he told of his being followed and assaulted and of all of Sheila's evidence having been destroyed, as well as of his adventure at Ground Zero and what he had seen down there, Augie nearly choked on his beer. "Whoa. You've got quite a story cookin' there, kid. There's got to be some way to help you get it out. But first, I have to go drain the main vein. I'll be right back. Don't go anywhere."

Augie, a resourceful, self-taught real estate maverick and property assessor, was the kind of person Nate had always classified as an "enzyme"—he knew virtually everyone and their business in Dutch Hollow and the surrounding hills, and specialized in getting people together just to see how things would turn out. As Augie was an amateur savant at reading people, things usually turned out well.

Nate looked around the smoky, U-shaped bar, and spied a pair of women opposite him, nodding in his direction and talking into their hands in a display of poorly concealed enthusiasm. He remembered seeing them a few pews behind him at Sheila's funeral, dressed in inappropriately short black dresses with spaghetti straps, like they had been auditioning for an '80s disco movie. He had no idea who they were. Both seemed to be in their mid-thirties and were reasonably attractive in a sun-wizened, countrified sort of way, with high, rose-colored cheekbones and wild manes of unfashionably permed, loudly dyed "Jersey" hair. With a twinge of private embarrassment, Nate became aware that he had been missing that sleazy coke-whore look in women for some time.

Realizing from Nate's barely disguised smirk that they had been discovered gossiping about him, they blushed and turned away. Nate figured they were probably local blue-collar horse people who had worked at Sheila's stables. He ordered another Jack Daniels.

Upon his return, Augie motioned to Nate to join him and a large, rumpled, bespectacled man hovering over a pint of Bass Ale and growling obscenities at the Yankees on TV. "Come here, Nate, I want you to meet somebody. Nate, this is Dave Sawicky. Dave, this is Nate Randall, Sheila's fiancé. Nate was with the Ex-Men, Dave, back when they were great. I used to go down and see them all the time at Tramps with Emma and Sheila. They were so fucking hot, I can't believe they didn't go all the way."

Despite being not a day under 50, with a faraway look on his face that indicated he wouldn't know the blues from a beer nut, Dave Sawicky nodded. "That was a great band, all right. I saw you fellas at the civic center opening for George Clinton. I don't know what was wrong with him that night, but you guys just kicked his ass. Nice to meetcha."

"Dave is a student of sixties and seventies soul, Nate. He has a record collection you wouldn't believe. Except for being a Red Sox fan, he's a great guy. He's also the editor of the *Dutch Hollow Chronicle*. I thought because of some of the things you told me that you might want to meet him."

* * *

The three talked long and drunkenly, discovering along the way that they were in the same leaky boat: middle-aged bachelors who had never grown up and gotten married. Most of their conversation was focused unprofitably on grossly oversimplifying the psychological problems of women. At 2 a.m., Dave Sawicky excused himself, but not before inviting Nate to meet with him the next morning to discuss employment opportunities in the community newspaper business. "Just so's you know, my friend," lisped Dave. "I'm not just the fucking editor of the fucking Chronicle; Augie doesn't know what the fuck he's talking about, God bless his freckled ass. I'm the fucking editor of the whole fucking chain of 10 motherfucking newspapers, that's what. If I make it home all right, I'll see you tomorrow at 11. Drive safe."

Augie, who seemed to be holding his beer a bit better than Dave, had sensibly thought to swipe Dave's car keys and managed to convince him to accept a ride home.

"So this is the country," thought Nate. "Neighbor helping neighbor. So beautiful."

He was interrupted from warm thoughts of his fellow man by a tap on the shoulder. "Are you Nate Randall?"

She was the taller of the women from across the bar. Her hair was a disconcerting day-glo orange, nearly matching the color of her improbably pouty lips. Her piercing blue eyes, had they not been concealed beneath an excess of mascara and eyeliner and partially crossed from the effects of too much drink, might easily have been called attractive. From what Nate could tell, she was in fine athletic shape, tending toward the muscular. Her legs, which he had first noticed at the funeral, were fantastic. "Yes, I am. And you are?"

"Natalie Johnson. I knew Sheila—I'm so sorry..." Her speech was slightly slurred, her voice artificially low and raspy from a lifetime of alcohol and cigarettes.

"That's OK..."

"...and Augie and I are old friends—the guy you were talking to."

"Yes, Augie. He's great. I knew him through Sheila. He seems to know just about everybody."

"Yes he does, yes he does. It's funny, Nate, we sort of have the same name. Nate...Natalie..." She placed her hand on his arm and left it there.

"Yes, I believe we do. Natalie's a nice name. I think I would have been Natalie if I was a girl."

"Mmmm." Natalie began to swoon, and Nate imagined himself cleaning her vomit off of his motel sheets.

"I'm sorry Natalie, but I'm a little bit drunk," he said, truthfully. "I'd really love to talk to you sometime, but right now I've got to get home and get some sleep. I have a big job interview in the morning. Could I get your phone number or something?"

Natalie Johnson too eagerly wrote her number on a damp cocktail napkin, adding the words, "CALL ME!" and underlining them twice for effect. To Nate, the effect was somewhat unnerving. As he walked out, he swore he could see her blowing him a kiss.

"Whatever," he sighed, wondering if he'd actually ever be so desperate as to call her.

Nonetheless, it was nice to have been hit on, even if it was by a grave-robbing, coke-addled associate of Sheila's who had been around the block more than enough times. Nate stumbled happily across the parking lot to the motel, which was virtually next door. A marauding herd of stray cats scattered in the misty light of the outdoor spotlight, reminding him through his drunken haze to be careful. On the way, toward the rear of the bar/restaurant parking area, he caught a strong whiff of a familiar, acrid odor, causing the muscles in the back of his throat to tighten. He squinted over his shoulder at the still-lit neon business sign out by the road.

"Delafield House, fucking Delafield House," Nate babbled to himself as he lurched toward his room, fumbling for the key. "Where the fuck I smell that shit before?"

CHAPTER SEVEN
BORN AGAIN

The 7:30 a.m. wake-up call was a bit of a surprise, as Nate couldn't remember having asked the pimple-faced night clerk for it. Shaking the kapok out of his ears, he implored his groggy consciousness to give him an update.

Things came back to him slowly. He had wanted to get up early to get ready for his 11 a.m. interview with Dave Sawicky, whom he dimly recalled having just about guaranteed him a job the night before at Sheila McNally's post-memorial blowout. He had met some people. He found a wadded up, ink-stained cocktail napkin on the nightstand, which when he unfurled it was completely illegible except for two runny, underlined words in block letters: "CALL ME!"

There was definitely a woman involved. He would get to the bottom of it.

He recalled being excited about his move to Dutch Hollow, which despite being where Sheila was born and raised, would be the perfect place to shed his uncomfortable latest skin and reinvent himself as a muckraking, middle-aged cub reporter.

He would need a makeover.

More than most people, Nate embraced change. He had successfully performed complete physical, mental and emotional metamorphoses a number of times before. He was delighted when two years earlier, in the midst of his dead-end run with the Ex-Men, he had attended his 20th high school reunion in Albany and was virtually unrecognizable to everyone

there, including his own sister. Nobody had known him at his 10th reunion, either, due to circumstances which were strangely similar to those
in which he was now embroiled. His ex-girlfriend had just blown her
brains out, snuffing herself and what she claimed in her suicide note was
his "love child."

Nate the Skate. Nate could, and often did, turn on a dime. He stood out
as a particularly nomadic sort, even among a nation of restless Americans.
In addition to his years on the road, he had lived in and left Albany,
Boston, Denver, Clearwater, Fla., Los Angeles and now New York. He'd
toiled, albeit temporarily, at more than 100 jobs—and had fucked more
than twice that number of women, according to his recently fricasseed
woman list. One of his favorite expressions to employ when rationalizing
leaving a girlfriend, a job, a city—or a best friend clinging to life under a
pile of rocks—was this: You can't hit a moving target.

It started with the physical, he thought. You physically alter your circumstances, and other changes will naturally take place. He had physically lifted himself out of Manhattan and plunked himself down in a venue
called Dutch Hollow. He had no ties here except the memories of one of
the many ghosts in his life. He would get over that. He would cut his hair,
shave his beard; begin a new career. Work his way out of it. Stay out of
woman trouble. He had a new goal. The rest would follow.

Nate looked in the mirror. He looked every millisecond of his 39 years,
if not much older. His face was a cut-up mess. He could tell he had lost a lot
of weight over the last few weeks, what with all the drunken mourning, running around being a psycho and getting the shit beat out of him. Up until a
month ago he was fifteen pounds overweight, slightly balding and bespectacled. No longer. He had lost his glasses looking for Sheila, and now that
his left eye was permanently dilated, he could actually see *better*. He hadn't
really needed glasses anyway. They were more of a prop than anything.

What had recently been a short Van Dyke goatee and a stubbly, nearly
shaved pate designed to hide his most obvious physical faults (creeping
baldness, weakening chin) had now grown out haphazardly into a pair of
matted, nappy clumps.

Yes, it was time for total change, he thought boldly. Physical, mental and emotional. Sure, and spiritual, too, if that's your thing. "Is it,

Nate?" he asked his reflection. "Do you believe in God? The Antichrist? Anything?"

The answer, as always, was no.

But now that he had not one but *two* dead ex-girlfriends, now that he had been a failure, a fugitive and fucking *followed* and nearly *killed*, he was more ready than ever for a change. He knew he could count on his physical chameleon quality, which before he began to age properly had been achieved mostly by sculpting his dense, fast-growing head and facial hair into permutations intentionally out of step with the fashions of the times. The Zappa-esque Fu Manchu and carefully tended Afro of his disco-era youth had given way to a full Grizzly Adams beard with attendant scraggly mop for the duration of the yuppified Reagan years, which subsequently were trimmed into an improbable walrus mustache and short, curly ringlets for the nerdy, aerodynamic early '90s. Then came the goatee, which was only radical for about three days until a much-revered tennis Mephistopheles successfully co-opted and popularized it among the Gen-X booboisie. The world had finally caught up with him, it seemed. Either that or he was getting old.

It really was time for a change.

Nate decided to keep his hair relatively short, and shave his face clean, for now. Doing so brought about a complete transformation. He was unrecognizable, even to himself. He looked like an out-of-work Nazi. He planned to eventually let his beard lapse into a stylishly unkempt 5:00 shadow—which for him would appear promptly each day at 2 p.m. All he'd have to do would be to hack at his face distractedly with a pair of dull scissors once every two days, and at his balding head once a week. He decided this new look would serve him well in his new incarnation as a reporter—certainly one of the lowest forms of life on the planet.

* * *

Nate was doubly pleased when Dave Sawicky failed to recognize him when he showed up for his interview at 10:45. When he pulled up, Dave was standing alone on the veranda of the lovely three-story, mansard-roofed gingerbread Victorian that served as the main office of the

Roosevelt Newspapers chain. He was enjoying the first of his many smokes for the day.

"Can I help you?" asked Dave, peering at him through the already filthy veneer of inky fingerprints smearing his thick, horn-rimmed spectacles.

"Hi, Dave. It's Nate. Nate Randall. I met you last night."

"Holy Jesus! Get a load of you. I hope you didn't think you had to get all cleaned up for me."

"Naw, I just needed a change, that's all. Am I late?"

"Nope, early. Come on in and let me show you around." He tossed his still-lit cigarette over the hedge into the quartz-pebbled driveway.

Stifling a strong gag reflex in reaction to the reek of stale Marlboros, body odor and beer wafting off of the beefy editor's unwashed hair and clothing, Nate was led upstairs to what Dave called the "newsroom." Running the length of the building, the loft-like space featured a well-worn, visibly warped wide-plank oak floor that dipped more than a foot toward the center from each end. Perched precariously atop most of the battered gray metal desks lining the walls were nine ancient MacIntosh computers. Six other desks scattered around the room—four of them large wooden corner units—sported relatively new Power Macs with large-screen monitors. Newspapers and scraps of paper littered the desks and the floor areas surrounding them.

The room would have been illuminated warmly by the morning sun, had it not been for the harsh, flickering banks of fluorescent tubes suspended in a crumbling drop ceiling overhead. A faded pincushion map of Roosevelt County was loosely taped to the far wall, underneath which bound volumes containing the progressively brown and brittle local news of Dutch Hollow from 2000 back to 1857 were stacked on sagging oaken shelves.

"This is it," said Dave Sawicky proudly. "Nobody's here yet. Reporters don't usually get in before 11 on a Monday."

It wasn't much of an interview. Dave was desperate—as he would turn out to be on a more or less permanent basis—to hire someone, anyone, to fill one of multiple chronically empty reporter positions. Having been a songwriter, a computer programmer and a music promoter in the past, Nate was apparently more than qualified for the job.

"When can you start?" asked Dave impulsively, before explaining what being a reporter for Roosevelt Newspapers entailed.

"Right away. Today, if you need me. How much does a reporter make?"

"Well, that's a good question," said Dave, his eyebrows rising nervously over the tops of his spectacles. "It may depend." He went on to explain that he also needed something he called a "paginator"—a person to lay out finished stories using one of the company's six "deluxe" computer stations.

"With your computer background and all, you could easily pick it up in a couple of weeks," said Dave. "Between being a part-time paginator and a full-time reporter, you could probably pull down $250 a week, which is usually what a 'bureau chief' makes."

Despite his having plenty of money for the foreseeable future, this came as a shock to Nate. He knew upstate New York was depressed compared to the City, but there *was* such a thing as minimum wage. He decided to push Dave a little bit. "Really? I don't mean to be rude, Dave, but how do people live on that kind of money? I've checked into rents around here and I couldn't find anything under $600 a month. Plus I'll need to buy a car. That's pretty tough."

Dave was far from offended. He had been through this before. Taking a deep breath, Dave gambled and, in hushed, conspiratorial tones, began to explain his ongoing dilemma to a stunned and skeptical prospect, for probably the thousandth time in his sad seven-year career as Managing Editor of Roosevelt Newspapers. Having met and partied with Nate the previous night, Dave was somewhat more forthcoming than usual, but the desired effect was to provoke sympathy and manipulate the coveted prospect to accept indentured servitude.

"Look, I got drunk with you last night," said Dave without irony, his red-veined eyes focused on the doorway behind Nate's head, "And I trust you. So don't tell anybody I said this."

Nate leaned closer.

"You're exactly right," Dave went on. "Journalism pays shit everywhere, but nowhere lower than here. Our esteemed owner, Winston Babson III, or 'Winnie' for short, is a benevolent despot; a millionaire politician. We call him 'Citizen Babs,' His mother was the evil queen in 'Sleeping Beauty,' remember her?"

Nate nodded, remembering.

"He's related somehow to the Roosevelts. He's married to a billionaire oil heiress. It's her money, really, that pays for all this." Dave waved his hand grandly around the room at the old furniture and the battered, outdated computers.

"He takes the low-rent mentality of publishing extremely seriously. His excuse is that he sincerely believes that any writer who is worth a damn would do it for free. Of course, what he really is, is cheap. He refuses to pay his reporters—or his editors either—a living wage. I'm the fucking managing editor of 10 newspapers. Whaddya think I make?"

Nate shrugged. "Thirty-five?"

"Funny. More like 28 thousand," said Dave, his eyebrows gesticulating wildly for emphasis. "A job like this is worth 45 anywhere else. But if Winnie likes you, he takes care of you, if you know what I mean."

Nate didn't, but decided to wait and find out for himself.

"Anyway, I like you. I want you. Here's what I'll do. There's space in the Dutch Arms. It's a big rooming house Winnie owns, out by the falls. Most of the reporters live there—the ones that don't live with their parents. It's 100 a month for a room, taken out of your salary. Winnie'll kill me, but I'll give you 300 a week, to do the Mohican Valley beat and to come in extra on Tuesday nights to paginate. You can use one of the company vehicles for four days a week until you find a car. That's my final offer. With the turnover around here, you'll be an editor in a month. Whaddya say?"

Having effectively increased his rate from $5 to $6 an hour, with dirt-cheap rent and a car, Nate was more than satisfied. "Winnie" was right. He would have done it for nothing. "You've got yourself a reporter," he said, reaching out his hand. "And a...what?"

"Paginator," confirmed Dave as he shook Nate's hand, his wide smile betraying a mouth less than brimming with nicotine-stained teeth. "Welcome aboard."

CHAPTER EIGHT
JIMMY OLSEN

Nate's half-day education at Dave Sawicky's foul-smelling altar of knowledge was fast, furious and, at times, side-splittingly funny. He learned that the 10 weekly newspapers, two monthly magazines and one weekly arts and entertainment rag published by Winston Babson III's Roosevelt Newspapers empire covered the goings-on in all of Roosevelt County's 18 suburban and rural towns and in Beaverton, a small Hudson River city tucked in its far southwest corner.

"Editorially, there are five bureaus, each with its own office," said Dave. "The central bureau here in Dutch Hollow houses the staff of the *Dutch Hollow Chronicle*, the *Pleasant Plains Inquirer* and the *Masada Voice*, which sucks. The *Mohican Valley Times*, my favorite paper, is the whole eastern bureau; its office is above a print shop down in Ostia. They have a sewage problem or something down there, though; the town stinks real bad.

"The northern bureau office is the nicest. It's like a fucking country club out there. It's in Kipsbergh, the so-called 'Hamptons of the Hudson.' The northern papers are the *Riverian Townsman*, which covers Indian Hills and Kipsbergh, and the *Roosevelton Eagle*. They're *Pennysavers*; not worth the paper they're printed on.

"Down south we have two bureaus: the southern and the USE country bureau. The southern is the *Beaverton Beacon*, our biggest paper, which covers the City of Beaverton, the surrounding Town of Waterkill and the Village of Waterkill, where the office is located. We're thinking of making it a daily again like it used to be. USE country papers are the *Echo Valley Guardian*, the *Lenape Falls Ledger* and the *East Waterkill Spectator*. They try to cater to USE engineers and suburban soccer moms, without much success—maybe 'cause they're all Chinese and Indians. That office is above the library in the Village of Lenape Falls. The five bureau chiefs and the editor of *Happenings* also work here Mondays and Tuesdays, editing and paginating on the six production machines."

Nate learned that the county's other, significantly larger city, Pinksterkill, boasted its own regional daily newspaper owned by the national Blodgett Publishing chain: the heartily maligned *Pinksterkill Journal*. Regrettably, said Dave, Nate probably wouldn't be covering very many stories in Pinksterkill. The Roosevelt company employed what Dave called a roving "editor-at-large," whose beat was the entire region including Pinksterkill, the county seat, and whose job it was to search for stories of universal impact for all the papers. It sounded to Nate like the perfect job for his purposes.

The mythical journalistic superman who performed this task, one Patrick McDuffy of Waterkill, apparently predated Dave, Winnie Babson and everyone else at Roosevelt Newspapers. He worked out of his home and the Waterkill office, sending stories via courier on ancient USE-formatted five-and-a-quarter-inch floppy disks that had to be reformatted on an old PC downstairs. "Give him a wide berth," said Dave. "He's so far up the Republicans' ass in this county he bleeds red, white and brown. He's a first class prick and a double-triple-dipper, and is a walking conflict of interest."

"What do you mean?"

"He's secretly on the payroll of three school districts, four law offices, two police departments, the sheriff's department, a minor league baseball team and a professional ambulance squad as a PR rep. I think he works for USE, too. He's like a one-man Pravda. He sells the same crap-ass stories he writes for us to the *Journal* under a different by-line and blats them out on his stupid radio show and on public access cable. He makes $180,000 a year with all these shenanigans. He's a knee-jerk, pro-business conservative hack and a festering boil on my ass, and there's absolutely nothing I can do about it. Winnie uses him to get re-elected."

"Re-elected?"

"Didn't I tell you? Your new massa is a Republican county legislator, with designs on higher office. He's a pal of the governor. If you move into the Dutch Arms, he'll be representing you, my friend, as well as writing editorials, directing news coverage, paying your wages and subsidizing your rent. How's *that* for a conflict of interest?"

Beneath his gruff, odiferous exterior, Dave was turning out to be quite the egalitarian, bleeding heart Lefty. He seemed obsessed with the plight of Pinksterkill. Shunned by the rest of racist, Republican Roosevelt County, said Dave, this heavily African-American, Democratic, riverside metropolis was in a class by itself. A sadly decimated former factory town and deep-water port, this once-proud "Jewel of the Hudson" was a victim of white flight from its increasingly poor black core, as well as of some mean-spirited urban planning.

The city's boarded-up downtown had effectively been cut off from the river during the 1970s by a monstrous six-lane "arterial" leading from its prosperous white northern and eastern suburbs to the sprawling exurban wasteland of "USE Country" to the south, with its attendant factories, subdivisions and shopping malls. The Italians, Irish, Germans and other white folks who had fled to the outer rim of their fair city went so far as to secede from it altogether in the 1960s, creating the aptly named "Town of Pinksterkill" in an obnoxious, gerrymandered ring around its forsaken namesake.

Dave was especially miffed at the city's waterfront "renewal" efforts. Most of the former factories and warehouses had been torn down 30 years earlier, and were dangerous concrete floodplains littered with broken glass and crack vials. Annual plans had been floated to turn the area into a wonderland of parks, restaurants, hotel and conference centers, amphitheaters and marinas, but according to Dave: "Someone's been making a lot more money by doing nothing." Millions in government backed "industrial development" bond issues had been sold to finance various projects, most of which came to naught. "These mobster lawyers split the take with their money-laundering pals, then they and their trader friends repackage the bad bonds with good ones and sell them on the open market, over and over, splitting commissions every time," said Dave. "When the bonds crap out after no one's paid them back, the county pays them off and they start all over again."

It was a recurring multi-million-dollar Ponzi scheme backed by county taxpayers. "Nice," said Nate.

The only thing industrial development bond money had actually ever built in Pinksterkill was a seedy industrial park toward the southern end of the city's riverfront which was dominated by the giant regional PECO Incinerator. The incinerator was a facility where garbage trucks from as far away as New York City lined up in long queues, 24 hours a day, to dump their contents in a yawning hopper to be cremated and turned into electricity for the hungry USE plant just downriver. "Damn racist, polluting motherfuckers," said Dave, slamming his beefy hand into the desk as his eyebrows did back-flips. "The people, the *black* people living near that plant have some of the highest asthma rates in the *country*. The *country!*"

Shades of Sheila, thought Nate. Clearly, Dave Sawicky would be an asset.

To its credit, Pinksterkill maintained a major regional railway station—"from which white New York City commuters scurry to their vehicles every night to avoid running into a Negro," said Dave. Pinksterkill was, for three months during the Revolutionary War, the temporary wartime capital of New York State, as George Washington holed up there and ground his teeth to dust while Kingston burned. The phrase "But will it play in Pinksterkill?" had been coined with regard to its fabulous, ornately gilded Globe Theatre in 1876. This landmark, said Dave, was still standing and drawing white audiences from the suburbs to indulge in locally produced culture—which included concerts by an under-financed symphony orchestra and a tear-jerking annual night of fund-raising cabaret entertainment performed by retarded group home residents. New York State's wildly popular Republican governor, Hiram Pollock, had been born, bred and, according to Dave, thoroughly corrupted in Pinksterkill. And of course, the city was home to the venerable *Pinksterkill Journal*, colloquially known in the acerbic Roosevelt newsroom as the *Sphincterkill Urinal*.

To the consternation of Dave and other Roosevelt editors, a *Journal* newspaper box appeared alongside nearly every mailbox in rural and suburban Roosevelt County. Winnie Babson, of course, was too cheap to get involved in home delivery. His 47,092 subscribers got their papers through the U.S. Mail, usually a day later than they appeared on the newsstands. Consequently, much of what appeared in Roosevelt's 10 weekly rags could hardly be called news. Most people read the weeklies for the local gossip, the bulletin boards and classifieds and the local sports that fell under the *Journal*'s radar.

But that was not for lack of trying on the part of Dave and a few other intrepid news-hounds. Dave confessed that there was a chip on the shoulder of every veteran Roosevelt editor regarding the hated *Urinal*, mostly due to the fact that they had each been turned down more than once for a job there. The mantra in the Dutch Hollow newsroom was, therefore, "Beat the *Urinal*," alluding to a stiff competition for breaking news that the editorial staff of the *Pinksterkill Journal* presumably was unaware of.

Since Roosevelt's 10 papers came out on Thursday and the *Journal* came out every day, Dave explained, Roosevelt's having the same story in one of its weeklies that had appeared in the Pinksterkill daily a day earlier—on Wednesday—was considered a "tie." If a story on the same subject came out in the *Journal* and, say, Roosevelt's flagship *Beaverton Beacon* on Thursday, said Dave, "we win." To actually print a major "scoop" that trounced the *Journal* by a full day or more—or even better, failed to appear in that paper at all—was an excuse for a night of free beer at the Delafield House for the intrepid reporter, on the tab of Winnie Babson. (Stories by Patrick McDuffy were barred from consideration, for obvious reasons).

Nate was beginning to see Dave's point about the millionaire publisher's 19th-century Andrew Carnegie-style paternalism. If one played his cards right, this job could have its perks.

It was one of Dave's jobs to scour the pages of the *Journal* each day for particularly odious typographical errors, and alert the "Pee-Jo" comment hotline of the bad news in a not-so-cleverly-disguised voice.

On one occasion, said Dave, chuckling maniacally, the *Journal* had announced the unexpected closing of a major regional mental institution with the 75-point headline: "PYSCH CENTER CLOSES".

Dave claimed to have dialed the hotline repeatedly, leaving the same message over and over: "Hi, I'm a regular reader, and I was wondering what a 'Pish Center' is. Because I'm sad the 'Pish Center' is closed and I really think I need one. Hello? Can anybody help me? I really need to take a pish!"

Despite Dave's room-clearing B.O. and his cornball humor, Nate was beginning to contract a mild case of hero worship. Besides being a wag, a music lover and a closet socialist, Dave was apparently an intellectual of sorts, and a man with an interesting history. He had been schooled by Jesuits his entire life, and had graduated from Georgetown at the top of his class. He had started in journalism in Manhattan as a crime reporter for the *New York Post*, but had quit in disgust in 1977 when Rupert Murdoch took over. After a series of stressful, alcohol-fueled mid-level editorships at the *Baltimore Sun* and the *Washington Post*, Dave decided he'd had enough, and returned upstate to his home turf to relax and drink himself to death.

"I'm a tabloid man, through and through," said Dave Sawicky. "And I can tell you're gonna be my Jimmy Olsen. Just don't call me chief."

"Sure thing, chief."

"Jimmy Olsen," for those unacquainted with Action, DC and Marvel Comics lore, was the name of the annoying, red-haired, dumb-as-rocks cub reporter for the fictional *Daily Planet* newspaper from the *Superman* series. The character was immortalized for baby boomers like Dave Sawicky by a spunky television actor named Jack Larson in the 1950s. The TV Jimmy Olsen would send his boss, the crusty editor Perry White, into apoplectic fits by calling him "chief."

"Listen, chief. I mean, Dave. You just gave me an idea. I need a pseudonym, what with people following me around trying to kill me and all. Would you mind terribly if I used 'James Olsen' for my by-line in the paper? I don't think anybody but you would notice."

"Probably not, kid. As long as Winnie doesn't catch on, it's cool with me."

* * *

Dave assigned Nate to a complicated series of "beats" for the *Mohican Valley Times* which, since it had been chartered in 1791 as *The Pepperton Trader*, was trumpeted in its own masthead as "Roosevelt County's

Original Newspaper." The *Times* was, due to its coverage area's relative remoteness and its longtime pit bull of a bureau chief, John Ianucci, the only rag in the Roosevelt empire to have a leg up on the *Journal*. The paper reported and commented on the municipal government, community events and news of four towns, as well as the redundant machinations of two village governments within two of those towns, and the news, events and sports of the area's three school districts. The ground to cover would be vast: a deep, verdant valley trapped between two ranges of high hills, running the full length of Roosevelt County's 43-mile-long eastern border with Connecticut. According to Dave it historically had taken four reporters, two part-time "stringers" and the beleaguered Mr. Ianucci to deal with it all, but since the company was short-staffed he knew he could count on Nate to assume a bit more of the load.

"No problem, chief," said Nate, with virtually no conception of that to which he was agreeing.

At the end of the orientation Dave drove Nate up the street in what would be his temporary vehicle—a 12-year-old, sky-blue, radio-less Ford Fiesta with a manual shift—to show him the Dutch Arms, an ancient, ramshackle building teetering on the edge of a cliff above a roaring waterfall. It had once served as company housing for an old textile mill next door, the stone remnants of which had been incorporated into another, much fancier apartment house also owned by Winston Babson III. It was a massive building, three stories tall, that looked as if it was divided roughly into two large duplex units. They entered the ground floor of the left-hand unit. "Dis is where de massa keep his work force," said Dave. "Keep a low profile, or Winnie might make you 'Master of the Arms.'"

"Master of the Arms?"

"It means you'll have to take out the garbage and enforce the house rules, which are pretty strict," said Dave, offering Nate a three-page handout titled "Rules of the Arms". "Don't worry. Nobody really pays attention to them."

That much was obvious; the place was a pigsty. A week's worth of dirty dishes clogged the kitchen sink and every available square centimeter of counter space. Massive dust bunnies rolled like tumbleweeds along the walls of the dingy downstairs "living room," with its four sagging '50s-era davenports and unmatched Formica coffee and end tables. The entire third floor of this unit was off limits: a suite occupied by the central bureau chief, Mark Zweiker, and his young wife Jill, a production artist on maternity leave, and their infant son. On the second floor were two bathrooms and six bedrooms—one lavatory, which Dave said was "for the girls," was relatively clean except for a small garbage pail overflowing with tampon wrappers and used tissues. The "boys" bathroom was predictably filthy, with a decade's worth of jet-black mold infesting the shower stall and walls.

Nate had his choice between three empty bedrooms, all of which would require considerable disinfecting to be made habitable. One room was festooned with the pellet-like turds of a miniature mammal—something smaller than a cat or a dog, but with a far more pungent stool. "The girl who lived in here had a fucking ferret," said Dave, shaking his head. "She lasted three weeks on the job. She was not only a health risk; she was terrible. She was fired a year ago and this room has been empty ever since."

"You wouldn't have had a thing for her, would you, chief?"

"Very funny, Mr. Olsen," laughed Dave. "Consider yourself lucky she's gone. I'm sure she would have found you attractive."

Another room was carpeted in cat hair, with the floor and wall in one corner rendered structurally unsound from feline urine. "Mona Levy just moved out of here into the sunny front bedroom," said Dave. "Mona is the Dutch Hollow reporter. She's a nice kid; smart, maybe a little contrary and opinionated and sensitive to criticism, but nice. She has two cats."

Uh oh, thought Nate.

Nate sensibly opted for the relatively unscathed back bedroom, kitty-corner to Mona's, as far away from her presumed contrariness and her smelly cats as possible. The room had the added attraction of being within earshot of the rushing waterfall 200 feet below, which would drown everything else out.

"Besides Mona there are two other people living in this unit now," said Dave, continuing the tour. "They're all probably out doing stories. Greg Callahan lives in here. He's a good, hard working kid—he's from upstate originally, like you. He and Mona have a little trouble getting along, but I have him working the Kipsbergh beat way across the county, so they don't run into each other too much."

"Sounds wonderful."

"Rex Nicholson kind of keeps to himself, and is hard to get to know. He's been the Pleasant Plains reporter for longer than I've been here, and knows more than most editors. He doesn't like noise much, and he's been 'Master of the Arms' since Vinnie Colello got fired for throwing a phone across the room and hitting Amy Vanderbilt with it, which made her quit. And now there's you."

"Hmmm." Nate began to wonder when he'd ever have the time or inclination to take a dump in "The Arms" —especially when it filled up to capacity. With this surly, profoundly unsanitary crew lording it over the place, he would definitely have to consider moving to his own apartment if something came up.

As if to second his emotion, a door slammed downstairs, followed by an irritated-sounding female voice. "Hell-*O?*"

"Hey, Mona. It's Dave. I'm up here showing the new reporter around."

"Great." The voice was dripping with snotty boarding-school sarcasm.

She came up the stairs, muttering to herself. "Mona, this is Nate Randall," said Dave, hopefully.

"Pleased to meet you," she said, without holding out her hand. "You seem clean, at least. Aren't you a little old to be a reporter?"

"Yes, as a matter of fact, I am. That's very observant of you. I've heard a lot of good things about you, too." Nate held out his hand, which she reluctantly grasped. They shook hands firmly, regarding each other warily with mutually steely eyes. Mona's frizzy red hair framed a haughty Mediterranean face dominated by a large aquiline nose and full, heart-shaped lips. Her eyes were green and fiercely intelligent. Beneath her shapeless art-school clothing, what should probably have been a knockout figure seemed as if it had been violently eroded through a blitzkrieg bulimic dieting plan. Her fractured fingernails and bloodied cuticles comprised a war zone all their own. "What do you think of Dutch Hollow?" asked Nate.

"I've never met a bigger bunch of assholes in my life," snorted Mona Levy, as Dave winced. "Dutch Hollow can kiss my fat, Jewish ass."

CHAPTER NINE
DEADLINE DAY

O
n his first full day of work, Nate came in Tuesday morning at 11 and met the five bureau chiefs and the Roosevelt central office staff. Tuesday, said Dave, was when the editors and production people "put the paper to bed."

Mona Levy's poisonous attitude notwithstanding, Nate took to his new life as a journalist like a duck to water. His immediate boss, John Ianucci, turned out to be the kind of hard-boiled, fast-talking wiseacre created by Hollywood during the 1940s, when reporters fashioned their images in the likeness of characters like Humphrey Bogart and James Cagney. Wearing a fedora and a trench coat whenever he stepped outside on the porch during breaks to chain-smoke Marlboros with Dave, Ianucci—known in the newsroom as "Nootch"—spoke out of the right side of his mouth and habitually kept his left hand shoved in his pocket as if he were hiding a gun. Despite this sort of foolishness and the fact that he was only 26 years old, Nate liked him instinctively.

Although he had grown up in suburban Echo Valley, Nootch was a true Italian-American child of the Bronx, a place to where his 48-year-old father still commuted for his job as a New York City firefighter. According to Dave, Ianucci was a scrappy, hard-working, funny, smart and soulful kid, who would be a dream to work for as long as you did your job. It added considerably to Nate's opinion of his new boss that the paper Nootch edited, the *Mohican Valley Times*, was consistently the most newsworthy, thought provoking and well laid-out in the pile of back issues of Roosevelt newspapers he had scanned on his first evening at the legendary Dutch Arms.

He was put to work watching the young bureau chief "paginate" his paper using something called "Quark." Nate had worked with similar desktop publishing programs back when he created his weekly music club ads for *Time Out*, the *Village Voice* and the *New York Press*; and before the night was through he took over an unoccupied production computer and fired off a few obituary pages and a sports front. The work was almost fun, like piecing together a puzzle, and both Dave and Nootch had to struggle to hide their appreciation of his being a quick study. It didn't hurt that after 12 p.m., when the threat of Winnie Babson showing up disappeared, the more jaded senior editors broke out the beer, wine and, it seemed to Nate, a smattering of psychotropic drugs. For the next six hours, until the business office people were due to come in, a party atmosphere ensued that exposed remarkable newsroom camaraderie—especially among Dave, Nootch and Rick Parton, the portly and demonstrably erudite Beaverton chief. Much of the humor derived from the scathing barrage of insults being leveled at absent reporters.

"Fuck, fuck, fuck!" Nootch would yell at the computer screen, throwing a sheaf of papers across the room. "Listen to this fucking lead! 'The Yonder Inn is a good place to meet and greet people who are as hungry as they are. That's why Bill and Nellie Johannson quit their job as librarians and truck mechanics to pool their savings and open the Yonder Inn on Route 33 in Pepperton.' What the fuck is this Mongoloid talking about?"

Nootch would then dial poor Bobby Hanrahan, still toiling away in the Ostia office on a breaking story about a secret halfway house for battered women, and query him as to what sort of medication he had overdosed on.

"Fools! Carrion!" Rick would bellow in a God-like baritone, looking and sounding like the fictional bombast, Ignatius P. Reilly, come to life. "Who told these people they could compose a sentence? This tripe befouls my finely tuned news sense! I cannot, and will not, continue without the proper chemical guidance!"

Outbursts such as these would bring peals of high-pitched, cackling laughter from Dave, Rick and Nootch, while Mark Zweiker and the rest of the editors would roll their eyes and smirk knowingly. "Is there something you people would like to share with the rest of the class?" asked Nate.

"Ah, grasshopper, you have not yet proven that you can be trusted," said Rick, inverting his "R's" and "L's" in a faux-Charlie Chan patois. "Only after the proper training and apprenticeship will you be allowed to join the dark side. Until then, would you care for a beer?" More cackling and snickering ensued.

"Sure, if you think it will help."

"Ah-so, correct answer, young grasshopper. You have the makings of a true Jedi."

The more stoked the editors got, the faster they worked, and the faster the bad puns, insults, sick jokes and social commentary flew. Every once in a while Nate would add a wisecrack or sick story of his own, which seemed to be appreciated. "You may do well here, grasshopper," said a red-eyed Rick at one point during the long night, only half in jest. "You think yourself funny, as do we."

Besides the six editors and Nate, five reporters were in attendance, finishing up their stories for the week well past the 5 p.m. Tuesday deadline. A gaunt, nervous Rex Nicholson was on hand; minding his own business and producing faint clucking noises with his tongue. Mona Levy was present, making loud phone calls in pursuit of a story about an illicit bed & breakfast operation. On the rare occasions when her attention turned to the constant hum of newsroom banter, she would instinctively argue with nearly every assertion made by anyone except Nootch, to whom she seemed to defer more as a matter of a carefully proscribed internal etiquette than out of actual respect.

The newsroom bristled with sexual tension as well. Dave was visited more than once by a reasonably attractive—although comparably unkempt—woman, from advertising production on the first floor, who rubbed his neck and invited him outside for a very long cigarette break. The brand new, week-old *Masada Voice* reporter, a sassy young dark-haired girl named Nicole Royal, was frantically typing in her last story, fending off the double-teaming sexual harassment of Mark Zweiker and "Aaron," a snotty, 100-percent assimilated Pakistani reporter from the USE-country office whose real name was Haroon Mahl. Aaron was a young hotshot fresh out of Stony Brook whom the central bureau chief, suffering from a case of arrested development, had apparently befriended in an attempt to resuscitate his fading frat-boy image. Nate wondered what Mark's young wife would think about his hitting on new meat.

Nate also caught Nicole stealing pretty glances toward Nootch, who would reward her with what he thought was a secret smile and an air-kiss. Mona caught them making google-eyes, and began to glower in Nootch's direction.

"What a snake pit," mused Nate to himself. "And I thought the music business was bad."

* * *

Tuesday night for the editors and production staff bled all the way into late Wednesday morning as they frantically inspected the final "flats" downstairs for errors and typos. No reporter with any common sense stayed in the office past noon. The less dedicated among them didn't even bother coming in; they knew their editors would soon be home sleeping. Nate, despite being up all night with the editors, was so jazzed to get going as a reporter—and primed from all the alcohol, caffeine and Krispy Kreme donut filling coursing through his veins—that he was wide awake, if a bit ill. As Nootch was getting ready to leave, Nate asked him if there was anything he wanted him to cover that day. "You crazy old fuck. Go home. Get some sleep."

"I'm serious. Fuck sleep. I'm having too much fun."

"Well, I can't sleep, either. Must've been something I ate. Come on, let's take a ride and I'll show you The Valley."

They rode in Nootch's fabulous battleship gray El Camino out of town the back way, past the Dutch Arms. "I heard you moved into the Arms. Welcome to the monkey house. I live in the north wing."

"Yeah? Do the same sort of weirdoes live on your side?"

Nootch cackled. "Are you calling Mona Levy a weirdo? Yo, that's my bitch, Holmes."

"Truly?"

"Yeah, truly. She's starting to get on my nerves, though. You want her?"

"Not with *your* dick. Oh, wait...I guess she's already got *your* dick."

"Motherfucker, you are some kind of wise-ass, aren't you, Jimmy Olsen? I do believe I like you. It's true, though. Everybody who ever came through the fucking Arms is weird as shit. Including me. Definitely including you. I mean, who the fuck in their right mind would live in that shit-hole, or work at a sweatshop like this all night for no money?"

"Mmmm. Point taken."

Explaining the significance of various rural landmarks along the way, Nootch drove eastward on a scenically undulating state highway along a high ridge with sweeping views of the rolling estate lands to the north and west. At the top of a high hill, he slowed down, heading for a sharp S-turn accompanied by a 15-m.p.h. speed limit sign. "Prepare yourself," said Nootch.

Halfway through the turn, the wall of pines on each side of the road parted like a curtain, exposing one of the most spine-tingling vistas Nate had ever seen: a deep, dramatic valley stretching for miles, both south and north all the way to two horizons. It was rimmed on the east and west by extremely high, steep, round-topped hills that flirted with mountain-hood. Along the valley floor could be seen a sinuous stream and a long, nearly arrow-straight two-lane highway crossing over the shimmering rill between every bend, passing through a number of picture-postcard, white-steepled villages shining in the golden morning sun. "This is unbelievable," said Nate. "It looks like fucking Switzerland."

"Welcome to my Valley," said Nootch. "Believe me, it looks better from up here."

Skillfully down-shifting the El Camino's manual three-on-the-tree into second, Nootch negotiated the four hairpin switchbacks descending what he called "Van Valkenbergh Hill," which was apparently "the site where the real Last of the Mohicans bought it; shot in the back while trying to steal a pig." On the right, near the base of the hill, he pointed out a high, Aztec-temple-looking stone structure. "That's what's left of the old Van Valkenbergh Furnace," he said reverently. "Where most of the iron for the Union Army's cannons was forged. It's part of Vitello's Country Club now.

"Big Nick Vitello is, like, the king of Ostia. The country club used to be an iron mine, then a gravel mine, then a dump. He covered it up and built a golf course when the pissants at the Dutch Hollow Golf and Tennis Club wouldn't let him play there because he's a Wop. Ya gotta love that. Big Nick still runs a bunch of mines in the mountains around here, and owns a landfill south of the golf course that's being capped. The townspeople treat him like God. It's basically, like, what he says, goes."

As Nootch spoke, a distinct and familiar smell entered the cramped confines of the El Camino, making Nate's eyes water. "Is that the dump?"

"I don't think so. I think it's from the restaurant we just passed. They've got a sewage problem, I think. The whole town does. It's worse some places than others. That restaurant's closed now, but it used to be a way better place to hang than the Delafield House. Owned by the same guy. It was a big music club; it had national bands and everything. When the sheriff started nailing the drunks coming over from Connecticut with DWIs, people got too scared to go. I think the real problem was the owner—Briggsy—had a falling out with Big Nick."

"What was the name of the place?"

"Sporty's Roadhouse. It's where Mona and I first hung out."

"Shit, my band played there back in '94."

"Get out! Dave told me you were some kinda rock star. That's true?"

"Yeah, I remember we couldn't find a fucking motel around here and we had to sleep in the bus in the parking lot, but it stank so bad we left. We always called it 'Stinky's'. I always wondered where that shit was."

"That's Ostia, alright. Stinkytown. There's even a part of town across the railroad tracks where the inbreds live, called Stinkytown. They used to grow onions there. That's how I made my fucking spurs, with a big exposé on daily life in Stinkytown. Nobody'd ever had the balls to go in there before. People thought the retards would shoot them with blunderbusses or fuck them in the ass. I got a fucking first-place NYNA award for that one. I tell you, Jimmy, you really gotta go see shit for yourself if you're gonna do a story right. That's my fucking wisdom for the day."

As Nate looked at Nootch, whose eyes shone black with the glory of his memory of journalistic immortality, he realized why he liked him so much. With his sleek, jet-black hair, his young Mussolini-like countenance and his innate ability to appear tattered and confused—which negated the possibility of him being taken for a foppish, good-looking dilettante—Nootch was the spitting image of Nate's best childhood friend, Anthony DiSalvo.

Tony had died in 1981, a victim of the left fender of a soundly sleeping nurse's aide's Buick LeSabre as it plowed through the empty front luggage compartment of his 1967 VW bug, severing him in half.

Nate and Tony had played together since they were six, building sand fortresses and organizing a small army of neighborhood rugrats to terrorize the hated Kleinfelds: the children of a local toy store owner whose back yard was set up like a miniature Disneyland. Forty-two kids would descend on the Kleinfeld property in complicated flanking maneuvers armed with dirt bombs and acorns, driving the spoiled brats from their land and annexing the jungle-gyms and expensive battery-powered children's vehicles until parental reinforcements arrived to repel them with threats of police action.

When a Bermuda-bound 727 landed 200 miles short of the runway in November 1978, killing Nate's parents, he had moved in with the DiSalvos. Nate and Tony had ridden their bikes to Lake George and back. They had beat off to Tony's father's *Penthouses*, fucked a gorgeous set of twin sisters at a drive-in movie, stolen cars together and driven them around all night at 100 miles an hour. They were going to start a band; take over the world ...

* * *

After showing him the Ostia office, a tawdry, broken-down affair sharing a foul smelling building with a poisonous vapor-spewing printing press, Nootch drove Nate the length of the Mohican Valley's Roosevelt County stretch, first turning north on Route 33 toward Pepperton. Dairy and sheep farms, public and private school campuses, apple orchards and vineyards lined both sides of the highway between Ostia and the Village of Pepperton, with still verdant October fields climbing halfway up the rising ramparts of the surrounding pine-green and burnt-orange hills. Local architecture veered dangerously close to the Tyrolean. Nate seriously thought he would hear the echoes of Heidi's grandfather yodeling for her to come home for lunch.

"This is the relatively boring part of the Valley," said Nootch. "Nothing much happens here, which is why I gave the beat to Hanrahan.

"Is he really that bad?"

"Worse than you can imagine."

"Shit. I hope you don't start to think that way about me."

"Unlikely, dude. I may be wrong, but you seem to have the spirit, which not too many people have. Why the fuck do you think I'm bothering to drive you around on no sleep? Can you write in complete sentences?"

"Yes."

"Then don't worry. I'll show you the rest. It's mostly about style, and it's not that complicated: never write *'over'* when writing about amounts, like *'over* 50 dollars,' or 'for *over* 100 years.' That's like saying *'on top of'* 50 dollars. Always use *'more than;'* that sort of thing. Get people you're interviewing to spell their names. I don't know how many times I've had to put corrections in the paper about Hanrahan's mistakes. He'll never, ever get it. There's no way you can pick up all his fuck-ups on Tuesday nights, crank or no crank. I fucking hate him."

As Nootch simmered about his ball-and-chain Pepperton reporter, he turned around and retraced his route, driving back south on 33 into Ostia. Once within the hamlet limits, he began again to relax and point out landmarks. "That's Max's Diner, where Big Nick gets his coffee. That's the entrance to the golf course. Nick's talking about selling it. That's the dump. This is where they have the cattle auction Thursday nights. You should go if you don't have a meeting; it's a real trip. Here's the town hall and the firehouse. There's a town meeting every other Thursday night. Attendance is mandatory, but you won't mind. It's free entertainment. The town supervisor is old Mabel McDonough, who's either senile or deaf, or both. There are four other board members, and she has no idea what three of them are up to. They basically out-vote her and run the town for Big Nick, approving all his projects. The rich weekenders come and complain to their one ideologically compatible councilman about the noise, dust, truck traffic and pollution while Mabel sits there and smiles and the three amigos ignore them all completely. Be sure to eat dinner first, 'cause you'll almost never get out of there before 11."

The southbound tour continued well into the afternoon, with Nootch providing illuminating, often rib-tickling commentary not unlike the hilarious musings one would hear from one of the wittier, more knowledgeable wags hosting a Big Apple double-decker bus tour. In between two populous towns—one of them gray and depressed and one nearly as lovingly restored as Dutch Hollow—they passed a vast, Medieval-looking stand of structures atop a series of low hills: a state mental institution housing 12,000 inmates. Another, similarly imposing small city of 19th-century buildings, gift-wrapped in 100 linear miles of coiling razor wire, turned out to be a maximum-security lock-up for violent teenage offenders. Both facilities had their own train depots on the Mohican Valley line to Grand Central Station in New York.

Nootch pointed out the scores of gravel pits, mines, landfills and recycling centers in this steep, relatively narrow section of the valley. "The Mohican Valley has been one of New York City's main toxic garbage dumps for years," said Nootch. "There are a lot of holes in the ground to fill. They hollow all the ore and gravel out of a mountain, fill it with garbage and C&D debris—which everybody knows is laced with toxic shit—cover it up and try to sell it to developers. So far not too much has been built up—the area's still kind of backward and undiscovered by the hoity-toity crowd. Too many inbreds, retards and escaped criminals, I guess.

"This is 'The Cut,' where a glacier stopped about a million years ago," said Nootch at a rocky, vee-shaped gap with barely enough space to accommodate the rushing Mohican River and the state highway hugging its bank. "And this is the end of today's tour."

They were at the southern terminus of the Roosevelt County segment of the valley, explained Nootch. "When the ice melted, everything north of here was an arm of an enormous inland sea called Lake Albany. Eventually the water broke through and carved out the rest of the valley going south. There's another cut just like it in the Hudson Valley, but much bigger and more dramatic, over at the Highlands near Cold Spring. These were giant natural dams, holding back a tank of water that went all the way to Canada. When the dams broke, they ripped New York a couple of new assholes and shit out Long Island. Robert Moses wanted to build a dam here and make a reservoir of my entire news beat, but luckily he died first."

Apparently Nootch was as much an amateur geologist as Nate, another trait that appealed greatly to him. Tired as his body was, Nate was thrilled that he had fallen in with such a crew of social misfits as Dave, Nootch and Rick, et al. For the first time in many years, after suffering so long as an emotionally disconnected, clinically noncommittal sociopath, he was beginning to feel like he had found a home.

Still, he knew the lush hills of Roosevelt County harbored evils and dangers both known and as-yet unimagined. He would be happy to settle into this new life as an apprentice to this interesting, intelligent, lovable group of low-rent sorcerers, but he knew he had a job to do. He would have to watch his back.

CHAPTER TEN
TO KILL A MATING BIRD

Located just north of the geographical center of Roosevelt County, Dutch Hollow was snuggled in a deep vale between sweeping uplands, with a churning chasm bisecting it in half. Five stone bridges and an old milldam spanned the Upper Lenape Creek at the most scenic point in its meandering, southwesterly 70-mile course from Mohawk Mountain near the Massachusetts border to the Hudson at Beaverton. The improbably picturesque village was, to Nate's untrained eyes, the very essence of frou-frou New England charm: a little slice of stuffy Connecticut conceit carved into a rolling horse country paradise. As had Mona Levy's, his opinion would soon change.

Nate was enchanted by the matchless beauty of his new surroundings, and paid little heed to the warnings repeatedly trumpeted in the *"Urinal"* and the various Roosevelt newspapers concerning the dreaded deer tick and other rural dangers. Something about these marginally tamed wilds warmed the cockles of his hereditarily English heart, and he spent many blissful early morning and evening hours walking the forbidden countryside alone, studiously ignorant of posted property signs, electric fences and other minor impediments.

All this "unblemished" natural beauty came at a price, as Nate had become aware through research at the local library and long talks with Nootch, Dave and especially Augie O'Malley, who seemed to know at least as much as his journalistic mentors about local lore. Roosevelt County was a world apart from the rest of New York State. A long vertical rectangle bounded on the west by the Hudson River and on every other side by rugged, ore-rich hills, fully two-thirds of the 802-square-mile county was a land of elegant viewscapes made possible through generations of brutal 19th-century harnessing of a once forbidding land. This brutality initially took the form of strip-mining for iron and the near-total deforestation of the county to provide fuel for the fires of smelting. The bulk of the armaments and ammunition used by the Union Army in the Civil War had been forged from the iron of the Mohican Hills.

After the iron ran out, most of the county segued into wheat and then dairy production, as landowners turned its denuded hills and vales into thriving farms. Vast tracts owned by less entrepreneurial-minded land barons in both the hilly northeastern and the northwestern riverbank sections of the county were eventually reforested and turned into beautiful English-style country estates. A full third of Roosevelt County, most of which was located in the southwesterly provinces surrounding the chronically depressed river cities of Pinksterkill and Beaverton and the vast USE industrial complex in the town of East Waterkill, slowly succumbed during the latter half of the 20th century to a virulent suburban sprawl.

By the time Nate—along with a gusher of September 11 refugees fleeing New York—descended on the place, Dutch Hollow and its northern Roosevelt environs was already becoming a magnet for disaffected, super-rich Manhattanites who could afford to buy large swathes of real estate from cash-poor old-line families. The barons of old had retained their dominion over the land they sold off by inserting clauses into the deeds banning further subdivision and most forms of land use. They insisted as well on clauses authorizing them to run their precious fox hunts across the new owners' properties in perpetuity.

Nate didn't begrudge northern Roosevelt's privileged few their tidy, hand-me-down land management system. As America's leadership seemed of late to be retreating from old Teddy Roosevelt's idea of unspoiled public land, having sold mining and drilling rights out from under a number of supposedly forever wildernesses, a feudal system seemed as reasonable a way to go as any. The only way to save land from over-development and ruination was to allow it to be hogged by rich, snobby horse people—who stood the best chance of letting it lie unspoiled forever. But that didn't mean Nate had to stay off their property.

* * *

While trespassing along the crest of a hilly estate near Dutch Hollow on the Friday evening of his first work-week, Nate witnessed a virtual swarm of helicopters heading up from the city and dropping one by one into the surrounding countryside. Although he didn't yet know it, this armada carried a small legion of commuting magazine publishers, movie actors, rock stars and chewing gum magnates. And one of these thumping commuter choppers, Nate would presently discover, routinely transported Sheila's old boss Arthur Schmidt, the legendary chairman and CEO of Universal Silicon Enterprises, to his 1,000-acre weekend Shangri-La which encompassed the very same Gunshot Hill upon which he was then standing.

Descending the hill as the sun set, Nate stumbled upon a disturbing sylvan scene. A red-tailed hawk, obviously distressed, was lying wanly on the ground in a clearing, trying in vain to right itself and fly. As it flapped its wings weakly, the creature opened its beak and convulsively regurgitated a foamy yellow liquid. Lying next to the flailing bird was the half-eaten carcass of a black starling. The hawk's mate circled overhead, making what sounded for all the world to be keening noises.

"I know how you feel, sweetheart," said Nate. "I know how you feel."

When he got home, he used Mona's phone to call a state wildlife hotline to report the possibility of a bird poisoning. The attendant took his information and referred him to something called the Mohican Valley Raptor Center, to follow up with them on Monday. Nate had the feeling he had stumbled on his first significant story.

Later that evening he went over to the Delafield House to eat a late meal of bad bar food and hang out with the Roosevelt Friday night after-work crew. Dave, Nootch and Rick Parton were there as expected, huddled at the bar trying to watch a basketball game on TV that was being drowned out by the caterwauling of a loud but serviceable three-piece cover band. Augie O'Malley was at the bar as well, deep in conversation with an artificially unattractive older blond woman suffering from a bad facelift.

Mark Zweiker and his sidekick Aaron were double-teaming a group of poodle-haired townies, hectoring them to dance. A large table, already laden with half empty pitchers, had been commandeered by a crowd of Roosevelt people, most of whom Nate hadn't met. Mona Levy was holding court at one end of the table; at the opposite end was a smaller, quieter group that included young Nicole Royal and poor Bobby Hanrahan.

Nate approached his bosses first. He told them about the poisoned birds he had discovered, and that he had contacted the authorities. "I smell a story. I know I have a town board thing and two Clover Schools stories to do, but I'd like to concentrate on the bird incident first—even though it's not technically on my beat. I'm going to try and go out there with a wildlife pathologist on Monday, and also see if I can find out how they got poisoned."

"Kid, animal stories rule! Especially dead animal stories," said Nootch. "You have my blessing, as long as it's OK with Big Dave, here. And as long as you finish your other shit."

"Follow your nose, Olsen," said Dave. "I'll deal with Mona and Mark. It's your story."

Nootch even gave Nate a series of leads and some mentor-ly advice. "Birds have been a problem in the Valley lately. A farmer down in Wheaton was arrested for poisoning birds that were *mang*-ing all his cattle feed. He was out of his mind. There's a dairy farmer in Haverfield who might have the same problem," he said. "Norm Poole. He was talking in the diner a few weeks ago about a bird invasion. They're shitting up his feed troughs. Haverfield is in Ostia, right up in back of Gunshot Hill where you saw your dead birds, which is in Jefferson Township. I'm pretty sure the land you were trespassing on is owned by a rich motherfucker: Art Schmidt, the head of USE. Go get 'em, kid. Just keep yourself transparent to the story. We don't make the news, we report it."

"Yo, grasshopper. I've got a fucking bird for ya," blurted a visibly drunk Rick Parton, nearly launching his 300-pound frame off the bar stool in a failed attempt to twirl around and flip Nate his middle finger.

* * *

On his way over to the main Roosevelt congregation, Nate was approached by a tall, familiar-looking woman sporting an incongruous pile of flaming orange hair, wearing a too-short skirt that more than showed off a killer set of legs.

"Hello, Nate. Why didn't you call me?" She didn't look particularly hurt.

"Because I have no idea who you are," said Nate, truthfully. "Have we actually met?"

"Right here, after Sheila's funeral. I'm Natalie Johnson, a friend of Sheila's—and Augie's. I could have sworn I slipped you my phone number, but I must have been drunker than I thought."

"Well, I'm certain that I was drunker than you thought, or I would have remembered you. Speaking of drinks, can I buy you one?"

"I'd truly love to sit and talk to you," whispered Natalie. "But unfortunately I'm here with a date who I don't like as much as you. Here, take my number again, and this time, don't lose it." She pressed a business card into his hand as she walked slowly by him, rubbing her flank against his thigh as she did so. "Call me."

Nate hesitated for a few moments before continuing over to the table of work cronies, in order to give his raging boner a chance to subside. It had been weeks since he'd even thought about getting laid, and here was a leggy Star Trek vixen all but handing him the keys to her fun-box. He would have to consider it. He looked at the card: Natalie Johnson, Equestrian Veterinarian. "Strange woman," he thought. "Nice legs. Nice name, too. I would have been 'Natalie' if I was a girl."

The rest of the night passed without incident, unless one could call Nootch trying to take Mark Zweiker's head off an incident. Stiffed by the local girls, Mark and Aaron had begun traumatizing sweet innocent Nicole again, and due to their drunkenness were losing perspective and coming on a bit too rough. Nicole ran to the ladies' room in tears, and Nootch must have noticed, because before Nate knew what was happening he was in Mark's face.

"You like picking on little girls, bitch?" he was yelling, thrusting his big jaw into Mark's skinny neck. "Where's your wife, bitch? Does she know you like shaved pussy? I guess she does, because she's got one, too. You wanna know how *I* know, jackass?"

At which point Mark took an ill-advised swing at Nootch, which was viciously countered by a blocking left hook to the temple, knocking him to the floor. In the ensuing melee both Roosevelt editors were forcibly removed from the premises and told to take two weeks off to think about how they were going to act before trying to enter the Delafield House again.

"I hate that jive motherfucker," said Nootch as Nate drove him and a brooding Mona Levy back to the Arms in the hiccuping Fiesta. "Jimmy, good luck with that fucking bird story. I want you to kick that motherfucker's ass."

"What bird story?" asked Mona. "What's he talking about, Nate?"

"Never you mind," said Nootch. "Nate, you just do what I say. Kick that motherfucker's ass."

Nate left the two star-crossed lovers bickering in the vestibule and went to bed, desperately hopeful that a Mohican Valley angle would pan out and save him from what he knew would be Mona Levy's eternal wrath for his stealing a story from her beat.

* * *

On Saturday morning Nate went down to the Ostia office, let himself in and started leafing through the ratty office phone book looking for the Haverfield number of Norman Poole, dairy farmer. He didn't find one. He walked over to Max's Diner, bought a *Urinal* and a *New York Times* out of the coin boxes outside, sat at the counter and ordered a bacon-and-egg on an English muffin and a coffee, black. After perusing the wafer-thin sports section of the Pinksterkill paper, he turned to the counter waitress and asked for more coffee. When she came back with the steaming pot, he popped the question: "Do you know Norm Poole?"

She was a tired-looking woman in her forties, with stringy brown hair and a shiner under her left eye. "You from around here?"

"I'm sorry, I'm Jim Olsen. New reporter at the *Mohican Valley Times*. My boss, John Ianucci, said Norm Poole was having bird problems. I'd like to talk to him about it. Do you happen to know his number, or where he lives?"

"Yeah, well, Norm's good people. Maybe you'll want to ask him your-self," she said, smiling and nodding toward a burly, leather-faced gentle-man in a filthy red Caterpillar baseball cap and mud-caked brown coveralls, sitting at the counter three stools down from Nate. "What a stroke of luck!" he thought.

The man eyed him suspiciously. "What do you want, exactly?"

"I'm doing a feature on how bird invasions are killing the dairy busi-ness in the valley," said Nate. "I'd like to visit your place and see for my-self. Take a few pictures. Interview you."

"That so? Well, I ain't got too much to say about it. But you got eyes; you just come take a look and see how deep the shit is, and make your own judgments. Four o'clock. You'll see."

"Where's your place?" Nate's heart was racing with excitement.

"Up on Haverfield-Ostia Road, just past the graveyard on the right. Haverfield Farms. You'll see the barns—and the birds. Can't miss it."

At 3:45 p.m. Nate drove up Route 31 out of Ostia past the boarded-up Stinky's Roadhouse and turned left on Haverfield-Ostia Road, which ran a crooked course behind the golf course and the dump, roughly parallel to Route 33. The sun had long ago disappeared behind the steep hills looming above, although the sky remained bright. After about two miles, the valley widened a bit and Nate came to a four-way stop sign with an old church and an overgrown graveyard on the corner. Just past the intersection on the right was an enormous barn surrounded by muddy fields, populated by a sad-looking herd of Guernseys. As Nate pulled closer he could see the immense bird swarm circling the barn and the herd. A wooden sign confirmed it: "Haverfield Farms."

It was cow-feeding time, and starlings, thousands upon thousands of them, were descending on the Poole property looking for an easy meal. Nate pressed "record" on the miniature tape recorder in his pocket, uncapped the camera Dave had given him, and knocked on the office door. A dour-faced Norm Poole appeared. "Come on out to the barnyard. Watch your step."

"Mind if I take a few pictures?"

"Suit yourself."

The sky was dark with screeching, flapping starlings. Every available perch on every rafter of the cow barn was occupied four-deep by sated birds, dropping the fruits of their digestion on Poole's unfortunate herd, which was trying gamely to finish its own contaminated supper.

"How much grain you think these birds eat every day?" asked Poole. Looking with pity on his feces-encrusted cows, he turned to Nate. "Just take a look at that. How would *you* like to eat bird shit all day?"

"What do you do about it?" asked Nate.

"I've tried just about everything," said Norm Poole. "Ain't a God-damned thing I can do about it."

* * *

Instead of taking the Fiesta down to Ostia Monday morning, Nate walked to the Dutch Hollow office at 9 a.m. He settled in at Nootch's Tuesday night desk and called the raptor center. The director, Marnie Hoag, said she'd already received a FAX from a state wildlife pathologist/investigator who was obtaining a blanket warrant for the two of them to walk the lands in the area, find the stricken birds and take them in for testing. Nate identified himself as a reporter as well as the discoverer of the birds and asked if he could accompany them and report on what they found. Following another flurry of phone calls, his request was approved by Randy Arnold, the state investigator.

The avian SWAT team arrived at the Roosevelt office at 1 p.m. Arnold the bird sleuth was a tall, loose-limbed man in his late 40s, with a salt-and-pepper beard, rimless spectacles and the humorless, no-nonsense manner of a math professor. Marnie Hoag was in her mid-50s, with a finely-lined, openly attractive face and a shimmering mane of gray-gold hair tied into a long tail which hung down her back nearly to her knees. The magic of the Summer of Love had kept its hold on her through the intervening years, as evidenced by the sparkle in her eyes, her tinkling turquoise jewelry, the aroma of patchouli wafting off of her and the way vestigial phrases like "far out" came tripping off her tongue.

They drove in Randy Arnold's state van to the spot on Route 31 that Nate remembered emerging from on his jaunt three nights before, and parked at the nearby parking lot of an ice cream stand that had been closed for the season. They trekked up a long hill to the point from which Nate had been watching the helicopters. "This is Gunshot Hill," confirmed Marnie. "We're on the Art Schmidt estate. The USE chairman. I've been here before. He's a falconer, and we've treated some of his birds. He lets the public on his land once a year for a groovy Fourth of July concert and fireworks. He's very nice for such a wealthy man. Very down to earth. He'd be devastated to know birds were being poisoned on his land."

Nate directed them to the clearing where the dying raptor had been. Sure enough, both the hawk and the half-devoured starling were still there. The hawk was dead, and its pining mate was nowhere in sight. "She's a female," said Randy.

As Marnie scanned the skies and treetops for the hawk's husband, Randy pulled out a camera and photographed the scene from a number of different angles. Nate started snapping photos as well. Randy knelt down, retrieved a kit from out of his backpack, put on a pair of rubber gloves and took a sample from the dead bird's beak with a medicine dropper, screwing it into an empty specimen bottle. With Marnie's help, Randy picked up the mangled starling and put it in a plastic bag. "This starling was already dead when the hawk picked it up," said Randy, as Nate activated the small tape recorder in his pocket. "It's covered in mud and manure. It was poisoned first, and probably dumped in a manure pile and spread in a field with a million other dead birds. This hawk ate poison meat. By now, the poison is moving up the food chain."

They carefully placed the dead raptor in another, larger bag. With a small hoe and shovel, Randy scraped the area in a 10-foot diameter around the scene and placed the dirt, leaves, twigs and feathers into other bags. He and Marnie labeled each bag.

"You two seem to have worked together before," said Nate.

"Many times, said Marnie. "Randy is one of the best wildlife pathologists in the country. He knows his birds, and he knows what they're up against."

"The large raptor population has expanded back into this region in the last 10 years," said Randy. "Even the bald eagle is coming back. There are four of them nesting in the marsh flats on the Hudson near Copenhagen. But that's partly because their prey population of small mammals and birds has exploded. Especially mice, which carry the deer tick, and starlings, which are on the rebound after having been nearly wiped out by DDT and other pesticides. Starlings eat corn, wheat and other grains, and without access to poison farmers have no chance of getting rid of them. Starlings tend to take over a place in large swarms, like in 'The Birds.' It can be pretty disgusting; even scary. The few dairy farmers left in Roosevelt and Columbia counties have been bearing the brunt of the starling explosion. They've taken to importing some pretty nasty poisons from states like Ohio where they're legal. I've already caught and fined a couple of farmers in this valley, farther south. They were using 'Kill-A-Bird,' which is 11-percent fenthion. Fenthion gets in through the starlings' feet, and paralyzes their central nervous systems. It's not a comfortable death.

"We've got to find us a farmer within two miles. That's the hawk's nesting and feeding range, if it's mating."

"I think I might already know of a farmer over the hill from here with a bird problem," said Nate. "But you can't tell him I told you about him."

"We don't lock anybody up," said Randy. "We just fine them and tell them to stop, and reduce the fine if they testify against the poison manufacturers in our lawsuits. The birds and rock-bottom milk prices usually drive them out of the business sooner or later."

"Yeah, well, he looks like he's just about out of business already. Take it easy on him. And please don't say where you heard about him from."

"Don't worry," laughed Marnie. "Whoever did this, Randy will find him, with or without your help."

"Haverfield would have been the first place I looked tomorrow morning, no matter what," confirmed Randy. "And I won't blow your cover. Although I'd like to get your signed statement in case I have to prosecute. The farmer'll never look at your signature."

"I guess. And can you please call me right away if you find something tomorrow? I've got a deadline tomorrow night."

"Sure. And thanks a lot for your help, Mr. Olsen."

* * *

The next day at 11 a.m. Nate got a call from Marnie Hoag. "Randy went down to your farmer friend this morning with a warrant. He found a field on the hill that had recently been spread with manure. Mixed in with the manure were thousands of dead starlings. Last night, Randy tested the birds you found for fenthion. They both tested positive. He's running tests on some starlings from the field and assumes they'll test positive as well. If so, Mr. Poole is in big trouble."

Nate didn't know whether to jump for joy or cry. He felt terrible for having outed the poor old fuck, but realized he had done the right thing. The man *was* poisoning the environment, after all. Norman Poole was a one-man avian holocaust. Still, he couldn't help but feel sorry for the ignorant fool. He decided to emphasize the wrenching duality of the situation in his story.

The story, titled "Anatomy of a Tragedy," which Nootch and Dave placed at the tops of the front pages of the *Mohican Valley Times* and *the Dutch Hollow Chronicle* early Wednesday morning accompanied by Nate's heart-rending photo of a group of skinny, shit-splattered cows staring forlornly at the camera as birds fluttered around them, was a hit. The papers sold out by Friday morning for the first time in recent memory, and another 3,000-paper press run was ordered on Friday afternoon. Winnie Babson himself called Nate in to the office Friday afternoon to congratulate him and invite him to speak about the story on his Saturday morning radio show.

Later that evening Nate was treated to a night of free beers at the Delafield House. With Nootch and Mark in the first week of their two-week suspension things were less overtly festive than they could have been, but Nate made the best of the situation by getting to know Nicole Royal, who turned out to be a smart, funny, soulful young woman. "All bullshit aside, I loved your story," she said, her eyes misting over. "You captured everything: the horror, the senselessness; the utter sadness of the farmer's life. I actually cried at the end."

"Aw, shit," said Nate to himself. "Here we go again."

CHAPTER ELEVEN
LEARNING CURVES

In engineering his glorious journalism debut, Nate had worked a 72-hour week for $300: just under $4.17 an hour. The new notoriety of "James Olsen" created a more or less permanent extra workload for Nate, who gladly accepted the pressure of his pen name's success. With virtually nothing better to do, he worked like a dog to complete breaking stories well past the Tuesday night story deadline, only to have to "paginate" the articles into his own paper in the early Wednesday morning hours before it had to be shipped to the printer.

What Nate hadn't bargained on was how much he was taking to the actual writing process, something he vaguely remembered having abhorred in school. It became a matter of pride for him to find the emotional "nut" of a story, even if it was about a cantankerous photocopy machine in the town clerk's office or a long, boring speech by a school superintendent to somnambulant seventh-graders. He learned to obtain multiple, varied sources for the more important stories, and how to let scumbag officials with whom he didn't agree hang themselves with their own words.

Nate learned to phrase sentences to get the point of a story across without bruising tender egos or unduly upsetting the delicate balance of local opinion. He strove to inject every one of the pieces with at least a smattering of conflict, humor, pathos and anger, stuff he remembered from reading New York-based rags like *The Observer* and *Vanity Fair*. Small-town politics frequently veers into the absurd, and Nate's jaundiced eye caught the sort of ironies a younger, less experienced cynic might have missed.

Yet, somehow, people on both sides of an issue assumed he was on their side, and tended to open up to him with juicy quotes. A fan base of sorts was developing, a phenomenon Nate thought was restricted to the baser forms of show business he had recently left behind. A few weeks into his budding career, a small cadre of mostly older, overeducated citizens and political busybodies seemed to be taking notice, and sent in a flurry of letters announcing themselves as kindred spirits. Even the ordinarily publicity-shy Big Nick Vitello called him personally one afternoon and asked if he wanted to do an interview profile on him. "I never trusted no journalist to get me right before, but I think you might have a shot, kid," said the King of Ostia and reputed mob associate. "Just treat me with the same, uh...compassion you seem to have for other subjects, and you got the job."

Nate jumped at the chance, and in a series of candid, intimate "Live at Max's Diner" interviews with Vitello, attempted to capture the man's unschooled wit and Bronx-bred charm. He apparently succeeded, because no one was dispatched to run him off of Van Valkenbergh Hill on the way home after the stories came out, and he heard through the Max's grapevine that Big Nick was having the articles framed.

As an added perk of James Olsen's burgeoning notoriety, hot news started being dropped in Nate's lap. A month after he started, a whistleblower at the Mohican Valley DDSO—the large mental institution south of Clover that Nootch had pointed out to him on his tour—called Nate and asked to meet him, again at Max's, which was becoming a sort of satellite office for him. Over a chocolate milkshake, the man—a supervising psychiatrist at the facility—handed Nate a thick envelope. "This is a confidential report of an internal investigation conducted by the state Office of Mental Retardation," he said. "It exposes serious physical and emotional abuses in the draconian environment created by our current director, who was brought in by the governor as a hatchet man to shut the place down. The director is quitting on Monday, but he's really being fired. A client was murdered on his watch, and they're scapegoating him."

"Holy shit."

The resulting series of stories was to cement James Olsen's reputation as a muckraker. Three full press runs sold out. The kudos rolled in. "You're the best reporter we've ever had," said Nootch. "Even better than me."

"This is the golden age of the *Mohican Valley Times*," decreed Dave. "You and Nootch; I've never seen anything like it. You're ripping the valley a new asshole."

"Let me know if there's anything you need," said Winnie Babson. "You're my guy."

Even the metro editor of the *Pinksterkill Journal* came calling, offering "James Olsen" a job as the paper's eastern Roosevelt reporter. "I didn't know you had an eastern Roosevelt reporter," said Nate. "I've never seen anybody at a meeting."

"We don't. We think you could give us the visibility we want in the Mohican Valley," said the editor.

Nate was flattered, but decided against it, knowing he'd probably be pigeonholed and that they probably wouldn't respect his cover. He didn't tell anyone at work about the offer.

* * *

Flushed with these unforeseen successes, Nate began to imagine an actual future at Roosevelt Newspapers. His short-term objective was to supplant Patrick McDuffy as the company's "editor-at-large," a situation which would give him the flexibility he needed to roam the county at will and root out stories, sources and information to support his secret jihad against USE and Janssen.

Nate had met McDuffy only once, at a county legislature meeting devoted to the prospective closing of the Roosevelt County Infirmary, a rundown old nursing facility for destitute old folks, located on a back road in the foothills of Clover. Despite trying to keep an open mind, he had found Dave's assessment of the man quite on target. A barrel-chested, heavily goitered walking heart attack swathed in what had to be a tailor-made three-piece business suit, McDuffy came off as an unctuous, shallow individual, dedicated to the status quo. On his improbably small feet, he wore a pair of crocodile-skin cowboy boots. He had developed a deep, basso announcer's voice to go with his annoying personality, along with an air of mock superiority that quickly evaporated when he slithered obsequiously up to power people like Winnie Babson or county legislature chairman

Herman "Hick" Vanderkamp to obtain their stock quote of the day. He was the word "asshole" personified, thought Nate.

When Nate read the story McDuffy wrote about the meeting in the *Beaverton Beacon* the next Thursday, he couldn't believe how much the man had left out. There was no mention at all of the 100-odd placard-carrying protesters hollering insults at the legislators as they rubber-stamped Infirmary Committee Chairman Winston Babson's proposal to close the neglected facility in three months, pawning the residents off on private nursing homes.

Nate had tussled with Dave over permission to run his own version of the story in the Mohican Valley paper. Dave eventually relented, but only with Nate's assurance that he wouldn't make Winnie look like a bad guy. Nate solved the problem by interviewing Winnie privately and placing his comments strategically to answer questions raised by the protesters. It worked, and everybody was happy with his "fair and balanced" approach, including Winnie.

Other reporters and editors, most of whom had never even seen Patrick McDuffy, were incredulous that he actually existed. "I always thought he was just a human head mounted on a big black box, like Commander Pike, hooked to a telephone and a dictation machine," said Rick Parton, who despite having to run McDuffy dispatches in every issue of his paper had never run across the man at a meeting or in any office.

* * *

In his spare time, and whenever possible during the course of his duties for the Mohican Valley paper, Nate tried to learn as much as possible about Roosevelt County, its people and its villages and towns. Dave, Nootch, Rick and Augie were indispensable, as were a growing number of disgruntled political insiders from Ostia and Clover, who would kidnap him after meetings to educate him on their axe-grinding viewpoints. On Fridays at the Delafield or at infrequent, Rabelaisian "Arms parties," he would grill other reporters about things they might know that they weren't reporting.

Nate soaked up information on local history, politics, personalities, businesses and their alliances, petty feuds and litigation, land deals, large

public and private development projects, who owned what, and where. He
learned about the various infrastructures in the county: where the garbage
and the sewage went, where people's power and water came from, how
two or three developers got hold of so much land.

He learned about the county's powerful Republican machinery and its
many links to the current governor's office. He learned that a small, inbred
clique of three Pinksterkill law firms handled almost every important client in the mid-Hudson region, including Big Nick Vitello, the Republican
parties of three counties, nearly every town government body and all the
banks, developers and construction firms, as well as Winnie Babson and
Roosevelt Newspapers.

Through Rick Parton, Nate became aware of the "Rocco Report," a
legendary document authored by Hamilton Canard, Esq., an old-school
New York attorney, concerning the machinations of the late Vincent
Rocco, who until he was found floating face-down in the Hudson in July,
2000 was an Echo Valley property tax assessor. Canard had been hired in
1990 by a citizen's group in Rooseveltion to handle its unsuccessful attempt
to sue Rocco for damages relating to his tenure as tax assessor there during
the '80s.

Since moving to Roosevelt County in 1968 from the Bronx to start a
housing construction firm, Vince Rocco had insinuated himself into local
politics. Starting in the Town of Pinksterkill and moving town by town
through much of rural central and southern Roosevelt over the next 32
years, Rocco would attain each municipality's tax assessor post. Once in
the position, according to Canard, he would manipulate assessments upward to the point that beleaguered farmers and old-line families would be
forced to sell their land or have it appropriated for back taxes. Commonly
one of three or four big developers would be conveniently waiting in the
wings to snap the property up for a song.

Canard's contention was that in each case Rocco was in covert partnership with a developer, and was almost single-handedly responsible for
much of the conversion of central and southern Roosevelt County from
farms to subdivisions. As his creepy act was discovered and the citizens of
a locality threw him out of office, Rocco would simply reappear the next
year a couple of towns over, backed by the development-happy countywide

GOP machine, to work his magic until he got caught again. He was never indicted for anything.

In the weeks before his death—which was reported in the papers as a "suicide"—Rocco had been nailed in a federal corruption probe and was a key witness against the boss of the county GOP, a portly Italian godfather type named Tony Costello. Rocco was due to testify before a federal grand jury in White Plains the next day.

Vince Rocco, Big Nick and Winnie Babson all had the same lawyer: a guy named Dick Strong from the venerable 150-year-old Pinksterkill law firm of Haberman, Wilson & Strong. So, too, as Nate found out one day flipping through files at the county clerk's office, did Janssen Movers.

Dick Strong lived in Dutch Hollow, where he was also the Town of Jefferson attorney. Nate had seen him in the checkout line at the local supermarket; a red-faced, white-haired blowhard, already half in the bag at 5 p.m. on a Monday, carrying on impatiently over the nervous fumblings of the zit-faced grocery clerk. "What a dick," Nate said to himself, even before encountering Strong again that evening at a Jefferson town meeting he was covering for Mona Levy.

Nate had prepared himself for the fact that he would be attending a meeting chaired by Sheila's father, William T. McNally. In addition to his job as head of Janssen Movers, McNally was deep into his first term as Jefferson's town supervisor, having left his earlier town position as highway superintendent to succeed the former town leader, his wife Edith. Her legendary fund-raising prowess for the state GOP had landed her a number of juicy no-show appointments in the nearly all-male regime of New York's Governor Hiram Pollock, starting in 1992. Following Pollock's sudden removal of Andrew Carlotti, the state's commissioner of Economic Development, in the wake of a financial scandal, she was appointed to the $350,000-a-year post. Over the past 20 years the McNallys of Dutch Hollow had quietly risen to become one of the wealthiest, most influential, most politically connected families in New York State.

Nate sat in the rear of the hall taking notes, slouching into his seat and hoping Bill McNally wouldn't recognize him. He needn't have worried. The man was so completely self-involved that he rarely bothered to look to the left or right, or further than three feet in front of him. Thankfully,

nearly the entire meeting was taken up with a closed-door "executive session" in which McNally and his fellow board members, accompanied by
the florid-faced Strong, filed out and reconnoitered in another room for
more than an hour. Only once did Nate hear anything verbalized concerning what the fuss was about: McNally, in announcing the executive
session, referenced a "highway department personnel matter." Nate made
a note to ask Mona about it.

* * *

It didn't take long for Nate to understand that Dutch Hollow was a burg
with a split personality. By night during the week it belonged to the
McNallys, O'Malleys and scores of other Irish, Italian and Portuguese
families, but would expand by day with legions of anorexic Frankenbabes
in boots and jodhpurs who descended from the surrounding hills to shop
at the village's many unaffordable boutiques. And on weekends it would
literally burst at the seams with obnoxious New York elitists who looked
down their noses at the locals as much as the locals looked down on them.
Class warfare was palpable, and smelled of sweat and gunpowder. To Nate
it was like watching a version of "Upstairs, Downstairs," expanded to in-
clude an entire town and its environs.

The rich themselves could be divided into classes. The first were old-
school folks called "hill-toppers," who had been around for at least a century and exhibited a relatively low-key gentility on their rare jaunts into the
village. The second was a newer class of "weekenders": interlopers who had
gotten suddenly and extremely rich during the recently expired economic
hyper-boom. Flush with stock market success, these newcomers had the
financial juice to wrest large pieces of estates from cash-strapped gentry or
to otherwise ferret out relatively good land deals in the dwindling undevel-
oped areas of northern Roosevelt. They were looking for relative peace and
quiet to mitigate the effects of their jarring working lives in the city.

A minority of these weekenders exhibited a taste in architecture and
landscaping that had apparently been gleaned from watching the Disney
Channel. Harassed by fusty neighbors and dragged into explaining themselves at impossibly long and unfriendly planning and zoning board

snoozefests, many of this group were beginning to tire of the game, and had plans to either flee back to the city or venture even further north where their monster SUVs and helicopter pads would be more welcome. Then the twin bombshells of the stock crash and September 11 broadsided them, and it seemed to Nate that there were more of them clogging the village streets with every new weekend. High-end lifestyle magazines were touting the two toniest Roosevelt County villages—Dutch Hollow and Kipsbergh—as "The New Hamptons."

Once an agricultural hub of regional importance and home to a second rate women's college, Dutch Hollow had at one time boasted its own movie theater, opera house and railroad depot. For a short period in the mid-1800s it was bigger than Pinksterkill. Dwindling steadily in size and influence since its 19th-century heyday—despite the valiant efforts of the third oldest Rotary Club chapter in America and the only marginally less irrepressible Dutch Hollow Businessmen's Association—the village had finally been reduced to just what it looked like: a fancy living toy for the rich to play with.

Despite commercial real estate being priced out of reach for all but a few empire-building Italian and Irish families, Dutch Hollow for the time being remained home to one grocery store and two hardware stores—which to Nate was a distinct plus. But the preponderance of estates in the area, each of them completely self-sustaining in terms of basic amenities like food and entertainment, meant that there were considerable gaps in services for the proletariat. The Dutch Hollow Central School District, even without the participation of the chronically underachieving "Shroomville" community on the wrong side of the defunct Lenape Valley Railroad tracks, would have been one of the 10 worst in the state.

Other than a serviceable pizza parlor and a picture-postcard 1950s-style diner that closed at the ridiculous hour of 7 p.m. every night, decent restaurants were in short supply. Until recently a wonderful Greek café had been struggling along to great fanfare, but the gifts of the chef/owner had attracted the attention of an ancient television diva who lived in the hills outside of town. She was so enthralled with his cuisine that she hired him as her private chef, providing Nate and the editors with one less tasty takeout alternative on Tuesday nights.

The Delafield was the one area venue that could properly be called a nightclub (and which, despite a discernible lack of competition, was unable to attract a crowd on any night other than Friday), and there was only one poorly stocked newsstand in town. This last indignity was the hardest of all for Nate to abide. Spartan rural laws of under-supply-and-demand often turned the simple act of buying a Sunday *New York Times* into a bloody struggle for survival against some of the most ill-mannered people on the planet.

The "downstairs" people of Dutch Hollow were Sheila's contemporaries, the sturdy descendants of Italian and, in Sheila's case, Irish and Portuguese immigrants who had long ago built and maintained the scores of baronial estates in the area. These families had transcended their once lowly status as indentured stone masons, ditch-diggers and trash-sloggers to become the American flag-waving mercantile backbone of the community: they were the shop-owners, entrepreneurs, contractors, bankers and lawyers of Dutch Hollow, and populated the fiercely Republican political machine.

The McNallys enjoyed the best of both worlds. While they hobnobbed with the hill-toppers, going as far as buying a hilly estate in the heart of horse country and joining the Dutch Hollow Hunt Association, they were also the undisputed king and queen of the proletariat; able to rub shoulders and drink draft beer with locals at the annual Dutch Hollow Firemen's Carnival.

According to Augie, Bill McNally was a prodigal son of sorts. He had been born in Dutch Hollow but had been sent to New York to live with his cousins following an incident when he was 13. Word was, said Augie, that he had raped a girl in the woods behind the school after a football game, and would have gotten away with it if the pesky junior high school principal hadn't happened by as he was zipping up. As was the case in those days, the crime was hushed up and surly young Bill was shipped off to attend a tough Catholic boys' school in Manhattan to straighten him out.

Which was apparently where he met Mickey Spillane.

When McNally returned to Dutch Hollow in 1973 he was a Vietnam veteran and a convicted felon, with yesterday's version of a Class-A CDL truck driver's license and a Teamster's union card burning a hole in his overalls. His Irish mob connections landed him a job with Conti Carting in Pinksterkill, and he wooed and married Edith Jardel, the girl he had raped in the woods.

* * *

When Nate grilled Mona Levy about the mysterious "highway department personnel matter" alluded to by Town Supervisor Bill McNally prior to Monday night's marathon executive session, she was initially somewhat evasive. She eventually produced from beneath her desk a sheaf of torn, crumbling papers given to her by Noel Preston, the local thorn-in-the-side political activist: one of a peculiar species of granola-eating lefties that Nate had noticed maintained a sparse but permanent presence in every town.

Preston's papers, discombobulated as they were, looked as if they had been stolen directly from Sheila's filing cabinet. "I could never make any sense of this stuff," said Mona, "and Noel Preston is just a huge pain in my ass. I never know what the fuck he's talking about. He runs for either the town board or the county legislature every year, and doesn't even get five votes. He wastes my time and takes up half of every town meeting ranting and raving about nothing. I can't believe you didn't see him there. He's the bald geek with the duct tape on his glasses."

"Nobody I saw. Can I take these for a while?"

"Be my guest. Don't bother calling Preston, though. He'll just talk your ear off for two hours, and you can't get rid of him."

The papers, when placed in some kind of date order, produced an incomplete story that nonetheless intrigued Nate. There were letters from the county health department and a New York City congressman to the Town of Jefferson calling for water testing to be done, and letters between various attorneys that seemed to be referencing some sort of litigation involving the town and its highway department. A group of individuals living off of Route 31 behind the Delafield House was suing the town for a public water district. And a town highway department employee, Sam Applebee, was being denied unemployment insurance after having been terminated for insubordination, and was also suing the town, for discrimination. He had been partially disabled while on highway department property when a truck backed over his foot as he was shoveling salt into a wheelbarrow.

And there was a poorly transcribed speech given by New York Congressman Evan Aldrich at Vassar College in 1997, in which he accused organized crime of a "vast conspiracy to poison the landscape of Roosevelt County with toxic waste, to line the pockets of gangsters and crooked politicians." In citing his long list of credits fighting the garbage mob since his days as a state assemblyman, Aldrich repeatedly referenced "my good friend and trusted right hand man, investigator Reginald Thurston Brown." In subsequent mentions, he kept referring to Thurston Brown as "Thirsty," as in: "Once again I called on my old friend Thirsty, and he didn't let me down."

* * *

As tickled as he was in being a star cub reporter for an obscure country newspaper, Nate was beginning to feel like he wasn't really getting anywhere with his primary obsession. He was afraid that the story was too big for him; that it would somehow evolve and elude him if he didn't devote at least 50 percent of his time to it.

Nate approached Dave and asked him if, should something terrible happen to Patrick McDuffy, he would choose him as editor-at-large. "My, you're an ambitious little squirrel, aren't you, my son? Actually, I've been hoping McDuff stumbles or drops dead, so I can slot you in there before we lose you to the *Daily News*. I'd have to clear it with Winnie first, and I'm sure he'd go for it. But there's no way he's going to let me get rid of that asshole without a major fuck-up. And the guy is too cagey to fuck up."

"What if we sicked another newspaper on him and had them expose all his conflicts?"

"That's a great idea, in theory. Don't think I haven't thought of it. You can't use the *Urinal*, though. He works for them, too."

"Yeah, but what if we forced them into it? They'd have to do something if they were publicly embarrassed into it. So would we. There's a stinker in every pot: a pinko activist in every town. There's gotta be some cracker out there harassing one of the school districts McDuffy works for who would just love to know he's working for them on the sly. We could make anonymous phone calls to these people, get them all riled up, and get them to start our war for us. Those meetings are televised on cable access TV. Reporters from RNN are at some of them. It might take a while to bubble up, but it might not."

"Olsen, you are a genius, and the personification of evil. I'd better watch my back."

"Don't worry, chief. I wouldn't have your job if it came with Marilyn Monroe's butt-crack."

Three weeks later a story appeared in the Albany *Patroon*, a political rag for state legislators and those who care about them, that a well-known mid-Hudson radio pundit and journalist was being censured by the Albany-based New York State Political Journalism Association for engaging in an egregious series of journalistic conflicts of interest. The story somehow made the Metro section of the *New York Times* the next Wednesday. It must have been a slow news day.

After fielding calls from *Times* reporters and fending off criticism from various civic and legal organizations, the *Urinal* finally relented and published an article concerning Mr. McDuffy, saying they had ordered him to cease all public relations work with newsworthy organizations or be fired. The radio station followed suit. Winnie Babson, embarrassed at his name being dropped unflatteringly in the *Times* and sensing correctly that the poor sap's reputation would be shattered forever no matter what, simply axed him unceremoniously. He refused to allow a story about it in any Roosevelt papers: he had a campaign to worry about. McDuffy's weekly TV show was public access, so nobody cared.

McDuffy was in a huge pickle. With three days to mull it over, he had to choose whether to give up a shit job as a stringer with the only newspaper that would have him, plus his half-hour weekly show at a reasonable hour for a fairly good-sized radio station; or face the loss of about $150,000 in annual income, which would probably dry up anyway as soon as he lost media influence.

Ultimately, he solved his dilemma by dropping dead of a long-overdue heart attack, which turned public opinion back in his favor for a few sad days until everybody forgot the whole thing and moved on.

"Jeez, chief, we didn't mean to fucking kill the guy," said Nate.

"Shut up, Olsen. You're scaring me. By the way, you're the new editor-at-large. It's $500 a week and you keep the car, but you still have to paginate on Tuesdays. Take it or leave it. I hope you can live with yourself. I know I can."

"You're my guy," said Winnie Babson. "Just be careful out there, and for God's sake, don't make me look bad."

CHAPTER TWELVE
IN SICKNESS AND IN HEALTH

Except for Friday nights at the Delafield, Nate had thus far completely avoided anything resembling a social life. He had avoided calling Natalie Johnson, Equestrian Veterinarian. For some reason she
frightened him, and she really wasn't so very attractive in his mind, once it
was stripped of its Friday-night beer goggles. Nicole Royal was a different
story, but he didn't feel ready for anything like that yet. Besides, he'd be
stepping on Nootch's toes. Nootch was mad enough at him already for
abandoning him in his time of greatest success in the Valley.

Nate didn't want to think about women at all, really. Neither did he
very often sit in his room at the Arms, jerking off to the few porn magazines he had left that hadn't been burned in the Gotham fire.

Even when he wasn't working, he worked.

Late one Monday night at his new desk in the Dutch Hollow office,
Nate was finally able, with much difficulty, to transfer Sheila's story,
"Adventures in Pollockistan: How USE, the Government and the Mob
Conspire to Give You Cancer," from off of its USE-formatted diskette
to a readable Word file on one of the company's Mac computers. He
printed out its 117 pages on the company's laser printer and brought it
home to read.

What Sheila and her friend Reginald Thurston Brown had written turned
out to be a report addressed to the U.S. Congressional Organized Crime
Task Force, whose chairman was Evan Aldrich, the liberal Democratic
congressman from New York City.

It began: "This will primarily be a chronicle of the mid-Hudson Valley region of New York State, and how its despoiling at the hands of industrialists and organized criminals has proceeded unabated for more than 60 years, despite all efforts to curb it. And it is a story of how the highest offices in the state, including the governor's office currently occupied by Hiram C. Pollock, a would-be candidate for higher office, are not only responsible for policies that perpetuate the process of illegal toxic waste dumping, but are intimately involved in proceedings at the meanest local level to snuff out all attempts to investigate and rectify known toxic waste dumps and prosecute the perpetrators."

"The story will culminate in an account of an unlikely series of events in rural Roosevelt County, N.Y., that serves as a window into this Byzantine underworld of mob hijinks, political favors, cover-ups and fancy maneuvering by high level government officials and connected law firms in the governor's inner circle, all in the name of toxic waste dumping for dollars."

The report went on to cast a wide net. It accused USE, Janssen, a phalanx of mobsters and, particularly, Sheila's father, of orchestrating schemes to dupe the taxpayers of towns around Roosevelt County, including Jefferson, into paying with their money and their lives for the privilege of having toxic chemicals dumped in their midst. And it accused the governor and his web of public officials and lawyer cronies, as well as the state police and county sheriff's department, of protecting the enterprise from being investigated and successfully prosecuted by state and federal authorities.

Sheila's father, back when he was the town highway superintendent, had over the years purchased many thousands of gallons of chemicals from Expo Chemicals, a distributor in Danbury. Reginald Thurston Brown, an investigator on the congressional payroll, had deemed the chemical distributor to be a bogus operator, whose real purpose was to move toxic waste for the New York-based Natale mob. Its president, Rolando "Ducky" Durso, had been convicted of a similar kind of racketeering in 1990, as part of a federal sting called "Operation Double-D."

The black market in toxic waste had been created in the 1970s with stringent new environmental laws that increased the cost of legal disposal of toxic petrochemicals to an average of $500 per 55-gallon drum. Seeing a vast new profit center, the mob moved quickly. Unscrupulous companies wishing to save money could contract with Ducky or another Natale associate to have their unwanted toxic waste carted away for $250 a barrel, no questions asked. By 1974, mobbed-up trucks were pulling into mobbed-up "sanitary" landfills like the Meadowlands, Atlantic Park and Roosevelt Sanitation in Pinksterkill, dumping toxic waste right in with the regular garbage.

As these manipulations were discovered and landfills were closed and garbage haulers prosecuted, the mobsters adjusted, and began "cocktailing" toxic waste in with construction and demolition (C&D) debris to be used for fill at construction sites or for filling tapped-out strip mines and such. Each day, thousands of filthy dump trucks containing toxin-laced C&D refuse began rumbling out of chemical and plastics plants throughout the northeastern United States, heading for places like West Virginia and the Mohican Valley to dump their loads. New York State tightened up its rules for the dumping of C&D, but left a 30-day loophole in the law that allowed a small landowner to have C&D dumped on his or her property for a month. Hundreds of small farmers and developers opened up their land to be dumped upon for a fee, gladly paid by mob operators like Ducky Durso.

As that loophole was closing, Durso and his cronies metamorphosed again. They began to double-dip, finding crooked markets to "buy" the chemicals they had already been paid by companies to dump. For example, Ducky would pull up to an industrial dry cleaning plant in New Jersey—or a Janssen warehouse for that matter—and load his truck with 50 barrels of spent perchloroethylene, or "perc," for which he'd be given $250 per barrel to get rid of. He could then turn around and take the same load of chemicals to, say, the Echo Valley town highway garage, as was proven in the "Double-D" case. There he would "sell" the dirty solvents to the town for $250 a barrel, slipping the shady highway superintendent a $1,000 bribe for the lot. The scheme was apparently lucrative enough that the grateful Ducky even loaded a group of on-the-take highway supers on a chartered bus for an all-expenses-paid junket to the Meadowlands for a Jets game.

Each highway superintendent would then have to deal with the constant flow of 55-gallon drums as best he could. Ostensibly purchased for routine highway department use for cleaning trucks and equipment, the growing hoard of solvent would sit in the department's garage and outbuildings until the barrels started to take over the place, rotting and leaking. Every once in a while the super would mobilize a crew of loyal workers to help him dump the stuff around the town. In Echo Valley, apparently, they dumped thousands of gallons through a couple of dry-well drains in the highway garage, which eventually formed a large plume in the aquifer, fouling the water supply and making the locals sick.

The water downgradient from the Echo Valley highway garage was tested in late 1992 and found to be very bad, indeed, but half-hearted attempts by the state to try and enforce a cleanup were met with stiff resistance by the town's all-GOP board, and the mess was never cleaned up. Thurston Brown alleged a far-reaching conspiracy by a web of politicos from the town supervisor all the way up to and including Governor Pollock, citing his cozy ties with the special cadre of Pinksterkill lawyers brought in to handle the town's problems.

The lead law firm was Zimmerman & Schmidt, with which Pollock was a partner until January 1993, when he assumed the governorship. A fellow Z&S alumnus was Charles "Chip" Seldon, Pollock's choice to head the state's Department of Environmental Conservation (DEC). Numerous attorneys seemed to glide effortlessly back and forth between working for Z&S and the law firm one floor down in the six-story FDR building in downtown Pinksterkill: Haberman, Wilson & Strong. Thurston Brown termed these two law firms "evil Siamese twins" and accused them of being essentially the same entity, dividing up business along lines of customer culpability. Z&S took all the above-board, law-abiding clients, while Haberman, Wilson & Strong specialized in mobsters and repeat felons of all stripes. Both firms would have a big hand in the fate of Echo Valley.

In 1995, a public water system was installed in the locality of the perc plume, piping water in from a vast housing subdivision in Lenape Falls that had its own reservoir and filtration plant. It was a two-million-dollar windfall for the housing division's developers, a consortium that included the Roosevelt County sheriff, Dean Hildenbrandt.

The Echo Valley town highway superintendent was eventually convicted of taking bribes, but died of a heart attack during the yearlong delay prior to sentencing. The feds could only manage to nail a Jonathan Wilson-represented Ducky Durso with a mail fraud conviction. After serving two years in federal prison, he was back in business as of 1993.

An Echo Valley citizen's group sued the town in 1994 for $5 million over their ruined drinking water. The town hired Jonathan Wilson of Haberman, Wilson & Strong to represent them, and the citizens eventually accepted a $250,000 settlement, half of which went to their "highly recommended" attorney from Zimmerman & Schmidt.

"None of this was any comfort to Echo Valley resident Trevor Jones and his late wife Angela, the citizens whose property was closest to the town garage, and who lived their entire adult lives in that location, bathing in, cooking with and drinking their well water," Sheila had written. "Angela worked for the town, right next door, for many years. Theirs was the well that was first to show significant amounts of perc in the water tests that set the Echo Valley toxic waste crisis in motion.

"Except, by the time her Echo Valley home was hooked up to a public water supply, Angela was already dead. She had retired early, in her late 50s, and went with Trevor on a trip of a lifetime to Hawaii. They had to cut their trip short, though, because Angela was bleeding internally. Six tragic weeks later she was dead, of liver and bladder cancer—the very same diseases that perc causes in rats and litigious USE clean-room workers."

"Angela Jones, however, was not a rat," concluded Sheila. "She'd never set foot in a USE clean room. She was a warm, loving country sweetheart who trusted in her government and her fellow man and felt safe in her cozy little small-town world. 'Echo Valley killed my wife,' says Trevor Jones, who netted just over $1,000 from the Echo Valley citizens' settlement—not even enough to replace his corroded appliances. 'Echo Valley killed my wife.'"

* * *

Elsewhere in their report, Sheila and Mr. Thurston Brown built a similar case against Bill McNally. With his twin roles as president of Janssen Movers and highway superintendent of Jefferson Township, McNally stood to make more in a poison-for-dollars scheme than your garden-variety corrupt official.

Sheila contributed voluminous insider knowledge of both her father's company's relationship with USE and her father's business at the town highway garage. And Thurston Brown used his investigator's savvy and experience in the workings of the Northeast mob to connect the dots. At some point, thought Nate, Bill McNally had to have become aware that his daughter was out for his blood. He wondered what that must have been like, and wondered how a man like that could continue to exist, with so much guilt hanging around his neck.

Once again, Ducky Durso was in business as a toxic middleman, having set up Expo Chemicals as his new front company. Although Durso's name wasn't recorded in his company's filing papers or on any of the false invoices he used, Thurston Brown had somehow traced to him the post office box address on a series of Expo invoices Sheila had spirited from the highway department files. With the congressional committee's funding, Thurston Brown also hired an out-of-state hydrologist to perform water testing of local wells around Dutch Hollow and its environs, looking for plumes of benzene, trichlorethylene (TCE) or perc—particularly in the neighborhood of the Jefferson town highway department.

While they didn't find any poison plumes beneath the highway department, they did find a big one containing all three chemicals and much more: behind the Delafield House, only a half-mile west on Route 31. It was not only poisoning the bar/restaurant's well water, but also those of the motel next-door and the Dutch Hollow Health Club, another quarter-mile down the road.

Again with Sheila's inside help, Thurston Brown located and interviewed three disgruntled former highway department employees, who independently confirmed that, yes, there were hundreds of barrels of chemicals stored at Mr. McNally's direction around the town highway property. And yes, these employees had on occasion been called on to assist their superintendent in disposing of toxic chemicals into the raw earth in selected spots around the town, usually in covert night drops. They told tales of pouring 10 truckloads of chemicals on the ground adjacent to the wetlands next to the state police barracks out on Route 56.

Sam Applebee, the plaintiff in the discriminatory lawsuit against the town mentioned in the Noel Preston papers, was a one-man wrecking crew. He testified that some of the stuff splashed onto his hand, searing it and leaving a permanent scar. He also told of performing a "rag test" to see if certain chemicals were flammable, whereupon they would bury whole drums of the most caustic stuff behind the garbage transfer station, also in the dead of night. And he told of pouring out barrels in the freshly bulldozed dirt behind the Delafield House for two weeks straight, before Paul Briggs covered it up with his new parking lot back in '95.

Most damning of all, he claimed to have overheard Bill McNally, while they were unloading an unmarked white truck full of drums, saying to his foreman: "These are from my warehouse. I usually don't do this, but this is some really bad shit. We've gotta get rid of it right away."

The report also included the results of a 2001 New York State Health Department study showing a sharp, unexplainable "spike" in both prostate and bladder cancers in the Dutch Hollow area in the last five years.

While full of facts and figures regarding past abuses by USE, and citing immense plumes of chemicals drifting along the bedrock beneath current and former Janssen warehouses, the report contained nothing except Sam Applebee's statement that came near to conclusively proving that the USE Corporation, through Bill McNally's Janssen Movers, was the source of the chemicals fouling these communities. A strong circumstantial case was made, but Nate knew that if he were to bring USE and Janssen down, he would need a smoking gun. He would have to witness the process in action himself.

The report was copyrighted in 2001. Nate wondered what, if anything, was happening with it. He decided to call on U.S. Congressman Evan Aldrich, and make a concerted effort to smoke out the mythical Reginald "Thirsty" Thurston Brown.

* * *

That Wednesday evening, either to reward himself for nearly 80 straight sleepless hours working on stories, paginating, researching and reading or, more likely, as a result of being certifiably addled in the head, Nate decided to call a woman, any woman. After wavering for five minutes, he dialed Nicole Royal. An answering machine picked up, and he left a garbled, exhaustion-slurred message: "Nicole. It's time for me to call you. You are very nice and I was wondering if I could ea- ... if you wanted to go

to dinner. It's Nate. Well, OK. I'm not drunk; just very, very tired. Maybe
some other time."

Without thinking another rational thought, he called Natalie Johnson.
She answered. "Hello?"

"Hello, Natalie. It's Nate Randall. I'm finally calling you."

"Well, yes, you are. How are you?"

"I know I sound drunk, but I've just been up for 78 hours working."

"Oh, my God! Are you all right? How can you be alive?"

"It's OK. I'm tired, but I'm hungry. Do you want to go to dinner?"

"Well, I happen to be making pesto tonight. Even though you've been
avoiding me, I could make an exception for a hungry zombie. Would you
like to come over and eat and watch TV? 'Six Feet Under' is on. It's my
favorite show."

Nate had never heard of it. "Sure. Where do you live?"

"On Route 56; the yellow house on the right just past the police barracks going toward Pleasant Plains."

"Great. I'll be there in a half-hour. I'll bring wine."

Yeah, great, thought Nate. Just don't drink the water.

When he arrived, Natalie Johnson opened the door wearing something
he hadn't seen since the 1970s: an elasticized "tube top" and hip-hugger
jeans. Her navel was festooned with a jeweled ring, the skin around which
looked a tad raw and tender. A large floral-pattern tattoo wound its way
from her neck and across her collarbone down beneath the starboard bulge
in her tube top, and her flame-red hair was bunched up in a bizarre knot on
top of her head like a blown-out Pebbles Flintstone. She was every inch a
Star Trek chick: typical Captain Kirk she-alien sex-bait. "Hi, there! I hope
you're hungry."

Indeed he was, and he glommed down every bit of her "pesto" despite
its being excessively oily and devoid of any trace of garlic. They sat on
her sectional sofa and finished the wine while talking about their jobs and
Augie O'Malley—who, it turned out, Natalie had once dated, as Nate suspected. He had meant to ask Augie about her, and wished he had. It would
be too late to get his opinion now.

Halfway through "Six Feet Under," as the show's homosexual funeral
director was making anal-retentive preparations to jack off to a gay porn

tape, Natalie leaned over, unzipped Nate's pants and started sucking his cock. Showing off another piece of hardware he hadn't noticed before, she noodled on the head of his dick with her solid silver tongue stud. Disturbingly, she followed this with a little trick Nate thought only hookers knew: she deftly unwrapped a condom with her free hand, put it in her mouth and manipulated the thing onto his turgid prong with her tongue and cheeks.

"Where'd you learn to do that? Veterinarian school?"

She laughed, then turned suddenly serious. There's one thing you have to know before we start," said Natalie Johnson. "I'm HIV positive. Is that OK with you?"

The blood drained from Nate's face and his cock simultaneously, racing for his electrocuted heart. "I...I'd like to say it's...well, no, it's not. I'm sorry, Natalie. I mean, thank you for your honesty, but I don't think I could deal with it."

Natalie looked less hurt than Nate would have predicted, as if she had been through this many times before. "Well, I can understand, but... You know that it's been proven to be perfectly safe with a good condom."

"Maybe, but...do you know how you got the virus?"

"Yes, from my ex-husband. He's Swiss. A salesman for USE. He said he was having unprotected anal sex with Brazilian girls on a business trip, but I always suspected he was gay."

"Does Augie know?"

"Yes, he wouldn't sleep with me either. He was nice enough to go out with me for a while and try other things. Toys and stuff. He's a nice guy. I thought he would have told you by now. I was hoping he had, and that you came over anyway."

"Sorry."

Suppressing the instinct to dive out of the nearest window, Nate sat and held her for an hour before leaving, while she cried and told her story, which included having been diagnosed with ovarian cancer a month earlier. She wasn't sick with AIDS, and didn't plan to get sick. She hoped to beat the big C and find a straight, compatible, HIV-positive fellow sex fiend to hunker down with.

Nate wished her luck.

When he got home, Nate washed his cock repeatedly in the blistering hot shower until the thing was red and sore. Drying off in his room, he was busy swearing off women for the rest of his life when he noticed the green message light blinking on his new answering machine. The message was from Nicole: "Hi, I'm sorry I missed your call. Are you all right, Jimmy Olsen? You sounded kind of low, to say the least. Call me and tell me you're OK, no matter what time. I'll be up."

Nate didn't call. Before falling asleep crying once again, this time for a woman he hardly knew or liked, he vowed to get an HIV test right away, prior to even thinking about starting something with someone he did.

* * *

The HIV test was negative, once again bolstering Nate's theory that you can't get AIDS from a blowjob. He was grateful to Natalie Johnson, probably the final nail in the coffin of his profligate former self, for being honest with him before allowing him entry to her seriously compromised inner sanctum. He wondered how many women involved with him during his past 20 years of nonstop, mostly unprotected sex had lied on that particular count. He would never know.

One thing he did know was that he had dodged his last bullet. If he ever got involved again, it would be for keeps. If it weren't about true love, it wouldn't be worth doing. Funny what it takes for a reasonably intelligent man to learn such a simple lesson, he thought. Still, much of the learning process had been fun. Someday he'd have to write a book.

CHAPTER THIRTEEN
AT LARGE

While he did have to be more careful than he had been in the Mohican Valley, Nate considered his new job a dream come true. He had to attend more—and usually longer—meetings than ever, as his job was to report on burning issues that less industrious or capable reporters presumably couldn't handle. Burning issues take a lot more time to sit through, as well as to decipher and write about in a coherent, compelling manner. The serendipity of being able to write about anything that caught one's eye was gone, with everything now being of such dire importance, but Nate didn't really mind.

His plate was full. Taking a break from Afghanistan, Kofi Annan and his United Nations were hosting the presidents of Greece and Turkey at a retreat in Ostia for a three-day peace conference regarding the fate of Cyprus. The entire Mohican Valley was besieged by state police, National Guardsmen and FBI agents in black helicopters. In between covering that story Nate had to deal with Winnie's bullshit and the fallout from the recent elections in which the Republicans solidified their hold on the county, as if that were really necessary. He also attended and reported on a celebrity-studded gala at Vitello's Country Club for the Clover Titans 2002 Class C State Champions football team.

Nate had earlier made a trip to the Carrier Dome in Syracuse to witness the team's 48-10 dismantling of a much bigger squad from Mount Calvary Boy's High in Rochester; his first and hopefully last foray into sports journalism. While he appreciated the combination of skill, determination and luck that had propelled this group of refreshingly small, steroid-free lads to a state championship over a vastly higher-rated set of opponents, Nate would not have looked forward to the hours and lifestyle of a full-time sports reporter. Nor would he ever again tolerate being trapped in the company of sports reporters, who from his short experience covering the game and hanging out at the hotel bar afterward were even more odiferous and prone to spouting mind-numbing esoterica than were road musicians.

The celebratory event at Big Nick Vitello's golf club was a different story. It drew a hefty contingent of local, regional and national big shots and politicos, all trying to get a sprinkling of the storied team's undefeated stardust. To Nate the event was a microcosm of the Roosevelt County power web in which he had found himself enmeshed.

Winnie Babson and chairman "Hick" Vanderkamp were there from the county legislature, sitting uncomfortably at a table with a wan and frail-looking Big Nick Vitello, county Republican Party chairman "Fat Tony" Costello, Sheriff Hildenbrandt, the lawyers Dick Strong and Jonathan Wilson and a couple of state assemblymen. Placed nearest to the head table containing the yawning, snickering Titans, their coaches and the guest of honor: former Green Bay Packers linebacker Merrill Stanhope of Lenape Falls, was a table at which Governor Pollock, Senator Rudy Viggiani and USE chairman Arthur Schmidt sat with their wives and security people, marveling audibly at the growing length of the proceedings. Sitting between the Pollocks and the Schmidts, curiously, were local stalwarts William and Edith McNally, smiling beatifically as if they were royalty.

Both seasoned pros at extemporaneous rabble-rousing, Pollock and Viggiani demonstrated why they were national figures. Pollock addressed the team directly: "I hope you appreciate all the people who have extended their hands to you, who were there when you needed help and support. When you get home tonight, take Mom and Dad aside, look 'em in the eye, give 'em a little hug, and say 'thanks.'"

There were few dry eyes in the house when Senator Viggiani approached the dais. "You're always a hard act to follow, Hi," he said to his protegé the governor, before showing his own mastery of the sports-as-metaphor-for-life genre of thunder-stealing rhetoric. Appropriating the

Titans' "Never Give Up" mantra, he elevated it to motto status for use in his upcoming re-election campaign against former Democratic vice-presidential candidate Imogene Maserato. "Never give up, especially when you're the underdog, like I will be in this struggle," said the Senator. "I may be a little guy, just like you boys were against the giants of Mount Calvary. But I'm gonna put my head down, stay low and try to apply the Titans' 'Never Give Up' attitude to myself, in my fight to whip Big Government and Big Taxes. Thank you, guys, for being my inspiration. Go, Titans!"

The biggest revelation of the evening, however, was that every one of the political and business operatives present was on a first-name, back-slapping basis with everyone else. It was as if there had been a direct hotline from Fat Tony's living room into the dens and home offices of the governor, the senator, the CEO, the sheister lawyers and all the local politicos and businessmen. Viggiani, Big Nick and Fat Tony carried on as if they had all emigrated on the boat together from Napoli. The governor and the Pinksterkill lawyer crowd huddled like they were plotting a hurry-up offensive series.

During a short intermission Governor Pollock, Arthur Schmidt, Dick Strong and three Mediterranean-looking gentlemen Nate didn't recognize went outside to smoke cigars—led by Winnie Babson and Bill McNally. Senator Viggiani went over and sat with a depressed-looking Big Nick, presumably to perk him up. Nick was being tended to by his two daughters, who seemed to glare at the backs of the cigar posse members as they headed for the exit. Nate, presuming he had gotten to know Big Nick pretty well in doing the "Live at Max's" interview series, took the opportunity to approach him.

"Mr. Vitello, it's good to see you. Jim Olsen."

Vitello brightened, and his eyes lit up. "Jimmy, *paisan.* You know my daughters, Angela and Fiona. Rudy, this is the kid who wrote that profile on me, the one I just showed you at the house."

Nate shook Vitello's bony hand, then the senator's.

"Pleased to meet you, Jim," said Viggiani. "Mr. Vitello is a big fan of yours. Did you know he had your story framed, and keeps a scrapbook of all your articles?"

Nate felt his face reddening. "Damn. I guess I should be flattered."

"Don't get excited, kid, I'm no pansy. You're a good writer, is all," laughed Big Nick. "Gimme a call sometime. We gotta talk."

* * *

Christmas was coming and the paper was closing down for a week, bringing for Nate thoughts of loneliness and loss. He had spent the last five Christmases with a few other disconnected, family-challenged East Village souls, holding a kind of annual bacchanalian anti-Christ feast on Christmas Eve. Sheila had always been away in Dutch Hollow for the week, engaging in a typical dysfunctional family holiday. Nate had never had an inclination to look up any of his own far-flung siblings and impose himself on them. His mother and father had been killed in a plane crash when he was 16, and his much younger brother and sister had been raised by an aunt while he had moved in with the DiSalvos. Christmas was a misty, uncomfortable childhood memory.

Winnie Babson threw an interesting holiday party at a fancy local winery, paying for it by what is commonly called a "trade." The winery owed Roosevelt's advertising department a few thousand dollars, and Winnie swapped the debt plus a bit of free advertising for a free catered meal and all the wine his staff could put away.

The party signified the passing of a torch, of sorts. Two days earlier Nootch had been called out by Mona Levy, who had given him a Channukah ultimatum: her way or the highway. He either had to scrap his little fling with Nicole Royal, which was apparently turning out to be not such a fling at all, or risk losing Mona, which didn't seem like such a bad idea to Nate. "Naw, man, I love Mona," Nootch had told Nate. "She's crazy but she's cool. We go back."

At the party Nicole Royal was solo, hiding among a group of girl reporters, looking uncharacteristically glamorous in a tight-fitting dress that revealed a stunning, modelesque figure with a booty that wouldn't quit. At work, most likely to protect herself from her obnoxious boss and co-workers, she was prone to wearing formless sweaters and oversized pants. "Yo, bro, you should go for it," said a half-drunk Nootch when Mona was out of earshot, nodding toward Nicole. "She's a lot of fun." Nate knew that already, having taken to conversing with her at every opportunity during breaks at the office. "And she's still a virgin. She never let me do her."

"What are you, her pimp?"

"Thass right," said Nootch woozily. "Pimp Daddy. Daddy Pimp. Smack dat ass."

"OK, shut up, Shaft. Here comes your girlfriend."

Nate ditched Nootch and his crabby girlfriend and approached Nicole. Their eyes met. She smiled knowingly, disarmingly. "Fuck," thought Nate.

"Hi. You look lovely tonight." He didn't have to lie. She blushed.

"Thanks. So do you." She was a smart-ass, like himself. He looked like shit in his three-day beard, with a wrinkled green golf shirt and grass-stained chinos under his old houndstooth jacket.

"I'm sorry I didn't call you back the other night. I don't know why I called you in the first place. I was almost unconscious. I'd worked for 78 straight hours."

"You're such a freak, Nate. Why do you do that to yourself?"

"Winnie's paying me so much, I feel guilty."

"So why did you call in the first place?" she queried, her eyes dancing.

"Because I was too tired to stop myself."

"I see." Her eyes continued to sparkle.

She probably *does* see, thought Nate, trying not to think about how much he liked her; worried that she might read his mind. Toward the end of the night, he realized he and Nicole had more or less paired off, having spent the better part of two hours talking. At first they had just gossiped about people they found mutually annoying, like her boss Mark Zweiker, his clueless wife and his idol-worshiping sidekick Aaron. Or amusing, like the increasingly bizarre Rex Nicholson, caught recently by Mona Levy at the Arms, buck-naked and fucking a pillow on one of the ratty living room davenports with an assortment of 1960s-era Playboy centerfolds splayed out before him.

Somehow they had steered themselves through a discussion on movies and popular culture into more serious topics like politics, religion and philosophy. They seemed to agree in principle on almost everything, including her being an atheist, a left-leaning anarchist and a cynic. He found it suspicious that someone so young, outwardly guileless and sweet-natured could have gone through the sorts of tortures he had endured to get to the same emotional place. She was 25, from Binghamton, of all places. He wondered what had happened to her, and if there was some dark secret in her past, of the sort that haunted Sheila and every other woman he had loved.

His tongue loosened by the wine, Nate not only told Nicole most of the horrors that had befallen him on September 11 and in the weeks after, he confessed his feelings about Sheila and what he had done to her. He told of his concerns over his own worth as a human being, and of his growing suspicion that he was bad luck, personified. "I feel like one of Anne Rice's vampires," he told her. "I'm outliving my time and my contemporaries, thriving and getting more evil by sucking the life force from them as they die. I don't really care about anything or anybody. Look what happened to poor old McDuffy. I'm bad news."

He wanted to ensure that, if this lovely girl was going to end up falling for him, as he was inexorably falling for her, she knew the sort of succubus she was getting entangled with. To his surprise and delight, despite all his attempts to scare her away, she was still sitting with him at the end of the evening. He offered to drive her home to the Arms; she lived in the other side. When he walked her to her entrance door, he did something he hadn't done since high school. He thanked her for a wonderful time, hugged her tenderly for a few moments, and let her go in by herself.

Time will take care of this ache in my chest, Nate thought to himself. If she's real, there's no hurry. If she's not, what the fuck. She would have far more to worry about from him anyway.

* * *

Being smitten didn't slow Nate down one iota from his workaholic ways. He and Nicole continued their slow-burning, platonic romance for weeks. She was becoming just as busy as he; upon the sudden exit of Mark Zweiker to a business-to-business hardware newsletter in New Jersey, she was tapped by Dave as the new central bureau editor. Freed and empowered by her promotion, Nicole rose to the occasion. She terrorized snotty young Aaron and the cantankerous Mona Levy into being better, more complete reporters, and spent Tuesday nights locked in verbal sparring matches with Nate, Dave, Nootch and Rick Parton. She was on the A team now, and easily held her own.

While Mona bristled at first from having to report to a younger woman—of whom she was naturally jealous for personal reasons as well—the chill was thawed somewhat when Nicole helped her achieve her first night of free beers at the Delafield by pushing her to do a story about the local "can man."

The Dutch Hollow can man, who would walk for miles every day clad in jeans and a red hooded sweatshirt, carrying a large garbage bag and picking up soda cans and bottles for redemption at the local supermarket, turned out to be an interesting character. He was hardly a "sinister, possibly dangerous bum," as Mona had first claimed in refusing to do the story. He had once been an engineer at USE, and had turned his retirement into a quest for longevity through long-distance walking. He walked 20 to 30 miles every day, rain or shine. While doing so, he thought he would perform a public service and pick up cans and bottles along his route. The $5 to $10 a day he collected from these activities went straight into the coffers of his church on Sunday; he had more than enough to live on from his retirement and savings interest.

The story was by turns corny, heartwarming and sad, and the positive public and workplace reaction to it was a watershed for Mona Levy, who had never before considered herself, nor been considered, an especially good writer. It also was an opportunity for Mona and Nicole to bury the hatchet concerning Nootch while getting drunk at the Delafield. They emerged from the evening fast friends, ushering in a short era of unprecedented peace and tranquility both in the newsroom and at the Dutch Arms.

* * *

When he wasn't chasing a story or putting papers together on Tuesdays, Nate would drive the rattling Fiesta around the county on what he called "reconnaissance missions," often south and west into "USE country" to check out the company's two manufacturing plants and the three giant warehouses of its waste chemical transporter, Janssen Movers. The older plant, located on the river just south of Pinksterkill, was burdened with a gated security system that prevented him from getting around the rear of the complex to see where Janssen trucks were coming from and going to. He did, however, clock their frequency at nearly one every two hours, and on a few occasions followed them to a Janssen warehouse in the northern leg of the horseshoe-shaped Town of Pinksterkill. The trucks would back their trailers into a fenced area behind the warehouse that harbored perhaps 100 other trailers and drop them, side-to-side, in sardine-can fashion. He knew they didn't contain furniture.

The other USE plant in East Waterkill was, for some reason, a much more open and accessible affair. Nate easily located the two main chip-processing buildings. Once he became acclimated and knew where things were, he began following Janssen trucks around, and almost immediately hit pay dirt. On the first occasion, he sat in a chip building parking lot from 6 p.m. to 8 p.m., watching workers roll barrels into three Janssen semi trailers, which backed up to a loading dock one by one. The trucks then headed out in a convoy, with a Janssen van in the lead.

Nate pulled out and began to follow the convoy as it wound around the inner road of the complex. Oddly, the van took a left turn at one intersection as the semis continued onward, toward the exit. Nate's nervous system reacted instantly as his mind struggled to catch up. What was the van doing? Was someone going to a business office to deal with invoices? Moments later he looked in his rear view mirror and realized the van had doubled around through a parking area and re-emerged. It was now following him, for fuck's sake. Giving up the chase, he turned right at the stoplight at the plant's main exit as the convoy went north.

The next time he dared venture to the East Waterkill plant, a couple of weeks later, Nate was more cautious. He verified that a convoy of Janssen trucks was loading and then waited in a parking lot near the USE exit, hoping against hope that the van would repeat its doubling act, proving the maneuver to be a routine one rather than a symptom of his amateurish surveillance being discovered. After an hour, three loaded Janssen trucks, led by a white Janssen window van, came coursing along the inner roadway. At the same junction as two weeks earlier, the van took a left, and looped around a parking lot, re-emerging a good distance behind the convoy. "A chase van!" thought Nate. "These people are afraid of something!"

Nate breathed a sigh of relief, and followed the convoy from a considerable distance, risking losing them, but anticipating where they were going to end up. They were heading in a beeline, straight toward a second Janssen warehouse in Lenape Falls, next to the Roosevelt County Airport.

Nate pulled into the visitors' parking lot as the three cabs were depositing their trailers side-by-side in a large fenced yard similar to the one behind the Pinksterkill warehouse. As he turned around to leave, his eyes were drawn to the main office/warehouse building, with its looming concrete and mirrored-glass façade. It struck him that the building's massive, almost monumental architectural style, so reminiscent of Albert Speer's work for the Third Reich, was identical to that of the main buildings of both USE plants. He wondered if this was a coincidence.

On the drive home, as he daydreamed about how he would conduct surveillance of the Janssen warehouses, Nate's neck-hairs stiffened involuntarily. Worried that he might have let his guard down and been spotted by the people in the white van, he looked in the rear-view mirror and noticed a late-model maroon sedan behind him, occupied by what looked like two men in business attire. He could make out their white collared shirts and ties, and not much else. He turned right into a supermarket strip mall complex, and proceeded to snake through the parking lot, pretending to look for a spot. The maroon sedan followed him, slowly. It was very clean, and did not look particularly ominous to Nate. Dull and unobtrusive, it resembled the government-issue shit-heaps Nate had once driven for the state.

Nate parked the car and walked into the store, looking back discreetly to see what was happening. The sedan backed into a spot parallel to the Fiesta, two aisles away. No one got out. On an impulse, Nate walked out of the store, and strode directly toward his pursuers. As he approached, too quickly for them to decide what to do, the occupants looked at each other and back at him, in apparent distress. He walked right up to the driver's side of the idling vehicle, and knocked on the flustered man's window. The window rolled down.

"Hello, fellas," said Nate, his heart thumping wildly. "I was wondering. Have you been following me?"

The two conservatively dressed men looked at each other, then back at Nate. "No," said the passenger.

"Actually, yes," said the driver, a look of sad resignation crossing over his freshly shaven face. Nate could feel no enmity from the man. He began to relax.

"Well, can I ask why? Who are you?"

The driver pulled a wallet from his inside jacket pocket and flipped it open, revealing a gleaming gold badge. "Charles Overlook, FBI. We were conducting routine surveillance, and we noticed you following a group of vehicles from the USE plant in East Waterkill to their destination. We wondered who you were and what you were doing."

"Routine surveillance? Of what? Shouldn't you be out shagging terrorists or something? I'm a journalist, and I was just conducting a little routine surveillance of my own."

"We are not at liberty to share that information. Are you in any way connected with USE or with the Janssen company?"

Nate couldn't see what there was to lose by revealing a snippet of truth. Maybe these two humor-challenged G-men would be of use to him if he played his cards right. "Well, I'd really like to talk to my lawyer first, but no. I'm a newspaper reporter sniffing around. I'm trying to find out what's happening with the chemicals in those trucks."

Overlook looked at his partner again, with raised eyebrows. "Look, Mr. ..."

"Olsen."

"Mr. Olsen. I'm afraid that under the circumstances you would probably be better off putting your investigation on hold. Your presence on the USE campus was a distraction to us, and could easily have compromised our surveillance. I would ask you to please refrain from further expeditions to the USE campus, which is in fact private property."

"Sure, but what if I had some information that might help you? I have evidence that USE and Janssen are dumping toxic waste illegally. They might be selling it on the black market. The mob is involved. Wouldn't you like to go have a drink somewhere and compare notes?"

The two investigators looked at each other again, shook their heads and sighed. Charles Overlook turned toward him again. "I'm not going to tell you what we're investigating, but it's not toxic waste. I would certainly like to talk to you about your concerns, at a later date. With your permission, I'd like to take your name and contact information."

Nate wrote down his pen name and his work phone number. "Could I have your card?"

"We'll be in contact," said Overlook, placing Nate's information in his wallet while ignoring his request. He looked Nate sternly in the eyes. "Meanwhile, Mr. Olsen, it would be wise of you to steer clear of the USE campuses and Janssen's facilities. You don't know what you're dealing with, and you are putting yourself at risk. Am I clear?"

"Yes, sir. Thank you, sir." Nate stifled the urge to salute. "And say hello to Thirsty for me,"

"What did you say?" The pair glanced at each other yet again, their eyebrows arching almost imperceptibly.

"Thirsty. Reginald Thurston Brown. I'm sure you guys know him. Tell him I said hello."

CHAPTER FOURTEEN
CHUMS

Meanwhile, the newsroom and the Dutch Arms population continued to evolve at a rate that would have made Charles Darwin blush. Hot on the heels of Mark Zweiker's departure, Nootch finally scored a job as a metro reporter for the hated *Journal*, after having been turned down on three earlier tries. Expecting to be promoted into his slot, Mona Levy was once again passed over for an editorship, this time in favor of Greg Callahan, her nemesis from the Kipsbergh office. As she had lobbied for a recommendation from Nootch that had apparently been less than glowing, a rift developed between the two constitutionally incompatible lovers, who already argued so often and violently that Nate dubbed them "The Bickersons." Within a week of Nootch's tearful departure at a lavish feast given by Winnie on a Hudson River excursion boat, he and Mona had broken up for good, an event that drove her and Nicole even closer.

Nate and Nootch still found a way to commiserate for a time as well, despite the fact that Nootch began to take on the unmistakable cigarette-fouled scent and dyspeptic demeanor of a lowlife reporter. They would often do mostly-liquid lunches together at Reilly's Tavern, an old-school Irish joint in the heart of downtown Pinksterkill, surrounded by tables full of city and county lawmakers and lawyers from the FDR building down the street. Nate would listen distractedly to Nootch's patented psychotic, stream-of-consciousness ramblings while trying to overhear conversations at adjoining tables, ready to tune in to his friend whenever the conversation came back to earth. Nootch claimed to have never wanted to be an editor in the first place, and confessed to having felt jaded and trapped by his life at Roosevelt and with Mona Levy toward the end. He was glad to be out of there. Nate hoped he wouldn't come to feel that way himself, and told Nootch truthfully that he missed him and was sorry he was gone.

Nootch had moved into a cheap $350-a-month apartment in Pinksterkill, next door to a crack house on lower Broadway near the river. He walked to work most days, and kept his El Camino in a city parking garage for $10 a month, one of the few perks for residents who were willing to risk their health living downtown. While putting up a devil-may-care front at first, Nootch was obviously pining for Mona and his old Mohican Valley life, as evidenced by his rising alcohol and cigarette intake. After a few lunch meetings he became increasingly pathetic, complaining about his new superiors and the horrors of a corporate news environment, and peppering Nate with incessant questions about what Mona was up to. Nate was less than sympathetic. "Look, dude. You wanted out, for obvious reasons. The job was starting to suck. The woman was a raving harpy. You made your deal with Satan, and now you're a fucking reporter for a medium-sized metropolitan daily newspaper. Be happy, and slow down with the drinking. You're making yourself sick. Someday when we're all working for the *New York Post* this will seem like kindergarten."

"Fuck you, Jimmy Olsen."

"Fuck you, too, chief. I'm serious. I love you like a brother."

"Yeah, I love you too, I guess. Bitch."

Despite being split up as a team, Nate and Nootch vowed eternal fealty to the cause, and promised to compare notes and be a secret source for each other for the rest of time.

* * *

A whole new slew of reinforcements moved into the empty reporter slots, and into the Arms. After just ten months on the job, Nate was now the senior employee living in the place, along with Nicole in the other half of the building. Upon clearing it with Rex Nicholson as a matter of protocol,

Nate moved his things into Mark and Jill Zweiker's sunlit third floor studio, which had its own bathroom and kitchenette. The new Masada reporter, Tawana Ornsby, a staff sergeant in the National Guard whose Marine fiancé was on tour in Afghanistan, moved into Nate's old room. Her thick Long Island accent reminded him of Rico. The first seriously dark-skinned person Nate had ever encountered at Roosevelt Newspapers, a pleasant Puerto Rican lad named Jose Cardinal, cleaned up the infamous ferret chamber and took over Greg Callahan's Kipsbergh beat. A wraith-like young blonde woman named Suzanne Finch, hired straight out of New Paltz State College, took over Nootch's room and the long-neglected Wheaton beat down in the Valley.

Other youngsters filled other cobwebbed rooms and long-empty beats. A new editor, Rochelle Moss, was finally hired to fill the dormant USE Country bureau chief slot, which Dave had been covering himself. To assuage the feelings of thrice-dissed Mona Levy, he made her a "senior reporter" with a $30-a-week raise. For the first time in recent memory, said Dave, the Arms was nearly a full house, and the Roosevelt news-rooms were almost fully staffed. The biggest problem he now had was filling Nate's former Mohican Valley beat, which the in-over-his-head Greg Callahan was temporarily trying to cover himself, with some trouble. The "golden age" of the *Mohican Valley Times* was effectively over, for the time being.

The new people were a varied bunch, uniform only in their yawning life inexperience. They were also extremely, almost excessively sociable. Nate was glad he had moved upstairs, because overnight the Arms was trans-formed into a 24-hour, post-collegiate, Club-Med-style party house. There would be someone organizing card games, Risk or Monopoly marathons, theme parties and "Truth or Dare" sessions almost every other night, all accompanied by plenty of alcohol, loud dance music, epilepsy-inducing strobe lights and junk food.

Mona Levy, freshly sprung from a bad relationship, became the mistress of ceremonies, with help from her new best friends Nicole and Tawana. When he wasn't working, Nate attended some of these soirees, if only so that he and Nicole could orbit each other slowly, testing out each other's gravitational fields. Rex Nicholson would shut himself in his room and fuck his pillow, and Greg Callahan, another of the social retards so often drawn to journalism, would sit in a corner and pout after being busted trying to touch a girl's feet.

In the newsroom, the as yet unmitigated enthusiasm of the new troops seemed to temper the dour cynicism of crusty oldsters like Dave, Nate and especially Rick Parton, who had been decimated by Nootch's departure. At least everyone in this bunch could write, making life easier for the editors. Greg Callahan had the only real problem child, as Bobby Hanrahan hadn't improved a whit. For all that he had yelled at the kid, Nootch had liked him and wanted him to succeed. He had handled Hanrahan himself and not bothered Dave with his troubles; and as Dave wasn't the most pro-active administrator himself, he tended to ignore an issue until it bit him in the ass. Greg Callahan had no such qualms, and badmouthed the wretched Hanrahan incessantly. Hanrahan's days were numbered.

With Nootch gone and Callahan a slow study at Quark, Nate took on a heavier Tuesday night pagination load. He was in his bedroom at the Arms one Wednesday afternoon, preparing to sleep off a particularly grueling all-nighter, when he heard a loud knock on the outside door. He wondered who it could possibly be, as everyone with any business at the Dutch Arms had their own key. It sometimes seemed as if half the population of Dutch Hollow had a key to the Arms.

Putting on a terrycloth robe and shuffling down the two flights of stairs, Nate saw in the vestibule window the bemused, smirking visage of a tall, slender young man with a shiny pink forehead and artificially straightened, heavily pomaded hair. He opened the door. "Hello, mate. Martin Brennan: journalist." Nate shook his outstretched hand.

"Nice to meet you. Jim Olsen. Editor-at-large. You the new reporter?"

Martin Brennan was dressed in a dark blue European-cut suit with wide lapels and heavy pinstripes, a white scarf and black leather driving gloves. He couldn't have looked more British, even if you added a bowler hat and a cane. Behind him on the stone walkway was a small army's worth of well-worn, obviously expensive luggage. A New York City medallion taxicab was pulling away. "Perhaps so. I'm an exchange student from Oxford, England. Balliol, actually. It seems I'm to be one of your journalists, in exchange for a room and a small, some might say niggardly stipend. And you are to be my mentor."

"Well in that case, my real name is Nate. Jimmy Olsen is my stage name. So Winnie Babson's trying to get some quality free help? I heard something about this scam."

"Yes, so it seems. I contacted one of my sponsors in New York City, hoping I'd be set up in an internship at *The Nation* or something. Winston Babson's was the only contact number he gave me. When I met your publisher, he was quite ebullient about welcoming me aboard and all that. He paid my cab fare, stuffed some American dollars in my pocket and told me I should come up here straightaway and look for you. I daresay this isn't so close to Manhattan, is it?"

"About an hour-and-a-half by car. Two hours by train from Pinksterkill or Clover. Hey, that's OK, New York City's not all it's cracked up to be. I just left after living there for the past 10 years, and barely lived to tell about it."

"Really? Were you a witness to the terrorist attacks?"

"Yeah. Twelve blocks and one dead girlfriend north."

"My word. I'm so sorry."

"That's OK. Listen, there's plenty of dirt up here for a leftist muckraker such as yourself to get into. I've been having a whale of a time. You'll be fine. You *are* a leftist, I presume?"

"I prefer the term 'champagne socialist.' My personal tastes are quite a few degrees to the right of my politics. In England that's not considered a problem. Look at Tony Blair, turning into Margaret Thatcher before our very eyes."

"Trust me, you'll be right at home here in Roosevelt County. Everybody here is a few degrees to the right of where they ought to be, even the Communists."

"Splendid, let's get started then. Where's the nearest pub?"

* * *

Although he'd never in his life encountered anyone quite like him, Nate instinctively liked Martin Brennan. The kid was obviously smart as a whip, and exhibited the gung-ho temperament and fiercely liberal opinions of a

Spanish resistance fighter. Having read a clip of one of Martin's opinion pieces for the Balliol College student newspaper, Nate knew he was a meticulous, persuasive writer, who could tiptoe to the end of a limb without breaking it off. He would, Nate quickly determined, make a great reporter.

It was a good thing he felt that way, because Winnie Babson, in a rare assertion of his authority, had decreed that Martin be placed under Nate's wing. He would be assigned to Nate's old Mohican Valley beat, and Nate would have to show him the ropes. Understood in the bargain was that Nate would be required to share the Fiesta with him.

Winnie's annoying and obvious fawning over his new, untested reporter exposed him as a hopeless Anglophiliac and sent temporary shivers of resentment through the newsroom, especially among the young women. "Winnie never offered *me* a fucking car," said Mona Levy. "I bet he can't even drive."

Even sweet Nicole was miffed. "Who is this guy, to walk in here and get treated like royalty? What's he done in his life?"

"He's English," said Nate. "He went to Oxford. It's so hard there, they give you a master's degree after three years of undergraduate study, so you have time to drink for a year before having to look for a job."

"Bullshit."

Nate didn't mind the British invasion at all. Tiring of the Fiesta's cantankerousness and reluctance to start on cold mornings, he had been eyeing a clean, comfortable-looking 1978 Cadillac Seville that was for sale out on Route 56 for a reasonable $2,500. More important, the assignment could be a blessing in disguise. He imagined feeding the clever young Limey leads, into which he'd sink his pearly teeth like a hungry pit bull. With the right guidance, he could be a prize piece in Nate's puzzle: a trusted ally in his crusade, who would gladly take a world of heat on his foppish shoulders before flying unscathed back to merrye olde England.

Nate had been trying to figure out how he would deal with some of the government corruption and mob-oriented information he had been hoarding—especially the toxic waste stuff involving Bill McNally and the dumping around Jefferson. He knew if he started hitting hard at GOP wrongdoing he would be quickly muzzled by Winnie; not to mention that he would risk putting himself in jeopardy. His worst fear was that McNally was already onto him; that he had known about Sheila's whistle-blowing ways and had loosed the big leprechaun on him to shut him up and destroy Sheila's files. Nate worried about what would happen in the unlikely event that he could slip a story into the papers about Bill McNally, Janssen or USE.

Once again, an opportunity had fallen in his lap. He could test the waters, using Martin Brennan as chum.

* * *

Nate groomed Martin Brennan carefully, focusing on an unfolding drama in Ostia as a starting point. Big Nick, rumored to have been in ill health, was cashing out; selling the golf course for $48 million to a company called International Leisure Entertainment. Its president, Edward Piazzo, was slated to speak to the Ostia town board Thursday night to start the ball rolling on applying for a liquor license and approvals for multimillion dollar improvements such as a hotel and amphitheater. Nate didn't trust the smooth-talking Piazzo; he had interviewed him once already and the guy smelled of expensive laundry detergent.

After adjourning Thursday to Snooky's Tavern in Ostia for a hamburger and beer while Nate briefed Martin on what to expect, the two of them attended the jam-packed meeting. The usual suspects performed admirably; led by addled old Town Supervisor Mabel McDonough, who sat with her eyes closed, mumbling to herself and asking people to repeat things she hadn't heard, which was everything. The "Three Amigos," town councilmen Denny Karner, Scott Barcheron and Herman Wozniak, led the local booster club for Mr. Piazzo, who dazzled the townsfolk with visions of a 21st-century Xanadu that would attract big-time entertainment like the Boston Symphony and Kenny Rogers, PGA tournaments, conventions and all sorts of other hokus guaranteed to "put Ostia on the map." To prove his points, he had brought along a cadre of perfectly coiffed young assistants, handing out hand-outs, flipping pages on flip charts and aiming a jazzy PowerPoint presentation onto an overhead projection screen. It was quite a show. All Piazzo was asking the town for was a liquor license, some zoning variances and building permits and a few million dollars in tax abatements.

A smattering of cranky pinko activists showed up to complain about excess development, noise pollution and traffic patterns, but were shouted down by the large pro-Vitello majority. One of the lefties was the duct-taped Noel Preston, who was apparently expanding his range in preparation for a hopeless stab at a New York State Assembly seat against a powerful Republican stalwart. He had been at the Infirmary protest as well, but Nate had somehow avoided him.

This time he wasn't so lucky. Preston had an eagle eye for anyone with a reporter's notebook. He kept staring at Nate and Martin from across the room, making strange head movements and exaggeratedly stage whispering that he would like to talk to them after the proceedings. Nate sighed and nodded, steeling himself for the inevitable.

Big Nick himself was there—albeit confined to a wheelchair piloted by his two homely, hook-nosed daughters—lending his support to the proceedings. Nate went up to him after the show to pay his respects and to inquire as to how he was feeling. Despite Big Nick's being an obvious, potentially murderous gangster, he had a playful sense of humor and the kindly, approachable bearing of a favorite uncle. Nate liked the old guy. He reminded him of Mr. DiSalvo, his surrogate dad.

"How you feelin', Nick?"

Vitello's face was hanging off its proud aristocratic bones, with huge purplish bags under his still sparkling eyes. His voice was weak and gravelly. "What, I look sick? Yeah, well, I've been better, if you know what I mean. My liver's actin' up. Listen, kid, I thought you was gonna call me. You did such a good job with that story about me. Maybe you wanna write my memoirs. I pay top dollar. You can quit this fucking newspaper racket. That fuckin' Babson's a cheap bastard. You got too much talent to waste on him."

"I'd like that," said Nate, simultaneously moved and frightened, attracted and repulsed. "I will call you, I promise."

"OK, good. Who's your sidekick?"

Martin's eyes were on fire, as if he were being granted an audience with The Godfather Himself. "I'm sorry. Martin Brennan, Nick Vitello. Martin's the new Ostia reporter."

Martin reached down and shook the ailing mobster's hand. "Very pleased to meet you, sir."

"A fucking Limey, already! *Madon'*, what'll they think of next? Good luck, kid. You got some big shoes to fill."

Noel Preston was lurking in the exit hallway, twitching nervously and staring at them imploringly. But Nate had a couple of other stops to make before having his ear chewed off. He motioned to Martin, still glowing pink from having shaken hands with a real American Mafioso. "Follow me, and take notes."

They approached the garrulous "Three Amigos" ringleader Denny Karner, who was always good for a few juicy quotes. Nate gambled and asked what was wrong with Big Nick.

"Liver cancer," said Denny, getting misty-eyed. "It's not good, if you know what I mean. We're all praying for a miracle. He's done so much for the town already. This new man, Ed Piazzo, is carryin' on Nick's dream of puttin' Ostia on the map, by Jesus. I hope Mr. Vitello lives to see his dream. He's a great, great man. Heart and soul of Ostia. And you can print that." Martin, employing some cryptic form of shorthand learned at Oxford, got everything down.

Mabel McDonough provided a quote that made the next Thursday's paper as well, the unedited form of which was: "Mmmm, well, ooooh. Aaaah, yes. Well, that's a good thing, I guess. Oh, yes. Mmmmm. For the town."

Finally Nate and Martin sidled up to Noel Preston, who by now had small droplets of foam forming at the corners of his thin, wound-like mouth. "Hi, I'm James Olsen, from Roosevelt Newspapers. And this is my associate, Martin Brennan."

"Jimmy Olsen? You're kidding! That's great!" blurted Preston, who had a much deeper, more sonorous voice than Nate would have expected coming out of such a sniveling nerd. "I've read your stuff. You're quite a writer. I've been wanting to meet you for a long time, but you never return my phone calls."

"Well, I have an assistant who screens my messages," Nate lied. "I don't get everything. You know how it is."

"Listen," said Preston, lowering his voice to a whisper. "I have a story for you. One of my people is a friend of the assistant town clerk here in Ostia, who has discovered something in the town files that should interest you. She hates the status quo down here and is ready to talk."

"Really?"

"Yeah, it's about an old toxic waste dump that was discovered on Nick Vitello's land south of the landfill back in 1992. There were hundreds of drums buried there, and the DEC was moving on it for a while until the whole thing got swept under the rug and forgotten about. Nothing's been done since Pollock's been in office. You should check with NYPIRG in Albany. They have old, pre-Pollock DEC site reports for every toxic dump in the state, and this one's sure to be there. The assistant clerk gave us a file of letters and memos that had been hidden in the back of the wrong drawer, that shows the whole history of the discovery, the testing, and the categorization as a class 2 toxic waste site, requiring immediate clean-up. The history stops in 1993, and for all we know, the stuff is still there."

After a difficult half-hour listening to Mr. Preston's opinions on everything from fertilizers leaching off of golf courses to the sad fate of county health care workers, Nate and Martin extricated themselves from his grasp and headed back to the Arms "for a little nightcap," as Martin put it.

"That was brilliant," he said appreciatively. "What a wonderful cast of oddfellows. I felt as if I had fallen asleep and awakened in a Scorcese film." Unfortunately, Martin had asked to drive the Fiesta, and was having some trouble managing the manual floor-shift from the left side. "Fucking American shitbox," he groused, grinding the gears as he sped through the left turn at the 33/31 intersection going at least 10 mph too fast.

As they barreled into Dutch Hollow, Nate yelled at Martin as he flew past an oversized stop sign at another major intersection at 45 mph, not even bothering to slow down.

"Motherfucker, that was a stop sign! We could have been killed!"

"Sorry, not my forte, actually."

"Do you even have a driver's license?"

"Of course! Well, I had just gotten my learner's permit in England, actually. Good thing my mum's got a '55 Jaguar in the garage with a manual shifter, or I'd have been shit out of luck here in America. What a backward country!"

With that Martin careened left off of Route 31 onto Mill Road, stalling the car in the process. They coasted down the hill and into the small lower driveway of the pulsating, strobe-lit Dutch Arms, coming to a stop with a jolt that nearly sent Nate through the windshield.

Nate would refuse to ride with Martin Brennan at the wheel ever again.

* * *

Normally on any automobile excursion, Nate would routinely check the rear-view mirror for potential pursuers, ready to take drastic evasive action at the slightest hint of being followed. This time, however, he wasn't driving, and had been so frightened by Mr. Brennan's wild ride that he had fallen out of his usual paranoid frame of mind.

If he hadn't, he'd have surely noticed the dark blue 1998 Lincoln Town Car that pulled out after them from the parking lot of the Ostia Town Hall, and that struggled to keep up with them all the way to Dutch Hollow.

And he surely would have noticed the car drive slowly by the Dutch Arms in two directions before turning right onto Route 31, heading back east toward the Mohican Valley. He probably would have tried to borrow someone else's car and follow it to where it was going, which in this case happened to be the long, gated, secondary driveway into Vitello's golf complex.

CHAPTER FIFTEEN
LOVE JONES

The party Nate and Martin stumbled into that evening was going full bore. A waxing three-quarter moon hung fat and low like a schooner under full sail in the eastern sky, making everyone act as if their genitals were in charge of their brains. Mona Levy was busy hitting on Jose Cardinal, who when Nate and Martin walked in tore himself away from her and made a bee-line toward Martin, as if swimming for a life preserver. For the first time, the thought entered Nate's head that neither Jose nor Martin might be prone to shopping in Mona's store. He'd have to keep an eye on that situation.

Both Nate and Martin had caught the sharp glint in Mona's eyes as she venomously regarded the young Englishman's entry. "I get the distinct impression that woman hates me," said Martin. "What have I done to offend her?"

"You're English," said Nate, excusing himself so as to leave Jose and Martin alone. "Maybe she knows you can't drive."

Rochelle Moss and Rick Parton were in the far corner of the large living room, engaged in a deep philosophical conversation about the place of hip-hop in the Western canon of music and literature, one of Rick's favorite subjects. Rochelle, a slightly stooped, raven-haired woman in her mid-thirties, with kind brown eyes and a pleasant smile, seemed to be enjoying Rick's company as much as any woman ever had. Rick seemed hopelessly entranced. Nate secretly wished his friend luck. He certainly deserved it.

Greg Callahan was similarly smitten by the feet of a visiting female friend of Mona's, which he sat staring at from across the room. The woman noticed, got up and walked away.

In what was normally the little-used "dining room," the table and chairs had been cleared, and Tawana Ornsby was writhing in the center of the room, sandwiched between a visibly astonished Mike Hanrahan and an unidentified, shirtless man, as a strobe light parsed their undulations into a series of hilarious stills.

Nicole was in the kitchen, talking to Suzanne Finch, as a small group of eager young male reporters hovered around them like angry wasps. When Nate entered, her eyes lit up, just as, he assumed, did his.

He nudged a swaying, cross-eyed reporter aside and stood next to the two women. "Hello, Suzanne. Good evening, your highness."

"What's up, Olsen? Long meeting, huh?"

"Yeah. Ostia's about to blow a gasket. Noel Preston gave me a big lead on a toxic dump and Big Nick's selling the golf course and dying of cancer. He wants me to write his memoirs. Martin's gonna be good, if he lives long enough. He's a quick study, but a fucking terrible driver. If it had been rush hour just now we'd both be dead." Nate must have still looked shaken, because Nicole's face dissolved into the picture of maternal concern. She touched his cheek.

"Poor baby. Are you all right?" Her voice was low and syrupy, in that slender register that never failed to stir a chord in his solar plexus. He had rarely been attracted to women with high, girlish voices. "Do you want to go sit down?"

"Sure."

Nate was falling in love. The pull in his chest and the fullness in his balls were becoming unbearable. For the past few weeks, maybe months, he couldn't remember, he had been trying to keep Nicole at arm's length during the day and out of his mind at night. It was a losing battle.

Tonight, he thought, I might give in. God help me. God help her.

* * *

They sat in the living room, across from Rick and Rochelle, who were head-to-head, nearly holding hands. "She likes him," said Nicole. "She told me today."

"Well I'm all for it."

Martin and Jose had disappeared.

"Do you think Martin and Jose are gay?"

"I have no idea. What, are you homophobic?"

"Hardly. I'm a lesbian trapped in a man's body."

"That's good, because I've been accused of being bi."

"Well, then. We're compatible."

"Nate." She held his hands in hers, caressing them. Chills raced up his arms and exploded at the base of his skull, sending shivers throughout his body.

"Nicole."

"Look, I don't care how damaged you think you are. I'm damaged, too. We all are. I don't want to scare you away, but I like you. As much of a pussy as you are, you seem to like me, too."

"That much is true." His rampaging pulse rate and swooning eyes gave him away.

"You don't want a girlfriend. I'm in no hurry to have a boyfriend. Or a husband. Or children. Someday, I'm sure. I'm young. There's time. But right now, tonight, I just need a kind, decent, smart, good-looking guy to make love to me. And you're it."

She leaned close and kissed him softly. His muscles turned to gelatin.

"Jesus, woman, have you been reading *Cosmo* again? You're scaring me."

"Shut up and kiss me already, you stupid asshole."

They kissed slowly, passionately. He wrapped his arms around her slender, perfect body, felt her tremble as he touched her neck and left earlobe with his right hand, running his left hand up her arm, around her shoulder, across her scapula and down her left flank, skirting her breast with his thumb. He resisted blurting out what was in his mind: "For fuck's sake, Nicole. I love you."

His hand was on her hip, heading for her matchless derriere when Mona Levy plopped down on the couch beside them.

"You two are disgusting. Why don't you get a room?"

Nicole refused to get flustered. "Hello, Mona. Nate and I were just talking. Where's Jose? I thought you two would be upstairs by now."

"Jose's gay. He and Martin just went into Martin's room and shut the door."

"Really? Maybe they're just talking, like us."

"Martin thinks you hate him," said Nate.

"That's because I *do*," she spat.

"Why, because he's upstairs sodomizing your boyfriend?"

"Nate! Ew!" He had never seen Nicole offended before. She started to pull away.

"Sorry! Sorry." She relaxed back into him, to his relief.

Mona was unfazed. "No, because he's such a fucking snooty prig, looking down his nose at people and thinking everything should come to him on a silver platter, just because he's a white man with a fancy accent. You're almost as bad as he is, but at least you don't flaunt it. You two get treated like fucking gods right off the street, and I'm supposed to be happy about it."

"She *is* right, you know," said Nicole. "There's a lot of macho chest-thumping going on in the newsroom. You guys rarely even listen to women, much less give them credit for what they do. And Dave's the worst offender."

"Dave? He *loves* women."

"Yeah, he thinks everybody should own one. If there was another man available, I'm sure I wouldn't have my job right now. And Mona's at least as good as I am, and *way* better than fucking Callahan, but Dave thinks she's too uppity. I can't believe he made that retard an editor. It makes me embarrassed to be one."

Mona basked in the warmth of Nicole's resentment, but Nate bristled at this shot across his savior's bow. "Jeez, don't be badmouthing my hero like that. Dave's no misogynist. He's just sensitive and doesn't like being harped at. Dave really likes you, Nicole; he's just shy around women and not good at saying what he thinks. And Mona, when I first met you, you never disguised your negative feelings about Dutch Hollow or your work. Dave happens to *like* Dutch Hollow, and *loves* the newspaper business.

I don't know if it's because that fuck-head Zweiker is gone and Nicole's bringing out your good side, but you've just started coming down off your high horse and becoming a great reporter. Don't be blaming Dave for not rewarding your earlier bad attitude. You'll get yours."

* * *

The unfortunate interlude with Mona had cooled things off temporarily, but Nate's and Nicole's raging pheromones regained control of the situation and manipulated them upstairs into Nate's apartment.

"This is actually nice up here," said Nicole, admiring the leather-bound early 20th-century medical encyclopedias arranged on the antique oaken bookshelves, all of which Nate had found in the vast attic space next to his apartment that occupied the remainder of the third floor of the Arms.

"Thanks. It's almost home."

Nate had also commandeered an old iron bedstead from the attic, which was brimming with ancient treasures left by former tenants and long-forgotten reporters. He had made a platform out of five two-by-fours and a half-inch-thick piece of plywood to suspend on top of the frame, and bought a fat futon to put on top of that. As Nate had been shorn of a lifetime of excess baggage by the Gotham fire, this was the first time he had ever lived alone in a clean, comfortable, uncluttered space.

"I like this bed, too. It's industrial." She sat down on it, looking like a tender morsel on an iron skillet, waiting to be sautéed. Nate put the disturbing imagery out of his mind and sat down next to her, kissing her forehead, her nose, her eyes, her cheeks and, finally, her waiting mouth. She caressed him with her indescribably soft hands.

Slowly their clothing came off, neither knew quite how, until they were naked on the bed, kissing and exploring each other's swollen erogenous zones. Nate had never been harder, and his *cojones* were fat from weeks of neglect. Nicole's breasts were high, round and firm, and her nipples erect and taut as thimbles. Nate slowly snuggled southward and went to work between her legs. Taking his cues from her soft moans and hip thrusts, he eventually settled into a rhythm that brought her to one, then two, then three explosive orgasms.

"Mmmmanu, mmmir, mmmir, mmir, sssssumbitch!" She squealed on the last one, dissolving into a mass of giggling, shuddering beauty. "No one ever did that to me before. Who the fuck *are* you, Jimmy Olsen?"

A quiet interlude talking about what to do next exposed the fact that, since neither of them had expected ever to have sex again, neither of them was armed with condoms. "I can't wait to make love to you," she whispered, "but we should have protection."

"That's true. If it's any consolation, I was worried a while back and had a full battery of STD tests, including HIV, and I'm clean as a whistle. I've been afraid of sex ever since. I have to say I consider myself lucky, and am ready to settle down and be a serial monogamist, at least."

"How romantic."

"Yeah, well, honesty is the best policy."

"I'm sorry, you're right. I had a big scare a year ago when a guy I was going out with caught herpes. That's the only thing I know about. I've been tested since and don't have it."

"I thought you were a virgin."

"Who the hell told you that?"

"Nootch, at the Christmas party. He said that's what you told him. He was trying to get me excited about you, I guess. Not that he had to."

"What a little weasel. I did say that to him, I guess. I didn't want to sleep with him, at least while he was still with Mona. It was the only way I could get him off me one night."

"I thought you liked him."

"I did at first, but all he would do when we were together was talk about Mona, and then get worked up and try to force me to fuck him. He wasn't gentle, like you. He has problems, believe me. Mona's told me stories..."

While she talked, Nicole had been stroking Nate's balls, working his faded erection back to half-mast. "Nootch, smooch. What's going on down *here*?" she purred, and kissed her way down his chest and stomach to his suddenly rock-hard phallus. "Hello, big boy. Mmmm."

What happened next cannot be related in a family publication, but was in Nate's addled estimation something that placed Nicole at the very top of his out-of-print woman list.

"I love you," he blurted.

"Tell me that tomorrow morning when you wake up and see what a pig you've been with."

"Shut up. I love you." And it was true. He really did. It wasn't merely his neglected manhood that had just exploded. It was his heart, his soul and his mind. He told her as much.

She sat up, wiped off her mouth with a tissue from her purse, and crawled up next to him, kissing his bad eye. A tear was rolling slowly down her cheek. "I love you, too, Jimmy Olsen. I have since the moment I saw you."

CHAPTER SIXTEEN
A GOOD WALK SPOILED

Being in love was beautiful, transcendent, rapturous. It also played hell with one's attention span and work ethic. After skipping work Friday and failing to roll in until 2 p.m. Monday, Nate and Nicole resolved to clean up their act, which was threatening to attract media attention. The only time they had ventured out of Nate's room in the preceding 86 hours was on Friday morning to Keenan's Pharmacy to buy condoms. Sheik Ultra Thins, thought Nate with a twinge, like the ones he and Rico used to stock up on.

"I'm sorry you were ill," said Martin. "Lucky for you Nicole was sick as well. I'm sure she kept you good company."

"How's it hangin', sick boy," said Dave. "I'd like a complete update."

"It won't happen again, chief."

Nicole was concerned that they should not publicize their romance in the office for the time being, and Nate agreed. Neither of them wanted to be typecast by their peers, especially as some kind of scheming power couple. Nate told the few people he was sure knew about their affair to shut up about it, and Nicole did the same, namely with Mona. They sneaked into each other's rooms at night, like horny coed boarding school seniors.

Nate was the first to mention their age difference. "So what do you see in a beat-up old fuck like me, anyway?"

"Shut up, I think you're handsome. I like men with a few dents. Besides, what do you see in a fat-bottomed, inexperienced girl like me?"

"Inexperienced? You've been driving me crazy here. And most men would kill to get next to a booty like yours. No, I'm serious. Aren't you at all worried about what people might think? About you and me?"

"I've thought about it, sure. It's not like you're my uncle or something. We'll see how things work out. If it turns out to be real, like it seems to be, then it shouldn't matter in the long run. But if you're just some kind of pervert, I swear..."

The lame attempt at seriousness deteriorated into a short-lived tickle fight, which Nicole won going away. Deep down, though, Nate was worried. Here was a woman who, for the first time since junior high school, had the potential to hurt him. Sheila had broken down the wall around his heart, and Nicole had just walked onto the job site and stolen it while reconstruction was still in progress.

Between the horrific time Diana Carmen jilted him in seventh grade and Sheila's even more horrific death on September 11, 2001, Nate had deserted every other woman he'd professed to love. "Never again," had been his secret motto. But he usually abandoned a woman only after she'd gotten weary of his cheating, pussyfooting act and was close to leaving him. Judging from his past performance, the odds that he could retain Nicole's interest were low.

But this time was different. He'd changed. It wasn't about sex, good as it was. He had been living like a monk, totally immersed in work that satisfied him and even, he dared to admit, made him happy—a brand new life development. Into this world, a woman had entered as an equal, not as a conquest or a diversion. Before laying a hand on her he had grown to love her more than he'd ever loved anything or anyone in his life. He wasn't going anywhere this time. He wanted her to stay with him. He might even say or do anything to keep her.

Nicole Royal had Nate by the balls. The difference between her and other women, he thought, might be that she was too good a person to notice.

* * *

Nate got busy traveling to the NYPIRG office in Albany to obtain his own copy of the old, pre-sanitized statewide DEC toxic waste site report.

It was similar to but in much greater detail than the one he had seen in Sheila's files. Extensive narratives describing all of the state's known toxic waste sites, including each of Roosevelt County's 120-odd abominations, were in the report. The scraggly public interest research activist who handed Nate the 100-page report was tickled that someone would actually be using the group's work. "Good luck, man. Reports like this don't exist at the DEC anymore; Pollock's Gestapo cleaned them all up. It's his final solution, man. Pave paradise, put up a parking lot."

Nate also set up a meeting with Ostia's assistant town clerk, who gave him his own copies of the letters and memos she had found buried in the archives. One item that jumped out was a letter to Ostia Town Attorney Jonathan Wilson from Janet B. Suss of Ecotest, Inc., advising him of the first steps to take in response to the DEC's Phase II report. One of these steps was to send a request to the DEC under the Freedom of Information Act for certain documents:

"1) Phase II Investigation Report for site no. 498074 (Ostia Town Landfill) including the final work plan and all supporting data;

"2) Correspondence, field reports and memoranda relating to the recommendation for reclassification of site no. 498074 as a Class 2 site;

"3) All correspondence from the NYSDEC to Nicholas Vitello, McCollum-Davies Corporation, Metal Metamorphosis Company, Haberman, Wilson & Strong, the Town of Ostia, the Town of Pepperton and any other agent for or former owner/operator of this site in connection with the subsequent investigations to date;

"4) Sampling results conducted by a USEPA contractor, Humboldt Geoscience Corporation, on February 22, 1993, and subsequent draft report/preliminary data of same, received by NYSDEC (EPA ID NYD989785276)."

Nate hoped this "Phase II Investigation Report" would be a blockbuster, detailing a major toxic waste dump. He filled out his own Freedom of Information request, went across the river to the DEC regional office in New Paltz and asked to see the file for the Ostia Town Landfill, site no. 498074. He was initially rebuffed by a surly records access officer named

Wanda Richtoffen, who told him after much huffing and puffing that the records he was looking for had been moved to Albany. He then went upstairs to the reception desk and asked to speak to Belinda Strossner, the DEC's regional director of media relations, with whom he had developed a warm telephone relationship in the course of his research on the bird-poisoning story. She buzzed him in.

"James Olsen, I've wanted to meet you," she said, shaking his hand. "I live in Pepperton and have admired your stories. You've been hard to find in the paper lately."

"I'm all over the county now, doing stories for every paper."

"Oh, that's good. I thought we'd lost you." Strossner was a pleasantly healthy, large-boned woman, whose ample facial features resembled the apple-cheeked subjects of van Gogh's "The Potato Eaters". "How can I help you?"

Nate told her of the alleged Ostia toxic dump, and how he was looking for evidence that the town had been involved in a cover-up and had stonewalled the DEC. He told her of his request for file number 498074, and of being cold-shouldered by Wanda Richtoffen downstairs. Strossner got up, walked to her door and closed it.

"This is off the record," she whispered. "Consider it background information. I've been with the DEC since 1984. I came in when Paul Greco became governor, as assistant commissioner, a political appointee. I'd worked on his campaign. Greco cleaned up this agency, which was rife with corruption. Until Pollock beat Greco we were going great guns, cleaning up many, many environmental problems around the state, especially here in the Hudson Valley. We were working with activists like the Hudson Fishermen's Guild and the River Guardians, who would identify polluters for us. We had scads of money from the Superfund, and were closing and remediating landfills, and bringing polluters to justice.

"When Pollock came in I was fired, and had to take a test for this job. It's not perfect, but I've been able to be a thorn in the side of his people's efforts to gut the agency, at least in the Hudson Valley. I can't tell you how many times I've leaked information, to journalists I trust, on what's happening in here. I think I can trust you as a person who wants to tell the truth, am I right?"

"You are right."

"Well then what you should know is that, with very few exceptions, this agency is thoroughly corrupt. Do not believe anything a DEC official tells you. Most of them are on the take, working for the polluters who pay them off. Your friend Wanda Richtoffen is the wife of a former DEC cop, Andrew Richtoffen. He was secretly in business for himself on the side, running an illegal toxic dump in Poston. He was found out by a local activist, brought to justice by the River Guardians, tried and convicted of fraud and taking bribes, and lost his job. He had a bogus checking account in Wanda's name, pretending the thousands he was depositing were from her fake candle-selling business. And she's in charge of finding your files? Good luck."

"Jesus."

"Anyway, if you come back here tomorrow, I'll have your files for you. If you ever need anything, call me first."

"Do you know a man named Reginald Thurston Brown?"

Her eyes lit up. "Thirsty and I are best friends. We've been tearing at the citadel from the inside for years."

"Well, I've been tearing at it from the outside for about four months. I would love to hang out with you veterans and pick your brains. Any chance?"

"I'm sure there is. Let's keep in touch."

* * *

Meanwhile, Nate had put Martin Brennan on the case to find out everything he could about Edward Piazzo and International Leisure Entertainment. And Martin succeeded beyond Nate's wildest expectations, finding out more about Piazzo in one short week than Piazzo probably knew about himself.

The first thing Martin did was go down to the Roosevelt County Clerk's office and enter the name "Piazzo, Edward" in the automated county court cases information system under the "defendant" field. He hit the jackpot. Piazzo had personally been sued in Roosevelt County for offenses like "nonpayment for services rendered," "breach of contract" or "default" on loans by no less than 53 plaintiffs over the past 10 years. He had lost or settled on all of those cases and had filed for bankruptcy once. He had owed and reneged on more than $2 million in local bills over that period.

Martin then attempted to contact each and every one of the plaintiffs he had unearthed and interview them about the circumstances of Piazzo's failure to pay them. He was successful on more than a quarter of his tries. One of them said that Piazzo had recently told him that International Leisure Entertainment was bidding for a hotel and casino complex in Las Vegas at the same time it was negotiating bank financing for the purchase of Vitello's Country Club. The son-of-a-bitch was using each of these as-yet-un-purchased entities as collateral for the loan to buy the other.

The picture that emerged of Edward Piazzo was that of a career small-time con artist suddenly going big-time, whose delusions of grandeur could hardly keep up with his ever-growing house of cards. The man had to be a front for a mob money laundering operation, thought Nate. Otherwise, how could he still be alive and in business?

* * *

The story Martin wrote for the *Mohican Valley Times* that week casting aspersions on Edward Piazzo's glittering reputation, titled "A Good Walk Spoiled?" after Mark Twain's ruminations on the game of golf, threw the town of Ostia into a tailspin, and Roosevelt Newspapers into a tizzy.

Edward Piazzo was predictably incensed, and got the town to hold a special public meeting Thursday night to lie to the townsfolk, deny everything and demonize the British interloper, Martin Brennan. The townspeople were ready to hang Martin in effigy.

Winnie, who had been away in London on business, returned Friday morning and was furious. "Who authorized this story? Why wasn't it cleared with me?" he thundered.

"It's all true," said Dave. "Martin didn't make one assumption. He let Piazzo's record, and the words of others, speak for themselves."

"This story is incendiary! For us to have run it is irresponsible! We could be destroying lives in Ostia here! People are going to blame me for this golden opportunity going down the tubes! We have to run an apology!"

For the first time, Nate witnessed Dave get his formidable back up. "This was a very well-written, well-researched story about a scumbag who is about to run a scam on the people of Ostia that may cost them millions. You talk about destroying lives? If you apologize to this motherfucker, you'll be doing it without me!"

Dave stomped out of the newsroom with his fists clenched, leaving Winnie standing there speechless. He then turned to Nate. "How did this happen?"

Inspired by Dave's outburst, Nate dug in his heels, albeit with more tact. "Ed Piazzo is a big-time grifter, Winnie. Someone would have found out sooner or later. Either the town will shit-can the deal right now or, more likely, they'll ignore the story and listen to Piazzo and his lies. Piazzo will eventually screw things up, stop paying his bills again, and a lot of pissed-off people will end up holding the bag for this so-called 'golden opportunity.' It may not look that way now, but it's good that it was us who ratted him out. If we stick with this, *you'll* get credit for saving Ostia. We need to talk to Nick Vitello and calm him down, too."

"Jesus Christ."

"Winnie, it's OK to stick your neck out sometimes. It was the right thing to do. They'll get over it. Dave's a great editor. You want me to go get him, or what?"

Winnie sat down and nodded his head.

* * *

Almost unnoticed in the fray were Nate's two stories. The first was about the old Ostia landfill, and ran below the fold in the same *Mohican Valley Times* issue in which Martin's golf course story was the lead. As promised, Belinda Strossner had delivered the goods. The DEC's Phase II Investigation Report for site no. 498074 described a toxic nightmare of disastrous proportions. Magnetic resonance imaging tests taken alongside Nick Vitello's helicopter pad just south of his landfill and the golf course had confirmed the existence of "upwards of 1,000 barrels" buried in the old landfill. Benzene, toluene, xylene, TCE, PCE and PCB's were leaching into the surrounding wetlands and the Mohican River. Tests had shown that the poisons were present in intense concentrations of up to 250 milligrams per kilogram; that the water was undrinkable and that wildlife was at serious risk. As no humans lived within a quarter-mile radius, no general health alert had been issued.

Nate's second story ran in all 10 Roosevelt newspapers. It had been a tedious job requiring a good 30 hours of work, but he had wanted it to run as a two-page jump sidebar in the Mohican Valley paper as well as a minor page one feature, with two-page jump, in the other papers. Dave went for it. Titled "Roosevelt County a Toxic Wasteland", the 5,000-word epic quoted and paraphrased NYPIRG's circa-1990 DEC report regarding the county's 123 toxic waste sites.

Winnie apparently did not deem Nate's two stories "incendiary," even though they whipped up a considerable public shit-storm. The "Wasteland" story, accompanied by a handy map of Roosevelt County clotted with black bull's-eyes pinpointing toxic dump locations, resulted in a flurry of phone calls from worried realtors, property owners and potential buyers. Although the Ostia landfill story presented nearly as difficult a problem for Big Nick and the Ostia boosters as Martin's story, it wasn't personal in nature. The story merely mentioned that if it weren't for "the initially unwitting investigations of a group of volunteer 'foot soldiers' recruited to gather information relating to the Mohican Valley Water Resource Evaluation Project," the DEC's damning Phase II Investigation Report for site no. 498074 would not have come to light. No aspersions were cast regarding the town's possible role in covering up a catastrophic toxic waste problem for seven years, and no assumptions were made regarding Nick Vitello's dominant role in Roosevelt's waste business. Nate figured correctly that enough people who were interested would read between the lines and start harassing the town to do something, and would connect the dots regarding Big Nick.

Nate had also gotten a quote from Vitello, after telling him that a story was running that had the potential to put him in a bad light. "How the hell would I know what's under my goddamn helicopter pad?" said Nick, somewhat believably. "I bought that land from Danny McCollum in 1985. That old dump was already closed. Nobody ever buried toxic waste in any of *my* landfills, I'll tell you that."

Wanting to nurture his burgeoning relationship with Nick as long as possible, Nate had covered his own ass, telling the mobster that Martin was doing a story on the golf course sale, but that he didn't know what it was about. Martin had called Vitello for his story as well, and as luck would have it, Nick never returned his phone calls.

Winnie worked fast to contain the damage. Winnie, Dave, Martin and Nate went down to Ostia on Friday afternoon and met with Vitello, Piazzo and Dick Strong, the walking conflict of interest who happened to represent both Big Nick and Roosevelt Newspapers. Nate didn't want to go, but Winnie insisted. "Take notes. You're my guy."

Piazzo's lawyer was there as well: a slick Westchester operator in a mustard-colored suit and gold Rolex named Dominick Chianni. In an earlier meeting, the Roosevelt contingent had gotten their strategy straight. Winnie would do all the talking.

Big Nick started things off. "Look, we asked you down here to try to clear a few things up. Mr. Piazzo here is, I feel, deservedly angry for having been lambasted in your paper. Whatever his problems in the past, he's more than made up for them. In coming in here, he has been able to put together a partnership that makes me feel good about the future of this club that I built with my own sweat. So what is the problem? Eddie, what do you think?"

"I am a legitimate businessman," said Piazzo, the veins on his neck straining against his starched white collar. "You people have libeled me and slandered my good name, and given this project a black eye that it might never recover from. I want to know what you're going to do about retracting these lies, before I have to take legal action."

To his credit, Winnie reared up to his full six-foot-three-inch height and went on the offensive.

"Nick, I consider you a friend. But first and foremost, I run a community newspaper. I'm sorry if you disagree, but my newspaper had a responsibility to run that story. There is not one libelous word in it, Mr. Piazzo. The facts regarding your record as a businessperson in Roosevelt County have been reported, without embellishment. Your record speaks for itself, and would have done so with or without this newspaper. It would aggrieve me to think that my reporter was treating you unfairly or somehow targeting you, but after careful consideration I have determined that he was not. He merely stated the truth. The fact of the matter is that your financial history is as full of unmitigated disasters as any I have ever witnessed. I can hardly believe that it would be in the best interests of the Town of Ostia or of Mr. Vitello to have critical information on your past business performances withheld from them. You are certainly within your rights to tell your side of the story; Martin here apparently gave you that opportunity before the story ran and you declined to comment. I'll gladly give you a full editorial page to explain your position after the fact, unedited. And if Mr. Vitello still wants to do business with you, and if the town continues to want to work with you, then that's their prerogative. Roosevelt Newspapers has no interest in destroying you or your reputation, such as it is.

"I will promise you this. There is no agenda on the part of my newspaper. There will be no further stories regarding this subject, except to report on the decisions made regarding your petitions to the town or changes in your relationship with Mr. Vitello. And if you should somehow be able to come up with viable information that contradicts the work of my reporter, the vast majority of which came straight from court records, then I will print as many retractions and apologies as it takes, on a point-by-point basis."

Piazzo had heard enough. "That's bullshit. I want a full retraction or you'll be hearing from Dominick here."

"Ho, ho, ho there, Ed, let's calm down a little bit." It was Big Nick. "Nobody's suing anybody. Come with me for a minute, Ed." He led Piazzo off to his private study.

What Piazzo was unaware of was the fact that Winnie and Big Nick, close personal and business associates in the past, had talked over what they were going to do beforehand. Winnie had apologized personally to Nick for letting the story slip through, but said the damage would not be undone with a retraction. If the paper retracted something that was patently true and obvious, people would notice. Winnie would lose credibility and lose value to Big Nick, whom he had always supported in the past, and would continue to do. Things would be worse for everybody by calling attention to the problem. They had both agreed that the best thing to do would be to drop the story softly and let things blow over. Winnie agreed to put Martin on a short leash and Nick agreed to calm Piazzo down. The way things went in the Mohican Valley, Piazzo would be forgiven his sins and given a new chance anyway.

In reality, Piazzo was a nobody; the available front man for a consortium Nick had created to buy the club from himself and hide some money. Big Nick wasn't about to let Piazzo ruin things over ego. He put him in his place.

"Look, you're my fucking fall guy, asshole," whispered Nick in Piazzo's ear. "Fucking get used to it already." There was no sense upsetting the status quo with Winnie and the newspaper, which Nick was able to use as his own personal PR agency, over a mistake by an overzealous cub reporter.

He had to keep a lid on these guys, though. Not just the Limey. That fucking Jimmy Olsen kid. Jimmy Olsen, my ass. One of Nick's informants in Bill McNally's outfit had recognized him at the Ostia town meeting. "That's the same funny little moother I was s'posed to take out with Bill's daughter's files at the storage bin in the City," said the big Irishman. "He cut his fookin' hair an' shaved his beard, but it's him."

What a ballsy fuck, thought Nick. Coming in here trying—no, succeeding—in getting on his good side. He had to give him that. The kid had a way about him. Jimmy Olsen. A fucking sense of humor already. And that busted face with the long, whaddya say, *aquiline* schnozz. Like Sammy's. The same Milanese prince thing going. A tough, hard-hearted fuck like he imagined Sammy would have been if he had lived to be a man.

Fucking Sammy...

Nick looked back over his long life. He had taken care of things the best he could. His family. His honor. He had done all right by people. But he had been wrong about some things. Big things. He had fucking liver cancer, for Chrissake. Sofia, blessed mother of his three children, dead of bladder cancer two years ago. All from living on top of garbage dumps for so long; he was sure of it. But who knew back then?

Other things. The drugs. It was wrong. That's what killed Sammy, no matter what the bogus coroner's report he had paid ten grand for said.

Nate Randall, huh? Gotta be half Guinea. At least a quarter. That's good enough, these days, with all these fucking Micks running around. Fuck them. The kid could write like a fucking angel, that was the thing. He was smart. "He has my voice down," thought Nick, starting to leak snot into his air hose. "He respects me like...a father. I can read a fucking face."

Big Nick called Bill McNally and told him he knew about his daughter's old boyfriend being in the area, sniffing around. He told the dirty fuck to leave James Olsen, a.k.a. Nate Randall, alone. "The kid is mine, capeesh? I'm gonna keep him close, turn him out by having him do some things for me. The cocksucker might be valuable. I'm gonna feed him some rope; see what he knows. See who's out there trying to fuck with us. If you touch the kid, you'll have me to answer to."

Nick was ready to unload it all. He was done. The girls would be well taken care of, he had seen to that. But he had a legacy to leave that went way beyond being Cousin Joey's fucking meat puppet or that Irish daughter-raper's steppingstone. He just had to hurry up before his air ran out.

What could he do that would outlast everything, even the granite hills of Ostia? What had survived through the millennia and would still be reverberating when the Pyramids had crumbled to dust? Words. The Bible. The Iliad. The Odyssey. Plato. Hammurabi's Code. Shakespeare. Dante. All those ancient leather-bound books lining his walls. His words would join them, a warning to future generations about the soul-destroying vicissitudes of The Life.

Or maybe not. Maybe he'd just take a broom to a few motherfuckers and straighten out the mess he'd let things slip into. Either way, "Jimmy Olsen," that sneaky little Sammy look-alike, was just the kind of smart, demented little fuck to help him do it, God bless him, or else.

CHAPTER SEVENTEEN
THIRST FOR KNOWLEDGE

One person who appreciated Nate's toxic stories was the DEC's Belinda Strossner. She called him late Friday, gushing: "Great job, Jim. People are going crazy. About the Ostia dump, of course; but especially about the accompanying story. A hundred and twenty-three sites, some of which even *I* have never heard of! Nobody's ever tried to explain all that in a newspaper before. It's absolutely mind-boggling. Of course there are many, many more that the DEC doesn't know about. How'd you like to come over for dinner tomorrow night? I've got a few people I want you to meet."

"Sure," said Nate, but it wasn't that simple. He was more than a little leery of Strossner, who came on in a way that made him uncomfortable. He wondered what she had up her sleeve. He also realized he had a problem he hadn't had to deal with for a long time, if ever: the feeling of obligation that comes with truly caring about someone else. Nicole had talked about wanting to go out to dinner and a movie Saturday night. His recently resuscitated conscience suddenly wouldn't let him just decide to do something else without involving her or consulting her, and it bothered him. He swallowed his discomfort, and asked: "Do you mind if I bring my girlfriend? She works with me. She can be trusted."

He detected a slight tone of disappointment in Strossner's voice. "Only if you swear her to secrecy. This is a social event, not a news story. I think you'll be pleasantly surprised at my guest list. They are people who won't want their names mentioned in your paper."

"Believe me, 'Discretion' is her middle name."

Nicole was tickled with what she termed Nate's "thoughtfulness," and the word stuck in his craw like a chicken bone. "I feel like such a fucking pussy," he complained, handing her a spray of yellow gladioli he'd picked up on a whim from the overpriced florist in the village. "I told you I've never cared about anything or anybody, and it's true. I can't say I *like* caring about you. It bites the blue-veined bag. But I can't fucking help it. Damn you to hell."

"Thanks a lot. I love you, too. Asshole."

"Will you marry me?"

"Probably. Let's practice first."

They made love without protection, for the first time. It was like sky-diving without a parachute, or walking the tightrope over a gorge with no net. They fit together like missing puzzle pieces, slipping into a seamless whole far greater than the sum of their parts. Long dormant synapses fired between their hearts, minds and sex glands, blasting open passages that had been shut and locked during past failures and disappointments. To Nate the experience was transcendent; far more sexually and emotionally exciting and frightening than anything life had thus far provided; even Sheila. Looking at Nicole's sleeping face long into the night, he wept.

"Only you can hurt me now," he whispered. "Only you."

* * *

Belinda Strossner lived with her two teenaged daughters in a remarkable California-style cantilevered octagonal glass house that jutted dramatically off of the top of an escarpment overlooking the Mohican Valley.

She answered the door wearing the full-length, flowing batik muumuu of an Ulster County earth mother, with a large quarter-moon medallion hanging off her neck on a beaded chain. She was living on the wrong side of the river for that get-up, thought Nate. "Your house is incredible," said Nicole.

"Thank you. It was a gift from my ex-husband. He got the beach house." Her ex was Michael Strossner, a well-known literary agent and former magazine publisher. Belinda Strossner was no ordinary mid-level civil servant. She and her husband had apparently traveled in some pretty lofty circles during their 15-year marriage, and she had endeavored successfully to maintain quite a few of those relationships after their break-up.

She led them into the living room, with its sweeping, unobstructed views of the valley and the mountains beyond. A number of expensive-looking people were lounging on comfortable furniture and a series of oversized, Native American-themed pillows, sipping on glasses of red wine. Belinda steered the newcomers toward a bald, gnomishly avuncular, light-skinned black gentleman in a suit and tie, perched on a straight-backed antique chair next to a tall, rugged, silver-haired man in a dark blue turtleneck and dress chinos, who was standing admiring the scenery out of the floor-to-ceiling, wall-to-wall bank of windows. It was 5:30 p.m. and the tops of the mountains across the valley to the east were lined with a brilliant gold, set against the darkening, moonless, unnaturally warm February sky. The lights of the Village of Pepperton and along arrow-straight Route 33 and the more sinuous Old Ostia-Pepperton Road could already be seen twinkling in the valley below. A hawk circled slowly overhead, reflecting the setting sun.

"Jim Olsen, Nicole Royal, I'd like to introduce you to Reginald Thurston Brown." The seated man stood slowly, smiled and shook Nate's hand. "I've been looking forward to meeting you," he growled in a curious South African-inflected accent, his gray-green eyes sparkling with mirth. "And I've heard from a number of my sources that you've been looking forward to meeting me as well."

"That is true, Mr. Brown," said Nate. "I've heard a lot about you, and read some of your work."

"Well in that case, please, call me 'Thirsty'." Maybe he was British, thought Nate. Whatever he was, he had already put down a few.

Brown then turned smartly, bowed and kissed Nicole's outstretched hand. "And you, milady. I am especially pleased to meet such a thoroughly charming young editor. I didn't think any such species existed. If your tenure with Mr. Olsen expires, I would be happy to replace him in your busy schedule."

"Thirsty, mind your manners," laughed Strossner. "Please excuse him; he's an incorrigible womanizer. And this is Congressman Evan Aldrich; I'm sure you've heard of his many exploits in battling organized criminals and polluters."

Nate shook the gnarled, callused hand of the tall, weather-beaten politician. Aldrich avoided looking him squarely in the eyes, and Nate had the distinct feeling that the man was uneasy; that he might be hiding something. Not having met many politicians, he wondered if it was perhaps an occupational condition to be habitually wary. "Pleased to meet you, sir."

"After reading some of your work Belinda has shown me, I can honestly say I'm a fan of yours," said Aldrich, still squinting over Nate's shoulder at an indeterminate point across the valley. "Welcome to the fight."

For the next ten minutes, Nate and Nicole were introduced to the other members of what was turning out to be a meeting of an informal environmental focus group—the word "coven" came to Nate's mind—made up of individuals from politics and the literary and entertainment worlds. Nate knew six of them by sight: Jack Danforth, the world-famous film star, race car driver and liberal activist; Bernard Esney, the ancient talk show personality and publisher of Incidental Books; Susan Jackson Smith, the aging television diva who had usurped the owner of the Greek restaurant in Dutch Hollow to be her personal chef; Allen Scott, the singing half of the 1970s pop-soul duo Byron & Scott; Gina Abramowitz, the celebrity photographer; and old Jake Striker, the banjo-playing, sea-chantey-singing Hudson River advocate.

Also present were a record producer, a best-selling author of political potboilers, the environmental attorney grandson of a former president, and the courtly Hamilton Canard, Esq., the author of the locally infamous "Rocco Report."

"These people all *know* each other?" marveled Nate to Belinda. Nate hadn't been in the same room with so many celebrities since the Ex-Men played at Nell's, where he'd shaken Tupac Shakur's hand, sold a CD to Julia Roberts and taken a leak next to OJ Simpson.

"Of course. Sadly, there is only a handful of wealthy, influential people who do more than pay lip service to environmental concerns. They tend to find each other."

The enigmatic Reginald Thurston Brown was the star of this party, however. Virtually everyone in the room stopped what they were doing and craned to listen in whenever he spoke; which at first wasn't often, but gained in frequency the more wine he drank. Central casting could not have come up with a more colorful character to play the role of a shadowy freelance gumshoe who had been called upon by the government over the years to investigate everything from the Kennedy assassination, Watergate and Iran-Contra to environmental disasters like Love Canal and Three-Mile Island. This droll little man had apparently toppled mobsters, tracked the international finances of terrorists and single-handedly brought down drug cartels. If everything being said about him by Belinda, Aldrich and some of the other guests were true—none of which he denied—Thirsty was literally a real-life, South African-American James Bond.

He told of his current project for the Congressional Organized Crime Task Force, exposing the Byzantine world of industrial development bonds. "People all the way up to and including the last three presidents have had their fingers in this bogus pie," said Thirsty, embarking on the first of his many long, languidly paced soliloquies for the evening. "These are billions of dollars in essentially worthless bonds, backed by public money, that are falsely marked up, repackaged with other bond types and sold as derivatives. It's a vast pyramid scheme, where the people who are connected on the front end get rich and the people down the line get left holding the bag. When the loans these bonds were financing aren't paid back by the mobsters who have long since spent the money, the taxpayers of the localities in which the bonds were produced foot the bill. If this ever became known by the general public, it would be a financial crisis that would make the Enron debacle pale in comparison."

Nate thought he had it figured out. Speaking slowly and precisely, pausing often for effect and over-emphasizing the accents of multi-syllabic words, Thirsty sounded like a slightly inebriated, South African Alfred Hitchcock. Despite the coffee color of his skin, there was a more than passing physical resemblance as well.

It turned out that Thirsty was the son of a white Liberal Democrat in the House of Lords and a black South African mother. He had spent a good part of his younger life in British Intelligence, where he hooked up with Aldrich on an assignment in South Africa during the congressman's former stint with the State Department. As a freshman in Congress, Aldrich lured the 35-year-old Thirsty to Washington in 1970, providing him with a job, free lodging and a reason to avoid returning to England. He had served as Aldrich's investigative right-hand man ever since.

The confab dinner party roared on, stoked by an endless supply of local Merlot and a serviceable meal of organic free-range chicken cordon bleu, brown rice and sautéed vegetables and tomato-basil salad. The guests were unanimous in their condemnation of the Bush and Pollock administrations, and in their acceptance of the thoroughly Chomskyan point of view that the United States was historically the biggest terrorist of all. Through its New World Order and its lavish support of soulless human rights violators and genocidal maniacs, the good old U.S. had caused untold suffering on earth, which led directly to the September 11 fiasco. But, being environmentalists, they reserved their greatest indignation for the corporations who sullied the land, water and air without a shred of conscience. The fact that most of them maintained vast, oil-heated upstate mansions and Manhattan pieds-á-terre, employed legions of dusky, underpaid servants and drove to the party in gas-guzzling SUVs didn't strike them as particularly contradictory. It was an earnest, irony-free gathering.

Nate was trying to take it all in with a grain of salt, but Nicole was visibly flabbergasted. The sensible, well-ordered world she had grown up with in Binghamton and college was being turned upside-down. She had teased Nate about his conspiracy-theorist tendencies, but now here was a roomful of people she recognized from movies, magazines and television, all talking excitedly about vast, nation-wrecking financial scams, international cabals of criminals who ran the world's governments and a shadow economy in toxic chemicals that was giving everyone asthma, cancer and AIDS.

"AIDS?" she couldn't stop herself from exclaiming during one of Thirsty's increasingly fantastic tirades. "Isn't AIDS caused by the HIV virus?"

"That's what we're all led to believe, love, but who decreed that to be the case?" drawled Thirsty between gulps, industriously adding to the backstory behind his nickname. "An American bureaucrat, Dr. Robert Gallo of the National Institutes of Health, who desperately latched onto someone else's research regarding a little known retrovirus and proclaimed himself to be the discoverer of the cause of AIDS. Rubbish. While this virus is indeed present in many AIDS cases, it is absent in just as many more, a discrepancy that has been conveniently ignored by the knee-jerk American medical research community. The fact is that in nearly 20 years no one has been able to show just how this single virus causes such an astonishing array of diseases in different populations. For example, Kaposi's sarcoma and pneumocystis pneumonia are common conditions in American and European gay men with AIDS, but not in women, Haitians or central Africans. Why is that?

"Research is now being studiously ignored which points directly to one ubiquitous modern chemical: benzene, and its many derivatives, as the cause of AIDS. Benzene is a petroleum derived industrial solvent that is used in manufacturing nearly everything that goes *onto*, *into* and *around* your firm young body, Miss Royal, including shampoos and conditioners, hand lotion, laundry detergent, clothing, asphalt, computers and drugs—both pharmaceutical and illegal."

All the males in the room gaped at the blushing Nicole with renewed interest, pondering her firm, young body. Nate reached out and pulled her close, protectively.

"Benzene is a known carcinogen that causes leukemia—bone marrow cancer. It also causes Hodgkin's disease, and lymphomas through inhalation. Chronic benzene poisoning starts slowly, with vague symptoms: fatigue, headache, dizziness, nausea and loss of appetite, loss of weight, and weakness. A lot like the much-ballyhooed Epstein-Barr syndrome, don't you think?

"Benzene was, and still is, the major ingredient in the kinds of sexual lubricants used almost exclusively by gays for anal sex. Kaposi's sarcoma and pneumocystis pneumonia started appearing in gay men in the major U.S. metropolitan areas in 1978, only months after the introduction of these new types of lubricants, which had been formulated and marketed for exclusive use by the gay community. Before this time, gays had been making do with Crisco, K-Y jelly, baby oil and such. The new, improved products were all based on denatured oils and contained very high amounts of acetone and benzoic acid. These poisons are introduced into the highly absorptive anus, where they pass directly into the bloodstream.

"Curiously, as gay men in other countries began mail-ordering these same lubricants, AIDS began to appear in those places as well.

"As for the Haitians and central Africans: A chemical called clioquinol, a benzene derivative, was routinely given to Haitians arriving in the U.S.A.

in the early '80s for parasitic infections. The same stuff is currently being heavily marketed in Zaire and Angola, along with other benzene-derived poisons to 'cure' tuberculosis. Haitians, you may recall, were singled out by the Center for Disease Control as being one of the biggest AIDS risk groups at the time. Zaire and Angola are currently hotbeds of full-blown AIDS. India and the Far East are being decimated as well now, as their populations are being turned into AIDS-scourged guinea pigs by the multinational pharmaceutical giants testing new benzene-based wonder drugs.

"AIDS is also found in drug addicts, of course, who comprise the vast majority of heterosexual cases in First World nations. The three intravenous drugs most implicated in immune suppression: cocaine, heroin, and crystal methamphetamine, are manufactured with coal tar derivatives like kerosene, which has an *extremely* high amount of benzene in it. Chronic intravenous drug use by itself produces may of the same sicknesses defined as AIDS.

"I could go on, but does that answer your question, young lady?"

Nicole nodded her head and shrugged, battered into a daze by Thirsty's informational blitzkrieg.

Nate finally spoke up. "Thirsty, there's something you should know. There's a reason I came up to the country and became a reporter. I'm following a trail that was willed to me by my ex-girlfriend, Sheila McNally."

For the first time, it was Thirsty who was taken aback. "You're Nate, the heartless musician?"

"The same."

Nicole, looking on intently, squeezed Nate's hand. He squeezed back.

"Well that explains your obsession with USE and Janssen Movers. Very unusual for an inexperienced community journalist to happen upon all that."

"How do you know about my obsession?"

"A little bird told me. Two little birds, actually. FBI birds."

Nicole looked at Nate quizzically. He hadn't told her everything yet, he realized. There was just too much to tell.

"Wow. I really didn't think they would know you. It was a shot in the dark. Why didn't you get in touch with me earlier?"

"You were an unknown entity. I have to be careful."

"Well, now that you know me, can you tell me if I'm on the right track with a few things?"

"Shoot."

"Number one, is Janssen Movers run by the mob?"

"Certainly. The president, Sheila's father, William McNally, has been a Natale family associate since his early days with the Westies, although the word on the street is he's getting a little big for his britches."

"Are they hoarding spent chemicals obtained from USE plants in order to resell them at a discount?"

"That is what we believe."

"Who are they selling these chemicals to?"

"Go to Janssen's three warehouses, and check out the businesses in each neighborhood. Ten paving companies within a quarter mile. Two major heating oil distributors. Two large chemical distribution companies, both of which supply USE as well as other regional factories and businesses. An oil-fired power plant a mile away. An oil-fired regional garbage incinerator a mile and a half away.

"There are other regional industries that use hundreds of thousands of gallons of heavy oil annually, and make it go a lot farther by cutting it with cheap, used benzene or similar stuff. An oil-fired, 300-foot rotating kiln in the hills above Waterkill, that blows up hunks of shale into feather-light meteors, which are crushed and made into the roofs of sports stadiums. There are plans to use these waste products in an abominable and messy gas mining process called 'hydrofracturing,' which I've just begun looking into.

"Then there are all the rural highway departments, who mix the stuff in with asphalt and the oil they use to maintain all those lovely dirt country lanes the rich weekenders so admire. They clean the salt off their trucks with anything that's not too strong to strip the paint off them. The state Department of Transportation's mid-Hudson facility out by the Thruway, just across the river, has a different Janssen trailer parked there every other day. What do you suppose it's doing there?

"But the biggest market, we think, are drug manufacturers. Besides distributing to local cocaine labs, we believe they're flying black market chemicals out of the nearby county airport to South America and the

Dominican Republic. There is also a burgeoning domestic market in meth-amphetamines, which is built from the same set of molecules."

"Holy shit."

"Holy shit, yes. The DEA has been shutting off all legal exports of chemicals to Andean South America since 1989; a year after the Chemical Diversion and Trafficking Act was passed. Before that, American compa-nies were the main source for the 20,000 tons of acetone, methyl ethyl ketone, ethyl ether, potassium permanganate, hydrochloric acid, methyl isobutyl ketone and sulfuric acid used annually to manufacture cocaine in the Medellin area alone. When that flow stopped, a vast black market was born. Incidentally, every one of the chemicals I just listed is used in computer chip processing in copious amounts. If you were a mob toxic chemical hauler with an airport next door, what would you do?"

"So if they're selling it all, what's in the drums that are supposedly buried under every shopping mall?"

"They can't possibly sell it all. Their market is expanding all the time, but the flow out of USE and the other businesses they serve: large indus-trial dry-cleaning establishments, newspaper and magazine printers, plas-tics manufacturers and so on, is so monumental they have nowhere near enough space to store it all. They probably are able to sell only a fraction of what they collect. And some of the stuff is just too fouled by industrial processes to be of any further commercial use.

"This isn't only being done in this region; it's all over the country, and the world. This area has a leg up on the competition, however, because the mobs are so strong and the infrastructure has been in place for so much longer. The New York area mobs control the flow of toxic waste and drugs within the United States. And Roosevelt County is ground zero, now that New York, New Jersey and Long Island have been picked over and weak-ened by the federales. Until ten years ago, the FBI didn't even know or care if the mob existed up here. Now the Roosevelt branch of the Natales is one of the richest and most powerful in the country. They're the tail that wags the dog, so to speak."

"Are you talking about Big Nick Vitello?"

"My, you've been a busy little beaver. No one will admit it, but Big Nick Vitello is the second most powerful don in the country, after his cousin Joe Natale. And Joe's in jail for at least five more years. Big Nick runs the show, in the garbage, trucking and drug businesses, at least, which are where most of the money is."

"How long has this been going on in Roosevelt County?"

"Since long before USE showed up. This county, if you look at a New York City watershed map, lies just outside the protected area where drinking water for the city is collected. There are no reservoirs up here. With swift access to the city via good roads, it has always been considered a prime municipal dumping ground, like northeastern New Jersey and Long Island before the feds cracked down. As I've said, the same mobs that control dumping in those places control it up here. You should listen to some of the wiretaps I have of conversations recorded in landfill and C&D offices all over Roosevelt County. Stuff that would curl your hair. Before they figured out they could resell toxic waste, the Italians would just dump it in with the garbage.

"When USE came in during the '60s and early '70s, they tried at first to ignore the Italians. They just dumped poisons down their own drains until they were caught polluting the aquifers. They paid those million-dollar fines and finally acquiesced, hiring mob carters to take their used chemicals away. The carters naturally were caught dumping them in landfills. When the landfills were closed the carters increased their 'cocktailing,' dumping toxin-laced debris as fill for construction projects, in short-term C&D dumps, in hollowed-out mines, on farms at night, anywhere they could slip someone a few bucks to look the other way. Over the past 20 years, of course, they've gotten smart and created a whole new industry out of it. The moving company was created to help them accomplish this. It's their golden age.

"It's not just Italians anymore, it's the Irish, too, along with a few Russians and other eastern Europeans. Your friend Bill McNally and his crew, known as the 'Route 77 Gang,' are almost equal partners with Big Nick; some say they're even more ambitious. They control the local coke and heroin trade, which is significant. They're building a meth business.

"Between them the two gangs also control the legal system and the local and state governments. Money from their covert industries flows into local and state GOP and Democratic coffers through the big Pinksterkill law firms, which split the money up into small, untraceable donations through hundreds of bogus businesses with bogus Post Office boxes. They pay off the police and the sheriffs, jump in and handle cases whenever there's trouble and cover everything up, and everybody's happy. The law firms also act as brokers for the industrial development bond pyramid scheme, which is where they make most of their big money.

"State government is rife with mob influence. In New York and most other big states, you can't get elected governor without the mob's help. Now, of course, the mob has the keys to the statehouse. Governor Pollock is Polish in name only. His father was three-quarters Irish and his mother is 100 percent Siciliano. His maternal grandfather was a capo in the Natale family, and his father's father ran a trucking and bootlegging racket for Dutch Schultz. He's every bit a product of the Roosevelt County Irish-Italian mobs as Big Nick and Bill McNally are. He has a foot in both houses.

"Up until the current Republican administration in Washington, we were building a case against the Natale and Route 77 mobs that was being looked at by the U.S. Attorney's office for the Southern District of New York. Now that the U.S. attorney has been reassigned to antiterrorist activities, it looks as if our case is dead in the water. The two gentlemen you met recently were working with me, on their own time off the FBI payroll. That's why they didn't give you their card."

"Has all you've just told me been proven?"

"Not all of it. The things you've read about in Sheila's and my report have all been verified, including the highway department stuff. Beyond that, it's a large job, and we don't have the resources in this climate where all the money is going to fight terrorism. The trade center attacks were a godsend to the people who commit domestic crimes, I must say.

"We have a world of circumstantial evidence, and enough hard evidence to open a case. Like you, we've followed trucks delivering drums from the USE plants to the Janssen warehouses, where they are presumably sorted and stored. From then on they play a complicated shell game. We have followed smaller delivery trucks from the warehouses to fenced-in, dog-patrolled yards behind auto repair shops, hardware stores and other businesses, where the trucks may sit unopened and unmoved for up to a week. Then another driver is dropped off who drives a truck to the loading dock of a paving contractor or a heating oil company or whatever. We've watched them unload drums from the trucks.

"We now are beginning to understand their patterns. We've followed trucks that leave the warehouse and drive around aimlessly, ultimately to end up doubling back to the airport, backing into a hangar building, out of sight. We've observed cargo planes emerging from the same hangar and taking off. We need to get someone inside to observe barrels being loaded onto planes. We have checked the license numbers of trucks and the registration marks of the cargo planes. They belong to shell corporations we've linked to the Route 77 mob.

"In conducting surveillance with our limited resources, we've located what we believe to be three of the Irish gang's local drug mills. We've videotaped traffic in and out of there, and followed vehicles to destinations throughout the mid-Hudson region where drug deals were observed. This was the crux of our case.

"With the FBI and the U.S. attorney's office out of the picture, it is unlikely we'll be able to get anyone else to investigate or prosecute. The DEA has all but closed their mid-Hudson office. All their agents are temporary sky marshals. The state police, sheriff's department and local police departments are all on Mr. Vitello's and Mr. McNally's payrolls. The county DA is Vitello's lawyer's best friend.

"Back to the governor; we think Pollock is involved in drug dealing. We've interviewed some of the illegal aliens he has working for him at his mansion in Indian Hills. They say the head of his state police security detail, a fellow named Commander Robinson, is running drugs right out of the governor's house, using Mexican and Colombian couriers. The Mexicans and Colombians are all donated to the governor by his friend and Vitello's associate Giancarlo Conti, owner of Conti Carting in Pinksterkill. So far we've followed some Route 77 vehicles up to the gates of Pollock's estate, but we can't get inside. State troopers wearing the special SS uniforms of his personal security detail are everywhere, and the entire compound is walled, floodlit and electronically secured. No one in our little group of activists here has ever been offered an invitation to one of Pollock's parties, obviously."

When Nicole excused herself to go to the bathroom, Nate leaned closer to Thirsty. "So, how did you start working with Sheila?"

"Through Congressman Aldrich, whom she approached after a speech he made at a fund-raiser in New York. She said she had information about USE and toxic waste disposal, and Evan set her up with me. She was indispensable, and actually got us focusing on USE, Janssen, and by extension the whole Roosevelt crowd with Big Nick. Before that, Evan and I had been focused on the downstate Natales and their Connecticut associate, Ducky Durso. She was a real firecracker, that one."

Belinda Strossner frowned, but Thirsty ignored her.

"I daresay, you really dropped the ball with that girl, old chap. She was awfully put out by your shenanigans, and was about ready to kick you to the curb more than once. I miss her dreadfully, as I'm sure you do as well.

"You seem to have landed on your feet, though," he whispered as Nicole returned. "Lucky bastard."

* * *

The evening deteriorated somewhat as a few of the remaining partygoers, including Thirsty, exceeded their personal limits. Most of the celebrity guests had long since disappeared, except for Jack Danforth and Allen Scott, who were battling inappropriately for Nicole's attentions while Belinda and Thirsty continued regaling Nate with far too much information for his overloaded, mildly pickled brain to process. They were apparently trying to recruit him into their informal network, to attend sporadic meetings and conduct surveillance from his position as a journalist. While flattered, Nate was pretty sure he didn't want to join any organization, no matter how star-studded or well meaning. He would be glad to share information with them, however.

Nate was getting progressively miffed at the behavior of the two celebrity mashers, who were beginning to act like a *Hollywood Squares* version of Mark Zweiker and Haroon, Nicole's former newsroom nemeses. She had been looking over at Nate with increasing frequency, pleading with her eyes for him to come rescue her. He was just about to do just that when Scott put his hand on Nicole's ass, causing her to back away and into Danforth's waiting embrace. The 72-year-old film star caught her and "inadvertently" grabbed her breast. Nate had seen enough. He excused himself from Thirsty and Belinda's swaying grasp, but was already too late. Nicole had responded with a couple of moves she'd learned in self-defense class, elbowing Danforth in the ribs and kicking Scott in the nuts, yelling: "Motherfuckers! Don't fucking *touch* me!" She was aiming for a blow at Scott's face when Nate raced up.

"OK, folks, I think it's time to break it up."

Danforth was being apologetic. "I'm so sorry, so sorry. Absolutely. I believe I've had a bit too much to drink. You're a lovely young lady, and my hand slipped. I'm just a filthy old dog."

But Scott, fully inebriated, had hardly felt Nicole's groin kick, and was unrepentant. "What the fuck did you do that for?" he slurred. "We were just getting to know each other. Fucking bitch."

That was all Nate needed to hear. He had always hated Byron & Scott for their watered-down, white bread appropriation of Marvin Gaye's sound. The blonde-mulleted Scott, always sucking his cheeks in and striking calculatedly gay runway poses, had been the worst offender. Nate would especially bristle when, back in the days before the Ex-Men when he was struggling as a solo act, women would come up to him after shows saying, "I love your voice. You sound just like Allen Scott."

Nate reached deep inside his resentment and sucker-punched the faded pop star in his permanent sneer, knocking him out cold. "Fool, you need to keep your hands off the ladies," he admonished the unconscious form splayed on the couch in front of him. "And don't be calling my woman a bitch."

Amid the ensuing confusion, Nicole smiled a little conspiratorial half smile that made Nate love her even more. He felt cleansed by his sudden act of violence. "It's OK," he said to the visibly embarrassed Jack Danforth. "I've been drunk once or twice myself. Just get home safe. Let's go, Nicole."

Tended by Belinda, Scott was coming to, not remembering a thing. After hatching plans with Belinda and Thirsty for them to steal Scott's and Danforth's car keys, Nate and Nicole left. Thirsty promised to sleep it off on Belinda's couch. Nicole had been drinking orange juice and tonic water mocktails for the past two hours in anticipation of having to drive home. "That was fucking unbelievable," said Nate, once safely ensconced in the passenger seat of Nicole's dark green 1998 Jetta.

"Poor baby. I'm sorry I caused you so much grief," said Nicole, still smirking. "I'm just not good at handling scumbags. You could have paid more attention earlier."

"I'm sorry, I thought you were OK. Danforth seemed harmless and Scott's just a washed-up old queen. I had no idea you were about to be raped. I was busy being brainwashed."

"No shit, Sherlock. I'm starting to get as paranoid as you. It's like we were being tag-teamed: divided and conquered. I'm sorry, Nate, but those people all scared me. Not just the two creeps. I felt like I was in *Rosemary's Baby* or something. Did you believe a thing they said? It was all just too outrageous."

"Well, I do accept a lot of what Thirsty says. I know too much already to discount it. And that guy Hamilton Canard is all right, too, for a Brahmin. Aldrich I don't trust. He's shifty, and I get the feeling he's playing both sides. Did you see how uncomfortable he looked when Thirsty started talking about that bond shit? I bet he's up to his ears in that.

"But that crowd of celebrity sycophants really disturbs me. I just think Belinda's got delusions of grandeur, and is trying to create a little cult of personality around herself and Thirsty, financed by a bunch of rich dilettantes who get to pretend they're secret agents. And if I didn't know better, I'd think old Thirsty was banging Mrs. Strossner. They act like alcoholic newlyweds."

"Yeah, well if you ask me, she likes *you*. Fucking Mother Nature. You know, it's no wonder fundamentalists and right wingers are taking over the world. These '60s rejects are all such fucking assholes."

He loved her, he loved her, he loved her. Beautiful, smart, sexy, funny, and tough. And loyal. Loyal Royal. At least so far. He'd had nothing to worry about from a couple of washed up has-beens, anyway. But what was he if not a washed up never-was? Nate still couldn't believe his good fortune, which naturally gave him the impulse to test it once again.

"It's true. I'd be inclined to give Thirsty a break, though. I don't think he's really one of them. He's just following what's left of his cock, and getting used by them. I'm not going to join their little club, but I'm going to take what I can get from them. Besides, I think I can learn more in the long run from hanging out with Big Nick. I think I am going to offer to write his memoirs."

"Jesus, Nate. You're crazy."

"Will you marry me?"

"No, not until you're through playing with mobsters. Is it really worth it, Nate? Even if the whole world is full of toxic shit, what can *you* do about it?"

"I don't know yet. I just think people have to know."

"I hate to break it to you, Nate, but nobody's going to believe you. It's too much to handle. What are people supposed to do, move to Mars? Stop buying computers and hair spray?"

"Maybe."

Nate thought about Sheila's troubled face, and remembered his solemn, secret vow. He thought about Rico and his cancer-plagued family and pictured the beautiful redheaded opera singer and the human bowler screaming in flames in the Gotham fire. He thought about how his father had told him of his boyhood diversion of diving into the Hudson for nickels. The old man had said he could see them floating all the way to the river bottom after tossing them in. Nate remembered his own thwarted attempts to reconnoiter with the river, which by the time he was born had been polluted into a thick, foul-smelling orange sludge. It had always irked Nate that this birthright was taken from him. He remembered when they flattened his childhood wonderland of sand dunes and scrub pines to make way for a gigantic shopping mall and a surrounding forest of McMansions.

He recalled the hellish scenes of industrial America from his many road trips, and the shock of having encountered them for the first time. The almost unbroken chains of poison-belching oil refineries, chemical factories and plastics plants lining Interstate 95 from New York to Philadelphia and beyond. The barren, sooty wastes of Pennsylvania and West Virginia. The brutal, breakneck urbanization and industrialization of vast stretches of Massachusetts, Connecticut, Delaware, Virginia, North Carolina, Georgia, Florida, Louisiana, Ohio, Illinois, Michigan, Texas, Kansas, Missouri, Arizona, New Mexico and much of the West Coast.

He recalled approaching Chicago and Gary, Indiana from the east on a sunny day, marveling at the mountainous black cloud in the distance.

The cloud loomed larger and larger until, upon entering it, day turned into night and, once through Gary, night turned to dusk. Hours later you emerged into sunlight on the other side, deep into the central Illinois farmland, looking back at the dark dome and wondering how anybody survived in there. He remembered flying into L.A. across the Sierras on a similarly cloudless day, encountering the endless sulfur-colored smog blanket for the first time. And an entire valley the size of Rhode Island east of Ventura, California, carpeted with greenish black smoke blown in from the offshore oil fields, and crowds of people milling about in the gloom at a festive carnival as if everything were hunky-dory.

These images, smells and sounds had been festering in his brain for years, eating at his helpless soul. Now he had a way to strike back.

And then Nate remembered something from even longer ago: a forgotten snippet of a song he had written as an angry, raw-nerved 16-year-old, before life had intervened and tempered his idealism. It was strange that he had ever felt anything so unabashedly:

Gone across the purple plains
My soul is drawn
To the breath of dark green forests I belong
To America
My flesh and bone have made their home with you
But my dreams turn to mud
You're a slave to wretched thieves who suck your blood
In your pain you shed a tear that turns to flood
I want to break those chains that bind you
I'm putting my life behind you
I'll help you
Scream your anger
Until I die...

Lies surround the castle walls where I was born
Between greed and God these troubled times are torn
Like a wounded heart
Divided creatures lay their claims on you

And the sky is turning brown
And I can't believe it hasn't tumbled down
Upon the heads of those whose conscience can't be found
In the weakness of their spirit
They don't have the strength to hear it
When you're trying to
Scream your anger
When you can't contain
The anger and the pain
I'll help you
Scream your anger
Until I die...

The passion that had prompted such a youthful burst of overblown hyperbole was back, and wasn't going away without a fight.

"Nicole, this is where I'm at. I've sat on my ass my whole life and watched them turn this beautiful country to shit. And now I've just been told that it's worse than I imagined in my wildest dreams. Somebody's dropped a gauntlet at my feet and I picked it up. I don't know what I'm going to do, but I'm going to do something, believe me."

For all her intelligence and sensitivity, Nicole had grown up in a time when the unacceptable was commonplace. Binghamton was already a land of supermalls, subdivisions and boarded up, PCB-infested government buildings when she was born. She felt no corresponding sense of loss.

"Please, Nate. You sound like a fucking martyr, and you're scaring me. We'll be all right. We don't take drugs. We don't use anal lube. We can drink spring water. We'll get an electric car. Please don't do this. The so-called good guys are assholes, and couldn't give two shits about you. And the bad guys are killers. You could get *killed*, Nate. I just found you. I love you, goddammit. I don't want to lose you."

"I don't know, baby. We'll see."

CHAPTER EIGHTEEN
FORGIVE ME, FATHER, FOR I HAVE SINNED

Sheila would have creamed herself over Nick Vitello's drawing room, thought Nate. It had a 20-foot-high, 40-panel mahogany beamed ceiling, massive Cippolino marble fireplaces at each end and four stately Georgian floor-to-ceiling windows overlooking a picturesquely hibernating English garden. From the sunny garden wall looking inward across a polished oak floor strewn stylishly with Oriental rugs and mostly Victorian and Edwardian antiquities, one was confronted with an imposing wall-to-wall, ceiling-high display of leather-bound English, American, French, Italian, German, Russian and Classical literature, bisected by an elegantly carved mahogany entrance arch.

The chamber resembled an interior on the A-deck of the Titanic. An ancient grand piano, perched on massive legs with carved claw-and-ball feet, hunkered like a potentate's funeral bier in one corner, guarded by a pair of life-sized, gold-turbaned blackamoor statues wielding wrought-iron whips. An enormous Victorian gilt-framed mirror hung over each fireplace on the north and south forest-green lacquered walls between recessed alabaster busts of a quartet of laurel-wreathed Roman emperors, making the already vast room seem even larger. The only thing Nate had ever seen that approached it in megalomaniacal, king-of-the-universe grandeur was the Monet, van Gogh and Picasso-bedecked entrance hall of *Penthouse* publisher Bob Guccione's East 67th Street townhouse mansion, where as a bike messenger he had once dropped off a package.

With his right hand, Big Nick fondled the joystick of his lilac-purple Jazzy 1103 Mini Power Chair, while his equally knobby, liver-spotted left hand, its emaciated pinky swimming inside a heavy diamond-encrusted gold ring, rested on a gleaming rosewood parquetry-topped Edwardian card table, wrapped around a tall glass of fresh squeezed carrot juice. His hairy nostrils were hooked via a plastic hose to an oxygen tank, jerry-rigged to the back of his hi-tech wheelchair with duct tape and adjustable hose clamps. A voluminous pale green silk bathrobe enveloped his slouching, birdlike frame, and on his feet he wore a pair of fleece-lined crocodile leather slippers.

Nate sat across from Vitello on a thickly upholstered mahogany settee, balancing his notebook and pen on his lap as he test-recorded a new 120-minute videotape in the hoary old Sony VHS video camera he had borrowed from Augie O'Malley. Big Nick had gone for Nate's suggestion that they videotape the sessions. "I respect your right to edit what I tape before I quote from it," said Nate. "We can erase anything you don't want in. It's just that it's easier to pick up what you're saying when I can remember what I've *seen* as much as what I've *heard*. You're fucking Italian, all right? A lot of what you communicate is visual."

That was putting it mildly, thought Nate.

* * *

Nate was not, as he had been urged to, wearing a wire under his bulky wool sweater, courtesy of his new roan G-man buddy Charles Overlook, to whom he had a fortnight before been re-introduced during the course of a drunken all-night brainstorming orgy with the British expatriates Thirsty and Martin, at a tiny back-street pub in downtown Hudson.

It had been a banner evening: a small group of stateless, disenfranchised alcoholics plotting murky deeds against the status quo of the evil empire in which they had found themselves trapped. The drunker he got, the more Nate had relaxed into his new persona as a low-rent international man of mystery: as border-free and devoid of patriotic impulses as any pan-Atlantic USE or BP executive, or Munich-based Al Qaeda cell member. Before the night was over, this fledgling ad hoc committee had sketched out hazy plans for a series of intelligence gathering assaults on three Janssen Movers warehouses and on a suspected illicit chemical export business at the Roosevelt County Airport.

The group was most pleased with the unexpected entrée into Nick Vitello's fabulous Georgian hilltop fortress, thanks to Nate's serendipitous invitation into the storied mobster's world. Thirsty and Overlook had been salivating over the prospect of the information Nate would provide them over the next few months, and were extremely persuasive in trying to get Nate to wear a wire so they could listen in. At one point before passing out, he had even agreed.

But after a spate of drunken nightmares in which he was either swimming naked across a lake stocked with carnivorous predators or hovering in flight just out of reach of the angry, outstretched arms of his dead father, Nate had awakened the next morning with mixed allegiances. He was not in the business of martyring himself for someone else's cause. Fuck them, he thought, this is *my* fucking neck. Besides, I *like* Big Nick. And he likes me; that much is obvious. I need to be straight up with him if I'm going to get the real story. He'll be able to sense if I'm being duplicitous and wearing a wire. As I promised—and failed—to do with Rico, I will dedicate myself to this man for the short period he has left, and hope he trusts me enough to tell me what I need to know between the lines. There'll be plenty of time for betrayal, should it ever come to that.

* * *

Here I sit, thought Nate, in the belly of the beast; or one of a growing number of beasts, anyway. Yesterday, sitting on the same settee during what was supposed to have been an air-clearing and negotiating session, he hadn't been so sure he'd be at this point 24 hours later, much less alive. He was relieved he hadn't been wearing a wire. The distraction of worrying about it might have gotten him killed.

"Look, you know what I am. I run some rackets: some good, some bad. I'm not proud of everything I do, but I take care of my *family*," Nick had begun, gesticulating with his left hand while holding Nate's writing, eating and bishop-flogging appendage in his spindly right paw and looking him squarely in the eyes. "You and me, we don't need a contract. My word is good. If I die before you're through, I've already left you a grand for every day this takes."

Nick then had tightened his grip gently, almost imperceptibly, and leaned closer. "But what I need to know is, who the fuck are *you*? This is my fucking *life* we're talking about. I want you to come clean with me. Trust is the thing. I know some things about you that you don't know I know. Tell me the rest, or we're done right here."

Vitello's kindly uncle visage had dissolved into an icy stare Nate had no desire to ever see again. Nate tried to sense whether there was someone standing behind him with a gun pointed at his head. "What do you mean, 'done,' Nick?"

"I don't mean that I'm going to hurt you. I just will not trust you with my legacy here, and you'll go home to the paper and shut the fuck up forever about me and my business. Capeesh?"

"Capeesh." Nate took a deep breath and let go of all trepidation. The precipice toward which he had been sliding had arrived. The only way out was straight down, and Big Nick was holding the parachute.

Something else in the man's eyes told him he'd be all right; not that it really mattered at this point.

"My name is not Jim Olsen."

Nick smiled and released his grip. The sparkle returned to his eyes. "Now we're talkin'. Continue."

"My name is Nate Randall. My parents were killed in a plane crash when I was 16. My father was a contractor. My great-great-great-great-grandfather on my father's side came over on the Mayflower. My mother was three-quarters Italian and a quarter Welsh."

"*Siciliano?*"

"*Napolitan.* She was beautiful, like Sophia Loren. I'm inbred, because her great-great-great-grandfather on her mother's side was the same fucking Pilgrim as my papa's ancestor. He wasn't a Pilgrim, actually. He was a grifter on the run from the law in London, and he started a mutiny on the ship because the fucking Puritans were hoarding all the beer and he was thirsty. He threatened to turn the ship back around. He extorted the Mayflower Compact out of them, bartering their religious freedom for beer and pretzels."

"*Madon.*"

"For the rest of it, after my folks died, I was raised by Italians; my best friend's parents. Mr. DiSalvo was all right. Tough and fair. Reminded me of you."

Nick nodded and began to smile, encouraging him to go on. Nate felt as if he had scored a go-ahead touchdown. He kept his story as personal and heartfelt as possible. The experience was transcendently liberating, like going to confession at the Vatican with the Pope himself ... or maybe the AntiPope.

"My best friend Anthony died in a car accident, and Mr. DiSalvo died of a heart attack a week later. Mrs. DiSalvo's in a home. That's my family. I've kicked around a lot. Social worker, computer programmer, messenger, whatever; but I always played guitar and sang in bands on the side."

"Those are fag jobs. You're not a fag, are you?"

"Yeah, right. No, actually, I'm in mourning. I'll get to that in a minute."

Nick chuckled. "OK, *che grande.* Go on."

"Anyway, I just became a reporter in October. I never wrote before; just read the papers every day, cover to cover, and a lot of books. Encyclopedias, literature, philosophy, history, whatever. Did crossword puzzles. That's my education. Before coming here I was in a rock band in New York for ten years. We had a contract with Arista. We were good. I came up here after my girlfriend died in the trade center. Sheila McNally. You know her father, Bill McNally."

Nate sensed a glint of enmity for McNally in Nick's eyes, and gambled with a truth he could easily have withheld: "Sorry if it bothers you, Nick, but I *hate* Bill McNally. I can't help it. It's personal. It comes from Sheila, who hated him because he fucked her virgin pussy twice a week until she went to prep school. She was working for USE when she died, and she was gathering inside information on the toxic waste dumping business of her old man. She tipped me off about it all just before she went down. I saw her die from her apartment up the street, while I was talking to her on the phone."

"Sorry, kid. Things happen." Nate thought he saw dampness forming in the corner of Nick's left eye.

"Yeah, they do. I read her files and got excited, and decided to come up here and bust heads for her. Carry on her work, so to speak. And while I was packing up to leave, somebody punched my eye out, firebombed my stuff and all Sheila's files, and left me for dead. I think it was one of McNally's guys. I hope it wasn't one of yours."

"How could you even think that? Kid, come on," Nick shrugged, palms up, and screwed his mug into a hurt frown. "I'm old school. We don't work like that. If we did, every reporter, cop and prosecutor in the country would be dead already. We only fuck with actual witnesses, scumbags and rats. It's bad business to hurt a civilian, unless absolutely necessary, in a kill-or-be-killed kind of way. It's in the code, which those fucking potato-eaters don't know from. We should never have allowed them in here."

"So you and McNally aren't friends, I take it?"

"Not so fast, kid," snapped Nick. "We were talkin' about *you*, here." Any shred of coldness was gone from his manner, however. If anything, Nate had begun to sense a cocoon of warmth enveloping him, emanating from the man's benign, smiling countenance.

Nate finished his story, telling Nick about nearly everything, including what he thought he knew about the mobster. He left out only that he had a girlfriend and that he was working with Thirsty and Martin and had been considering wearing a wire provided by a loose-cannon FBI agent.

"I don't blame you for your life," said Nate, courting disaster one last time in the name of full disclosure. "I'm nobody to judge. But I do know that some of what you do, with toxic waste particularly, is giving people cancer, including yourself, and probably me, someday. It pisses me off. This is what I came up here to fight against."

Nick did not flinch. His face retained its warmth.

"So now I have all this information about what a fucking clusterfuck we're living in here, and I don't know what to do with it," said Nate. "I feel like the only thing to do is write about it. Not in a fucking newspaper or magazine somebody will toss in the garbage and forget. In a book. I don't want to change the fucking world. I just want people to hurt as bad as I do about what kind of a fucked up place this world is."

"All right, you can shut up now. We're good. We're on the same fucking page, kid, believe it or not. I'm not proud of everything I've done, like I said. I don't have much time to make it right, but I'm tryin'. I'm glad you came down here, whoever the fuck you are."

"Nate."

"Yeah, Nate. I think I'll call you Jimmy anyway."

"Sure."

"I don't know if you noticed in here, but I love books."

"Yeah, I did. That's some collection."

"What you don't know is I have read most of them. I taught myself, like you."

"That's something."

"Yeah. And the books I've been attracted to lately, I gotta wonder if I've gone soft. Ethical philosophy. Plato. Aristotle. About waking up and starting to do good, no matter that it took a world of shit to get you to where you were able to think about it. This guy George Soros. I just read a biography of him, hot off the press. He's like a fucking billionaire, already, more dough than God, and he's out there spending millions on building a fucking water district in the middle of a fucking war zone so snipers won't be able to shoot women trying to fill their fucking jars in the town square. Now *that's* a life well lived, right? That kind of shit inspires me.

"But I'm old and sick. I'm almost out of gas. Like I said, I've done a lot of good things; and some not so good. I feel like if I could get some of this off my chest and into a book... Not just about me, but about where I fit in the proper con... con..."

"Context?"

"You're a smart kid. You got a gift. Context. If I could do that, write a book, teach some things, I would feel a lot better about dying."

"Why did you choose me? I never wrote anything bigger than 5,000 words in a newspaper."

"Because you got a spark, kid. What I see in all those books on the wall there. That bird story, for starters. You didn't just cut that farmer a new pussy, you saw what he went through and told his side. People cried for him, even though they wanted to wring his skinny neck. That's fucking art.

Put all your newspaper stories together and that's a book already—in what, five months you been at it?"

"A year," corrected Nate.

"Whatever the fuck it is. You'll be all right. I don't know if you notice, but I'm not surrounded by rocket scientists around here. Angie and Fiona are good girls, with hearts of gold like their mother, but they're dumb as rocks. My son Sammy was smart like you; he was tops in his class at Dutch Hollow Prep School and had a scholarship to Harvard already, but he's gone."

"Gone?"

"Dead. Sixteen years old, of a heart attack."

"Jesus. I'm sorry."

"Like I said, things happen. I could have gone outside, but I'd lose control. I don't like any of these so-called writers today. Hemingway's dead. The book business is run by PC dicksuckers and women, and accountants with no balls. When we do this, I'm gonna publish myself, through my own network. Fuck Oprah. Barnes & Noble's will put my book in the window, or face the consequences."

Nate imagined the consequences.

"By the way, if you do this, I can't have you workin' at no newspaper no more. I'll be buyin' out your contract, like George Steinbrenner. You'll be mine for a year: eight hours a day, five days a week, five grand a week. That's over a quarter mil for sittin' in that chair there, listenin' to me talk and makin' me sound as articulate as I feel inside my head. You want to do this or what?"

Nate didn't have to think twice. This was what he had dreamed of; to gain the confidence of the one man who knew everything. Sheila had given him the map to the Holy Grail; this motherfucker *was* the Holy Grail. He had learned all he could from the outside looking in; he now had the considerable resources of a veteran congressional gumshoe and a disgruntled FBI agent to draw upon on the investigative front. What did he need the newspaper job for now, except more useless ego massage?

"Yes, Nick. It would be an honor. You know I'd do it for nothing. Can you give me a month to give notice and tie a few things up? We can start part-time until then."

"Sure thing, kid. Just one more thing." Nick was throwing out another line, now, fishing for something else. "I'm gonna have a man on you, for protection. McNally knows about you by now. I don't trust what that fucking Mick scumbag might try to do to you on your way home. You know that if his daughter hadn't gotten crushed in the trade center, he was ready to fucking *kill* her? *Kill* his own flesh and blood, who he had already raped and deflowered?"

Nate's blood, which was already running hot, began to boil.

"He said she was out of control," continued Nick, hooking his prey like the professional he was. Of all the emotions, the desire for revenge was the most malleable. Sure this kid was just a writer, but he had something else going, he could tell. First of all, he was fearless. Something violent was lurking in his gut, waiting to explode. Even if the book didn't work out, he would be useful in other ways.

"He told me he'd had his boys watching her 24/7 and was moving in 'any day now,'" continued Nick. "He was pissed because he heard she tried to sell her story to *90 Minutes* and the fucking *Times*. Who knows, he might have even paid for the towelheads' flying lessons and plane tickets, whaddya think about that?"

In his paranoid state, Nate had already thought about that. Until now the idea had been too ridiculous to contemplate.

"So you might even think about moving in here for a while, for your own good. I got a spare bedroom."

The offer of protection was unexpected, but not entirely unwelcome. Sure it would put a crimp in his lifestyle, but what good was personal freedom when you were using it to destroy yourself? Nate imagined himself relaxing into the bosom of Nick Vitello's paternal embrace, free from fear and free to pursue the knowledge that he would later use to save the world from itself. The only problem, and it was a big one, was what he was going to tell Nicole about all this.

"And by the way," said Nick. "I'll know if you're fucking with me. If you are loyal and show me respect, I'll treat you like the son I lost, I promise on my mother's grave. But if you fuck with me, I will make you regret it before you die. Capeesh?"

Nate's head began to hurt.

"Capeesh."

CHAPTER NINETEEN
MORE MOVING AND STORAGE

On his way to work Monday morning, where with a heavy heart he would hand in his resignation and ask Dave for a light workload for his last two weeks, Nate kept the sadness at bay by plotting and re-plotting his immediate future. He had effectively one month in which to wrap up whatever business he thought he could get away with before his self-imposed exile to Big Nick's Ostia fortress. Most important, though, he had to formulate a plan of action regarding Nicole, whom he was suddenly acutely aware had become a liability, at least for the duration of his intensifying jihad. Her caring about him could constrict his freedom to act rashly and decisively, and his caring about her could get her killed. He had to harden up quick, which would mean cutting her loose for the time being. He was not looking forward to it.

As an act of appreciation for his success in making his publisher look especially good recently, Nate had been invited by Winnie Babson to accompany him to a St. Patrick's Day bash at the governor's riverside mansion in Indian Hills, where he planned at the very least to do some serious reconnaissance between bites of shrimp and caviar. And he had a number of felonies planned with Thirsty, Martin and Charles Overlook: one a break-in at the Roosevelt County Airport hangar owned by 7&7 Associates LLP, a shell entity set up by William T. McNally. They would be sampling the contents of drums and photographing any documents in the small business office there that might verify 7&7 business involving exotic destinations in or around the Gulf of Mexico and points south. They would also be installing telephone wiretaps and listening devices.

If that one succeeded, another criminal operation was to be a similar break-in at whichever Janssen warehouse that, following a preliminary investigation, would be deemed by the group to possess the highest potential for smoking-gun evidence of illegal misappropriation of waste chemicals.

And then, of course, there were the headaches. They had started the afternoon of Nate's pivotal confrontation with Big Nick, and they weren't going away without help. Refusing to think about it, he bought a big bottle of aspirin and began drinking more heavily. It seemed to do the trick.

* * *

"Jesus. You're *sure* about this?" Dave trembled and arched his eyebrows in grief.

"As sure as I can be about anything," said Nate, the emotions welling into his head, ratcheting up the already considerable pressure behind his eyes another notch. "Look, I'm going to miss you guys. I'm going to miss this place. It's the best life I've ever had. You, Nootch, Rick, Nicole. Everybody. All the money and power and prestige..."

Dave laughed and snuffled, reached into his shirt pocket and pulled out a filthy, wadded-up ball of Kleenex, blew his nose in it and dabbed at the ducts beneath his smudged glasses.

"But this is what I came up here for. I don't have any choice. The motherfucker really *knows* everything. Outside of McNally, who I'll never get close to, he's the key."

"Yeah, I guess so. I was pretty sure you weren't long for this place. So are you just going to write Nick's memoir and be done with it? What about the rest of the story?" Ever the journalist, Dave had long dreamt of publishing something worthy of a Pulitzer. He had seen it happen with lesser stories, to lesser news organizations.

"I have a book in mind," said Nate, half lying to himself, as well as to Dave. In fact, a book was no longer his number-one priority. Along with the growing pressure in his head had come the kernel of an idea that he was suddenly in a position to make a very real difference in some as-yet-undetermined, but ultimately concrete way. *Real* change, through action. He was a mere vessel, really, wasn't he? A vessel through which change would come. I mean, look at what eight fucking amateurs did to the fucking trade center, he thought. They very likely had started something that, as did the little band of 22 comparably amateur Bosnians who conspired to kill Archduke Franz Ferdinand in 1914, would bring down an empire and change the map of the world forever. Could he not do the same? Was he not getting closer to the soul of the monstrous evil that held the nation, and perhaps a good part of the world, in its thrall? Wasn't he attending a party Monday night with *at least* three participants—Hiram C. Pollock, William McNally and USE chairman and CEO Arthur Schmidt—who were responsible for the waking nightmares of countless millions?

"I think I'll call it *Wasted*."

Dave laughed. "That's great. Maybe we could run a few installments."

"Maybe," said Nate, his head pounding. "Maybe."

* * *

Nate had been studying Janssen Movers relentlessly, even before joining forces with Thirsty and the gang. He had looked up its history in the Roosevelt County Clerk's files. He had traveled to the state college library at New Paltz, using its free Lexis/Nexis system to ferret out news, court cases and business profiles on the company and its principals. He had hit up Nootch to do some clandestine snooping in the *Urinal's* automated morgue files and had already spent hours physically casing each of its facilities. He had become as expert an authority on the history and current state of the company as anyone on earth outside William T. McNally himself.

There was a tantalizingly challenging aspect to the specter of Janssen Movers, Nate had discovered. It was a puzzle to be solved. These people were not your garden-variety, wetlands-polluting lowlifes. They were highly intelligent, resourceful and extremely self-aware, to the degree that they had left a dizzyingly complex trail of clues to their identities, motives and activities. Or maybe, thought Nate, he was just going insane.

He wasn't. One Tuesday evening, Thirsty called Nate at work. "Can you get away for a cocktail tomorrow? I have someone I want you to meet."

"How about dinner at the Delafield? Pick me up in back of the Dutch Hollow Deli at 6 o'clock."

Nate and Thirsty had devised a series of stock plans for shedding the surveillance that Big Nick was intermittently putting on Nate. This particular plan involved Nate riding his bike to work, as he did on many days, then taking a constitutional health ride around dinnertime. Being a picturesque walking town, Dutch Hollow was blessed with a maze of back alleys, pathways and pedestrian-only thoroughfares through which a cyclist could easily traverse to lose a car-bound pursuer. Behind the deli was a parking lot fed by an alley that ran parallel to Market Street, serving the delivery traffic of its westward blocks of businesses. When Nate locked his bike on a fence pole next to the deli's dumpster, Thirsty was there waiting in his car with an elderly passenger wearing a red hooded sweatshirt. Nate recognized the stranger immediately. He was Mona Levy's Dutch Hollow can man.

* * *

Joe Aquino had toiled at USE in Pinksterkill from 1962 until 1980, when he went to work for his fellow chemical engineers Loveland and Judith Aiche, in an exciting new venture. The duo was forming a USE spin-off company: Amorphous Recycling.

"They saw a crying need and filled it," mumbled Aquino as he munched unappetizingly on a chicken wing, picking at his dentures with a fork between bites. "They formed a company of trained chemists like myself working outside the box, using our skills to thwart what we all thought was a cumbersome and stifling environmental bureaucracy. We took used chemicals that would be wasted by being burnt to cinders in some far off incinerator, diverted them and began figuring out what wondrous applications we could find for them through results-oriented engineering. We were an experiment in recycling technology. We had no idea at the time what it would turn into."

"Of course, none of what you were doing was legal, even then, I presume," said Thirsty.

"Technically, no. But, like I said, it was experimental, supposedly funded by USE. During the course of my employment I became aware that they were using our technological advances and selling the fruits of our labors on the black market, without going through an approval process with the EPA and so forth. They were hiding what we were doing under the umbrella of a reputable 'moving' company, with its own warehouses and fleet of trucks. They were making drugs."

Nate already knew about the Aiches through his research. Their names were on their company's recording documents in the county clerk's files, and Thirsty had told him they were former chemical engineers at USE. "Amorphous" was such an odd name for a moving company that it had led him to wondering. He had imagined the Aiches' sense of nerdy, esoteric humor influencing their choice of a name. He had embarked on a long, digressive web search for clues to the Aiches' personalities. In the course of traipsing down many a fruitless research cul-de-sac, some of it within the labyrinthine domain of USE's own web presence, Nate had discovered many obscure facts, few of which made much sense until now.

"Was 'amorphous' a possible reference to 'amorphous silicon technology?'" asked Nate.

Aquino looked at Nate with astonishment. Thirsty smiled the smile of a proud uncle. "How would you know that? Amorphous silicon is the display technology that's the benchmark for every computer, video and TV screen in the world. I worked for Loveland in the 1970s in the group that developed it. It was his crowning achievement."

"I thought it was something like that."

Aquino shook his head. "The Aiches were quite a legend. Did you know how they got their last name?"

Nate's head began to hurt. He took a swig of beer. "No. Tell me."

"They weren't married in the early days, in the '60s. Judith was Loveland's assistant. He was Loveland Breen, and she Judith Greenfeld. They were sex fiends, totally in defiance of company policy. We'd always find them with their pants down, rutting in the corner of a storage room or something. They both legally adopted the name upon marrying. 'Aiche' is an acronym."

"Wait. Does it mean 'American Institute of Chemical Engineers?'" Nate had recently done a Yahoo search on "Aiche," which brought up only the names of three Frenchmen in the midst of more than 50,000 hits for the institute's acronym, "AIChE." He had thought it was more than a coincidence, but he was sleepy and half in the bag at the time and had forgotten about it.

Once again Aquino's mouth dropped open, this time exposing a disgusting glob of masticated chicken. The degree of this young fellow's obsession was almost frightening to him. Thirsty just sat and chuckled, like James Earl Jones in a Verizon commercial.

"Yes, yes it does. I'd say you've been doing your homework. I'm surprised you didn't already know about *me*."

"Sorry. I'm just getting up to speed. I haven't been doing this that long. So what 'applications' did you work on?"

"Well, everything the company does now. Simple filtering, some denaturing. Research into common industrial applications for USE's primary waste chemicals: benzene, acetone, perchloroethylene, trichlorethylene, trichloroethane, toluene, polyvinyl chloride and methylene chloride. Cheap, simple solutions for preparing waste for reintroduction into the economy wherever possible, as opposed to just throwing it away. You'd be surprised at what can be made from waste solvents. We made wallboard, floor tiles, asphalt, all kinds of cheap stuff to cut fuel oil with, gasoline additives like MTBE, pharmaceuticals, you name it. Somebody made cocaine and methamphetamines as a joke. It wasn't a joke. The Aiches started finding markets for our work. I didn't pay too much attention to the business side, until Bill McNally started sniffing around."

Nate's heart was racing. He felt faint, and took another gulp.

"I grew up in Dutch Hollow. Bill McNally was bad news. In 1988, he started coming by at odd hours, talking to Loveland and Judith. Our results-oriented engineering breakthroughs had apparently attracted him. He was salivating over the potential bonanza of waste chemical sales. Of cheap solvents to make drugs. I'd already started getting spooked about what we were doing, and when I heard his intentions were serious, I knew I'd better get out. I took an early retirement."

"McNally was the top dog at Upstate Carting at the time," interjected Thirsty. "The Route 77 gang's suburban New York flagship. It's now part of Scientific Waste. Upstate had taken over Conti Carting, where McNally had come up. They still handled 50 percent of USE's toxic business the old-fashioned way—dumping it in landfills. McNally must have talked his bosses into it because in 1988 Amorphous was bought out by McDonald Movers, a New Jersey company also run by the Route 77 syndicate. They renamed it 'Janssen,' and made it look like a real moving company, paying a franchise fee to Associated, the big national chain. They painted 'Associated' logos on all their trucks. The Aiches were kept on as partners."

"That much I knew," said Nate, essentially talking to himself.

"In fact, the Aiches and their USE patrons resisted at first," continued Thirsty. "But McNally sent his boys over to strong-arm them and they ended up giving McDonald 60 percent of Amorphous. Records show that McNally left Upstate Carting and was given the title of President and Operations Manager of the new Janssen Moving and Storage, which was awarded an exclusive, multimillion-dollar contract to 'transport' all of USE's chemical waste. It was either that or the Aiches and a few USE executives would have been singin' with the fishes."

"So I was right," said Nate, musing about the birth of Janssen Movers. The company now had everything, he realized—the technical know-how to exploit and find new uses for its bottomless trove of unnatural resources, and the mob muscle to do the "marketing" and "business development."

"Could I ask you a personal question?" said Nate to Aquino, who was wiping reddish stains off his puckered chin.

"Sure."

"How come you don't have cancer from monkeying around with chemicals for all those years?"

"Who said I don't?"

"You look pretty healthy to me."

"I battled prostate cancer ten years ago. I've been living as healthy as I can. I drink carrot juice. You never know."

He knocked twice on the polished oak dinner table.

"Well, good luck with that. What about the others in your group? The Aiches?"

"I have a lot of dead ex-co-workers, that's for sure. But have you ever *seen* the Aiches?"

"No."

"Well, you should. They're a sight to behold. They were always be-lievers in scientific solutions to health and longevity. They belong to an immortality spa in California. Biotechnology. Regenerative medicine. Telomerase activation. Cryonics. Both of them have had so many facelifts and body lifts and plastic pieces installed that there's almost nothing left of their original equipment. I heard she had a bone marrow transplant recently. She has non-Hodgkins lymphoma. He's got a platinum septum, a pair of titanium hips and God knows what else. He survived a bout with brain cancer while still in his 40s, don't ask me how."

Nate's head was really throbbing now. It hurt so much he began to swoon.

"But Janssen, Janssen," said Nate deliriously. "Why would they name such a thing 'Janssen'?"

"Finally, something you *don't* know," said Aquino, obviously pleased. "Back in the late '50s, Loveland was a precocious teenager in Europe on a scholarship. He was a research intern under Dr. Paul Janssen, the Belgian super-chemist. He was part of Janssen's team that discovered diphenoxyl-ate, a highly addictive treatment for diarrhea. He idolized Janssen for his work, even though he always said he hated his guts."

"Enough to name an evil, cancer-spreading company after him," said Nate, not noticing the spit shooting out of his mouth onto Aquino's half-eaten chicken wings.

No amount of beer could wipe away Nate's headache. Had he slowed down long enough to examine himself, episodes such as these would have indicated the degree to which his obsessive-compulsive brain had become infected with the very thing he was fighting against. He was becoming toxic.

Thirsty merely smiled, remembering when he had encountered such a phenomenon before, though to a far lesser degree, to be sure. Nate Randall was turning out to be what he had needed all along. A heat-seeking missile; a martyr for the cause. He would have to hurry to get the most out of the poor sap before he spontaneously combusted.

Thirsty didn't know it, but he was not the only one thinking along those lines. He would have to take a number.

* * *

Since being formed, Amorphous/Janssen had been housed in a constantly shifting array of warehouse facilities, all convenient to USE sites. The original Amorphous warehouse/laboratory was adjacent to the East Waterkill plant campus on USE-owned property, rising out of filled swampland with an array of high tension wires soaring overhead. It was torn down in 1983 to make way for a new high school, which was closed for a year in 1986 until drinking water could be piped in from neighboring Lenape Falls. The aquifer beneath the school had been completely fouled by what the DEC termed a "dense, non-aqueous phase liquid."

By the time of the great Route 77 gang takeover in 1988, Amorphous had two facilities, one near the airport in Lenape Falls and one on the border of the towns of Pinksterkill and Rooseveltion. The Rooseveltion warehouse was eventually torn down when the state appropriated the land upon which it sat for the widening of Route 11. The aquifer beneath it was similarly polluted, according to DEC reports, but nothing was done about the vast plume of chlorinated solvents, because the DEC was "not sure" where any of the poison had come from. As filtrated Hudson River drinking water was already being piped into the area for a new shopping center and subdivision being built along the widened roadway, the site was "de-listed," i.e., swept under the rug forever—despite the fact that the air in the vicinity continued to smell like ass-hairs singed with a hot rubber dildo.

Since then, every new Janssen warehouse had cleverly been erected upon the site of a former toxic waste dump abandoned by a long-defunct entity, with its cancerous effluent draining into an already polluted wetland. There currently were three facilities, the first being the imposing flagship home office and warehouse complex in Lenape Falls next to the airport. The second was a large, faceless steel portal framed storage building in a Pinksterkill industrial park, and the newest space was housed in a massive, mall-sized building that the Janssen Company leased from the Town of Pinksterkill.

The Aiches, who by the mid-'90s had cashed out of the black market toxic recycling business, had built the building in 1997, selling it to the town in 1999 for $5.8 million. The town refitted it to house its police department and court facility in one-third of the building, leasing the warehouse two-thirds to Janssen, which was fast running out of room at its other two facilities.

Almost immediately, cops, judges and other people working there complained of bad smells, headaches and dizzy spells. In March 2000, according to the *Journal,* a newly elected Pinksterkill town board finally started to act, hiring a firm to test the air quality in the building; results were found to have been "inconclusive," but the health problems of current and former employees continued to mount. The police union filed a class action suit in January 2001, and that June the police department and court offices were temporarily relocated to a mothballed elementary school until further notice. Janssen quickly leased the remaining third of the building.

The building the Aiches had built, with its history of shakedowns of contractors by the drowned tax assessor Vincent Rocco and others during the $2.5 million retrofitting for town use, was the focus of the federal case against Roosevelt County GOP boss Fat Tony Costello. Over a late breakfast at the Pleasant Plains Diner in the afternoon before the group's first mission, Charles Overlook, who had worked on the Costello case, filled in the many gaps in the *Journal*'s reporting for Nate.

"It was a fucking mess," said Overlook, whose face seemed to be getting progressively puffier every time Nate saw him. "There were so many cans of worms, we ran out of can openers."

Overlook had recently either been dismissed by or had quit the agency; he wouldn't say which, and Nate didn't ask. He was being paid a retainer through Thirsty's congressional task force, which couldn't have been much. He didn't look good. The crisp white shirt and tie and dark suit had been replaced by a threadbare, coffee-stained yellow turtleneck and a plaid sport jacket, and his florid cheeks were glistening with the sticky remains of a Krispy Kreme donut. It looked like dried sperm.

Nate caught sight of himself in the bronze tinted, marbleized mirror tile on the wall of their booth. He didn't look any better. He was hollow-eyed and sallow complexioned from lack of sleep and constant headaches, and his nerves were shot from his having worked very hard to lose his tail all morning. He had finally taken to driving the Seville like a maniac at 50 miles per hour over a series of bone-dry dirt roads through the pleasantly

rural town of Poston, leaving his pursuers in a literal cloud of dust. He had
sideswiped a young deer, watching it limp off into the woods, probably to
die. The coffee wasn't helping the throbbing behind his eyes. He bought
a beer, and used it to swallow three aspirins. His stomach began to hurt
more than his head, so it was an improvement. He was saving the Tylenol
3s he had scored from Rick Parton for later.

"We had a lot of irons in the fire, but we concentrated on their organized bribe-generating network because it was quick and easy to prosecute," Overlook was saying. "We were turning everybody out. We flipped
Rocco, who was just a gofer and a bagman, but they fucking got to him
the day he was going to testify. But luckily, he had already given us this
guy Lindros, the county water commissioner, who gave us Tony Costello.
We were hoping to flip Costello to get to who was behind it all: Big Nick,
McNally and the lawyers and maybe the governor, but the fat fuck took
the heat like a mensch. Sentencing was delayed for eight months until just
last week. When he gets out in a couple of years he's gonna be a fucking hero, and will move up in the organization somehow. What a fucking
waste of time."

"What about the Aiches?"

"They're in with the big boys now. Financiers. But get this shit. They
were a couple of real psychos; sex freaks. Had a swap ring going with
the water commissioner, Lindros. Lindros was the head of it, a real cowboy, with an Elvis pompadour and everything. Elvis brings in this crazy
bull dyke from the Catskills and already has a mistress who's the town
clerk of Pinksterkill, and the five of them—the Aiches and them—have a
five-way *manage-à-twat* with an 8-ball and a bottle of Viagra down at
the Roosevelton pump-house party room. They videotape the whole ugly
thing. It looks like a fucking geriatric cattle stampede."

"Lovely."

"But wait, it gets crazier. Lindros is negotiating with us, and is scared
shitless. He's worried about his mistress, who knows enough to put him
away for a lot of other shit even if he cuts a deal with us on the bribery
stuff. He contracts with the bull dyke to have her kill the bitch, in the parking lot outside of her choir practice at church, right down the street from
here. She shoots her in the puss and dumps the gun by the old Conti dump.

We've been on her and the town clerk as well as Lindros, so we see all this go down, from a respectable distance. We're not supposed to interfere. We see her meet with Lindros right here in this booth we're sitting in a week later, and when they split we move in on her with the state police, and arrest her. We've got the murder weapon, which Lindros had been tearing his hair out looking for in the bushes by the dump. It's his fucking gun. A stupider motherfucker I've never encountered.

"Later, after the dyke confesses, we're trying to beat the state police to Lindros's house, because we know that *he* knows he's in deep shit. We're too late. They run in there like assholes with a whole SWAT team, knocking his door down, and he shoots his chin off while they're coming up the stairs. He misses his fucking brain, so now he's Elvis with no chin and no fucking mouth, either. No tongue. Just a pompadour and a pair of beady eyes looking at you. After three months we're finally able to get him to write down his testimony on a legal pad, so we can fuck with Costello.

"Of course by now Rocco is a dead river rat and Lindros has compromised his testimony by co-murdering his mistress and shooting his chin off. This put a big hole in our case, which was why Costello got off so easy. And we never were able to get anything going on the real shit: the drugs, the money-laundering, the toxic waste black market, the political connections, the governor. I'm sure somebody was putting the screws on us from the top: Senator Viggiani, probably, or maybe somebody even bigger."

"What do you mean?"

"You know what I mean. I'm not stupid enough to say it."

CHAPTER TWENTY
CON AIR

Later that same evening, Charles Overlook and Nate met as they had planned with Thirsty and Martin, who had shed *his* tail by packing a travel bag, careening the Fiesta through every changing red light on Route 31 between Dutch Hollow and the Pinksterkill railroad station and hopping the 5:58 to New York. He got off the train at its second stop at Beaverton, where Thirsty retrieved him.

The four international spies dined at the crowded Ground Round in the Roosevelt Galleria at 7:30 p.m. Overlook handed out the toys, which he had gift-wrapped for the occasion: wireless micro-mini in-ear receivers and miniature voice-activated transmitters for everyone, and a miniature color video camera and head-mounted infrared illumination lamp for Nate. Two pairs of night vision goggles for Nate and himself. High-powered binoculars for Thirsty and Martin. The retired G-man had also put together a small kit of fast entry tools for breaking into just about anything, and was packing a holster-mounted stun gun at his hip beneath his hellish sport coat, along with a .45 caliber semiautomatic with a silencer in another holster under his left armpit.

"What would you gentlemen like to drink?" asked the anorexic, pock-marked waitress, frowning at the mess of exotic electronica and cheap wrapping paper littering her number-seven four-top booth. An old *Popeye* cartoon flickered silently on a screen behind her.

Cognizant of the ordeal ahead, Nate, Overlook and Thirsty curbed their alcoholic tendencies and ordered iced teas. Having been weaned on James

Bond films, Martin under the circumstances couldn't help himself. "One vodka martini, please. Shaken, not stirred."

At 9 p.m. they set out for the airport. Nate had gobbled down a couple of Rick's codeine-laced Tylenol 3s along with his overcooked steak, and he felt sufficiently sedated and pain-free for the first time in a week. Someone had thought it would be a good idea for Martin to drive Overlook's flimsy, nondescript red Saturn alone from the mall to the airport. Actually it was more complicated than that. The job required two cars. Overlook and Thirsty needed to ride together so they could finish plotting strategy. Nate didn't feel comfortable operating machinery with all the contraindicated opiates swimming in his bloodstream, and he made it clear that he would not ride anywhere with Martin at the wheel. In the end, Martin drove Overlook's car by himself, almost without incident. He tailgated Thirsty the entire way, bobbing and weaving conspicuously, terrified of getting left at a traffic light. "Hope you don't care about your car," said Nate. "Martin might be the single greatest highway menace I've ever known. Worse than a Chinese Gypsy cab driver."

"That's OK. I stole it from my ex-girlfriend last week after she threw me out. That's what she gets for registering it in my name."

It was an unseasonably warm Thursday night in March and the Roosevelt County Airport was virtually empty and wide open; too wide open, thought Nate. There was a faint sliver of a fingernail moon in the western sky. The small municipal airport had no commercial passenger service; it was all private planes, charter companies and freight carriers. There was no security to speak of except for an extremely intermittent sheriff's patrol—the group's earlier reconnaissance had verified that happy fact. The airport tenants each took care of their own security needs; most of the hangars and airplane parking areas were ringed by fences, some of them topped with coils of razor wire, and they all had alarm systems.

To Martin's chagrin, he and Thirsty were to be lookouts, while Overlook and Nate were going inside. Thirsty dropped Nate and Overlook off on a lonely stretch of perimeter road outside the southeast corner of the complex, across a chain link fence and a long, dark stretch of tarmac from the Route 77 hangar. He and Martin proceeded onward: Martin to an auxiliary parking lot behind a bustling Irish pub adjacent to the airport's main north

entrance, and Thirsty to the parking area of a paving contractor a quarter of a mile down the back road from the targeted hangar, between two
large, boxy step vans. From Thirsty's vantage point, he could survey the
whole south and east flanks of the hangar and any approaches from the airport's secondary entrance to the southeast, and was close enough to sweep
in through that entrance and pick the two intruders up if anything went
awry. This was assuming Martin's slightly alcohol-impaired brain would
be able to recognize in time whether anyone coming from either direction
on Route 247 would be turning into the airport's main gate.

The entry was flawless. Overlook may have been in the throes of a
health-destroying midlife crisis, but you never would have known it to look
at him in action. In his jet-black second-story-man's ensemble: ball cap,
windbreaker and ultra-light infrared gear taking the place of the silly plaid
sport coat; with the puffiness in his jaw seeming to disappear as he tin-
kered effortlessly with various industrial-grade locks and security devices;
he looked like the consummate pro he was. Once inside, through an access
door mounted in a larger hangar door, Overlook instantly found the alarm
box and disarmed it. They scanned the area and were pleased to note that
the entire rear wall of the hangar bay was stacked with 55-gallon drums
and bottles of plastic coated glass. Shining his infrared light on some of the
containers, Nate could see they were labeled. Acetone. Methyl isobutyl
ketone. Methyl ethyl ketone. Hydrochloric and sulfuric acid in the large
bottles. Ethyl ether. Potassium permanganate. Everything needed to make
cocaine except coca leaves.

"Bingo," said Nate, a rare feeling of euphoria—ironically, very much
like a good coke high, he thought—spreading through his synapses. He
lingered over the treasure, recording every label with the video camera.

"You got enough pictures?" whispered Overlook, all business. Nate
nodded. "Then let's go."

Before taking any samples of the drummed solvents to later test for
telltale chip-production contaminants like PCBs and silicon, they broke
into the small hangar office. It was like Christmas all over again. While
Overlook planted bugs in the phone system and around the office, Nate
opened drawers and rifled the two desks for evidence. An unlocked file
cabinet in the corner yielded a trove of documents. Flight plans and

fuel receipts in one drawer identified U.S. destinations ringing the Gulf of Mexico: Tampa/St. Petersburg, Panama City and Scholes Field in Galveston. Bills of lading were specific, down to the liter, for every chemical being transported. Documents in another drawer identified transfers of material to larger cargo planes bound for destinations unknown. A large Rolodex on one of the desks contained names and phone numbers, including those of Bill McNally and the three Janssen warehouses. A smattering of Florida and Texas numbers. Some of the numbers were international, written in a hard to read chicken-scratch. Carlos — 011-57-4-2309232. Venezia — 011-57-4-2307888. Chuck — 011-507-430-2283. Juan/Klaus — 011-506-221-7524. Santi — 011-809-221-7524. Nate videotaped as many documents as he could at close range. He was moved almost to tears by the bounty, and started to babble under his breath like a fashion photographer. "Beautiful. Beautiful. Hold it right there, baby. Just like that."

"Nate, shut up."

"Sorry."

"OK. Let's take samples."

"Right."

They were attempting to pry open the tamper-resistant plastic cap cover of a drum advertised to contain acetone when the call came. "A-four here." It was Martin. "Truck approaching from the west, slowing down. OK! Turning into main entrance. Proceeding south, past first building. A-one, do you pick it up?... Thirsty?"

They didn't wait to hear his reply. "We're moving," said Overlook, pointing to the door. "Nate, go!"

"A-two and three." It was Thirsty. "You have 30 seconds to find a hole to wait it out in. I'll look for you at south gate, 2300. If no show, I'll go back and wait for your call. Out."

In 15 seconds, they were out the door, Overlook having re-armed the alarm. There was no time to jimmy the deadbolt into a locked position. Lights were approaching from the north. They ran for the stacks of wooden pallets in the southwestern corner of the fenced lot, arrayed behind an ancient twin-engine DC-3.

The white box van was familiar to Overlook. "Hold on," he whispered. "Let's wait and see what we got. Keep your camera ready."

Two men were in the van. The driver emerged and opened a set of motorized, telescoping gates wide enough to let the DC-3 through, then got
back in and drove the van inside, turning left and heading straight toward
Nate and Overlook. "Sit tight and shut up," said Overlook, reaching inside
his jacket to retrieve his .45. The van passed them, parked nose-in on the
far side of the DC-3, and the driver again got out. He walked toward the
far end of the row of pallet stacks, as Overlook fingered his gun nervously. A few seconds later a small engine coughed to life and a gas-powered
forklift emerged from behind the pallets, and parked behind the van. The
driver returned to the van and waited, leaving the forklift idling. An annoying Kenny Rogers song, "She Rides Wild Horses," rattled from the van's
blown speakers.

A strange, muffled drone buzzed Nate's earpiece, followed by Martin's
mellifluous voice, mangled by the odd trans-Irish-Sea drawl he sometimes
lapsed into when he got really drunk. "Sorry? ... Just waitin' for me bird.
She refuses to go in a pub alone. Warm up a pint for me, will ya? I'll
be gummin', time she gets 'ere... Fuck no! Name's Brennan. Oirish to
the bone, mate. Too many years among the fooking Tans, that's what...
Awright, bang on!"

Whatever Martin said, it seemed to do the trick. "You OK?" queried
Thirsty.

"All clear," replied Martin in a shaking voice. Another drone: this time
from the sky. Kenny Rogers' caterwauling was soon drowned out by the
growing throb of turboprop engines from the east. A boxy four-engine De
Havilland emerged from over a line of trees, flew low over the hangar as the
van blinked its lights, then veered south almost out of sight before making
a wide banking turn, descending fast and disappearing behind the hangar.
Within minutes, the plane taxied into the yard, guided by the van driver
with a large flashlight. The other man opened the van's roll-top rear door.

As the four turbos sputtered to a halt, a cargo door opened in the rear
of the plane and the forklift rolled up slowly, lifting its prongs into the wide
bay. It emerged with a full pallet, loaded with cardboard boxes. Just like
in the movies, the van driver flipped out a knife, slit open the top of one of
the boxes, fished out a plastic package and made a small incision in it. He
sniffed at the tip of his knife and nodded.

Seconds later eight other men appeared from inside the plane's cargo bay and jumped one by one to the tarmac. They were small, stocky, dark grayish-brown in the dim light. Dressed in faded work clothes, some wearing brimmed hats. Latino or Indian, thought Nate. Central or South American. Supervised in Spanish by the driver of the van, the eight men silently offloaded the pallet of boxes and two more from the plane and transferred them to the van. They then clambered into the back of the van themselves. The driver barked something else in Spanish, then lowered and locked the vehicle's rear door. From his hiding place behind the pallet stacks, Nate videotaped the entire sequence as best he could.

No money changed hands. No briefcase or satchel was given to the pilot, who got back in the plane and, once the van and forklift were cleared away, maneuvered to a parking spot on the other side of the DC-3. He and the original two participants then got in the cab of the van, which, after the gate was closed and locked, sped south toward the airport's rear entrance.

"A-one? A-two." It was Overlook, using codes for Thirsty and himself to be used by the group when unfriendly parties were in range.

"A-one here."

"Hot load coming your way."

"OK. Change of plans. Heat coming from the south. I'll follow, if I can. A-four?" Thirsty was hoping Martin remembered his pre-arranged code name.

"What? Oh. Right. Martin here." He was still rattled.

"Wait 10 minutes, come to where we dropped. Pick them up. Proceed to rendezvous and wait for me."

"Got it."

Nate and Overlook exited the compound through the small hole they had cut in the fence on the southeast corner of the hangar property. As they proceeded to the pickup point on the access road south of the airport's rear gate, they heard a last transmission from Thirsty, whose voice crackled as he passed out of range. "Heat is an escort. We'll see. Call you later."

Martin chimed in. "Convoy heading west on 247. White van and county sheriff's car. Thirsty in pursuit. All clear. I'll be down in a jiff."

* * *

Overlook took over the wheel of the Saturn. Nate got in back. Martin bubbled with a nervous post-traumatic enthusiasm that seemed to irk Overlook. "A sheriff's deputy escorting a truck full of drugs and wetbacks? Magnificent! I say, how *was* it in there, chaps? What else did you find?"

"We got a lot, hopefully," said Nate. "Destinations, chemicals, phone numbers. Offshore contacts. Charles planted a few bugs."

"Calm down, everybody," said Overlook. "We'll see what we got later. I'm pissed that we didn't get a sample. Labels don't mean shit in court. There's plenty of time to fuck things up, and I'm afraid we already might have done so."

"What do you mean?" asked Nate.

"Three things. One, in hurrying out of there, we probably left a trail. I couldn't lock the deadbolt. There's a hole in the fence. I'm missing a screwdriver. I think I left it by the can we were trying to open."

"Shit."

"Two, I'm worried about Thirsty. I'm not sure I should have let him follow that caravan. He's great at legwork, but he's lousy at surveillance, especially mobile surveillance. He's not trained, and he sticks out like a sore thumb."

Like me when you caught me following the Janssen convoy the day we met, thought Nate. He started to worry, too.

"Plus we were talking too much on these transmitters. I know we were using a pretty high band, but on a night when they're doing a drop, with a police escort, somebody's probably out there scanning every frequency. Toward the end there, a few of us were pretty specific about things." He frowned at Martin, who flinched. "They might know they're being followed."

Overlook realized he'd come down a little hard. "Good job getting rid of the interference at the pub, kid. You're all right."

Martin smiled wanly. "Thanks. It helps being Irish."

Forty-five minutes later, the three edgy, irritable sleuths were sitting at a booth in the Roosevelt Diner when Overlook's cell phone rang. "Charles. Thirsty. I'm near the governor's compound. Indian Hills. That's where they went. I'm about to be pulled over by a sheriff's deputy on Route 11G. Wasn't speeding. Don't hang up. I'm leaving this phone on."

Nate watched Overlook's worried face as he listened. Martin started to say something, but he shushed him. As the waitress came by with more coffee, Overlook's expression went blank. He hung up the phone.

"Fuck. Thirsty's been caught."

* * *

"You're going to *what?*"

Nicole was premenstrual, which didn't help mitigate her reaction to being blindsided by Nate's ridiculous proposal. It also didn't help that he had called her in the middle of the night and asked her to pack his clothes, toiletries and a tattered wad of traveler's checks in a suitcase and meet him in the parking lot behind a diner in Pleasant Plains. Worse yet, he had told her to watch and make sure she wasn't being followed, and to return to the Arms and call him at a pay phone if she was. This cloak-and-dagger shit was getting a little tiresome.

When she got there, he looked like death. He had tried to hug her but he smelled like a jock strap after football practice, and she had recoiled. He then made her follow him over twisting, foggy, deer-infested back roads to the seedy FDR Motor Court on Route 11 in Rooseveltson, where they were now holed up like a pair of interstate child molesters. This was bullshit already, and suddenly it was getting worse.

"Quit Roosevelt and go to work for Big Nick for up to a year," answered Nate. "Write a book about him. Maybe live in his house for a while. Find out the rest of what I need to know."

"What, are you going to pretend you're joining the fucking mob? You think you're a fucking double agent or something? You've been doing this, what, *a year and a half*, Nate? *No ... not even! 15 months, maybe?!* You're no fucking Donnie Brasco. Does this guy know what you've been *doing?*"

Like *you* really know what I've been *doing*, thought Nate.

"Mostly. Except for some stuff with Thirsty and the FBI guy, Overlook. Nick doesn't care that I've been working against USE and Janssen. He's contrite, even apologetic about drugs and toxic waste, all the cancer stuff. He's dying, and having a moral crisis. And *he* hates Bill McNally, too. The Irish gang's been stepping all over his shit, and he wants to get rid of them."

"Jesus Christ, you even sound like a fucking wiseguy already, do you hear yourself? What, are you going to help Big Nick *whack* your dead girl-friend's father?" This last cruel dig was delivered along with a pair of ironic two-fingered "quote" signals framing the word "whack."

Nate ignored her attack. It wasn't her fault. There were many things he had been keeping from Nicole, so as not to worry her unduly. One of them was the airport junket earlier that evening. Another was that Thirsty had been caught, a mere 20 miles up the road from here, and was probably be-ing tortured and killed as they talked. Yet another was his earlier suspicion of almost having been slain by one of McNally's men, which he had re-cently found out was horrifyingly true. The fact was, he and anyone close to him had always been in danger, and would be until this was over. Nicole had only a small inkling of the jeopardy Nate and she had been in all along. It was time to scare her silly, for her own good—and to shut her up.

"No. But Nick will protect me from McNally while I figure out how to take him down. There are some things you don't know about me. When I was in that storage-room fire in New York, it was no accident. There was a big Irish goon who tried to kill me that day; he punched my lights out and started the fire. I just found out that he was McNally's guy, Nicole, and he had followed me there to silence me and destroy Sheila's files. I've been in real trouble for a while now.

"And now I've been recognized by *all* of them, the Italian and Irish mobs, as Sheila's old boyfriend, who at the very least can finger his at-tacker, and who at the worst can bring down their whole fucking world. Luckily for me, Big Nick is willing to overlook these flaws, because he wants me to write his memoirs so bad. My Jimmy Olsen name was not a joke; it was to protect myself. Before you met me, I drastically changed my appearance, but my cover is blown. Now I find out the Irish gang's on my jock, and Nick has called them off, because he fucking *likes* me, all right? So basically, I've painted myself into a corner. Going with Big Nick is the only thing I *can* do, unless I quit and leave the country."

Nate had thought long and hard about what he was going to say next, but he still had trouble getting it out. "So I guess you might want to find yourself a new boyfriend for a while, at least until I get myself out of this. I love you too much, baby. I don't want you to get hurt. I haven't told Nick

I have a girlfriend, and I don't want him or McNally to find out. So after tonight, I can't see you anymore, for I don't know how long—maybe a year. Because I love you. Because I want to marry you. If you love me like you say you do, then wait for me. I'm so...fucking...sorry."

Listening to Nate, Nicole's anger over his relationship-killing obsession had first dissolved into shock, then fear, then a hopeless, blinding sadness to match his own. She began to weep in a soft, guttural moan that emanated from deep in her heaving breast, triggering Nate's own emotional breakdown. The two doomed lovers entertained the traveling salesmen, extramarital sodomites and welfare cheats in the adjoining motel rooms with a series of stereophonic banshee wails. When they finally calmed down they ignored their shabby surroundings and Nate's sinus-clearing B.O. and made sweet, matchless love one last time, after which they both blubbered and snuffled in each other's moist arms like colicky infants through the night.

"I *will* wait for you," said Nicole.

"You don't have to."

"I will."

He knew she wouldn't.

CHAPTER TWENTY-ONE
BOOK OF REVELATION

"Have *fun-un-un* last night-ight-ight?" Big Nick's disembodied voice caromed off of two-and-a-half stories of Giallo Provenza marble. His wheelchair humming angrily, Nick had rolled himself at what seemed at least 20 miles per hour, right up into Nate's face as he entered the soaring vestibule. He was obviously cranked on some sort of amphetamines.

"How's that?" Nate had anticipated something like this, but didn't see any other choice.

Nick lowered the volume a few decibels, but his eyes still smoldered like miniature induction coils. "Listen, smart guy. You can give me the slip all you want, but I know what you been up to. And I know who *with*. Your moolie friend got nabbed last night by McNally's crew. He's not doin' so good. Except for me, you wouldn't be doin' so good either. Billy boy went over to the airport and found out all about your little adventure. He said he knew you were in on it and I should put a stop to you. I lied."

Spittle drooled onto Nick's joystick. Steam wafted out of his nostrils around the oxygen hose.

"I lied and told him I was watchin' you all day and night, so how could you be there? Thing is, he knows it was you. How am I supposed to look out for you when you pull shit like this?"

As Big Nick expectorated and wheezed, a large, extremely unfriendly, spud-shaped man poked at Nate's tender lymph nodes like a rookie acupuncturist with his beefy fingers, looking for a wire or a weapon. Nate again was left wondering if he'd survive the next 24 hours. He was beginning not to care.

"I'm sorry. It was a way to get at McNally."

"Yeah, well. I wanna get McNally, too, but not like that. I mean, right now his business is *my* business. You fuck with *him* you're fucking with *me*, until I get this thing straightened out. *Stunad!* What the fuck did I *tell* you?"

"I'm sorry."

"You're fucking *sorry*. You crazy fuck. So who else? Somebody planted bugs all over the place, and it wasn't you."

"The black guy that got caught was a lookout. There was an ex-FBI guy: Charlie something. He and I were inside."

"Charlie *something*? You fucking pussy... . Yeah, we figured he was still around. A stinking drunk, but a pretty good agent. *Too* fucking good. We had to get him retired for putting away Fat Tony. So how'd you get out of there? Your *melanzana* lookout was busy following a truck. It's a long walk to the Roosevelt Motel."

"Jesus, how'd you know I was there?"

"How do I know a lot of things? Look, half—no, three quarters of the people in this county work for me, *capeesh*? So how'd you get out of the fucking airport?"

Nick motioned for Nate and the no-necked bodyguard to follow him into the drawing room.

"Charlie had a car."

"What kind of a car? A little red piece of shit with a Limey fuck driving, maybe? Because McNally told me a little red car was sittin' behind McSorley's Tavern last night with a Limey motherfucker in it, trying to pretend he was Irish with a fucking bullshit English accent. Kind of didn't belong there, you know? It's like *Mick*-Nally central in there. One of his boys comes out and asks the little fuck what he's doing there, and he says he's waitin' for his girlfriend. Were *you* his fucking girlfriend?"

"I guess so."

Nick stopped and threw the wheelchair into reverse, backing it into its usual spot across from the settee, where Nate's video rig was still set up from the last session.

"That's right. So you see, McNally, who is not so stupid for a stupid Mick, puts two and two together later when he's at McSorley's asking if anybody's seen anything suspicious. When somebody tells him about your Limey boyfriend in the parking lot, a big light goes off in the head of *another* dumb Mick standin' there; you might remember him, the guy who tried to fry your monkey ass in the City. This guy remembers the Limey and you from the town hall in Ostia. Remember that night, Jimmy Olsen? I do. You were very respectful to come over to me like that. I remembered that. And I remember your Limey friend who almost fucked up my golf course deal. And so does McNally. Which is why he thought of you being at the airport last night. Which is why I don't look so good right now for protecting you."

"Shit. Martin's his name. Nobody's going to kill *him*, are they?"

"That would be stupid. I'm gonna have him sent back where he belongs on the next plane, with a warning from me."

"What about Thirsty and Charlie?"

"Don't worry about the FBI guy. He can take care of himself. Nobody will listen to him, though. He's *persona non grata*. The banana-eater I can't help you with. McNally's got him on ice for the time being. He's a pest. Only that fuck Aldrich will miss him, anyway."

"Yeah, well, *I* might miss him. I happen to *like* that guy."

"No accounting for taste. Look, I'm not mad at you, fuck-up that you are." Nick had finally started to relax, the paternal slackness returning to his ravaged cheeks. His eyes looked almost normal, like shining black coals set deep in his emaciated skull. He waved the big goon away with a cock of his head. "To tell you the truth, I'm fucking amused. You're like a fucking video game already. Super Mario. And now you want to be a fucking hero; I'll put a hundred bucks on it. You're going to the governor's St. Polak's Day party with your boss on Monday, right?"

I have no secrets from this man, thought Nate. He's like God, or Santa Claus. He knows everything. Fuck! He knows about Nicole...

"Doing a little fucking around on the side, right? Who knows, maybe there's a coupla tons of dope in the garage or maybe your moolie friend is locked up down in the cellar, too. Maybe you even got bigger ideas..."

Nate stiffened.

"Well, you know what? You're right. But here's a little tip. Fuggedaboudit. Everybody in the place works for McNally. As if you didn't know already, the governor's a fucking prop."

"I know."

Despite having downed two Tylenol 3s ten minutes earlier, Nate began to feel the pain behind his eyes again.

"Yeah, you *know*. Well here's something you don't *know*. The game is over. Checkmate. You belong to me. And I don't have time for writin' bestsellers right now, because that fucking potato eater and his mulatto friend the governor, they're up my ass. I gotta, whaddya say, *neutralize* them, capeesh?"

Nate nodded painfully as what felt like a red-hot glob of mercury bubbled back and forth across the interior of his cranial dome with each small movement.

"Look, kid, siddown. Like I said, I'm not mad at you. Look at me. *Look at me.*"

Nate looked at him dazedly. With the light of the garden windows as a backdrop, Big Nick's face was luminescent and ringed in shimmering oxygen tubes. He resembled a wizened, robotic Mother Teresa with a butch haircut. Nate suppressed a sudden, psychotic urge to cross himself.

"Turn on your fucking camera. I wanna give a statement." Nate turned on the video camera, put in a new tape and pressed "record."

"When I started in this business, it was basically the garbage business. That was all we had that was legit. All they would *let* us have. That and masonry—building foundations and walls.

"*We* were the fucking moolies. They treated us like shit. But over time, garbage became more and more of a big fucking deal. What once seemed like a shit job nobody wouldn't let their dog do was startin' to make more dough than John D. Rockefeller. Through garbage, we could rule the neighborhoods, whole cities. We got control of the trucks. Garbage, cement, freight, you name it. They couldn't fucking move without us.

"And then it got even better. Every time the regulators try to regulate something: landfills, chemical disposal, recycling, whatever, it makes something more expensive to do. We were there at the back door to take the pressure off—make things copacetic for the capitalists who run this fucking country to exist without being put out of business by all the fuck-ing regulation. We was doing good for people, for the economy. We even learned, we *thought* we learned, how to do garbage right, as clean as gar-bage could possibly be done. We didn't need the fucking feds to tell us how to do our fucking job.

"But like you said, we fucked up. We were wrong about some things. We thought the chemicals would wash away. They don't always. We got into sellin' drugs. These are cancers we started; I admit that. It's too late for me, for my son, for my wife. For a lot of my friends; for my cousin Joey Natale, who's dying of lymphoma right now in a fucking prison hospital. And at this very moment, I couldn't stop it if I wanted, from here. I'm old. Isolated. I still got the downstate rackets, but my power's shifted. It's all about garbage and oil and drugs and chemicals now, and it's all McNally's and the Jersey crew's. It's not just here; it's all over the country now. It's international. Turn the camera off."

Nate hit the "pause" button.

"It's off?"

"It's off."

"So how come the little green light is still on?"

"I 'paused' it. It's better than 'stop' because when I turn it on again it'll be smooth, not shaky."

"Yeah, well, turn it the fuck off."

Nate hit 'stop' and turned the camera off.

"All right. You and me, we want the same thing. You want the dump-ing to stop. I want McNally neutralized. Dead, disemboweled, or just disgraced and dismissed, I don't give a fuck. Neutralized. And I decided you're just the motherfucker to help me do it."

Nate was dumbfounded. "Shit, Nick. Nothing would make me hap-pier than fucking with that asshole. But what makes you think *I'm* your man? I'm nobody. I'm a writer, for Chrissake. I never 'neutralized' any-body, at least on purpose. Don't you have people who do that kind of thing for you already?"

"Nobody tailor-made to keep the heat off *me*. I been watching you. You're fucked up over your dead girlfriend. You're pissed off about ev-erything. You're suicidal, and if you aren't, you're homicidal. Fratricidal.

Genocidal. *Something*-icidal. I seen this shit before. You need to do some damage, right? Fuck shit up. Fuck *writing*. Writing is too slow. Nobody'll believe you, you're thinkin'. Am I right?"

Nate couldn't disagree. Through the blur of his excruciating, opiate-twisted intra-cranial agony, the unholy little motorized gnome before him was making perfect sense.

"And you're gonna help me, because I got nobody else I can get next to McNally without makin' me look bad. Nobody knows you work for me. McNally thinks you're a lunatic. Everybody thinks you're a lunatic. And you *are* a fucking lunatic, am I right?"

Nate nodded, agreeing.

"Plus, if you don't do this for me, I can't promise what's gonna happen to your new girlfriend on the way home."

* * *

The icicle had come in high from out of left field, plunging straight through the pain and drug haze and into Nate's chest, missing his aorta by inches. Nick was looking at him matter-of-factly, without any particular sense of menace. But the halo of kindness, if there ever really was any, was gone. Somehow Nate summoned the will to speak, even before he could formulate a clear thought. "Now *that* sucks, Nick. What the fuck? Why do you feel the need to threaten me?"

"Was I threatening you? Because, you never know. I need this done. I can't have nobody backing out. It's all set up. So you gonna do it, or not?"

Big Nick's threat had unleashed a powerful surge of pent up resentment in Nate that had been building for some time. Resentment against God for the deaths of everyone he had ever loved. Against the great, crushing futility of it all. Against the tendency of every semi-educated man to choke the life out of himself and everything around him for the sake of greed, power-lust and double-digit investment returns. Against his father for dying without preparing him to deal with these assholes. Quasi-religious, rebel-without-a-cause shit from deep in his pre-adolescent subconscious. Whatever it was, he went with it. "Jesus, fuck! It's *already* what I wanted to do, Nick! Why you gotta bring my woman into this? That just pisses me off. *Fuck you!* I would do this for *myself.* You stay off my girlfriend, or I'll have to come back and neutralize *your* skinny Wop ass, too, you fucking old cripple!"

Nick laughed, and shook his head. "You're a fucking pisser, you know that? All right, all right. Relax, already, nobody's gonna fuck with your girl, I was just testing your, ah, *resolve.* Are you with me?"

Nate glared at him, imagining crucifying him and tearing his black, squirming heart out.

"Look, I'm sorry, but I got a fucking business to run. I don't have time for this shit. *Are you fucking with me, or not?*"

"Yes, I'm with you. Just leave my fucking woman alone."

"Yeah, yeah. You have my word." Nick paused, heaved a rattling sigh and took a long sip of what looked like two-day-old carrot juice. He closed his eyes. "So where were we? OK, here's what we gotta do. A coupla things. We gotta kill McNally and make it not look like a fucking hit. It's either gotta be an accident or like a freak of nature, like a fucking lunatic got him. Better yet, we gotta kill him *after* we strip him of his juice by telling the world what a fucking scumbag he is."

Nick's eyes opened, boring into Nate. "Or, more precisely, *after you, the fucking lunatic that's gonna be at the governor's party with the fucking suicide bomb strapped to his chest, tells the world what a daughter-raping, drug-dealing, toxic waste-dumping scumbag Bill McNally is.* And, by the way, what a scumbag, wetback-smuggling, crooked dope dealer that rat Hiram Pollock is. Right in front of the TV cameras who are gonna be there filming for the Channel 7 News, because the governor has a bunch of New York City firefighters and the fucking pedophile Cardinal Buttfucker over for St. Patrick's day dinner."

Despite his lingering anger, the anarchist in Nate couldn't help smiling at the thought.

"And then you, crazy lunatic eco-fuck that you are, can march the hostages, the TV crew and McNally and the governor and whoever else you want down to the cellar of the north garage, where your moolie friend is locked up, and set him the fuck free to go eat bananas or whatever. And then youse can all go upstairs to the garage and take a look at the governor's latest drug shipment."

Nick smiled and spread his arms in a welcoming papal gesture, his final summation complete; his case in the bag. A beam of sunlight appeared, bathing him in a golden aura.

The headache and the anger were disappearing as Nate let go of the last remaining dock-line to his sanity and drifted into the ether. Over Big Nick's left shoulder, outside in the garden through the windows, a fire-engine red cardinal flitted on a dogwood branch. Nate stood up and started pacing. "This is perfect. Perfect! I'm you're man. Hundred percent. But you're wrong about me being suicidal. I'm a stealth bomber, not a Kamikazi. I have a couple of questions. Like how do I get this fucking suicide bomb in there without anybody knowing? And how do I kill McNally and get out of there alive?"

Nick frowned. "I can't say there's no risk to this; it's about 50/50. But I got things worked out. You'll have inside help."

"Inside help, who?"

"You better sit back down, kid, I have a confession to make. You know that big Irish motherfucker who sucker-punched you? He's one of McNally's enforcers. But he's been on *my* dole for a while, because of something McNally did to his kid brother. He was supposed to kill you that day, McNally's orders. But he liked you, and gave you a fighting chance. He said you were funny. He was easy on you, and even helped you down the stairs after you woke up."

"Jesus." Nate sat down.

"He was checking you out at our town meeting that night for McNally, who suspected you was around. But after he recognized you and followed you home, he came over here and told me about it first. He's the one who put the idea in my head to use you to get McNally."

"That's fucked up. So what's he gonna do for me?"

"He's got clearance at Pollock's house; he's almost family. His name's Tommy Dongan, by the way. His fucking ancestor was the first English governor of New York when the Dutch got evicted, except he was Irish. You and him are probably kissin' cousins. He runs dope and Colombians in and out. He hangs around at almost everything important McNally does, for muscle. He'll be in and out of there all week. He'll smuggle the bomb vest and a .45 in and plant them in the shitter."

"OK, what then?"

"Hang on." Nick pressed a button on a control panel mounted next to his joystick. "Freddy, come in here."

The large, unfriendly man returned, this time carrying a lethal-looking apparatus: a lightweight vest wired with 20 pounds of C4 plastic explosives, from which a hand-held, push-button detonator switch dangled dangerously. Another looming disciple followed closely in Mr. Potato Head's considerable penumbra, stepping into Nate's full view only when the pair was nearly upon him. It was Tommy Dongan, the giant, laughing, eye-crushing leprechaun from Gotham Mini Storage, complete with aerodynamic sunglasses.

"Sorry about your face," said Tommy Dongan in his curious singsong baritone lilt. "It waren't personal. 'Twas a fookin' job."

"You pulled me out of there?"

"I guess so."

"Well, thanks, I guess. I can see better now, anyway."

"A sight better'n me, I reckon," said Dongan, pulling off his shades to reveal a badly scarred wormhole of a right eye that was more than a match for Nate's damaged left orb.

"Who did that to you?"

"I'd rather not say."

Nick interjected. "This is heartwarming, you two gettin' to know each other like this. Maybe you can talk later. But right now we got a job to do. Freddy?"

Nick's bodyguard, if that's what he was, was incongruously well spoken, exhibiting the slow, deliberate loquacity of an Episcopal bishop. While he still appeared as mountainous and dour and forbidding as a Grand Seraglio eunuch, the sound rumbling from his barrel chest was warm, deep and brimming with complex emotional overtones, like that of the ubiquitous voiceover narrator of independent film trailers. Like God Himself should sound.

"We'll go over this a number of times over the next couple of days, until you have it down cold. I understand you'll be going to the governor's house with Mr. Babson in a rented limousine, is that correct?" said Freddy, slowly and deliberately, Godlike.

"That's what they tell me, yes."

"Good. Now here's what we're going to do..."

CHAPTER TWENTY-TWO
THE LAST SUPPER

Of course, nothing ever goes exactly as planned. The 50/50 odds of success Big Nick had estimated for this stunt should have been more like 85/15 against. Still, to Nate, it was worth a try. At the very least, he would create a kernel of awareness in the mind of one of the WABC cameramen, perhaps, or convince a visiting corned-beef-and-cabbage-stuffed fireman that a homegrown evil far greater than any Saracen terrorist threat was loose in the land. In risking sacrificing himself, he would achieve what Sheila had failed to do: raise into the public consciousness the specter of wholesale chemical carnage being wreaked on an unsuspecting populace by these people. If the lemmings didn't get it when it was being jammed in their faces, then fuck 'em, they deserved to die.

Anyway, he had a more than sneaking suspicion that the mind-erasing blitzkrieg that was raging in his head was probably a symptom of something fatal he had acquired from inhaling far too much benzene over the past few months, and he preferred going out in a blaze of glory rather than wasting slowly into a living cadaver like Rico or Nick. Compared to the alternative, a suicide bombing mission would be downright fun.

On the day of the big gubernatorial St. Patty's day fete, Nate drove from Ostia up to the Babsons' hilltop gentleman's farm in his reconstituted Cadillac Seville, knowing he might never again sit behind the wheel of an automobile. He relished the moment, going the back way up a winding gorge via a black-market-benzene-oiled dirt road, past the old Van Valkenberg mine and the ancient, rusted remains of the long-abandoned

Mohican Mountain House tramway. He parked for a few minutes at an outcropping where the burned-out chimney stacks of the 19th-century cliff-top luxury hotel still stood. Walking to the edge of the escarpment, he drank in the beautiful valley through squinting eyes, filtering out the details until he could pretend he was a Lenape Indian encountering its untarnished splendors for the first time.

"Yeah, right," he said aloud to himself, and returned to his car, as a chemically compromised red-tailed hawk circled overhead, preparing to swoop down on the scraggly, emaciated, PCB-and-perchloroethylene-infested field mouse that had wandered up the hill from the tainted golf course below.

* * *

The limo was already there, with Freddy, Big Nick's factotum, standing by the open passenger door looking like a misanthropic titty-bar bouncer in his black tuxedo. The day's first case of collateral damage, the rented auto's actual driver, was presumably lying in the trunk amid the 10 portable plastic cans of gasoline, drugged into unconsciousness and heavily trussed-up—and quite possibly deceased from breathing toxic fumes—as per the flexible battle plan that had been cooked up by Freddy and Nick. Winnie, rheumy-eyed and mumbling to himself as usual, was standing atop an open dumpster by the carriage house, jumping up and down on the unruly contents. He reminded Nate of a dotty former PGA Masters champion in his bright green sport coat.

Nothing in the man's quirky demeanor contradicted Rick Parton's oft-quoted opinion that the Roosevelt Newspapers publisher exhibited all the characteristics of a screaming pothead. Rick even claimed to have smelled THC on Winnie's breath one Wednesday morning as he paranoiacally checked the flats for embarrassing stories. Dave was purported to have caught him once rolling around on his back on the grass behind the hedge, squirming and laughing like a boysenberry-drunk bear cub.

Winnie's remarkably well-preserved Texas oil billionaire wife Marjorie, somehow having aged gracefully without the benefit of plastic surgery despite her involvement in a series of horrific one-car accidents, wore a simple lime green frock under a slightly darker spring jacket. She limped

slightly, from injuries sustained in her last crack-up, during which she was
flung down a 100-foot embankment in the snow fourteen months earlier.
She had been rescued by her Dutch Hollow neighbor Jack Danforth, the
film star, who had seen her in his headlights as she dragged herself along
the snowy shoulder of Route 31 on her elbows, her two useless broken legs
trailing along behind her. "At first I thought she was a dead deer," he was
quoted by Mona Levy as saying. The quote didn't make the paper.

"Remain glued to Mr. Babson at all times, through the cocktail hour and
into dinner," Freddy had instructed. "McNally won't try to mess with you in
public, but he'll probably have Tommy here assigned to keep an eye on you."

That was the first problem. Winnie was a nervous, paranoid wreck, and
probably high, to boot. Keeping "glued" to a man in his state wouldn't be
easy. Nate wondered whether the man knew something was going down.
"Mr. Olsen, Mr. Olsen," Winnie had babbled upon descending awkwardly
from the dumpster to welcome him. "I invited you to this party, first of all
as a token of my appreciation for all you've done for me this year. Thank
you, and thank you again. But sadly, I just heard from Dave that you're
thinking of leaving us, is that true?"

"Yes, it is, unfortunately."

"Well, if I don't see you again, thank you from the bottom of my heart
for all you've done. You're my guy. I wish I had ten of you." Winnie
looked Nate nervously in the eyes and held his hand for a moment too
long, as if he really were saying goodbye.

The ride to Indian Hills was nearly uneventful, if profoundly uncomfortable. Nate had taken a handful of prescription medicines and con-
trolled substances in anticipation of the long evening ahead. He needed to
stave the headaches off, calm his nerves, suppress the urge to puke, piss
or shit, and stay alert. He was cranked as well on Dunkin' Donuts coffee
and Krispy Kreme glazed donuts from the shops in Clover and Ostia, the
same toxic combination that had worked so well during band road trips
and marathon Tuesday all-nighters at the newspaper. He would be fine as
long as he avoided eating or drinking anything at the party.

As he checked over and over beneath the waistband of the late Sammy
Vitello's olive green double-breasted suit for his money belt stuffed with
hundred-dollar bills, and in the inside jacket pocket for his wallet, fake

passport and brand-new Radio Shack burner phone, Nate tried to keep his mind focused on the job ahead in the face of Winnie's constant prattle and Marjorie's rolling her eyes at her husband and her coy flirtations with himself. He had always wondered what it would be like to fuck a seriously older woman, and found it ironic that a geriatric Mrs. Robinson fantasy would be presenting itself on what could very well be his final day of existence.

As he knew they wouldn't, neither Babson recognized their limo driver as one of Big Nick's associates. Nor did they notice the stray black detonator wire for the 100 pounds of C4 explosives packed beneath the front and rear seats, dangling carelessly out from under the plush-pile floor mat. Stifling the reflex to gasp upon noticing it, Nate had to stretch himself in an odd, nearly spread-eagled position to cover the thing with his foot. The ungainly come-hither pose seemed to incite Mrs. Babson to further advances, making the ride that much more uncomfortable. Winnie, thank God, never had a clue.

The limo passed through the governor's security checkpoint effortlessly. Freddy was a downstate Natale, a cousin of Nick's who was not very well known among the Roosevelt County Route 77 crowd; nonetheless the decision to have him pose as the driver carried the operation's biggest potential risk. As a result of Bill McNally's unofficial palace coup and Big Nick's illness, the Natales had been conspicuously uninvited to everything of late, and were feared in their absence. Someone at the party would be on the lookout for Natales. Still, Freddy was the only person Nick felt he could trust, so that was that.

The governor's private mansion was a grand Queen Anne style affair on a bluff overlooking the Hudson, a long stone's throw north of the recently refurbished and re-opened Copenhagen train station. It had once been the northernmost terminus of a string of family "country seats" carved out of the original Astor family's vast riverfront holdings, and was the only one of the fur fortune's remaining legacies that hadn't been turned into a museum, convent or nursing home. Winnie and Marjorie seemed charmed rather than rattled when the limo came to a halt and Nate lunged chivalrously for the door to open it so that Freddy could remain behind the wheel and not have to expose himself to the scrutiny of the guests mingling on the portico. As Freddy drove off to the side lot to lay low and await Nate's summons, the newcomers wended their way into the pasty-faced crowd of power brokers and sycophants, all clad in various shades of green.

At first Nate struggled to keep up with Winnie, who was bouncing from asshole to asshole, shaking hands and making a gentlemanly nuisance of himself. Nate eventually resigned himself to tagging along with Marjorie, who due to her lingering leg injury was relatively immobile. They moved inside into a high faux atrium, where drinks were being served. Nate declined, but ordered Marjorie a double Chivas with ice. A trio of fiddlers in the corner played annoying Irish jigs as an idiotic mime dressed in a neon green court jester's outfit pranced by with a tray of green hors d'oeuvres.

Then he saw her.

Nicole was resplendent in a tight-fitting dark green crushed velvet dress, her dark hair piled on top of her head like a black-Irish princess. She appeared thinner than he had remembered her from a week ago, less plush, but still beautiful. As he caught her eye she blushed, and his mind raced as to how he could keep her out of harm's way. He turned to Marjorie. "I'm sorry, Marjorie, I see a friend, which is unusual in this crowd. Don't go far, I'll be right back."

He left the aging, hobbled temptress and started toward Nicole, feeling the woman's estrogen-supplement-fueled gaze drilling holes in the back of his neck. As he approached his lost love, a strong hand grabbed him from behind and spun him around.

"Nootch!"

"Jimmy, my brother."

The two friends embraced heartily.

"Jesus, what are you doing here?"

"My date invited me." He nodded toward Nicole. "Don't be pissed, buddy. She said you two had broken up."

"It's OK; no foul. She was right, we're done. It's a free country." His heart was beating fast and way too hard.

Nicole walked up. "Hello, Natie." Nate kissed her on the cheek and embraced her tenderly, as Nootch looked away.

"Shh," he whispered in her ear. "In this crowd, I'm Jimmy Olsen. I still love you. I see you didn't waste any time..."

"Nate, I..."

"Shh. It's OK. I understand."

He backed away, and addressed them both. "So what brings you two to Chez Pollock? Isn't this scene a little tired for a couple of fancy muck-rakers such as yourselves?"

Nicole blushed again, then hardened improbably into a glossy, smooth-talking, corporate-smiley-faced caricature of herself. "I guess you didn't hear. A week ago I got offered a job at USE. I'm starting in Arthur Schmidt's executive PR department in a week. He wanted me to come today to get my feet wet."

Her eyes glowed with pride of accomplishment and a deep, mercantile satisfaction with the quadrupling of her salary.

"Great! Congratulations."

"Fucking traitor," thought Nate to himself, fighting the urge to scream. "I thought you were different. Can't you see what they're trying to do? Divide and conquer. You're in Satan's thrall, and you're going to drag one of my best friends down with you. Wake the fuck up!"

He said nothing. Nicole regarded him quizzically and with a palpable degree of fear, as if she were encountering a foul-smelling, homeless sub-way pusher.

"I'm just here to keep her out of trouble," said Nootch. "And maybe get a scoop."

"Well, here's a scoop, you two," said Nate, looking around furtive-ly. "Whatever happens today, pretend you don't really know me, or you might catch something and get sick. It might be fatal."

Nicole rolled her eyes. "Oh, Nate. Is this another one of your conspir-acy theories?"

"Just stay away from me today, and pretend you don't know me. Capeesh? I love you both."

He spun stiffly on his heels and walked away, looking frantically for Mrs. Babson, who had disappeared. Feeling a chill, he turned around and spotted Bill McNally and his wife glaring at him, along with the dou-ble-crossing, shade-wearing Tommy Dongan. Nate hoped against hope that the big motherfucker wasn't a triple-crosser. Just in time, Winnie hur-tled by, and Nate attached himself to his boss as the guests were herded into the dining room for dinner.

* * *

The high-school and college-aged wait staff looked as if they had been stamped from the same mold: tall, raw-boned, angular, blonde (when their hair was not dyed in bright, unnatural colors) and nervous as young racehorses. Bits of painful-looking metal protruded from the most tender and vulnerable parts of their facial anatomy: eyebrows, nostrils, lips and tongues. Nate figured there was enough inbred Astor, Vanderbilt, Whitney, Roosevelt and Clermont blood still percolating through the northern Roosevelt gene pool to afflict the local population with horsy good looks, rare diseases and mental instability for generations to come.

Nate spent the entire meal being mauled by a billionaire septuagenarian oil magnate, eschewing eating one of his favorite dishes and avoiding the glances of the most beautiful woman in the room, all the while pondering how and when to excuse himself to don a suicide vest laden with high explosives. The singularity of his situation, which had begun to dawn on him during his abbreviated commando training sessions in Big Nick's subterranean boot camp, now hit him full force. With the total absence of his now-familiar head pain, he began to suspect that he might be dreaming. He pinched his wrist, and it hurt.

Freddy's droning instructions came back to him, and he followed them to the letter as they scrolled through his brain. "As the dinner plates are being cleared, you'll excuse yourself to go to the lavatory. It's out the north door of the dining hall, in a long hallway that accesses the kitchen."

Nate excused himself, and glanced around to see if he was being followed. Eyes followed him, but not a soul moved. Tommy Dongan was standing mutely by the dining room's main exit, watching.

"The bathroom is on the left, just past the kitchen and the pantry. It's single occupancy. You go in, lock the door, take off your jacket and hang it on a hook. Then stand on the toilet seat, raise the center ceiling panel and feel for a box, toward the rear wall. *Carefully*, take the box down." Like Laurence Harvey in *The Manchurian Candidate*, Nate did as he had been programmed, slaloming through the traffic of dessert tray-bearing wait staff barreling along the passageway. The bathroom was occupied, and he waited for what seemed like an hour, but was actually 45 seconds. An elderly red-faced gentleman in a green plastic bowler hat finally emerged scowling, a foot-long length of shit-stained toilet paper dragging from his shoe. The restroom smelled like dog farts.

Nate entered, locked the door and went to work. This was nothing like practice. The toilet seat was unstable, the ceiling panel rained ancient mouse turds and sneeze-inducing particulate matter and the box was nearly too heavy to lift out without dropping it; Tommy Dongan was a much taller, stronger man.

The bathroom door handle jiggled. "Hello?" A woman's voice.

"I'll be right out."

Flustered, Nate had to recapture his place in the mental scroll of Freddy's lesson plan, amid flickering, unwelcome thoughts of Sheila and Nicole, one on each side, both kissing him and sticking their tongues in his ears. "Place it on the sink, remove the vest, and put it on. There's an arming switch in front on the left side. Don't touch it until later. There will be a small roll of duct tape in the box. Tape the detonator wire down your left arm. You're right-handed?"

"To write with, yes."

"To fire a gun?"

"As far as I know, yes."

During this exchange Nick had been sitting in his wheelchair, smiling inscrutably like some crippled Yoda action figure. Tommy Dongan had stood in silence, holding up the killer vest as if he was some extra-large stone-faced flight attendant miming distractedly to a canned air safety spiel before takeoff. Nate remembered how Tommy's passive countenance had seemed to reflect a sense of peace, now that the long-plotted demise of his blood enemy was finally within reach. Nick had promised him an elevated position within the revamped Natale/Route 77 family hierarchy if the purge went as planned. *Please let it be true*, thought Nate.

"A holster will be attached near the armpit on the side of the vest *opposite* your shooting arm, probably on the left side," Freddy had said. "Tape the detonator wire to the arm that's on the same side as the holster."

"OK."

"There will be a fully-loaded .45-caliber automatic in the box as well. We'll get you used to handling it in a few minutes."

"Nice."

"You'll take the safety off and put the gun in the holster. Pick up after yourself. Put the duct tape roll back in the box, put the box back in the ceiling, close the ceiling tile. Put your jacket on, tuck the detonator into your jacket cuff and make sure you can grab it with no problem. Be careful not to set it off. Button your jacket. Look in the mirror and adjust everything so it's not showing. It will feel bulky, but it won't look bad for the short trip back to the table. Nobody but Tommy here will be watching you."

Despite having practiced these moves fifty times, Nate felt as if he were moving underwater. Donning the vest, with its pouches full of plastic explosives augmented by a couple of hundred 8d carpenter's nails sewn into the front for effect, was like donning a wheelbarrow full of cement. With the gun in its holster under his armpit and Nick's dead son's suit jacket stretched over the whole mess, Nate was nearly immobilized from the waist up. He was sure he'd be caught; that SWAT teams of snipers were waiting to vaporize him along with the hapless and expendable Colombian kitchen help before he got back to the table.

"What the hell, you only live once."

He opened the bathroom door, and stared into Nicole's face. She looked at his bulked-up frame in horror. "Nate, what are you doing?"

He looked around. No one in the hallway save two fey waiters, hurrying to the kitchen. He pulled his lapel aside, revealing the death machinery strapped to his chest. "Reality TV, news at 11. I'm today's host. Stay the fuck away from me. Don't come back to the dining room, and stay out of this hallway. I love you. I'd love to kiss you, but I might blow us up. Goodbye, sweetheart."

"Nate!"

"Shh! Don't you get it? These people are *evil*. They're *killing* us, Nicole. Please get out of here, and for God's sake, don't *work* for them. Goodbye."

He touched her lips with his fingers, spun around and nearly sprinted down the hallway, suddenly unaware of the weight on his shoulders and torso. A tray-toting waitress took one look at his face, recoiled in horror and fled into the kitchen.

"Pollock will be making a speech for the cameras during the dessert course, giving some token gift to the firefighters," Freddy had said. "At the moment the firefighters get up from their seats, you'll get up, too. As you do you'll arm the vest, lower the detonator switch into your left hand, unbutton your jacket and pull the gun out with your right, and yell: 'This bomb is armed! No one moves or we all die!' as you reveal the vest's fire-power and grab the nearest celebrity hostage, which will hopefully be the cardinal. We'll practice the necessary moves many times."

There was no time for that. Nate looked back and saw Nicole running after him down the long, suddenly busy hallway. He unbuttoned his jacket, baring the bomb vest, reached up into his left cuff and pulled down the detonator switch, armed the vest, yanked the gun out of his holster and burst into the dining room through the swinging doors.

"HOLD IT! This bomb is armed! No one moves or we all die!"

The room froze. Pollock was on the dais, preparing to speak. Gun in the air, Nate walked quickly over to the cardinal and pointed the weapon at his head. "Get up, your grace."

"Nate, no!!!" Nicole burst into the room.

"Stay where you are or I kill us all!" screamed Nate, trying—and, beyond his wildest dreams, succeeding—to convince everyone in the room, including Nicole, that he was insane enough to pull the ripcord on 150 lives.

Nate fast-forwarded the tape in his head. "The governor's security force is not particularly tight when he's inside his own home," Freddy had said, slowly and deliberately. "They'll be a little slow on the uptake, but there will eventually be guns pointed at you. It'll be up to you to calmly, loudly and firmly inform the assemblage that any small disturbance of the ultra-sensitive detonation sensors on your suicide bomb will result in the certain obliteration of everyone present. Hands should be in the air, guns should be lowered and placed in a pile on the floor, and all voices but yours should remain silent unless spoken to. If your orders are followed exactly, no one will be hurt. You cannot repeat these caveats enough; some of these people have extremely short attention spans."

"Pardon me, but this sounds pretty suicidal to me," Nate had responded.

"Actually, this is the least dangerous part of the operation. You have the upper hand, and you are in a room crowded with frightened people who don't want to die. All they will want is for you to leave, taking as few of them as possible with you. When you do *that* is when things will become more dangerous for you."

Freddy, you are *so* full of shit, thought Nate.

"Everyone stand up, move away from the table, and keep your hands in the air where I can see them!" shouted Nate. *"This bomb is very powerful, and very, very sensitive!!!* It will explode and *vaporize everyone in this room* if I am *shot, punched, grabbed at,* or *jostled!* And if I *see* something I don't *like,* I can detonate it, like *this!!!"* He thrust his left arm abruptly forward and upward, making the crowd flinch in unison. Hands shot into the air.

"No one moves an inch or speaks a word unless I say so! Do exactly as I say or I will kill us all!"

The crowd was mute, paralyzed with fear, except for a few steely pairs of eyes regarding him with condescension and contempt. Bill McNally glared at him menacingly, his hands hovering lazily in front of him as if considering some sort of rash action. Nate pointed the gun at him. "Hands on your head, McNally, you fucking child-raping, drug-dealing greaseball, or I'll kill *you* right now! I've got nothing to lose! *Move it!!"*

"Bill, please," said the governor. Nate was beginning to get high on the power he was wielding over the assemblage. He suddenly realized how Rico must have felt every night for five years, and how the heady experience had turned him into an insufferable, self-idolizing blowhard until the cancer slapped him down off his pedestal. We humans are such fucking assholes, he thought. Why even bother?

"You, in the sunglasses! Put your gun on the floor, right there! Then *slowly* go over and disarm your boss and everyone else in the room, and put the guns on the floor with yours where I can see them! Take cell phones, too! *Now!!"*

Tommy Dongan did as he was told, as reluctantly as he could manage. He removed McNally's gun from its shoulder holster and moved around the room, lightly frisking each of the revelers. Nate was amused, although not particularly surprised, at how much firepower had been deemed necessary by the Republican guests of a holiday party on friendly turf—more than two dozen in all. Mrs. Babson was packing a pearl-handled Derringer in her purse. Arthur Schmidt was carrying a pair of guns, one in a spiffy ankle holster.

This was another weak point in the program. Surely someone would succeed in hanging onto his or her piece, thought Nate. To require Tommy to comprehensively pat everyone down would take too long and likely blow his cover. "Hurry up!" he barked, a paranoid and manic gleam in his eye. Meanwhile, Nate could sense activities beyond the four doorways of the large dining hall. He knew dark forces were massing.

"If I see *one* SWAT team member or sniper or cop or jar-head appear at any door or window, *this bomb goes off!!! DO NOT FUCK WITH ME!!! There will be no stupid heroics! This is not a Neil Young song! Someone go tell them to back off, NOW!!!*"

He addressed Nootch. *"You!* Urinal *reporter! Come here!"*

Nootch approached gingerly, his hands in the air.

Nate spoke quietly. "There's a cell phone in my right jacket pocket. Take it out and punch in this number: 212-714-3340. That's the CNN as-signment desk. Tell them there's a bomb-toting terrorist who has taken over the governor's mansion and is holding the governor, the cardinal and the CEO of USE hostage. Tell them there's a WABC crew in here with a satellite feed truck outside, and I'm taking the crew with me. Tell them one of my demands is that CNN send a helicopter right away, and that they negotiate a deal with WABC to broadcast a little manifesto, or I blow the joint and everybody dies. Got it?"

"Got it." Nootch did so, having to wait on hold for two excruciating minutes but finally getting through to a responsible person who took the story. "Now, take a member of the WABC crew outside with you and tell them what we've just done, and that they need to call CNN and set up a feed. If I don't get a phone call from outside in 10 minutes telling me they're watching me on CNN, this bomb is gonna blow! *Got it?"*

"Yeah, I got it."

"Good. *Now go, and take your sell-out bitch with you!* Tell every moth-erfucker outside what's going on in here, and to back off, or everybody dies! Tell them to have Mr. Babson's driver back his limousine up to the north garage of this mansion! Tell him to make sure it's the same car, with the same fucking license number. I'll *know*, I marked the car. And it better be the same stupid fucking mook driving, and no funny business, or I *will* know! Tell 'em how fucking thorough I am! No fucking surprises or everybody dies, *got it?*"

Nootch nodded. He put the phone back in Nate's pocket and walked away.

"Everybody else, STAY WHERE YOU ARE!!!"

Nootch went over to Nicole, who was weeping softly, and led her out the main entrance by the hand. Nate realized their relationship with him would compromise them forever and possibly even lead to them being targeted for extinction if this thing didn't work out. But it was better than their being blown to bits with him if events turned sour. He had needed to be firm.

As Tommy continued about his business and while Nate waited for a phone call from Charles Overlook, who was watching CNN at the nearby Kipsbergh Hotel bar, Nate occupied himself with colorfully brandishing the gun and detonator switch and making further brief, threatening pronouncements while letting Freddy's training spiel play on in his head: "Anyway, proceed carefully with Cardinal McCall to the dais, telling the WABC film crew to keep their cameras rolling. Once you are in place next to the governor with a gun to his head, and with the detonator in your hand visible to the crowd, you can proceed with your speech which, according to Nick, you'll have had no trouble drafting."

"No trouble at all," Nate had said.

"Well, if you need an editor, I'll be available. I have experience."

This had tickled Nate. He remembered thinking how fascinating it was that so many people, from all walks of life, harbored dreams of being wordsmiths, while he had simply stumbled into being a writer without ever having given it serious thought. He couldn't believe how bizarre this was; that here he stood, about to give an address that, like Lincoln's, Churchill's, Gandhi's or Martin Luther King's shining orations, could quite possibly change the world. "More like Charlie Manson or Ted Kaczynski," he abruptly and bitterly contradicted himself in his deteriorating mind. "I am such a fucking megalomaniac right now. Someone should shoot me and get it over with."

He shook himself free of these unclean thoughts, as the crowd cowered and gasped at the manifestations of obvious insanity playing across his face.

His cell phone rang.

"No false moves! This bomb will go off if anybody fucking moves!!!

He carefully put the gun in its shoulder holster, reached in his pocket and answered the phone on the fourth ring.

"Jimmy?"

"Yo."

"They're reporting it, but there's no feed yet."

"OK, whatever."

He hung up, put the phone away and pulled out his gun. There was no time to wait: a bluff would have to do.

"Members of the WABC television crew! Please relax and go about your business. I want this entire process to be recorded for posterity. CNN is on line. Start filming, *NOW!!! Or else!!!*" With the cameras rolling, or at least pretending to roll, Nate walked with the cardinal to the dais, released him and grabbed Pollock, pointing the gun at his bad comb-over. "'Ello, Guvna. I'm about to tell these fine folks a little story.

"This is live television, folks. Uncle Jimmy's Texaco Dinner Theater. What you are about to hear, upon pain of death, is how the governor here, the man in whose palace you have just gorged yourselves, the workingman's friend, the tireless champion of education reform, sustainable business development and the environment, is a high-level criminal. A cocaine importer, smuggler, toxic waste dumper, Mafia shill and all-around scumbag. *Please remain still!!! I'm VERY NERVOUS, AND NOT MYSELF LATELY!!!*"

Nate was developing a sore throat already, and was afraid of losing his voice. With his gun, he banged loudly on the gooseneck-mounted microphone, adjusting it downward from the lofty position it had been set at for the taller governor's aborted speech. With each deafening tap, the room filled with an even more ear-splitting feedback screech. Nate paid no attention. He gazed around the room, studying each face intently. Mrs. Babson looked horrified, all postmenopausal yearning extinguished for the time being; Winnie just seemed deflated, like he'd been eviscerated alive and left to die. The McNallys continued to glower, Mrs. McNally while chewing voraciously on her lower lip like an angry steer. Arthur Schmidt stuck his massive CEO jaw out bravely, the effect belied by the worried crinkle behind his bushy eyebrows, as mascara-blackened tears streamed down his fourth trophy wife's jutting cheeks, making her look like Alice Cooper in a blonde fright wig. Tommy Dongan stood a reasonable twenty feet from the oil-black pile of guns and phones, trying his best to look angry and put-upon through his visage-deadening eyewear.

A cluster of men and women his own age and younger whom Nate could only assume were 9/11 surviving firefighters and their stoic spouses looked on almost distractedly, as if this were just one more ho-hum crisis in their skewed, hopelessly aggrandized post-traumatic lives. Scanning the crowd for trouble, he continued.

"The governor's very good friend, the former Westie gang member and current Natale family associate William T. McNally, whom I've already introduced, is among us today. Mr. McNally, please raise your hands even higher, for those among us with our heads up our ass."

"Fuck you."

"That will be all, fuckface. Mr. McNally's biggest problem is not that he is a sexual psychopath who met his future wife Edith while raping her behind the Dutch Hollow goal posts, and who repeatedly and systematically violated his eldest daughter in her bedroom from the time she was nine years old. *Do not move a muscle, Mr. McNally! I would really LOVE to kill you right now! I am a very good shot! I have been PRACTICING!!!*"

As McNally simmered and steamed and got ready to burst a vein, Edith, who had presumably not been completely unaware of her husband's indiscretions, began to assert herself. Nate did not stop her from whispering angrily in her husband's ear. Whatever she said seemed to sedate him.

"Thank you, Mrs. McNally. You just saved your husband's life, for the time being. Now if you'll allow me to continue, maybe we can *all* get out of this alive." The firefighters twitched and snickered. They may be plotting something, Nate thought. Heroes, maybe, although he wondered how many of them had looted stores in lower Manhattan during their heroic search for their brethren. He had heard stories of firemen in a poor section of Brooklyn ordering an entire block of families out of their homes when a smoke alarm went off, hacking down doors with their axes and stealing TV sets and fancy electronics from people they considered helpless welfare frauds. But then, he was feeling especially uncharitable at the moment. Maybe it was just him.

"*QUIET!* As I was saying, William T. McNally has much bigger problems as a human being hoping to get into heaven. It is not because he is a wholesaler of cocaine, methamphetamines and other dangerous drugs, which he is. It is not because he smuggles Colombian, Mexican and other illegal immigrants into this country to work for subhuman wages, which he does. It is not because he is a dangerous, ruthless mobster with no ethical sense, which he is. It is, however, because he has been personally responsible for the cancer deaths of thousands, if not hundreds of thousands, of his fellow human beings.

"How has he achieved this death toll, which is greater than the human loss of life on September 11 and in the ensuing year and a half of bombing and devastation in Afghanistan, Israel and Palestine combined? Through the wholesale, indiscriminate dumping of millions upon millions of gallons of toxic waste into the landscapes and fresh water aquifers of Roosevelt County, Ulster County, Orange County, Sullivan County, Putnam County and Columbia County in New York State, the counties of Litchfield and Fairfield in Connecticut and in the counties of Passaic, Hudson, Union and Bergen in New Jersey.

"His multimillion-dollar company, Janssen Movers, does not move household furniture. The scores of Janssen trucks you see each week rumbling along the lower and mid-Hudson region's highways rarely, if ever, contain furniture. They contain hundreds of barrels each of cancer-causing toxic waste, much of which comes from one source: the computer manufacturing operations of USE, right here in Roosevelt County. We have USE chairman Arthur Schmidt here to verify the fact of Janssen's $50 million annual contract with the world's largest computer manufacturer, am I right, Mr. Schmidt? Mr. Schmidt, *am I right?*"

Schmidt nodded his head.

"People, keep your hands up! *Up! Up!!* Rest them on your heads if you must! This will all be over soon!

"Now. Instead of recycling these poisonous chemicals properly, William McNally and his Janssen Movers store them in three vast warehouses until they can be resold and shipped out, to Colombian and Dominican drug lords for the manufacture of cocaine, to paving companies so they can cut their asphalt with cheap, dirty solvents, to anyone and everyone who doesn't mind poisoning a few innocent suckers to increase their profit margin.

"The thing is, my friends, that Bill McNally can't unload even half the toxic chemicals he has amassed, so he needs to find ways to get rid of the excess, to sweep it under the rug. And so, he and his mob friends have devised schemes to dump and bury the stuff under every large construction project, down every drain in every highway garage, and into every wetland and freshwater stream. Even in graveyards, packed around grandma's cancer-eaten bones. Toxic waste is under every superhighway, parking lot, high school, shopping mall, golf course, children's park and sports stadium, making the air above them dangerous to breathe and the water below them undrinkable.

"Right here in Roosevelt County, there is not one town in which unfiltered, unprocessed well water can pass muster with any health agency except Mr. Pollock's thoroughly corrupt Department of Environmental Conservation, which is virtually owned by Mr. McNally's mob. Strange, lethal solvents have been found in the groundwater everywhere, and water must be piped in from the Hudson to entire communities. Rooseveltown. Pinksterkill. Lenape Falls. Beaverton. Waterkill. Echo Valley. Pleasant Plains. Sunnydale. Kipsbergh. Right here in beautiful Indian Hills. *The PCB-infested Hudson is cleaner than your water here under these green hills and valleys! Why is that? Why do children in Roosevelt County have a cancer rate nearly three times this disgusting, toxic country's national average? Why are there huge spikes in prostate cancer, leukemia, Hodgkins and lymphoma in southern Roosevelt, the Mohican Valley and the horsy town of Jefferson, of all places?*

"Because of one man's tremendous efforts. William T. McNally, take a bow. Never mind, Bill; just stand there and squirm. Because here's what's happening right now, folks. We're going on a little televised tour of Mr. Pollock's lovely house. Call it a suicide *MTV Cribs* episode. And seeing as our great governor Mr. Pollock is basically a paid employee of Mr. McNally here, we're sure to find some very interesting stuff. In order to keep things simple, I'm taking only a handful of hostages with me. Mr. McNally, come up here, please."

McNally finally came unhinged. "Blow me, faggot." Edith nudged her husband's raised elbow violently with her own.

"*EXCUSE ME? How about I blow your fucking head off, huh, asshole?*"

"Fuck you. You don't have the guts, faggot."

Nate didn't even have to think about it. He aimed carefully as the governor and the cardinal cringed beside him. "*Everybody stand PERFECTLY still! Mr, McNally's about to take one for the team!*" Even as he spoke McNally ducked, but Nate had anticipated his movement perfectly and on the word "*take*," fired a round into his shoulder, collapsing him to the floor. Moans and cries erupted from the crowd.

"*SHUT UP! Nobody move! Sunglasses man, pick your boss up and bring him here! MOVE IT!!!*"

Dongan, working hard to suppress a smile, moved quickly and scooped up his bleeding employer. He got within ten feet when Nate stopped him. "That's far enough. Stay right there. Wrap his shoulder up, it's making these people sick. *You!* Give the man that scarf."

Tommy took a woman's green peacock satin scarf and tied it around McNally's shoulder, stuffing a wad of cloth napkins inside the wound to stanch the bleeding, as the mobster swallowed a scream—the effect of which was the sad, muffled sound of a drowning man crying for help with water in his lungs. Perhaps in sympathy with the agony of his nemesis, the pain receptors in Nate's brain chose that very moment to switch back on. He shook it off.

"Shut up, McNally. I'm tired of your whining. Mr. Schmidt, I don't believe I'll have to shoot you to convince you I mean business. Come up here and join the party. Governor, Cardinal McCall, if you would please join the entourage as well? Thank you. I also need the WABC camera crew. Please bring your most portable equipment that can send a signal out to the truck."

"Our portable equipment won't send, sir."

"Oh, well. Do you have a portable video camera?"

"Yes."

"Then bring it."

They quickly got together a portable package: a Sony BVW D600 Betacam and a small light tripod.

"Note to CNN and all who are watching. If these people get out of here alive, they will be carrying a videotape of our tour. I am hoping not to have to kill them, but if I am attacked *they will die* with the governor, the cardinal, this bleeding scumbag and myself. If all goes well I will be letting this crew out first, with the videotape in hand. If anything happens to the crew or the videotape after I let them go, you can blame the governor and his Mafioso friend here, Mr. McNally, along with the state police and sheriff's department they have outside working on their payroll."

He addressed a swarthy, diminutive busboy in a white shirt and black pants. "And you, sir, *habla Español?*"

"Si."

"Do you speak English, can you translate?"

"Si. Yes. I think so."

"Good. *Nobody move a muscle! We're almost through here!* Everything will be..."

Just then a flurry of activity erupted outside of the main dining hall entrance. Nate brandished the detonator switch and the crowd cringed in anticipation. A door opened.

"Nate!"

It was Nootch.

"What's up?"

"They want me to negotiate. They're holding Nicole."

"What for?"

"They know about you two. They think you care about her, and that she's had your ear. They're threatening to arrest her and prosecute her as an accomplice if you don't give up."

"That's absurd. They're full of shit. That bitch is a sell-out."

"That's not what she told them. Anyway, there's a whole division of troop Q out there in combat gear, with helicopters. They want to know what you want. They gave me a cell phone."

"I don't want anything, yet. Tell them to go fuck themselves."

"They told me to stick with you, no matter what."

"They probably think I'll think twice about using *this!!!*" Nate brandished the detonator switch once again. "They're wrong!"

"Come on, dude. Calm down. What will it hurt?" Nate could have sworn Nootch half winked at him. "Just let me come along. I won't be a bother."

"Yeah, sure. You might as well die with me. They'll probably kill you anyway."

On Nate's instructions, Nootch and the Latino busboy cleared a table, tore off the tablecloth, picked up the guns and phones and placed them inside, and tied up the four corners into a makeshift duffel bag. "You're going to stand in front of me carrying this sack," said Nate to the busboy.

"Nootch, you walk with him and watch him like a hawk."

"Sure thing, chief," Nootch whispered.

"Don't call me chief."

"OK! *When I say 'go,'* everyone except this small group here—Mr. Sunglasses, you're coming with us—please proceed with your hands up and facing me at all times, toward the main dining room door, over *there. Stay away from my Latino friend!!!* You will not be getting your guns *or* your precious cell phones back today. Your busboy, if he is still alive, will return them to you at a later date. *Wait!! Do not move until I say so!!* Mr. Sunglasses, please release Mr. McNally into the custody of the cardinal, so he can succor him, maybe give him last rites or something."

Dongan did as he was told.

"Nootch, call your friends outside and tell them we're letting everyone go but a small group. The governor, the cardinal, Mr. Schmidt, Mr. McNally and his henchman, a Colombian illegal immigrant and a crack camera crew from the city. Tell them to stand back and keep away from the doors of this room, or there will be bloody mayhem involving the severed body parts of a very popular, environmentalist governor with vice presidential aspirations."

"*All right! Everyone but our little ragtag team here, slowly, carefully, hands up, no stupid moves, back across the room and out the door! Slowly. Carefully. Easy does it. One by one! Don't crowd! I'm still VERY NERVOUS!!!*

"*So long, everyone! It's been a gas!*"

When the last man and woman—which happened to be a shell-shocked Winnie and Marjorie—had exited, Nate grouped the remaining party ahead of himself in a sort of flying wedge formation, pointing them toward the north hallway doors, and said the thing he had been waiting all evening to say.

"OK, class. In the words of our Commander-in-Chief, *'Let's roll.'*"

CHAPTER TWENTY-THREE
OLD MAN RIVER

The lethal phalanx advanced slowly down the north hallway with Nootch in the vanguard, whispering to the busboy to keep cool, and that things would be all right. Cardinal McCall of the Catholic Diocese of New York followed, with Tommy Dongan on his left. The wounded Janssen Movers president, William T. McNally, sagged along fitfully, supported on his right by New York State Governor Hiram Pollock and flanked by USE CEO Arthur Schmidt on his left. Nate and his bomb occupied the rear, along with the two trembling WABC journalists, their Betacam whirring and visions of a Peabody Award—or a memorial statue with their names on it—dancing in their brains.

They passed the kitchen, where through the porthole windows three of the wait staff who had been too curious to run off could be seen huddling, the dayglo-hued tops of their heads bobbing comically above a gunmetal-gray countertop.

"Halt!" said Nate. "Nootch. Open the door here and check for anybody with a weapon. Ask those nice folks hiding behind the counter if anyone's seen SWAT teams or other police activity in the hallway here or the elevator lobbies."

Once again Nootch complied without complaint. He could now be considered a full-blooded accomplice, if anyone was splitting hairs.

"Yes, they say people with guns have been in the hallway, but they left when they saw us coming. They said they went out through the back stairwell. No sign of anyone else in the kitchen."

"OK. Shit. Ask one of them for a flashlight, and tell them to get the fuck out of the building."

Dusk had fallen outside, and although the hall lights were blazing, Nate didn't trust leaving anything to chance. A flashlight appeared at the door: a sturdy green Coleman camping lamp. "Nootch, make a call. Tell them we're going down the elevator to level B, and if anything *at all* happens: lights going out, elevators shutting down, doors being locked, gas or smoke seeping into a vent, gunmen appearing, *anything at all*, I'm blowing this joint to Kingdom Come. I'm getting very, very tired of this, and my thumb might slip if I get upset."

As he turned around to talk to Nootch, Nate smiled, nodded and winked at his friend reassuringly. While McNally, Pollock, Schmidt and the cardinal hadn't seen the gesture, it did not escape the camera.

With his reporter's gifts, Nootch was a natural as a negotiator, able to transmit Nate's unfolding demands word-for-word. Although he was still scared shitless, Nootch had earlier decided his former protégé knew what he was doing. He knew Nate was *acting* loony-tunes, but despite what Nicole said he was convinced it was all a front to keep the hostages and the police from getting comfortable enough to try something. For sure, the crazy old fuck had a bomb strapped to his chest and had shot someone, but he had heard Nate's rant on the WABC monitor outside, and had been convinced that he had a point, wacked as it was.

In fact, Nate was reminding Nootch of his secret hero during his inner-anarchist-awakening college years: Ted Kaczynski, a.k.a. the Unabomber, an intelligent, dispossessed loner who had waged an 18-year terror campaign as a sick but effective means to attain a platform—*The Washington Post* and *The New York Times*—for exposing the evil of the industrial-technological status quo. When Nootch was a raw freshman computer science major at Yale, the bomber had targeted one of his professors, David Gelernter, a guy who was semi-famous for making up a programming language and naming it "Linda," after deep-throat porn queen Linda Lovelace. Since seeing his teacher running down the hallway with his face and hands dripping blood, Nootch had followed news of the Unabomber's exploits and read everything he wrote, including his famed "manifesto." He basically ended up agreeing with everything Kaczynski wrote, which was what predicated his abandoning computer science for journalism in his junior year. He had never adequately explained the reason for his mid-semester career switch to anyone.

If everything Nate said was true, thought Nootch, old Bill McNally deserved to be shot. McNally, it seemed, was a real-life manifestation of the sort of Machiavellian villainy epitomized by Noah Cross in *Chinatown*, complete with the pedophilic, incestuous streak. This was a very bad man, whose callous and mindlessly greedy actions were turning a former earthly paradise into a cancerous, post-industrial nightmare of shit. The public would be forgiving of Nate if he somehow got out of this foolishness alive and could continue to pump his story. "Good luck, brother," Nootch ESP'd to Nate, forming both hands into surreptitious, protective *i corni*. "Sacred hearts of Jesus and Mary protect..."

* * *

Nate and his nine hostages wended their way clumsily down the hallway, turning right through a set of double doors at the end into a large storage room with a utility elevator.

"One floor down is the north garage, outside of which the limo will be waiting," Freddy had said. "Two floors down, off the warehouse where the cocaine stash is, is the brig, where your associate Mr. Thurston Brown should be languishing, if he is still alive by then."

"Thirsty!" Nate had blurted.

"I'm sure he will be," Freddy had cracked, in his slow, deadpan fashion. "Dead or alive, the scene should make great television. Just watch out for snipers, make an announcement as the doors open and have your translator translate it, loudly. Remain visibly agitated and cultivate an aura of unpredictability throughout the proceedings. That look you have on your face right now should do fine."

Waiting for the elevator to arrive, Nate could see his reflection in the darkened window of the door, sandwiched between those of McNally and Schmidt, and was pleased to note that he continued to appear certifiably insane to the naked eye. Strong drug doses, lack of food, periodic gushers of fear and anxiety hormones and the strange, complicated rush of shooting a man had seen to that. The problem now, as he saw it, was to avoid actually falling into madness via the repetitive imitation of insane acts.

It wouldn't be easy, mused Nate. He had seen with his own eyes how seemingly innocuous actions or circumstances become predictors of fate. For example, he once knew three smart Schenectady boys with the bestial surnames Wolf, Fox and Partridge. They could have become anything when they grew up, but they didn't. They not only became veterinarians within three years of each other; they joined in a four-man practice with an older doggie doc named Doctor Lamb. Similarly, at least a dozen successful, competent rock musicians Nate had known through the years had become so not through any development of natural talent, but because someone in their distant past had told them they *looked* like rock musicians. A slender torso, long skinny legs, ratty hair and a sallow, pockmarked complexion do not an accomplished musician make. But because of the sheer power of suggestion, these talent-less creatures had each taken up an instrument and gutted it out to the point that they were eventually able to realize their highly unlikely dreams.

Nate considered himself to be in the same boat as these name-destined veterinarians and physique-destined rock stars. Through the coincidence, bad timing and even worse luck of having bedded down a beautiful martyr and witnessed her destruction, he had stumbled upon a worthy cause and become an anarchist zealot himself. Having painted himself into a corner with his obsession he had somehow allowed himself to be talked into posing as a martyr as well. Since taking the plunge, he had succeeded so grandly in *pretending* to be a suicidal maniac that he was in serious danger of *becoming* one. He was very glad Nootch had tagged along. As his only link to his former, better self, his friend was part of a very slender membrane of humanity keeping his left thumb from pushing the little red plunger button.

* * *

"I have to go to the bathroom," said Pollock.

"Pee in your pants, Governor. This isn't high school, there are no hall passes."

McNally moaned something unintelligible.

"What the fuck does *he* want?" This could easily get out of hand if he relaxed his resolve for even a split second, thought Nate. He didn't know if he could keep the crazy act going for the time it would take.

"He said he's thirsty," said Schmidt. "Look, friend, why don't you stop this charade? You haven't killed anybody yet, and if you give yourself up I'm sure..."

"*SHUT THE FUCK UP, YOU PIECE OF SHIT!* I am not negotiating with you! You are a fucking *prop*, understand? I don't give a fuck if you *or* I live or die! Your only chance is if you keep your yap shut and do as I say!"

The elevator arrived from a lower floor. "Now *MOVE!!!*"

The freight elevator, empty as a dowager's womb, was large enough to accommodate a semi trailer. The party easily fit inside. "Nootch. Press B2, please."

Nootch pressed B2. Nothing happened. Nate already knew why.

"Nootch, check these people's pockets for keys, starting with Mr. Sunglasses here, then the governor. I believe B2 is accessible by putting a key in that little round hole there."

"I wouldn't do that," said the governor. "That's where my security is. It's probably crawling with police by now."

"*Do you want to shut the fuck up, asshole, or do I have to put you down, too? Shut up!!!* Nootch! Do as I say!"

Nootch complied. He fished a keychain out of Dongan's left-hand pants pocket, inadvertently grazing the man's nut-sack in the process. "Sorry, dude."

Dongan just stared at him mutely through his shades. Nootch found three cylindrical-shafted barrel keys on the chain, and tried them one-by-one in the circular hole. The second one worked. Nootch turned it, punched B2 again and the doors closed. The elevator began to descend, slowly.

There was an access door on the north end as well as at the south where they had entered. Nate turned to Dongan. "You. Which door opens at B2 level? And what will we see? Are there places for snipers to hide? Don't lie or I'll blow your brains out."

"Both doors," said Dongan evenly. "The shaft is in the middle of an open warehouse level. There are stacks of boxes on shelves, with room to drive a lorry around."

The red LCD on the control panel changed from "G" to "B1."

"Can I choose which door to open?"

"Aye. Those buttons right there."

"Which one opens the door in front of us?"

"That one, on the left."

"What about B1, when we go back up?"

"The door in front of us opens into a big open garage bay."

The elevator thudded to a halt at B2.

"Good. You better hope you're right. Push the left button."

A wet streak began to darken the inside of the governor's olive green left pant leg. The elevator door opened into a well-lit underground warehouse.

"We're coming out now! This bomb will blow if I am shot or jostled! If I see guns or smoke, or smell gas, or if the lights go out, we all die!"

After each phrase, Nate had the busboy yell it in Spanish. He herded his charges over to the nearest storage rack, loaded to the ceiling with boxes, which, according to Tommy's earlier briefing on the mansion's subterranean layout, contained nothing but premium grade Colombian cocaine. Other racks were laden with barrels and plastic-coated bottles, just like at the airport.

"Pull a box down and open it, Nootch."

Nootch walked over and reached up to the top of the first tier, just over his head. He pulled at the corners of a heavy 200-lb. box with his fingernails and slowly shimmied it out until it dropped of its own weight on the cement floor. McNally sagged further, and the governor winced and peed again as Nate's gun casually grazed the back of his head. Viciously ripping the packing tape off, Nootch tore open the top and exposed the contents: twelve clear plastic bags containing about 16 pounds of cocaine each. Nate did a quick mental calculation: 45 grand times 16 times 12. There was more than $8 million street value in that box!

He looked up and down the lofty rack system. Three tiers of boxes, stacked four wide, two deep and five high. Eight times three is 24. Times four is...96? Times two is 192. Times five is...shit. Almost a billion dollars in coke was staring him in the face!

Moving forward toward Nootch, Nate turned around and faced his captives, still pointing his gun alternately at Pollock, McNally and

Schmidt while addressing the WABC crew. "Take a good look, kids. This rack contains nearly a billion dollars in high-grade Colombian cocaine. What you're looking at is a major, if not *the* major distribution center of coke for the entire northeastern United States. This is a large-scale criminal operation. Those racks over there contain toxic chemicals from USE, which are to be sent to Colombia to manufacture cocaine. Again: this wounded man here is the ringleader, and these fine gentlemen are two of his many stooges. The state police and sheriff's departments have been employed by Mr. McNally's mob and the governor to protect the operation. They are gathered outside in a multitude in order to kill me, cover up this investigation and safeguard their investment from prying eyes. I am sorry, but your lives are as much in danger from them as from me. Are we clear?"

The camera crew nodded.

"Nootch, c'mere."

Waving the gun wildly and brandishing the detonator, Nate put his left arm around Nootch's shoulder and the detonator in front of his face, as the group cringed. *"Nobody fucking move!* We're gonna have a conference, here!"

The sound of nearby compressors hummed in the vast space. Nate hadn't noticed them before. He whispered. "Look, buddy. I'm sorry I got you into this, but it's real. These people are crooks and killers. Now listen to me. As far as any of them killing us, they're bluffing. So far they have no fucking idea that I'm bluffing, too, and we have to keep it that way, *capeesh*? That was the fucking Cuban missile crisis up there and they had their chance to gun me down, and they blinked. As long as we stay together and have the governor and McNally, we'll be all right."

Nootch nodded.

"Look, this guy over here, Mr. Sunglasses, he's good. He's my mole in here. We're getting out of this, OK, man? I'm not crazy. I'm having them send the car down. It's packed with gasoline and dynamite. I'm gonna let the cardinal, the busboy and the camera guys go, blow up those three motherfuckers while pretending to blow up myself, and escape out the back door while Mr. Sunglasses mops up. You can either split with the camera crew and help them get the video out of here alive or find Nicole or whatever, or come with me out the back door into Big Nick's witness protection plan. You're in this pretty deep, so it's your call."

"Jesus Christ, what a fucking ass-fuck you've got by the tail! This is stupendous! Dude, if we get out of this, I swear I'll get your story out somehow."

"Yeah, well, just remember to use the past tense when referring to me. It's a style thing. Oh, and P.S., chief. You and Nicole enjoy your lives together. I love you both. I mean that."

Nate's embrace tightened, and Nootch's eyes began to tear.

Nate raised his voice. "Now, Nootch. Who are you talking to when you call the outside?"

"Sheriff Hildenbrandt."

"Fucking scumbag. Did you know USE paid him five grand to let them dump 50,000 gallons of PCBs and other shit on his beef farm in the '60s? Mr. Schmidt here probably knows about that, don't you, sir? Anyway, I digress. Give the sheriff a call, and then hand the phone to me."

Nootch got out his phone and tapped in the number. "Sheriff? John Ianucci. The bomber wants to talk to you."

He held the phone out to Nate. Nate traded the gun for it, and Nootch kept it trained on the three main hostages.

"Howdy, sheriff."

Nate had always wanted to say that.

"Listen, there's been a change in plans. Remember that limo I asked for? It should be waiting right now with the driver in it, backed up to the mansion's north garage. Is that happening?"

"Yes. Listen, Mr. ..."

"*Shut up!* It had *better* be Mr. Babson's car, the one I rode here in. Make sure it's the *same car*, with the same license number—525 DHL— and the same fucking driver! Do you hear me?"

"Yes, yes. Please calm down, Mr. Olsen. I can hear you."

"*I'll fucking calm down when I'm good and ready, motherfucker!* Now send the fucking car down the elevator to B2 level *now!* Then clear the fuck out of the garage and shut the door and wait for further instructions, got it? I'm taking these people for a little ride! Just *send the fucking car down, NOW!* Goodbye!"

Nate traded the phone back to Nootch for the gun, and turned to his bleeding nemesis.

"Good. Now, Mr. McNally, can you speak?"

"F-f-fuck you."

"Fine, then." Nate walked over to him and put the gun to his forehead. "Mr. McNally, I want you to tell me in which room here you have incarcerated my friend Reginald Thurston Brown. A little old chubby mulatto with a British accent. You have five seconds. One, two, three, four..."

"No!" It was Pollock. "Please. I'll tell you. Look, I had no idea all this was going on down here. My security people told me they were holding an intruder for questioning. Their office is down that hallway on the left." He pointed past the last storage rack where there was a set of double doors in the wall.

"Excellent. Then that's where we're going. Company, harch!"

Nate steered the group toward the door in the adjacent wall, 50 feet away. Suddenly the door cracked open and a hand bearing a white flag appeared. Then a slender white arm, followed by a curvaceous body in a green dress, capped by a frightened, tear-streaked face framed by a partially fallen hairdo. "Nicole!"

The sound of the same woman's name being blurted from Nate's, Nootch's and Schmidt's mouths surprised and disoriented nearly everyone.

But not as much as what happened next.

Appearing through the doorway behind Nicole, holding a Luger to her head and using her as a human shield, was the most bizarre looking human being Nate had ever seen. One could only assume the man was kidding, dressed as he was in the Nazi-inspired get-up of a tricked-out New Jersey state highway patrolman: jodhpurs and shiny knee-length boots, an ornate high-peaked SS cap, tight-fitting belted jacket with epaulets, shoulder braids, bandoleer and what appeared to be a rack of medals glinting behind Nicole's left shoulder. A Salvadore Dali mustache and a Dishonest John sneer completed the improbable picture. Robinson. Behind the crooked commandant and his hostage was an apparently empty darkened hallway, but Nate could imagine the anti-terrorist SWAT team of helmeted men with body armor and submachine guns lurking in the gloom.

Beyond any hope of turning back from his suicidal bomber persona, Nate stayed the course. *"Back off, motherfucker! Let that woman go!"*

"No, my friend, it is you who will back off. I am Commander Robinson of the New York State Police. This woman is an accessory to your crimes, and is under arrest. Put your gun down, and release these people at once. If you detonate your bomb, she dies. If you rush at me and my finger slips, or if my men in the hallway are drawn into a shootout, she will die as well. Either way she is in grave peril. Is that what you want?"

Nate knew what he did next would bring either victory or Armageddon. He gambled on the thin shred of hope that Commander Robinson was more interested in protecting the billion dollars worth of cocaine twenty yards behind him than anything else.

"NO!!!" he thundered. He raised the detonator and cocked his thumb, and aimed the gun at the commander's face. Oh, well, he thought. Here goes nothing. "State police, my ass! You're as big a fucking criminal as the rest of these people. I'll give you ten seconds to let that woman go, and back the fuck out of here, or you're getting one between the eyes before I *PUSH THIS FUCKING BUTTON!!!"*

"Jim, do what he says! He'll do it! He's fucking crazy!" It was the governor.

Nate kept walking forward. *"TEN! NINE! EIGHT! SEVEN! SIX!"*

The commander cowered behind Nicole, a look finally crossing his face that indicated he realized he was dealing with a seriously deranged individual, and that he had gravely miscalculated what he thought was his natural advantage.

"Nate, no..."

A muffled thud, then a single shot exploded, followed by a burst of automatic gunfire from deep in the hallway. Commander Robinson crumpled to the floor, his Nazi hat and what looked like the top half of his head wobbling off to the left like a badly thrown, blood-drenched frisbee. Nicole collapsed to the floor as well, having caught three slugs in the back below her right clavicle. There was another short burst of gunfire and Nootch, who had been running toward Nicole, took one in the ribs.

Seeing all this, Nate finally lost what was left of his marbles.

* * *

With such an inauspicious beginning to the proceedings, coupled with the presence of a madman with a powerful bomb and live rounds being fired off in many directions, it was a miracle that the ensuing melee produced as little carnage as it did. But sometimes life—and death—don't play by Hoyle's rules.

Actually, it would later be sorted out that it was not Nate but Tommy Dongan, impatient with the slow progress of peace negotiations, who had broken the impasse. With Nootch partially blocking him from the eyes of the other hostages, he had stealthily moved to the right and unsheathed his auxiliary weapon, a 9x19mm Beretta 92 FS with a silencer, and with a clear shot over Nicole's left shoulder, fired it at Robinson's noggin. As Nootch and Nate rushed at the front like Kamikaze doughboys, Dongan then turned and, noticing that Schmidt and the governor had dropped McNally and were running, fired three quick rounds, one grazing the governor's shoulder, one missing Schmidt's ear by inches and the third catching him in the buttocks. He paused and fired once more into McNally's forehead, before taking a stray bullet in the thigh and collapsing himself.

Earlier, as Nicole fell away from the commander, Nate had gotten a shot into the man's skull as well, an act that, in conjunction with Tommy's bulls-eye, had apparently been enough to wrest the man's hat and a bad toupee from their moorings, sending them spinning.

Foaming at the mouth, Nate then charged at the open doorway like a deranged Moses, nearly emptying the magazine of the gun in his right hand. With his left arm raised high and his thumb still on the red button, he screamed: *"Hold your fire!!! Hold your fire or die!!! Raaaah!! RAAAAAAAAAH!!! RAAAAAAARGH!!!!!"* … while somehow avoiding the ricocheting bullets of the initial, knee-jerk burst of gunfire from the jittery SWAT team still not visible down the darkened hallway.

Whether Robinson's backup team had retreated in fear or was just biding their time and baiting a trap was unclear, but the shooting subsided, at least for the moment.

Nate ventured carefully to the corner of the hallway and peeked around it into the gloom. There was no movement, and no one shot at him. He retraced his steps slowly, checking doors on the way. Trying one and finding it locked, he stood clear and fired at the doorjamb, smashing the lock. As he opened the door, a fetid dead-animal stench threw him back. He stifled the urge to vomit and lunged forward again, groping along the inside wall for a light switch. He found one and flipped it on.

It was Thirsty, or what was left of him. A bloated, oozing corpse, his eyes were empty sockets, caked with dried blood. His face had obviously been beaten savagely, and his fingernails were missing. Nate turned around and walked away.

He returned from the hallway and closed the access door. The warehouse floor was stained with blood leaking from the dead and wounded. The elevator doors opened and a gleaming Cadillac limousine nosed out into the warehouse. The WABC cameramen, who had run for cover behind the lofty stack of cocaine, had re-emerged and resumed filming.

"You want *real* war footage? Down that hallway, second door on the left," said Nate. "His name's Reginald Thurston Brown. He may not look like much now, but he's my friend, and a hero. They tortured him to death. There's your fucking state police. But I'd hurry if I were you. Those troopers are still down there somewhere, plotting their next move."

The cardinal and the busboy were nowhere to be found. A parallel trail of CEO and gubernatorial blood streaked off in the direction of another set of doors in the concrete wall to the south. McNally lay motionless on the floor, blood oozing from a half-dollar-sized hole in his head.

Freddy Natale emerged from the driver's side door, with his gun drawn. "What the *fuck* is going on down here?"

Tommy Dongan, having quickly stanched his own wound, was already administering crude medical assistance to Nicole. "Chill out, Freddy, everything's under control. That car got a first aid kit?"

Nootch was sitting beside Nicole, holding her and stroking her hair as Tommy ripped her dress down from the neck in back and fashioned a makeshift body tourniquet. Nate walked over to them, put a finger on Nicole's jugular, and felt her pulse. It was strong. "How is she?"

"She's alive," said Tommy. "She's not bleeding too bad; if she's lucky she'll only have a punctured lung. We'd better hurry, though."

"How is *he?*"

"*Him?* I didn't know he'd been hit."

Nate moved Nootch's jacket aside, revealing the widening bloodstain on his shirt.

"*Motherfucker*, why didn't you say something?"

"F-fix her up first," said Nootch. He swooned and passed out.

Freddy returned and went to work on Nootch. "Where are the governor and Schmidt?"

"They ran," said Tommy.

"Well, we've got to work fast and get out of here. If they find out McNally's dead, we're blown." Freddy finished dressing Nootch's wound. "We're going to have to leave these people here for their own good. We'll take McNally. He's our only excuse, now. Help me get this bastard in the car."

"Wait!" said Nate, pointing at Nootch and Nicole. "I want these two to come with us."

"It'll never happen," said Freddy, matter-of-factly. "We take them, we all lose. They'll bleed all over the fucking tunnel and slow us down. They're better off going with the camera crew like we said."

Nate's heart sank even lower, knowing he was about to abandon two more loves of his life.

Freddy and Tommy got up and hovered over McNally's lifeless form. The two cameramen returned from their side mission, shaken.

"That's it, you two," said Nate, holding out his hand. "Show's over. Give me the tape."

They blanched. "What..." said the taller of the two.

"Shut up and fork it over. It's for your own good. You think these people are going to let you get out of here alive with this?" Nate took the videotape, then leaned down and rummaged in Nootch's jacket for his cell phone. He put it in his pocket and handed his own cell phone to the cameramen.

"We're leaving now. If you can, get these two to that far door over there, where there's probably a stairway out of here. Stay as far away from this elevator as you can. After you hear an explosion, use this to call your people and tell them where you are. Tell them we let you go and went up the elevator with McNally and the video. It's your only chance. Then get these two to a hospital."

Nootch moaned and awoke.

"Nootch, you OK, buddy?"

"Not really," he croaked.

"OK, listen. I'm leaving you and Nicole in the care of these nice newsmen. Here's my gun. Use it only if you have to. You need to get upstairs through those doors and find a safe way out of here, preferably with a TV crew or in an ambulance. I might never see you again. Thanks for everything, little brother." He kissed him on the forehead.

Nate bent over Nicole, who smiled weakly. "I'm sorry, sweetheart. Please don't die on me. Take care of my friend here and make lots of big-nosed babies. I'll always love you."

He squeezed her hand, and she squeezed back.

Tommy and Freddy had finished hauling McNally's carcass and a box of cocaine into the back seat, and had gotten in the limo's front. Nate climbed in the back with the dead man, and the car backed almost silently into the waiting elevator. As the doors closed, the two WABC cameramen stared after them quizzically, wondering what had just happened.

"Don't even try to figure it out," said Nootch softly, not quite realizing he'd been left to die. "Just help us get the fuck out of here."

* * *

As the elevator slowly ascended, Nate carefully took off his jacket and bomb vest, laying them atop McNally's corpse. He took out his wallet and laid it on the seat, and put his fake passport and the small video in his pants pocket. Using a pocketknife, he cut off a chunk of his hair and a piece of his thumbnail and sprinkled them around, then slit a small incision in his index finger and let it bleed on the plush carpet and the seat. Tommy and Freddy, meanwhile, had gotten out of the car and gone to the trunk and opened it. They lifted the limo's real, quite dead driver out and lugged him into the front passenger seat. They also took out the 10 cans of gasoline and arranged them around the rear passenger compartment.

When they reached B1 and the elevator doors slid open, the conspirators and corpses were all sitting in the idling limo as if waiting for a light to change. The large garage was seemingly empty, and its three 25-foot-high outer doors were closed as well. The other two garage bays to the left accessed a wide loading dock, beyond which were two doors in the wall. Freddy edged the long Caddy out into the right-hand bay.

Tommy and Freddy got slowly out of the car, guns drawn. They checked the perimeter of the room. As Freddy returned to the limo, Tommy walked over to the handle-less door on the far wall, put a key in and watched it spring open. He turned on the light inside, illuminating a stairwell. He then walked up the side stairs of the loading dock to a bank of switches, turning the garage lights off and leaving everything in darkness except the limo's running lights and the illuminated doorway. Freddy dragged the dead limo driver across the seat into position behind the wheel and closed the driver's-side door. The engine purred softly. It was eerily quiet, save for muffled noises that could be heard leaking in from outside: some shouting, the wailing of distant sirens, the thumping of helicopter blades.

Nate got out of the car, closed the door and pressed "send" on Nootch's phone. The sheriff's phone rang. "Sheriff Hildenbrandt here."

"Howdy, again, sheriff," said Nate, walking with Freddy toward Tommy's massive silhouette framed in the doorway. "I have two hostages left: Your boss, Mr. McNally, and his big Irish lackey. Everyone else I have let go."

They reached Tommy and began walking down the stairs as he pulled the door closed behind them. He turned on a flashlight, shone it on the steps in front of them and dowsed the lights.

"Escaped, you mean. We have the governor and Mr. Schmidt here. They said you shot them. What..."

"*I don't give a fuck what they said! I let them go!* Now, Mr. McNally is not feeling too well. His big friend here says he needs to get to a hospital. So what I need is clearance to travel unhindered to St. Mary's Hospital in Kipsbergh. There is a helicopter pad there, where I want a CNN copter to land in the open, with no police presence, so I can hand them the videotape I have in my hand. Then, when I am satisfied that my documentation has escaped your clutches, I will release Mr. McNally and give myself up."

As they descended, the cell phone signal weakened considerably.

"We don...fi...heli...nowhe...and!"

"I can't hear you! You're breaking up! I'll have to call you back!"

The stairs ended and they continued into a downward-sloping passage that looked as if it was hewn out of solid rock. "We need to book," said Tommy, breaking into a limping jog and grunting from the pain of each left footfall.

The tunnel banked to the left, then straightened out for what seemed like a quarter mile before veering sharply to the right again. It dead-ended at a concrete block wall with a metal door in the middle.

"Freddy, you first. Check it out."

Freddy pushed on the long bar handle, and the door swung open slowly into a dimly lit chamber. "It's clear. Come on."

With enough light from halogen street lamps outside, there was no need for a flashlight. They were in the north annex of the Copenhagen train station. Through the high arch windows near the ceiling they could see the helicopters circling the governor's property on the bluff to the north.

"Come on, hurry."

Tommy led the way to an exit door at the end of the building. It was locked from the outside, but pushed open from the inside. They stood on a handicapped access ramp to the platform on the left. Tommy kept his foot jammed in the door to hold it ajar. As Nate hit "send" on the cell phone, Freddy took a transmitter out of his pocket.

"Sheriff? Hello. Did you hear what I said before?"

"Yes. But we can't find a..."

"Hey, what are you doing? Give me tha..."

Nate hit "end." At the same time, Freddy pushed a button on his detonator transmitter. Two seconds later a massive explosion lit up the sky over the bluff to the north.

"Here's where I get off," said Tommy. "You know the way from here?"

"Yeah, chief. And thanks for everything. You saved my ass back there. You gonna be OK?"

"Fook you, ya crazy shite bastard," said Tommy, as the door closed behind him.

"Let's go. This way."

Five miles upriver, a train could be seen winding down along the river's edge from Hudson to the north. A faraway whistle blew. They peered around the corner of the building: a young couple from the nearby college was standing on the south end of the platform, waiting for their ride to the city and staring dumbfounded at the conflagration on the hill. A stone bridge just to the north afforded Copenhageans access over the tracks to a riverfront park and boat launch. Vaulting the rail onto a darkened section of northbound track, the two men hurried north until they reached the other side of the bridge tunnel, then scooted across both sets of tracks in the shadows afforded by the bridge. Keeping to the shelter of bushes and trees, they wended their way to the water's edge, and were picking their way south across a levee of boulders when the train arrived. They waited until it pulled out, and continued south beneath the dark, foreboding cliffs of Copenhagen. After ten minutes of difficult progress they found what they were looking for. A flat-backed canoe with a small gas-powered motor at its stern was pulled up on the shore between two boulders. Crouching next to it, smiling broadly, was Martin Brennan.

"Thank heavens. I thought you people would never show up. Where's Thirsty?"

Nate shook his head, incredulous. He had been expecting one of Nick's men. "Thirsty's dead. Good to see you, mate."

* * *

The river was mercifully calm in the moonless night. More than a mile upriver, helicopters still circled above the orange and black beacon where fire brigades were presumably battling to save what was left of the governor's Queen Anne mansion. "That was quite a blast," said Martin. "You had all that dynamite packed into a little vest?"

"Not quite. So what are you doing here? I thought you were on a plane to Liverpool."

"I leave tomorrow, from Newark. Meanwhile your boss gave me a chance to redeem myself. He said I was to rent this boat for the day at Musselman's in the Rondout and pretend to go fishing. I came upriver under the bridge, waited until sunset and crossed the river at the lighthouse. He said that you were springing Thirsty loose and would be needing a ride to the city, and that I was to be your guide and forever keep my mouth shut upon pain of death. So what happened to Thirsty?"

"Sorry, Martin. I don't want to talk about it right now. Maybe later. Let's get ashore."

They were a quarter of the way across the river, drifting swiftly south with the outgoing tide. Nate and Martin were in the front and rear seats, paddling slowly, as Freddy hunkered his bulk low in the center and struggled with a fish-hook stuck in his pants, trying not to move and upset the flimsy craft. Besides being too large for the canoe, he was deathly afraid of water. He couldn't swim, and Martin had only brought one tiny seat cushion as a life preserver.

They agreed they would have to remain quiet and avoid using the motor for as long as possible. Police helicopters were making wider sweeps of the Copenhagen area, with searchlights. They occasionally veered south over the train station and out across the water, although so far not close enough to spot a small dark canoe in the middle of the river.

Farther south, the pearly necklace of the Kipsbergher Bridge twinkled across the Hudson. Soon another set of twinkling lights separated itself from the bottom of the expanse, seeming to move toward them steadily. "Is that a boat?" said Martin.

"I don't know, and I don't want to find out. We'll have to risk starting the motor. Let's go."

Martin pulled at the small cord, making the canoe wobble slightly and causing Freddy to complain. The engine sputtered to life.

"Take us over there," said Nate, pointing to a battery of black oil tanks on the western shore.

As the small canoe puttered slowly across the river in a southwesterly direction, the lights to the south grew larger, higher and brighter. They were halfway to their destination when they began to discern an outline against the deep azure background of the evening sky. "It's a ship," said Nate. "A big one. Maybe an oiler. It's heading straight toward us. We'd better move it, or we might get swamped."

It seemed the farther west they went, the farther the ship turned along with them. As they neared the shore the big, empty tanker, riding high in the water, was obviously heading for the same spot, a sheltered cove bordered by the rusting hulks of a defunct oil storage depot.

No more than a quarter mile away, the ship slowed considerably. They made landfall as the gigantic hulk stopped dead in the water in the middle of the cove, and began to turn in place, reversing its engines. In the lights emanating from the deck far above, a Moldovian flag could be seen waving at the rusting ship's stern. An enormous anchor dropped into the water from the bow beneath the ship's moniker, which couldn't be made out clearly but looked like "Katrina" or Katrovna." The escapees clambered ashore and pulled the canoe up onto a rocky, oil-stained beach just as a series of waves came crashing in. They ran to higher ground, hid behind a gnarled tree stump and watched.

A loud roaring sound began to emanate from deep in the belly of the ship, followed by a louder roar as two gushers of gray foam began spewing from the superstructure just above the waterline. "I think I know what they're doing," said Nate. "I read about this. They just brought a load of oil to Jersey from Venezuela or Aruba or somewhere like that. Instead of going back empty, they're cleaning out their tanks with river water, so they can go up a little farther and fill up with more river water to take back and sell in Aruba."

"You mean Arubans drink Hudson River water?" mused Martin. "With all those PCBs and whatnot?"

"That's life," said Freddy, taking off his chauffeur's cap and tossing it in the water. "Let's go, you two. I've got a dinner date."

Black water lapped gently at the oil-slick shore. They pulled the boat up into the woods, climbing the slippery slope to dry dirt above the high water mark. Staying near the shoreline as much as possible, they traversed the four miles of junkyards, abandoned brickyards, oil tanks, cement plants, foul-smelling sewage pipes and other post-industrial wreckage. Through chain link fences, past gasoline-drenched boatyards, under the soaring Kipsbergher bridge and over another two treacherous, tetanus-filled miles, they stumbled and groped until they finally reached Martin's rented white Chevrolet in the crowded Rondout parking lot.

Couples walking arm-in-arm were discussing the news. "The bartender said they shot Pollock and blew up his house."

"That's crazy. Was it Al Qaeda?"

"I don't know. Let's go home and see. He said it was on CNN."

CHAPTER TWENTY-FOUR
ANONYMOUS

I n the five and a half months Nate Randall had been back in the city, only one person had come close to recognizing him. All he had done was let the beard grow out and wear a black market FDNY hat and sunglasses. His name was now "Steve," and he had on very few occasions run into anyone who had the attention span to contradict that fabrication. This was, after all, New York City, where a person's relative visibility can change radically from day to day or even from block to block—and where a six-month absence from the scene may as well be a lifetime. City people have a hard enough time picking out their best friends in a crowd, much less identifying a habitual loner they may have met or fucked once or twice a year or two ago.

During the ride to Newark, Martin had lobbied hard for Nate to come with him. "You can stay at my parents' home in the Cotswolds, rest up in peace and quiet, write a book and plot your next insurrection."

It was true. Nate could easily have left the country, using the ersatz "Stephen Jenkins" passport and Social Security ID card Big Nick had provided. But when he really thought about it, there was no place else he wanted to go. He was nothing if not a New Yorker. It had been the end of a frighteningly sultry March—spring and baseball season had ejaculated prematurely in the thickly carbonated air—and he told Martin to drop him at the Newark PATH station on his way to the airport. As he pulled the car to the curb, Nate handed him the videotape. "Use it how you want," he said. "But be careful not to get yourself killed."

Martin's eyes shone. "I will do that. I shall never forget our adventures together, James Olsen," he had blurted, for a moment considering jettisoning the gray future of upper-class security and government service his parents had reserved for him in favor of disappearing with Nate into the exotic bowels of lower Manhattan. He stifled his emotions and pressed a piece of paper into his friend's hand. "Please call or write sometime. It's been a pleasure. Good luck to you."

Nate swallowed hard. "Thanks, mate. You were a lifesaver, more than once. Now get the fuck out of here, before I change my mind. Stiff upper lip and all that."

Neither CNN nor WABC had carried live coverage of his jihad; someone had gotten to the producers in time. Aerial views of the burning governor's mansion and of ambulances leaving the compound had been accompanied by grainy sequences of himself holding a gun to the cardinal's pate, and a bald-faced head shot of him that Winnie had provided. The story was a decent diversion for five days or so, but it was no 9/11 or anthrax scare.

Three days afterward, Hiram Pollock was already helicoptering around to ribbon cuttings as if nothing had happened, seemingly no stiffer in the shoulders than usual. The cardinal also was back at work, although he might have wished he wasn't, with all the pederast priests in his diocese being unmasked on the front page of the *Post*. Arthur Schmidt nursed his wounds in a private suite at Westchester Medical where he had been airlifted, while his name kept popping up as a deep-pocketed supporter of President George W. Bush and a vocal proponent of U.S. military intervention in Iraq.

There was virtually no news of the fates of Nicole and Nootch, which was not necessarily bad. The two WABC cameramen, the Colombian busboy and the slightly injured Tommy Dongan had disappeared into the yawning media blackout as well.

Reginald Thurston Brown might as well have been the top-secret X-files corpse of a marooned space alien. Perhaps that's what he was all along, mused Nate.

The only detailed information of any kind was about the death of himself and his victims: Commander James Robinson of the governor's special

New York State Police detail, Jefferson Town Supervisor and GOP stalwart William T. McNally and limousine chauffeur Paul Coons of Pepperton. Bill McNally was eulogized by Pollock as one of the party's premier fundraisers along with his surviving wife, Edith, who was mourning him gracefully with the help of her recently divorced daughter and four lovely grandchildren.

James Olsen, AKA Nathan Randall was portrayed by the networks and newspapers as a confused madman; a copycat criminal who had been traumatized by his fiancée's death in the World Trade Center disaster. Dark rumors that Nate's obsession with McNally was due to his daughter's hatred of him were circulated, but were dismissed by the family, who spoke of Bill and Sheila's "loving father-daughter bond." Witnesses Nate barely knew—including an equestrian veterinarian named Natalie Johnson—were found who verified that he had fallen off the deep end into drugs, and was constantly besieged by nightmares and conspiracy fantasies. A flotilla of professional talking-head shrinks analyzed his crime, coming to the consensus that in addition to post-traumatic psychosis, televised images of the escalating violence in the Middle East had triggered Randall's attack on the governor's mansion with a suicide bomb.

The one proof Nate imagined could possibly clear his name was the Betamax tape he had given to Martin. He had no idea yet if he'd ever bother with a stab at redemption. He felt a sense of relief at being presumed dead, if he indeed had gotten away with it.

* * *

Roosevelt County Sheriff Dean Hildenbrandt cradled his massive gray-pompadoured head in his calloused hands. He was having a hard time keeping the media and the feds sidetracked while his boys tried to figure out what really happened. They had interrogated Winnie Babson and his wife, who swore up and down that the Randall cocksucker was clean when they arrived at the party. "He couldn't possibly have smuggled a bomb without Marjorie fucking noticing," Winnie had told him. "She was all over him like a cheap suit."

Hildenbrandt knew what Winnie was talking about. He had been down that road with Marjorie himself.

Plus the blast and fire were much too large to have been caused by the amount of explosives in a fucking bomb vest. But that meant the little fuck had had help. But who?

Pollock had been clear. *Everyone* was suspect, even himself. Find out how this went down, and fast. Interview everyone, and keep any real witnesses clear of the feds. If anyone had seen anything, find out what they knew and either pay them off or get rid of them.

It wasn't that easy. His boys had interviewed and disposed of the little Spic, before he had a chance to blab to his wetback friends. The cardinal and Schmidt he didn't think he would have to worry about, as up to their ears in the business as they were. Along with the governor, they gave him valuable information about what had happened up until their escape. Schmidt said Robinson seemed to have popped a cork, coming out and threatening Randall with the girl like that. He had always wondered what Hiram had seen in that idiot. He was such a preening, tightly wound closet queen, he probably thought he had the guy in a Mexican standoff. But the fucker was so cranked on pills he had rushed Robinson and blew off his stupid hat and toupee, and all hell broke loose.

What a nightmare.

The big thing was, the 9X19 mm slug that came out of Schmidt's ass didn't match his and Pollock's description of Randall's .45 automatic. It could have been a stray from one of Robinson's chicken-shit SWAT crew, but both Schmidt and the governor had sworn somebody was shooting at them on purpose.

The most likely candidate was that Ianucci character, who they said was dragging around a tablecloth sack full of guns. He and his girlfriend had gone missing, along with the two WABC camera people. Any one of them might be walking around right now with a fucking tape of what happened in the cellar. If that got out, the jig was up.

Hopefully they were all trapped down in B2 or had been killed in the explosion. The blast and fire had destroyed the entire north wing of the house, including the elevator shaft and stairwell access to the B2 level, which hopefully had withstood the conflagration. Crews from one of McNally's outfits were working to clear the debris and secure the exits, while he himself was coordinating efforts to keep the feds out until

Monday at least. He hoped that was time enough to move all traces of the dope operation out of the place.

That left Dongan, who had showed up after the blast with a bullet in his thigh and scratches on his face, saying he had escaped from the limo during a fracas between Randall and McNally, and flown the garage through the governor's secret passageway. That lame explanation produced a spike in Hildenbrandt's well-oiled bullshit meter, and he had his boys put the big Mick on ice.

He was beginning to smell a bigger rat in all this, and the rat was Nick Vitello. During their necessarily rough processing of the uncooperative Dongan, his boys found Big Nick's phone number in a text on his phone. Dongan tried to explain it away, but that and the fact that he had failed to put any hurdles at all in Randall's path was enough to put the big Irishman on the sheriff's shortlist of probable accomplices.

Hildenbrandt had never heard of any secret passageway from the governor's garage to the train station below. When he asked him about it Pollock seemed surprised, and said he had never told anyone but McNally about it. "Tommy Dongan knew. That's how he escaped," said the sheriff. "I don't know how to say this, Hi, but I think somebody else might have gotten out of there with him."

"Fuck. I want that motherfucker found and killed. I don't care what you have to do."

* * *

After six days in hiding, Nate had ventured out to Kinko's to perform some Yahoo searches. He entered the names "Ianucci," John Ianucci," "Royal" and "Nicole Royal." Nothing relevant came up. He checked the on-line *pinksterkilljournal.com* for any stories during the week by or about John Ianucci. There was nothing. Against his better judgment, he clicked the "Obituaries" icon. Scrolling down, he froze before he got to "I," momentarily unable to go on. He psyched himself up to expect the worst, as he had done so many times before.

If they're dead, they're dead. Life is for the living.

It wasn't working. He felt dead inside himself.

He took a deep breath, and scrolled: Hoag, Hopper, Jackson...Lindsay, Orenstein, Randall. Randall, Nathan. Who would have thought to put his obituary in the paper?

He scrolled, slower.

Randall, Rogers...Sidwell, Travers...

He sighed with relief. No news is good news.

...Vitello.

Vitello, Nicholas, age 76, after a long illness.

It was an extended obituary, full of anecdotes lifted verbatim from Nate's articles about the man. He paused and reflected on Big Nick's flawed legacy. Was it a life well lived?

Yes and no.

How about his own legacy, now that he was a certified memory? Was Nate Randall's a life well lived?

As things stood at present, definitely not.

Still, he had to pat himself on the back for one thing: Nick's obituary was much livelier and better written than his was. Seeing the words staring back at him in an unfamiliar context after so much time, space and tragedy had intervened, Nate finally saw his own writing objectively. He actually wasn't half bad. Almost as good as Sheila on her worst day.

Nate hardly noticed as his mind began to wander, backtracking aimlessly and touching down every so often like an Oklahoma twister, kicking up puffs of disconnected data and addled notions. Freddy Natale would be the family boss now, he thought uselessly. Charles Overlook would be looking for a new job. What on earth could a man like that possibly do? And what the hell had happened to Tommy Dongan, God bless his mutilated eye? He might never find out. Time to move on, time to move on. Just forget about the whole fucking thing and move on.

And then Nate remembered Nick Vitello's death-grip handshake and warm, basset-hound eyes, which brought back vivid flash-card memories of his father and mother and Mr. DiSalvo and Anthony and Annie and Sheila and Rico and Nicole and Nootch and... he began to weep, which brought on yet another pounding headache. He paid the Kinko's bill, dry-swallowed a morphine pill, and went across the street to wash it and his aching sadness down with a freshet of bourbon.

* * *

Dying isn't always as easy as it looks. After five-and-a-half months of drowning himself in drugs and alcohol fully expecting to die, Nate had to admit failure. He resigned himself to the fact that, short of putting a bullet in his brain, he might be around a while longer. Maybe he didn't have cancer after all. Maybe he was just crazy. The headaches hadn't gone away, but they hadn't gotten any worse either, and Nate realized one day he could ease up on the morphine dose by seventy-five percent with no corresponding increase in discomfort. This was a good thing, because at the rate his wad was dwindling from payoffs to the five-finger-discount pharmacist up on First Avenue, the money would be gone long before he was.

Other behavior modifications ensued. Once he succeeded in rolling back his daily intake of Jack Daniels from nearly a fifth to four shots at mealtimes, he felt his appetite returning, and as he was able to get and keep more food down he felt his strength increasing. He went on walks around the neighborhood, bought an old stationary bike off the street and started pedaling in his room while looking out the window at the woman sunbathing on the roof next door. As the globally warmed dog days of August became unbearable, he traded in the Jack habit for vodka, mixing it over lots of ice with carrot/orange juice for an extra antioxidant kick.

After about a week he reached a sort of plateau, where further experimentation failed to produce any improvement but there was no regression either. The headaches would come and go during the day; he could mitigate most of them without medication by exercising. When his condition inevitably worsened after dark, he would pop a couple of morphine pills, suck down a shot of something or other, smoke a bowl and go to sleep. He hoped he could eventually wean himself off morphine entirely, as it upset his stomach. But pot by itself was too weak by far to deal with the worst of it.

He still figured he was effectively a goner, and blamed what he assumed was a brief remission on the sturdy genes of his maternal grandmother, who had beaten back breast cancer at 35 and gone on to bear his mother at 40 and live another 57 flinty, smart-mouthed years. His pessimism was borne out by a convulsive attack one Saturday morning in which he threw up blood and green bile. Strangely, though, it abated as quickly as it had begun.

Rather than check into a hospital, he calmed himself down, went to the corner and picked up a *Times*, a *Post*, a *Voice* and a Bic pen and brought them over to Tompkins Square Park, relaxing among other humanoids for the first time in months. Within twenty minutes he was rejuvenating himself with the delicious trivialities of *Page Six*, box scores, musicians' classifieds, personals ads and the crossword puzzle. If he was to die today, he would die doing what made him happy.

Eventually as he worked his way backward through each publication, Nate began to catch up on the world he had effectively stepped off of five months earlier. It amused him that life, like a television soap opera, can be skipped for an awfully long time without missing terribly much. The major characters—war, disease, famine, religious and corporate fanatics, errant priests and politicians, pregnant, drug-crazed, homicidal teenagers, pouting millionaires in cornrows and collagen-injected movie stars—hadn't gone anywhere. Like hoary old Erica Kane, they seem mired in a recurring plot line by bad, repetitious scriptwriting.

And then he saw it.

It was a story on a public flap concerning the publication in the current issue of the virulent Leftie rag *The Nation* of an article potentially damaging to New York Gov. Hiram Pollock, currently angling for a vice presidential nod to replace an aging and physically hobbled Dick Cheney on G.W. Bush's re-election ticket. Tucked away on the second-to-last page of the Metro section of the *Times*, the article stated that Pollock and his handlers were incensed at the "slanderous and deleterious lies" being promulgated by the *Nation* piece's British author, who accused the governor of having run a multi-million-dollar cocaine ring out of his Hudson Valley mansion prior to its being torched by "St. Patty's Day Bomber" Nathan Randall in March.

The author of the *Nation* article, which was liberally peppered with unnamed, confidential sources but contained no mention of any Betamax tape, was listed as Martin Brennan, an ambitious young assistant to the socialist writer Alexander Cockburn. Nate ran out to the news store at Second Avenue and St. Marks and bought a *Nation*, and it was all there, including eyewitness stuff that couldn't have been caught on videotape and could only have been provided by someone like ... Nootch? Nicole? His heart jumped once again with something approaching hope.

* * *

The trick, as always, was to keep moving.

After all that had gone down, it felt good to be back on a bike again, hustling packages. The bicycle was a good one, a brand-new fifteen-speed Peugeot Manhattan mountain/road hybrid that Nate had bought for 50 bucks off a hustler on St. Marks and scuffed the shit out of to make it look old and beat. He bought a mondo bike chain for it and an indestructible American lock; and a new helmet, aerodynamic goggles, skin-tight suit and bag. With his hair and beard now a wiry thicket, no one on earth would recognize him.

Or so he thought.

On a good bike, Nate was still a speed demon. Rico, who used to be a messenger, too, always told him he was pretty fast for an old man. He was right. When the two of them would ride uptown together Nate would kick Rico's skinny ass, as well as the spandexed asses of more than one pro messenger—he was reckless.

Nothing much had changed, except there was no one worthwhile left to race against.

The headaches were under control through diet and exercise, and the hurling fits were infrequent. He rode downtown to a company he hadn't worked for before: Bust-a-Move, an improbably busy messenger service on the fifth floor of a building otherwise full of Chinese rag trade sweat-shops. He easily passed the silly bike messenger quiz—a cross between a Post Office exam and a driver's test.

The business took up the entire floor, a light and airy loft bustling with the activity of messengers coming and going and dispatchers taking calls and droning instructions to their serfs out on the streets. The own-er was Jack, an artificially relaxed lapsed yuppie, who reeked with false integrity and the odor of stale pot. As he interviewed Nate he seemed perplexed that a 40-year-old man with a résumé that read better than his own would want to be a bicycle messenger. Jack hired "Steve" anyway, and set him up with a dispatcher. "You're real lucky to get Stewart," said the boss. "He'll give you as much work as you can handle, and he doesn't play favorites."

Stewart turned out to be a pathologically impatient, intensely moody dreadlock brother who enunciated like an Uncle Tom but bristled with spiky Afrocentricity. Sensing his new dispatcher eying him suspiciously, Nate wondered just how in the name of Judah they were going to get along. Still, as he sat around being ignored for more than an hour trying not to think about anything, he couldn't help noticing that Stewart worked far more efficiently than did any of the other people jabbering into their headsets. He would browbeat his riders when they screwed up, yelling and hanging up on them; but afterward he would call them right back and say he was sorry. He seemed able to keep a lot of balls in the air.

Eventually Stewart handed Nate a Bust-a-Move "manifest" pad with a few addresses scrawled illegibly on it, and told him to get moving and call him when he'd made the first three pick-ups.

The first address was an organic-looking block-long maze of somehow still extant artsy dotcom offices on Broadway in SoHo. It had two identical entrances, and Nate knew from experience that if you took the wrong one you could get lost in there for hours. Luckily he found the place right away—a modeling agency crawling with big-boned young ladies and beady-eyed boys with spiky, heavily moussed N-Sync haircuts. One of the latter pushed two giant black cloth-bound supermodel portfolios at Nate across the counter—neither would fit in his bag—and sneered that they were going to an ad agency on 57th and Broadway.

The Bust-a-Move slip he gave Nate screamed: "RUSH!"

Nate dragged the things into the hall—they each weighed about 70 pounds—and tried to recall how he once horsed a similar burden uptown while riding a bicycle. He remembered the method of using his big chain to hang the portfolios off the handlebars, saving his back and neck during the ride. It was still slow going due to reduced leg motion and a high center of gravity, not to mention the thought of an unidentified cancer eating at his brain. Lugging the things up and down five flights of stairs for the next two pick-ups had Nate ready to pack it in.

When he called Stewart, the first thing out of the surly dispatcher's lips was: "Where the hell are you?"

Nate told him about the two-portfolio "RUSH!" job.

"Shit," he said. "We should have sent a truck. Just get up there and call me when you're done. Put down 'overweight' and 'long distance' on the manifest and you get triple for the trip. You all right?"

This sudden hint of genuine concern took Nate aback. "Yeah, I guess."

"All right then. Just don't wreck the portfolios. If you do, you're dead."

"Sho' thing, boss."

"Whoa there, looks like we got ourselves a real honky smartass. Go fuck yourself."

"Thank you, sir. You, too. Just keep me working."

Nate mapped out his route of drop-offs to give him the quickest, most level ride. He had one stop to make that wasn't on his manifest, the U.S. Post Office on 8th Avenue, to mail a long letter to Martin Brennan. The letter detailed specifics that filled in the blanks in his article and could help him continue his work. He provided names and phone numbers of contacts like Charles Overlook, Belinda Strossner and Hamilton Canard, Esquire. He revealed where he had hidden a stash of documentation in the attic of the Arms, including a computer disk containing the opus: "Adventures in Pollockistan: How USE, the Government and the Mob Conspire to Give You Cancer," by Sheila McNally and Reginald Thurston Brown.

His missive concluded:

"Great story, Martin, and thanks for keeping me in the grave where I belong. I am not germane to the story, which is yours to run with. By the time you read this, I shall be either actually dead or removed to sunnier climes. I do not wish to be exhumed from the crypt only to be prosecuted and die in Guantanamo. Take care of yourself, and please do not burden Mr. Iannucci or Ms. Royal with any news of me or my whereabouts, should they be in touch with you.

Thank you, and kisses,

J. Olsen

P.S.: Please burn this letter."

When Nate finally got uptown and unloaded the twin monstrosities at a pretentious ad agency staffed by a snooty, shellac-haired receptionist in a mauve power suit, he felt like Atlas after his big shrug. He called Stewart again and was rewarded with a flurry of well-timed uptown pick-ups—nothing bigger than an envelope—that would last him the rest of the day and wind him up a mere three blocks from the Bowery hotel where he was holing up. "Don't call me again until you're done," said Stewart. "I'm sick of you."

"Thanks, chief."

"Don't call me 'chief.'"

* * *

On Saturday, September 6, in the morning after throwing up, Nate felt a strange, serendipitous pull from the past. He went downtown and found the new pedicab headquarters, which had moved from its East Third Street garage to a former gas station in SoHo. There he renewed his acquaintance with Arnold, a Don Quixote-looking cadaver who apparently had a bottomless well of trust fund cash for propping up what would never in a million years be a moneymaking concern. With the five thousand a month he was paying in rent, on top of the four thousand each month for liability insurance that was guaranteed to be canceled the first time somebody got hurt, on top of being slammed by the post-911 tourist slowdown, Arnold was hemorrhaging daddy's cash.

He owned ten pedicabs manned by an average of eight drivers a day who would give him five dollars an hour to rent one. It was easy to see the business would never last, but Nate didn't care. For one thing it was anonymous, and under the table. Neither scatterbrained Arnold nor any of the pothead veteran drivers remembered him distinctly from four years before, and when he reminded them that his name was "Steve" they'd bought the lie without so much as a furrowed brow. If hustling packages was easy, healthful work that cured a cancer headache, pushing a few thousand pounds of lipstick lesbians and German S&M tourists around a park on a blistering Saturday afternoon in early September would be Nirvana.

A pedicab is a garishly painted 200-lb. tricycle with a two-passenger seat in the back, five speeds, disc brakes, and running lights powered by a car battery. It has a virtually useless convertible top, and a lovely bell that attracts customers but has little effect on Manhattan traffic. The fleet owned by Arnold was once active in Honolulu, until they were banned after a couple of drivers were convicted of selling the coke they had stashed in the handy under-seat storage compartments.

Nate was immediately conscripted into pedaling downtown in a convoy of cycle freaks to wait by Trinity Church for a wedding party. He was not enthralled with the prospect of hanging out with this particular group of drivers, most of whom he recognized from the old days, even if they didn't remember him. Sally, the lone woman in the group, was, when not driving a pedicab, apparently an actress and children's clown. She was loud, talkative, literal-minded, and dressed like a Harlequin. Arnold's most experienced driver, Jerry, a brillo-haired cretin with bad teeth and one leg at least six inches shorter than the other, was a fount of bad stories and worse advice. He leered at women, and would routinely frighten away potential customers. Another poor soul named Dave was so painfully shy and pockmarked that he would refuse to ring his bell, and would look the other way when someone approached to ask a simple pedicab question. The group reminded him of the cadre of misfit journalists he had left behind in Dutch Hollow—a far cry from the hordes of fancy, well-dressed people he somehow had successfully avoided rubbing shoulders with for his entire life. Nowadays Manhattan was overrun with shallow-hearted mercantiles. Nate swore that if he donned a pair of special sunglasses—like Rowdy Roddy Piper in "They Live"—that the crowds walking these sidewalks would be exposed as the lizard-faced space aliens they really were.

As soon as the drivers hustled the wedding guests to a nearby Irish restaurant for their beer-soaked reception, Nate separated from the group. He cruised the streets around the fallen Trade Center, pretending to be a viable form of transportation. "Cheaper than a cab, and ten times more fun," he squawked at pedestrians, ringing his bell furiously and making irony-tinged eye contact whenever possible. The mood, however, was somber, as tourists had come downtown in droves on the eve of the second anniversary of Sept. 11 not to revel in the city's charms but to gape at the hole in their collective consciousness and gawk at the blocks of sad, faded memorials.

Nate did much better just sitting at the corner of Broadway and John Street and looking morose. It was easy picking, as downtown traffic patterns and reduced and confusing subway access were still difficult for out-of-town pedestrians to cope with. To amuse himself, Nate regaled his passengers with first-hand narratives of the carnage, devastation and eerie aftermath of that horrid day. It was oddly liberating.

Before sundown Nate ventured north up Sixth Avenue through the Village, with the eventual intent of hanging out by Bryant Park where there was always a profusion of drunken yuppies and a dearth of cabs. In the old days he had scored his biggest coups out of that park, once charging a fat lawyer $300 to haul him over the Brooklyn Bridge as kids on trick bikes buzzed around them offering fist pumps and hooting dated, Arsenio-Hall-style encouragement.

But he never got that far. As he pedaled past the blackened stone hulk of the Limelight—which last time he'd heard about it had been closed forever due to its being a notorious drug bazaar—a pair of revelers flagged him down at the 21st Street red light.

The woman was stunning, an almond-eyed chocolate delight in a skintight red dress with a thousand-watt smile. As incandescent as she was, her sugar-daddy escort easily outshone her in his deep purple velvet suit, tall, feathered Toussaint L'Ouverture admiral's hat, cashmere scarf and solid gold eye-patch.

Mo' Better strode over, exuding the confidence and bearing of an African prince. He smiled, revealing a mouthful of new gold caps. "My mans, could you please get us to Gran' Central by the most scenic-est means possible? Money is no object... it's a lot o' little ones."

Cracking himself up, Mo laughed a long, braying Eddie Murphy laugh.

"Yes, sir, step right in."

Mo hesitated, and studied Nate's face intently with his good eye. "Hold up a minute. Where I hear that voice before?"

His juicy companion beamed delightfully.

"Yo, Mo," said Nate.

"Shorty? Is dat you?"

"Yes and no. Hop in, before I get a ticket for blocking traffic."

Mo and his date clambered aboard as the light changed, and settled in romantically, he with his arm around her fabulous shoulders and she caressing his bony knee and snuggling under the absurd brim of his hat to nibble lasciviously at his diamond-encrusted left earring. Nate pedaled furiously, eliciting a squeal of delighted laughter from the woman.

"Looks like you've done pretty well for yourself since I last saw you," said Nate. "I'm glad things worked out for you."

"Yeah, well, I went back down near where we was and staked a claim, so to speak. It ain't what you think, though. I found some more *liquid* assets, if you catch my meanin'. Alarms and shit don't work so good when the power's out, heh, heh, heh. Yo, I found some gold, too, but it was too damn heavy to drag around. I got a motherfucker to *pay* me for a map to where it was..."

Nate had reached 23rd Street and taken a right toward Madison Park. He slowed his pace, turned around and looked from Mo to his date with a questioning expression on his face.

"That's OK," said Mo. "She's from Senegal or some shit. Only English she knows is 'Yo, bitch, down on de wood.' We in *love*, right, baby? Down on de wood, yeh, dass right."

The woman laughed, cooed something musically unintelligible and stroked the edge of Mo's crotch lustfully. Nate pedaled faster and wondered where he had gone wrong in life.

"It wasn't so good for us," he said, stopping at a light. "Rico was nailed in a tunnel collapse, and I had to hide out for a while. You hear about that?"

"Yo, G, that shit was *fucked up*," said Mo, reaching inside his jacket with his free hand and fishing out a solid gold cigarette case. "We was supposed to meet at the corner at St. Marks that time, remember? I'm sorry I missed that shit, but I freaked out. Them motherfuckers seen *me* down there, too, an' I didn' figure I should be hangin' out wit' y'all in plain sight, dig? Sorry, man." With one hand he deftly flipped open the case, withdrew an English Oval with his thumb and pinkie and lifted it to his mouth, closing the case simultaneously. His hand returned the case to its nest and re-emerged with a gold-plated version of the same silly Mickey Mouse Pez dispenser lighter he had lit up with in the tunnel nearly two years earlier.

"No, I understand, believe me."

"So, yo, watchoo been doin', shorty? I coulda swore I seen some mad bomber motherfucker on TV looked just like you. Heh, heh, heh."

"No, man, I've just been laying low," lied Nate. "'S good to see you, though. Especially under these circumstances. Kinda gives a smug white cracker hope for the plight of the long-suffering negro, you know?"

Mo laughed so hard he nearly blew his cigarette out. His beautiful girlfriend laughed at his laughter. Somehow, thought Nate, things were as they should be.

Nate rode up over the sidewalk and into Madison Square Park, where couples huddled under the stilted Op-art taxicabs. He meandered northeast through the park, once known as "Needle Park," but now as clean and bright and well patrolled on the perimeter as a suburban shopping mall.

The middle section of the park was relatively unpopulated. "Whoa, Trigger, stop right here," said Mo. "We'll be right back..."

He reached in his pocket. "Yo, here's a down payment. Keep the meter runnin'. Heh, heh, heh." Mo thrust a C-note into Nate's hand, and he and his sweetheart alit from the carriage and disappeared into a copse alongside the pathway.

While the lovers amused themselves, Nate sat on a park bench. His head was remarkably clear and pain-free. He could feel his heart pumping and the blood pulsing through the veins of his neck, groin and extremities. "I am alive," he thought. "How and why that is so, I haven't a clue. Maybe there's a reason beyond my comprehension. If I didn't know any better, I'd think somebody was looking out for me." He gazed heavenward, open for suggestions.

As had happened on the handful of occasions in his life when he allowed himself to think the unthinkable, an involuntary *frisson* spread through his entire nervous system from his head, down his spine and out to the tips of his fingers and toes. This time, however, he did not stifle the feeling with logic. He let this sense of spiritual ecstasy, or whatever it was, overwhelm him. He shuddered and began to cry the tears a child sheds upon first realizing that the hairy giant hovering over his crib all the time loves him. He sniffled and gagged.

"Hi-ho, Silver, everything awright?"

Mo had returned, and was carefully checking his pants for stains in the soft park-light.

"Yeah, I was just sitting here having a religious experience, knowing you were getting your cock sucked." Nate retched and coughed up the phlegmy mass that had gathered in his lungs as a result of his reverie.

Mo's date returned from the bushes, looking none the worse for wear. She and Mo both looked at Nate quizzically. He coughed again, spat, ferreted out a tissue from his pocket and blew his running nose. "Really, man, you awright?" asked Mo, his eyes bright.

"Yeah, fine. Grand Central, right, boss?"

"Yeah. Take it easy, though. Don't strain yourself."

Emerging from the park at the northeast corner, Nate went east on 26th. As he turned left onto Park Avenue, Nate's canoodling passengers were treated to the classic Woody Allen panorama of a fabulously lit Grand Central Station, with the MetLife building looming graciously behind it as a sparkling backdrop. Behind them to the south, a pair of massive searchlight beams, which had been temporarily re-lit for the week of the 9/11 observance, stretched into outer space, nearly illuminating the darkened new moon.

Park Avenue between 26th and 34th streets is as lung-taxing an uphill stretch as Manhattan offers to a biker, even when he's not dragging nearly 500 pounds of weight behind him. It is also a notorious hooker stroll, and as Nate stood on the pedals in first gear Mo' Better struck up conversations with some of his acquaintances on the sidewalks. "Yo, blood, I'm from the ghet-to, and this is *my* lim-o. We just rode in from *Flo*-rida, and we don't know *what* to do."

Laughter and catcalls erupted. Whores and their cell-phone-toting pimps stopped in their tracks to watch the slow procession. "Ooooweee! Lookin' good, Black."

"Yeah, booooey."

Nate struggled mightily against gravity and the burning in his lungs, trying to trick his mind into not quitting by giving it the busywork of counting his leg pumps between lights. "Thirty-nine, 40, 41, 42, 43, 44... 33rd Street."

He paused and breathed heavily, waiting for the light to change—only one more block until things leveled out for a while.

"You OK, Holmes? Shit, I got a bet on you. Heh, heh, heh."

The woman giggled. Nate nodded and gave a thumbs-up sign. The light turned green.

"One, two, three, four, five, six, seven..."

A searing fireball exploded in Nate's head. Somehow he kept counting.

"Eight...nine...t-...elev-..."

An image of his mother, holding his head, stroking his hair, smiling.

"...22...minus 35... plus 13...equals..."

And then there was nothing.

CPSIA information can be obtained
at www.ICGtesting.com
Printed in the USA
FFHW021039201119
56093510-62150FF

9 781948 796309